THE
ADMINISPHERE

John Prather

© 2016
All rights reserved.

ISBN: 1533202028
ISBN 13: 9781533202024

The following is a work of fiction. Anyone attempting to identify himself or herself in this narrative is working too hard.

To my Mom, my first teacher, who taught me to love words and stories. And to all the teachers who toil at such a noble task—your efforts make our world a better place.

I must begin by acknowledging the contribution of my wife, who patiently endured my relationship with this narrative. She is also a fine teacher and a great mom. This book began during a How to Write a Novel class at Scottsdale Community College. Thanks to moderator Rob Hall, brilliant source of countless ideas, and to my classmates for their valuable critiques and words of encouragement. I hope each of you finished your novels as well. Thank you to my readers for your honest and thorough comments which (I hope) made this final draft better than the first. I am delighted to have so many literate and literary friends.

Cover art by Elettra Cudignotto.
Author photograph by Intrinsic Imagery.

2005 – 2006

1

THE WOLVERINE

Mix equal parts vision and tyranny. Season liberally with pathos, obstinacy, and illogic. Cook in a small dish at intense heat for eighteen hours per day. Serve very chilled. Garnish with ample helpings of processed sugar and caffeine.

Such was the recipe that made up Dr. Connie Rumsford.

She had not killed anyone, not literally anyway, not yet. But as principal of newly opened Shadowcliff High School, she had made them ponder their mortality, question their sanity, and, occasionally, contemplate the essential questions of mankind. This particular problem had vexed them for more than a month, since mid-August.

Three teachers now shared a table at Wingding's, a spacious local tavern whose dark wood interior was illuminated by the glow of ubiquitous neon signs and unrelenting televised sports, and by shafts of Arizona glare injected into the darkness with each opened door. For years, Wingding's had been popular for cheap Happy Hour beer, hot wings, and free peanuts, and now it had become the unofficial watering hole for Shadowcliff High School faculty.

A cheer arose from a distant table. Jimmy Clayton's head swiveled instinctively, but he was unable to ascertain the cause of the excitement. So he turned back to face his colleagues.

"Let me tell you how it is," Clayton announced, sitting tall in his chair. He dramatically sipped his Bud Light as he waited for all to quiet, then began, "I was watching *Animal Planet* last night when it came to me—"

"—You were watching *Animal Planet*?" interrupted Bob Cockrell, a tall, jovial, rumpled man who moved like a bear with sore feet. "What happened? You get tired of the women's bass fishing tournament on ESPN?"

"I watch more than ESPN," Clayton argued. His dark mustache twitched at the indignity of Cockrell's assertion.

"Yeah, you watch ESPN2, too."

"So? You spend all your time watching the fucking Rowboat Channel. I bet you actually know who won the women's bass fishing tournament."

"Of course I do. Eliza Carney," Cockrell said matter-of-factly. "She was my lab partner in college."

"First of all," Clayton explained, grabbing a handful of peanuts, "the University of Eastern Oregon is not college. It's more like Fred's Camping Outlet. The Unabomber was probably your history professor—"

"—Math," interrupted Keri Tanner. "The Unabomber was a math professor."

"Whatever. Second, bass fishing is not sports. It's like watching a fruit fly masturbate on PBS."

"Oh, lovely," said Keri dryly, pulling her blonde hair back from her face.

"So is that the answer that came to you? The masturbating fruit fly?" asked Cockrell. "Seems like a mouthful. 'I have a meeting with the masturbating fruit fly.' 'The masturbating fruit fly wants me to turn in my lesson plans for the next twelve years.' 'I have to change my socks because the masturbating fruit fly doesn't like yellow.' I thought nicknames were supposed to be short."

"Jesus, Bob, I was just making a point...."

"And that point was?"

"It does have sort of a catchy ring to it," Keri decided.

"The point was—" His attention was suddenly drawn to the TV overhead. "He was safe, you moron! What a lousy fucking call." His gesticulations spewed peanut shells into the beer mugs being carried by a passing waitress, who eyed him contemptuously as Greg Samson—who taught four different classes, coached cross country, and sponsored two clubs—finally arrived, slipped into a vacant chair, and casually pitched a peanut shell into Keri Tanner's cleavage.

They were an unlikely bunch, a group which otherwise would probably not spend that much time together. But like those who had endured shipwrecks, World Wars, and Monday morning queues at Starbucks, they had forged an alliance of survival. They had persevered through interviews, questionnaires, and psychological screenings. They had watched the video by master teacher Elden Ray Fong and pretended to read every page of his book. They had filled out two hours of District paperwork and signed the following statement:

> I, _____ (hereinafter referred to as "Teacher"), do solemnly pledge to be trustworthy, vigilant, and beholden. I further vow to uphold the laws of the State of Arizona and to support and abide by the policies, procedures, and directives of Sweetwater Unified School District No. 43. Most important, I promise and assure my unending loyalty to the Constitution and the democracy that is the United States of America.

Having therefore satisfied the late Senator McCarthy, they were now first-year teachers as part of the most innovative educational setting in the state of Arizona: the newly opened Shadowcliff High School. A school which employed block scheduling, Mentor Time, and heterogeneous grouping. A school with carpeting, snack time, and Mozart piped-in over the intercom before first period. An environment of student-centeredness, shared decision-making, and esteem-building. All theories espoused, and now presided over, by Dr. Connie Rumsford.

"So, another week goes by at Shadow Valley Cliff Ridge Desert High School. Which one are we at?" Greg asked as he leaned forward.

"Shadowcliff," Keri helped. She reached for the peanut shell inside her shirt. "And no, I don't need your help with this."

"I can't keep 'em straight," said Greg, settling back into his chair. "Maybe it's the fourteen-hour days. You'd think the legislature could pass some sort of law that required school names to have some originality. I guess they were too busy sanctioning the sexual deviancy of Catholic priests."

"My future ex-husband is Catholic," Keri added, offhand. A slight smile creased her lips. Clayton was now absorbed in a game on the television on the other side of the bar.

"Who's playing?" Greg asked.

"WKU and ETSU," Clayton replied, never taking his gaze from the inch-high figures on the television fifty feet away.

"Who are they?" Greg asked.

"No idea," replied Clayton.

Greg shrugged and turned back to the others. He was tall and tanned, with a thin frame and thinning hair. His sharp features included a craggy nose and prominent cheekbones on a gaunt face, softened occasionally by an impish smile. As he once explained, "Women don't necessarily run away from me in sheer terror, but they are always careful to maintain a safe distance."

On a TV much closer to the group, a man in an ill-fitting suit sat in an uncomfortable chair and spoke woodenly to the camera. The words "Actual Client" appeared beneath him. He explained that his was a "real success story" in which he had won millions, "all thanks to the wise and ethical representation by the law firm with teeth: The Lyon." This last part he said with great drama.

"Cute slogan," Clayton said. WKU and ETSU were at halftime.

"I went to law school with that guy," Greg said.

"Wait a minute," Cockrell demanded. "You said you went to business school."

"I did both," Greg replied. "It was a joint program, MBA and JD."

"So why aren't you a lawyer?" asked Cockrell, genuinely confused.

Greg chuckled. "After law school I was lucky enough to get a college teaching position. That lasted three years, and it was great. Then, when I moved back here, I just didn't want to work sixty hours a week."

"How's that working out for you?" asked Keri, already knowing the answer. Greg's wry smiled affirmed the irony.

"At least I get to 'share the privilege and responsibility of guiding America's young people,' in the words of some pamphlet I picked up in Human Resources. That's worth something."

"Yeah," said Clayton, wiping the beer from the lower edges of his mustache. "About thirty-two thousand a year."

While the waitress delivered a sandwich to Cockrell and a basket of fries to Clayton, Keri turned to Greg and asked, "What were you saying about school names?" It took him a moment to process, as he found himself captivated by her sky-blue eyes and curious about the slight bump on her nose that somehow made her all the more desirable.

"One year, new high schools in Sweetwater, north Phoenix, and wherever the other one is, and absolutely no identity," Greg resumed.

"What, you don't think Cactus Valley, Shadow Valley, and Shadowcliff are original?" asked Cockrell.

"I grew up in this district. Bonanza High School, class of '86. Every single school had a western name. Eldorado High School was our rival. I went to Sierra Elementary School and Cimarron Middle School. But nowadays, it's like they name 'em using those poetry magnets for your refrigerator, except due to the budget crisis they bought a defective set. Only had four words to choose from."

"But our fearless leader was able to convince the School Board to make Shadowcliff one word," noted Cockrell.

Added Keri, "As she reminds us, every single week."

"No doubt about it," Greg said, contemplating a mustard label, "she's a true educational visionary."

Indeed, Dr. Rumsford was a champion of innovation, reading educational journals with the voracity of a buzzard on a roadside carcass. She constantly exposed herself to the most cutting-edge theories about learning styles ("Brain Engagement is No Myth!" *Southern Educational Review*, vol. 1, November 2003), the most passionate practitioners of child psychology ("Johnny Hates Himself," *Children's Mental Health Quarterly*, vol. 17, Spring 2004), and the most vociferous critics of American education ("Why American's Can Not Spell, *Journal of English in Action*, vol. XXIX, March 2005).

"Now Greg," Bob cautioned. "Be more nurturing. You must be more nurturing."

"Please," Greg protested, filling his glass. "Two weeks ago she asked me to go through all the footage of the school being built, and then put together a video to show on the announcements. It took days, then another couple hours actually editing. I thought it was pretty good, considering I didn't have much to work with. I even added music. 'School is In' by—"

"—Josie Cotton," Clayton jumped in. "I know my eighties music."

"I'm not sure that should be a point of pride, but anyway, Rumsford comes in to watch the finished product, and I show it in front of the entire class, and when it's over she frowns and turns to the class and says, 'I thought it was terrible. What do you guys think?'"

Greg's parents had moved to Sweetwater when the town was still a sleepy suburb of Phoenix, no more than a passel of farms just beginning to sprout tract homes. Back then, people still came to Arizona for the healing quality of the warm, dry desert air. But the farmland had long since been paved over, and the process of turning fields into parking lots had raised a nasty brownish-gray haze, a dreary mixture of dust and exhaust fumes that loomed over the city both night and day and, on the worst of days, obscured the views of the craggy mountains to the east. Meanwhile, Sweetwater's small-town feel had been exchanged for an uptown ambition which remained largely unfulfilled. Greg often described it as "the traffic of Los Angeles, without the beach."

Now, pristine desert was being systematically destroyed, supplanted by massive gated communities that abrogated native wildlife in favor of divorce lawyers, plastic surgeons, and software entrepreneurs, each lounging around backyard pools or inside five-thousand square foot air-conditioned plywood-and-stucco palaces while they complained to their Homeowners' Association or relatives in New Jersey about the displaced javelinas roaming the neighborhood.

Greg stood up from his chair and walked past the space where the cigarette machine used to be, back when he first came to Wingding's as a college student, before Sweetwater's no-smoking ordinance thankfully made the air in local bars less toxic to healthy lungs. Now the space was filled by a giant cardboard cutout of the Arizona Cardinals cheerleaders, the team's schedule plastered across the girls' stomachs. Greg paused to examine both the schedule and the cheerleaders before he pushed open the creaky bathroom door.

When he returned to the table, Greg said, "Anyway, I asked Lydia Scanlon to do some research." Lydia Scanlon, Shadowcliff High School's sixty-year-old school librarian, was the most brilliant person Greg had ever met. Her insatiable thirst for knowledge encompassed world politics, medicine, law, and science. She knew the words to Lou Gehrig's farewell speech, the Magna Carta, and "Lydia the Tattooed Lady"—the last of which she adopted as her personal theme song during her wilder graduate school days. In Greg's mind, Lydia Scanlon may have been the school's most valuable resource, a human wellspring of information, opinion, curiosity, and quirky genius. She certainly offered a skill set unique to the challenge at hand.

Greg pulled out several sheets of paper and began to read. "It seems 'dangerous animals' is an official subject heading in library world."

"I did not know that," Keri said, reaching for the salt.

Greg continued, "An ordinance in Urbandale, Iowa makes it illegal to keep a dangerous or vicious animal within city limits." He read forward a bit. "Dangerous animals include wolves and coyotes, mink, weasels, elephants ... ah, that's boring. Let's see what else. The city of Aurora, Illinois also includes jackals and bison."

"Yeah, I'm sick of bison attacks," Clayton interjected as he cracked a peanut. Just last week—"

"—Hey, I actually got attacked by a bison when I was hiking in Montana one summer," argued Cockrell.

"What a surprise!" added Keri. "But I'm sure he was intimidated by your degree from Eastern Oregon University."

"Actually, he was more scared by my pistol from ... what did you say ... Fred's Camping Outlet?" Cockrell responded.

"Here we go," Greg continued, finally locating the appropriate page. "Here's a list we came up with. You guys ready?"

Cockrell belched. "I am now," he said.

"Black widow, death adder, barracuda? *Dracinculis medinensis,* cane toad, Australian tick? Box jellyfish, bulldog ant, tree-dwelling tunnel-web spider, candiru? Africanized—"

"—Wait a minute." Jimmy Clayton was intrigued. "What the hell's a candiru?"

Greg smiled. "I am so glad you asked." He turned to another page. "Allow me to quote." He paused for the sake of drama.

"Candiru (*Vandellia cirrhosa*). Found almost exclusively in the deep, dark waters of the Amazon River, the candiru is a tiny parasitic catfish, no bigger than a toothpick, with an affinity for human urethras. Candirus, which often attack when the unsuspecting human is urinating in the water..."

Beer dribbling from his nose, Jimmy Clayton tried to contain his laughter. Biting his lower lip, he emitted a strange fzzz sound, like a punctured bicycle tire.

"... have an equal attraction to both men and women. Upon entering, they immediately erect their backward-pointing spines and painfully affix themselves to the inside of the victim's urinary tract."

Both Keri Tanner and Bob Cockrell instinctively doubled up in agony. Greg noticed, smiled slyly— that had been his first reaction, too—and continued.

"These spines serve two important functions: to hold the fish securely in place, and to start a blood flow that will serve as the candiru's food supply."

Clayton pounded his beer mug on the table, while Greg's cadence grew more rapid in his excitement.

"The pain, it has been reported, is absolutely magnificent."

"Magnificent!" cried Clayton, loud enough to cause a woman on the other side of the bar to miss her shot at the eight-ball and then stare at him angrily.

"Once in place, a candiru cannot be removed without surgery. Unfortunately, since medical care in the Amazon is quite primitive, tribal doctors often treat the affliction by ... are you ready for this? ... amputating the victim's genitals."

Bob emitted an involuntary, guttural groan and Keri crouched even lower, both probably unwilling to sit up lest a stray candiru catch them unaware. Greg paused for a moment to let the full magnitude of agony sink in, while two businessmen at the bar pointed and chuckled.

"Is that a wonderful animal or what?"

"I think I'm gonna throw up," said Keri.

"I mean, how many animals' descriptions actually make you double over in pain?"

"I'm sorry," Cockrell said. "It is a wonderful animal. It gets you in your most sensitive parts and it hurts like hell. Just like Rumsford."

"Basically, it's a cocksucker," summarized Keri.

"Just like Rumsford," Cockrell continued. "But I don't think I can give her a nickname that makes my penis hurt every time I say it."

"C'mon," argued Greg. "We could all wear cod-pieces to a faculty meeting, and she wouldn't have the slightest idea—"

"—I don't even know what a codpiece is," Cockrell objected. "But I do know what a urethra is, and I don't want to think about some bloodsucking fish living there." Unconsciously, he waved a toothpick for emphasis.

"Fine," said Greg. "Anyone have any other ideas? Although I'm telling you, the candiru is now my favorite animal of all-time."

"I'm sure that will earn you a free pass next time you're peeing in the Amazon River," Keri said.

Bob Cockrell inhaled deeply. "What's that mascot for that one school? The woolavino?"

Clayton shot back, "It's the wolverine, you idiot. And it's the University of Michigan."

"I don't watch football," Cockrell admitted. "I don't really care. But a wolverine—isn't that a short, hairy, mean fucker?"

"I hate their fight song," Clayton interjected, knocking over his beer. "Goddammit!" Everyone scattered.

By the time they had cleaned up the mess, it was settled. A short, hairy, mean fucker was exactly what they were searching for.

"Henceforth, Dr. Connie Rumsford will be known to one and all as The Wolverine."

They clinked their mugs together in victorious affirmation. Business completed, they now got down to some really serious drinking.

For Greg Samson, the nightmares had already begun.

2

THE MASTER TEACHER

Summer in Arizona is hot. Greg used to occasionally train with a guy, originally from upstate New York, who had made the grave error of relocating to Arizona in the summer. This guy was no stranger to difficult conditions, having once finished eleventh at the Boston Marathon on an 85-degree day. Still, he said that when he first arrived in Arizona, he felt like his face was on fire, melting like the Nazis at the end of *Raiders of the Lost Ark*.

This particular June day was a killer, 114 degrees in the shade, one of those face-on-fire days.

Greg pulled his pickup truck into the parking lot of Sierra Elementary School. The concrete shimmered from the heat, waves of oppression rising up to make the red brick buildings look like a Salvador Dali painting. But Greg knew both the heat and the buildings were real. He knew every brick of this place. He smiled, recalling the friends and the experiences from his six years as a Sierra student years ago. He knew how many buildings there were and how many classrooms were in each. He still remembered his favorite teacher, Miss Randall, room 17. He remembered writing a skit about The Lone Orange at a picnic table under the mulberry tree and building rockets in a science class on the other side of campus. In this place he had learned fractions, Greek mythology, and indirect objects. He had also, unknown to him at the time, begun his competitive running career one unusually cold winter day, when two friends suggested they run laps at lunchtime simply to stay warm. So many memories.

Even as a boy, Greg knew that Sierra was the pride of Sweetwater Unified School District No. 43 and Sweetwater was the pride of the Arizona Department of Education. But as attendance in this part of the District had diminished in the past few years, migrating to the wealthier areas of northeast Sweetwater, some of Sierra's buildings had been repurposed as centralized pre-K classes or for District in-service meetings. And now its parking lot housed a trailer which served as temporary office space for the soon-to-open Shadowcliff High School, the newest and most dynamic facility in the District.

As he walked the hundred feet toward the Shadowcliff trailer, Greg could not help but start to perspire. It was damn hot.

Dr. Connie Rumsford welcomed Greg into the trailer, whose air conditioning was invigorating, actually chilling him due to the perspiration on his skin. "I don't like you and I don't want you here," she began, formalities be damned. "And I don't like people who sweat."

"If I become your cross country coach," Greg replied politely, "I'm afraid that'll be unavoidable."

Strewn with papers, textbooks, boxes, and chocolate bar wrappers, the temporary space gave the appearance of a Gulf Coast town after a late-summer flurry of tropical storms. "But Maurice McCullough and Randy Smith are both strongly advocating on your behalf," Dr. Rumsford continued, "so I owe it to them to give you fair and unbiased consideration." Maurice, a Shadowcliff assistant principal, was a former sprinter from inner-city Detroit and now coach of a local track club. Pushing fifty, he remained fit, handsome, and well-dressed. Randy, meanwhile, was Greg's oldest and dearest friend, his partner in driveway hockey games, lunchtime escapades, chemistry experiments, and Led Zeppelin albums since first grade. He was now Shadowcliff's Athletic Director, and he urgently needed coaches. Greg relaxed, until she added, "Although there's no way in hell I'm hiring you."

Somehow, Greg managed to overcome Dr. Rumsford's initial reticence and proceed with the scheduled interview. Actually, it was not really an interview but more a recitation of Greg's shortcomings, which Dr. Rumsford had mystically divined from the two-page résumé she held in front of her. Between bites of her Snickers bar, she pronounced him "unfocusedable," "distantory," and "digressient." At least, he thought, the quality of her manufactured words was admirable. Greg was not above admitting he had flaws, and had frequently been informed of them by former girlfriends. But like the twisted wreckage of some terrible automobile accident, the audacity of this person he had just met was somehow both sickening and strangely compelling. Besides, as much as he wanted to tell Dr. Rumsford to stuff it, he was pretty sure he could be an effective teacher and, moreover, he ultimately realized that a year of part-time work landscaping houses while caring for his sick father had stretched him pretty thin. Truth be told, he was nearly broke, and needed a job desperately.

Master teacher Elden Ray Fong says: *Never leap to rash judgments.*

While working on his MBA/JD several years earlier, Greg had relationships with three different women who had already accepted lucrative corporate positions with east-coast companies. He came to call it "futility dating." Yet here he was, a week after his meeting with Dr. Rumsford, adjusting his tie while he awaited an interview before other members of the Shadowcliff English department. Surely, he thought, based upon Rumsford's solemn assertion, this was no less futile than a third-party presidential campaign, the eradication of cockroaches, or his own love life.

Yet as a result of this interview, Department Chair Ramona Thurlow, a twenty two-year veteran of Sweetwater Unified School District No. 43, sent Dr. Rumsford the following memo:

> Very bright and energetic. Although inexperienced in a high school setting, his college teaching experience is a plus. Exceptional subject matter knowledge. Fine sense of humor and rapport. Does not understand all the newest educational theories, but will easily learn and adapt. Strongly recommended.

He received an urgent phone call two days later, and was told to report for a second interview with Dr. Rumsford at eleven a.m. He spent the morning rearranging his schedule and ironing another shirt, arrived at the trailer a few minutes before eleven, and helped the office aides staple parent newsletters until he was called into Dr. Rumsford's office promptly at 12:45.

"The reason you're here," she began, scowling at her watch, "is to tell you that your interview with the department didn't go particularly well."

"I don't quite understand why I needed to cancel my dental appointment—"

"—But I wanted to give you one last chance," she continued, "out of courtesy to Maurice and Randy, who are both advocating strongly on your behalf."

Greg was bewildered as to why they were still pushing for him. If they were, their support demonstrated either an inspiring level of friendship or a blithely masochistic approach to their own careers. More likely, Greg realized, their "advocacy" was probably nothing more than an elaborate fiction perpetrated by Dr. Rumsford.

"So you need to really impress me in this interview." She stiffened noticeably and crossed her arms. "Or else. Understand?"

This second interview was a wide-ranging, almost dizzying compilation of questions focused almost entirely upon his knowledge of all things she knew he did not know.

"Tell me your opinion of Blake's Eight-Tiered Model of Esteem," she posed. He had no answer, so she spent five minutes berating him for not understanding that we must utilize positive talk to build a strong self-image in others. "How would you construct an effective rubric in order to accomplish District curricular objectives?" Greg replied that it would have to begin with a clear understanding of the District curriculum guide, so she thrust a heavy red notebook in front of him and ordered him to memorize it while she enjoyed a snack of cookies and a Sprite. "In ten words or less, explain your use of alternative assessments and their impact on objective performance measures." When Greg offered that it would be impossible to do in only ten words, she launched into another tirade, explaining her philosophy and the philosophy espoused by Podkevnik, Andrews, and Torre, *et. al.*, taking eleven minutes and approximately five thousand words to do so. And finally, "What do you know about scaffolding?"

Even a desperate man has his limits, thought Greg, as he smiled slightly and began his answer. "Made of either metal or wood, or some combination thereof," he said, "scaffolding is used to reach the upper levels of a building, typically for construction or maintenance functions. Michelangelo lay on his back on a scaffolding while he painted the ceiling of the Sistine Chapel, which I understand is an impressive piece of work, and one for which he should be praised." Then he added, "Under Blake's Eight-Tiered Model of Esteem, or otherwise."

Dr. Rumsford stood up, the universal sign that the meeting was finished. Turning her back, she announced, "I don't know why you want to be a teacher anyway."

"Thank you for your consideration," Greg said as he unfolded himself from his chair. "I look forward to hearing from you." She stared at him as if he had just offered to sacrifice a live goat. Walking out the door and into the blazing Arizona summer, Greg smiled of liberation and decided he was in the mood for a turkey sandwich from Caratelli's Deli down the street, where he could read the Help Wanted section in peace.

Master teacher Elden Ray Fong says: *Cultivate a sense of team unity.*

Toward the end of July, Greg received a most unexpected phone call. "Hello?"

"This is Dr. Connie Rumsford from Shadowcliff High School," she explained, as if Greg had undergone some sort of shock therapy to erase his memory of her. "My Yearbook teacher decided to take a job in Michigan, so I'm stuck with you. You'll also teach Video Production, English II, and English III in a block. Welcome to the team. If you screw up, heads are going to roll."

And that was it. She did not ask if he had found another job (he hadn't) and did not even wait for a reply. With a click on the other end, Rumsford hung up, and Greg was now a high school teacher.

One week later and one week before the school was to open its doors for business, the faculty and staff of Shadowcliff High School gathered in the school cafeteria for orientation. "Welcome to Shadowcliff High School," announced Dr. Rumsford, her voice slicing through the buzz, "the best high school in Arizona." There was a smattering of applause. "I said, the best high school in Arizona!" Oh, Greg realized, this is a Tony Robbins seminar, so this time he hooted and hollered along with his new colleagues. "That's better. This will be unlike any challenge you've ever encountered. It will be a year of chaos and fatigue. Yet, I am confident that I have hired the finest group of teachers in the world. Each one of you was hand-picked, and I am absolutely confident in your abilities because you are the best."

Greg fought mightily against the urge to raise his hand and say, "Dr. Rumsford, you forgot about me!"

What took place over these three days was a multitude of team-building activities Rumsford had designed. There were games of chance and games of skill, activities that demanded physical dexterity or child-like imagination. Some, like charades, were old favorites. Other activities incorporated a new twist, like the game of Pictionary® in which the answers were all famous teachers. This one fell flat, to Rumsford's chagrin, and was ultimately suspended when nobody could identify Saint John Ogilvie from a sketch of a stick figure with what appeared to be a slice of toast on his head. Randy Smith's suggestion of a glove hockey tournament was dismissed, but there was a combination tricycle relay/spelling bee that most of the teachers agreed was kind of fun.

What did not take place over these three days was any activity that might help them become better teachers.

During this time, Greg met his colleagues, shared stories with them, and threw Nerf balls at them. Like himself, many were new to the profession. Others were transplants from distant states, drawn by the weather or by a lifestyle change to the wild-west image the city purposely cultivated even as its every political decision conflicted with that image. Still others were veteran teachers who wanted to finish out their careers with a little juice. Greg teamed with one such veteran, Jeanette Candelaria, during the Three-Legged Color War, missing out on a likely podium finish when they stumbled through the Hula Hoop station and lost valuable points. However, they soon learned from Dr. Rumsford that the scores did not matter anyway, because scores create hierarchies of success and failure which jeopardize children's positive self-image.

Later, he partnered with Keri Tanner for some sort of numerical personality self-analysis exercise moderated by an off-duty policeman and the woman

recently hired as Shadowcliff's head fry cook. Greg
had actually spotted Keri across the room earlier in
the day while she was talking with Randy Smith. As
it turned out, she was a math teacher, so Greg felt
they might have an advantage in this particular exercise. And she was the prettiest woman in the room,
so he did not really care if they had an advantage or
not. Their score was seventy-four, which was higher
than some and lower than others but, sadly, meant
absolutely nothing to him or anyone else at his table.
Of course, that was probably for the best, since he
now understood that scores create hierarchies of success and failure which probably would have jeopard-
ized his own self-image and the self-images of those
around him.

He met Bob Cockrell during lunch, when teachers were seated alphabetically according to their
place of birth. Born in Wyoming, Cockrell decided
he did not want to sit all alone, so he opted for the
Texas table at which Greg and one other teacher were
seated. They were soon joined by Jimmy Clayton,
who bypassed the introductions and immediately
pulled out a newspaper column proclaiming "This
could be ASU's year," as if his efforts in spreading
the gospel would simultaneously get him into heaven
and the Sun Devils into the Rose Bowl.

But the orientation was not all fun-and-games.
Policies were to be decided. Procedures were to be
discussed. Expectations were to be enumerated.

Master teacher Elden Ray Fong was to be introduced, praised, and put forth as the ultimate role model in education. And "the finest group of teachers in the world" was to be reminded, constantly, that they had better be perfect or else they would face the wrath of a five-foot-three, fifty-two-year-old former nurse who still knew how to draw blood and who probably still kept a rusty scalpel in her top desk drawer.

Late Thursday, as fatigue had taken over and the teachers just wanted to be done for the day, Rumsford began to talk about goals. She explained that effective goals needed to be realistic, measurable, and timely. She defined the terms and provided examples of each. She described the difference between short-term and long-term goals. She checked for understanding and asked the teachers to discuss the value of goal-setting at their tables.

Those teachers at Greg's table seemed clear enough on the concept. They could easily have been divided into two distinct groups with two distinct short-term goals: about half of them had their eye on the last chocolate chip cookie on the dessert table, while the other half were clearly motivated by making it to the bar before Happy Hour was over.

Greg understood goal setting, and as a former elite athlete probably could explain the process as well as anyone in the room. Among the most important points, he knew that goals were worthless unless accompanied by action, that the true purpose of a goal is to allow the person to formulate a plan to achieve the goal, and then to get moving when his alarm went off at five a.m. and it was already hot as hell outside and his legs were sore from a hard workout just nine hours before and he had to get twenty miles this morning because the Olympic Trials were only eleven months and four days away and there were still about six thousand miles he needed to run. All the rest was bluster.

He also knew that not all goals were met. He had done the five a.m. runs but still came up short on his Olympic dream. And now here he was in a hot cafeteria, yawning and hungry, in the midst of a fundamental shift in his world. The vicissitudes of life.

Greg's reverie was broken by Rumsford's sharp whistle. She announced that each person would present one personal goal to the group, and that the day would not end until everyone had done so. The Happy Hour group looked at their watches, then each other, downcast, their most immediate goal looking dubious. The cookie group continued to eye the dessert table, until finally a custodian walked past and snagged the last one to render their immediate goal unattainable. And now everyone, faced with crushing defeat, was going to have to impress Rumsford or else face the prospect of an all-nighter.

One teacher offered, "I want to be the best teacher I can," and everyone applauded, even though the goal was neither measureable nor timely. Another suggested, "We should try to be the best school in

Sweetwater," and Rumsford smiled, even though this was stated more like a Disney movie than a goal, and it was neither measurable nor timely, nor even personal. And so it went, inanities offered mostly as a tool to move the teachers toward their freedom, with an occasional good one thrown in.

Soon it was Greg's turn. He had actually been thinking about this all week; such was his nature. "As a classroom teacher, my goal is for my students to achieve the highest scores on every standardized test, while never teaching to the test." A smattering of applause at best. "And as a coach, my goal is to hang Shadowcliff's first state-championship banner."

"We do not teach to the test," Rumsford said curtly before she moved on. Greg mumbled "Like I said" as he sat down.

"My goal is for students to develop a love of learning in a nurturing environment," said one teacher. Rumsford, delighted, failed to notice the teacher pointing out to a colleague that she had lifted those exact words from the District's mission statement.

"Now, one final thing," Rumsford said. "A goal is meaningless unless it's yours. You need ownership of your goals. Nobody can tell you what your goals should be. It needs to be something *you* thought of and *you* want to achieve. So with that in mind, here is my goal: to make Shadowcliff the best high school in Arizona. I'll see you at eight a.m. sharp tomorrow, and we can all start working on making my goal a reality."

3

THE INSURRECTION

Master teacher Elden Ray Fong says: *Your colleagues are your greatest resource.*

Friday began with a brief greeting from Rumsford and a reminder of her individual goal. While it was neither measurable nor timely, and perhaps not even realistic, it was hers. And now it was everyone's: Shadowcliff's collective goal by virtue of executive fiat.

The rest of the morning was reserved for department meetings, so Greg dutifully walked down the hall toward Ramona Thurlow's classroom. This was no easy task, as the hallway was blocked by huge rolls of blue carpeting and stacks of white plastic cans of carpet glue. While not a major problem for Greg, who simply hurdled the obstacles, it forced many of his Language Arts colleagues to find a different route. I sure hope they get that carpet installed before Monday, he mused, watching them scatter.

Greg and the others obediently filed into a room with the hope of learning more about collaboration in heterogeneous groups, ideas for writing instruction, and the proper sequencing of activities in block versus single-period classes. Ramona Thurlow, the department chair, stood before the sixteen English teachers. Slight of stature, her close-cropped hair and sharp tone gave her a commanding presence that strangely mirrored that of Rumsford. Indeed, Greg wondered if all the department chairs were short, shrill, cryptic women.

"I know you all want to work on some curricular approaches, and we'll have time for that later," she said. "But now, I think it's important that we get our supplies and work in our rooms."

"But Ramona, I have a concern," said Katherine Bogard, a veteran teacher. "For the past three days, I feel as if we've been rushed through everything. With all these new programs, I'd like some help. I'd like to work with my colleagues on block strategies, and I'd certainly like to discuss some ideas for Mentor Time. I have no idea what to do with that."

"You can move students around, do lots of small group work," offered Ramona. "There's always the questions in the text. Have them read a story and then answer the questions. Strong students should help the weak ones."

"But how do we do that if we're not supposed to label kids?" replied Katherine. There was a certain tone, Greg noticed, which suggested these two had a *history*.

"And Mentor Time is for connecting with a group of kids. Mentor them."

"In what?"

"Activities. You've got the notebook."

"I've looked through the notebook." She pulled it out. "Working in groups to put shapes together is supposed to help me connect with kids?"

"Why are you always so negative?"

"Why are you always so evasive?" The other English teachers glanced among themselves, sinking down into their chairs almost in unison.

"I resent that!"

"I don't care if you resent that. If you had any ambition, you—"

"—Ambition? I have plenty of ambition. I helped plan this school, and I'm department chair."

"So what? All that means is that you kissed somebody's butt."

"That's unprofessional, Kate. I—" But Katherine was already halfway out the door, and it was obvious she was crying. "Everyone get your materials and go to work. I have an important Department Chair meeting."

The teachers quickly gathered themselves and hurried from Ramona Thurlow's classroom. "Greg?"

Greg stopped and turned around. Teachers had filed out so quickly that he was now the only one, besides Ramona Thurlow herself, left in the room.

"Greg, I said nice things to Dr. Rumsford about you," Ramona said. "I was a big reason you got this job."

I don't like where this is going, Greg thought.

"So I'd like you to write a statement about what just happened. That it wasn't my fault. And sign it. Can you do that?"

"Sure," he replied, barely masking his discomfort. It was like being asked by guards at Guantanamo Bay if he would mind too terribly much being waterboarded.

"I'd like it by lunchtime. I'll pick it up after my important Department Chair meeting."

Greg went immediately to his classroom. He could pick up his supplies later, and maybe his desks could magically arrange themselves, since he was having no luck in making them fit his sharply rectangular classroom. But none of this mattered now. Instead, through some combination of obligation and circumstance, he been implicated in the most remarkable example of Cover Your Ass he had ever witnessed.

He turned on his computer, wondering if he should put the statement on Shadowcliff letterhead. Best go to the source, he thought, so he walked down the hallway to Ramona's room, just in time to see her slip out the back door wearing shorts, a T-shirt, and hiking boots, the noontime sun winking at him as it flashed off her silver water bottle.

Master teacher Elden Ray Fong says: *Consensus builds trust, and trust builds ownership.*

The week's events ended with a high-level staff meeting, either one final team-building opportunity or a time of homage, depending upon one's perspective. Regardless, it was mandatory. So Shadowcliff's teachers shuffled wearily into room 4122, hoping to fill the seats toward the rear but finding, much to their dismay, that the oblong shape of the room prohibited anyone from hiding in the back. They rubbed eyes made tired from having read too many articles, adjusted necks made cranky from too many meet-your-neighbor activities, and massaged shoulders made sore from trying to throw too hard during the Great Nerf Ball Rally.

Greg sat at a table by himself, as he often did. He had never been particularly socially adept, which made it easy to immerse himself in the solitude required of a national-class distance runner. Plus, he had chosen to purposely avoid the rabble of coaches who always congregated; their side conversations and inattentiveness were tolerated by Rumsford, but Greg just knew he would somehow manage to get in trouble if he joined them. Instead, by virtue of sitting by himself and then being joined by whomever happened to wander past, he had managed to meet most of the staff over the past few days. Now he scanned the room, recognizing virtually every face, the activity during which he met them, and some vital characteristic that was supposed to help break the ice.

There's the guy who goes to Denny's every Tuesday morning, Greg thought. The lady who collects chopsticks. The dude with the ear afro. (While not what the man had offered, his ear hair was the characteristic that stood out the most.) Only trouble was, as he tried to match names to faces, Greg mostly drew a blank.

"Hey," he heard, breaking his thought. And now he would have to remember one more.

"I'm John Woodacre," said the new guy. "I teach Social Studies." He slid into a chair.

"Greg Samson. Language Arts, Yearbook, Video, Cross Country coach.... I think that's all. For now anyway."

"Nice to meet you. My friends in Indiana call me Woody."

"What do your friends in Arizona call you?" Greg asked.

"I only been here a week," Woody replied. "I had a girlfriend back in Muncie. She got into grad school out here, so I applied for a job. Now here I am."

"And what do you think?"

"It's a nice campus and all that, but so far I took a seven-thousand-dollar pay cut to spend three days playing children's games."

"You don't find it worthwhile to write on balloons with Sharpies?" asked Greg.

Just before lunch that day, each teacher had written something pithy and inspirational on their balloons, then blown them up and released them from the second-story walkway. It was meant to be a symbolic exercise of giving wings to their feelings.

"I guess the long-distance flight competition was OK," said Woody. "Being how it just proved what we already suspected."

Greg laughed, knowing from his tone and his gaze toward the front of the room what he meant. Rumsford's balloon flew further than all the others. She was full of hot air.

"Plus I think she's bipolar," Woody added. "And my girlfriend broke up with me and went to the University of Colorado instead."

"That sucks," said Greg. Before he could elaborate, Rumsford called for everyone's attention and the room grew quiet.

Rumsford invited each member of the planning team to say a few words, to share their thoughts about the opening of the new school, about what it meant to them both personally and professionally. Ramona Thurlow, who had helped select textbooks and who had somehow acquired a sunburn since the morning, said she was honored to be here. Edie Walker, a counselor who had helped select furniture, explained how excited she was. Samantha O'Bradovich, head of Special Education who had helped select paint colors, offered a tribute to the vision of Dr. Rumsford and the others on the planning team, a heartfelt wish to the faculty for a safe and successful school year, an appreciation of the District for allowing their dreams to come to fruition, and a tearful, seventeen-minute thank you to her husband, children, parents, pet Chihuahua, and first piano teacher. Finally, Kim Purcell, the school nurse who had helped select a case of Band-Aids from the stockroom at Walgreen's, told everyone that they were not allowed to send students to the nurse before school, during first period, during either of the lunch periods, and after school. Kids would just need to get sick at a convenient time.

Greg eventually began to call this group as "The Politburo."

The meeting was now delegated to Rumsford's minions. The tardy policy was addressed by Maurice McCullough, who was apparently in charge of attendance issues. Greg knew that four years ago, Maurice had been hand-picked for grooming by Dr. Rumsford at her last school, and it was clear he had become her pride and joy. Rumsford's frequent deference to him throughout the afternoon made it clear that he was also going to be in charge of discipline, parking, athletics, student government, standardized testing, and accommodations for kids with Attention Deficit Disorder. The other assistant principal, Zoey Crandall, was never allowed to speak and was, Greg later concluded, apparently in charge of ordering lunch.

Ike Gravenstein, a teacher with twenty-six years in Sweetwater Unified School District No. 43 who had chosen to join the faculty of Shadowcliff High School because of its innovative approaches to learning, raised his hand.

"Connie, you keep mentioning the 'No Hats' policy. I was wondering if we could discuss this."

"Sure," she responded, a little defensively it seemed. Greg had never heard anyone call her anything besides Dr. Rumsford before. "What would you like to discuss about it?"

"I think it's silly."

"Silly? Hats constrict blood flow to the human brain, which gives the wearer migraines and leads to hair loss and strokes. I was a nurse. I know this for a fact."

"So most baseball players are bald and dead by the age of thirty?" Gravenstein inquired. He turned toward Jeff Dunleavy, the baseball coach. "Coach Dunleavy, are you aware of this?"

Dunleavy just laughed, noncommittally, so Gravenstein found someone else to query. "Kim, what about you? Have you ever heard of this?"

"Well, I...," the nurse stumbled.

Continued Rumsford, "And all the latest research indicates that hats are a distraction to the learning environment. An article by—"

"—How are they distracting?" Gravenstein was relentless.

"Gangs, for example. They can indicate gang affiliation."

"That's a valid concern in some places maybe, but Officer Mike said there is no known gang activity in this part of the city. You're gonna have to do better than that."

Greg shifted uneasily in his seat. While he knew this could get interesting, he also thought it best to remain as inconspicuous as possible. But not Gravenstein.

"Besides, I assume teachers are going to be the ones enforcing this policy on a day-to-day basis?"

"That's right."

"And why would we enforce a policy that many of us don't agree with?"

"Because I say so. That should be good enough."

"But is it necessary?" asked Gravenstein. "Is it good for kids?" And then, pulling out one of Rumsford's pet phrases, he added, "Is it 'student-centered'?"

Rumsford was struck silent. Greg considered it a Hale-Bopp moment, one of those which, like the comet, comes only every few hundred years. But her trusty lieutenant, Maurice, apparently knew his role well.

"Ike, what do you suggest as an alternative?" he asked, smoothing his Ferragamo tie.

"I think we should ditch it. I think it's a stupid policy, and I'm willing to bet most of the teachers agree."

"You want to vote on it?"

"Yeah, I'd like to do that. We're supposed to be the cream of the crop, and all week we've heard phrases like 'shared decision-making'. I'd like to see you put your money where your mouth is."

"Fine," shot back Rumsford, filling quickly with spit and vinegar. "Anyone who supports the hat policy as it's now written...." As a smattering of hands went up, she stared directly into the eyes of each and every new teacher and added, "... a policy we worked months on, and which has the absolute backing of both the local parents and the District administration..." Nice touch, thought Greg, who personally believed it was a stupid rule mostly because the issue was so utterly insignificant. Besides, if boys wanted to wear the same hat every day, even as it grew more sweat-stained and stinky, who was he to impose his standards of personal hygiene on others?

Yet as he watched many uncertain teachers being intimidated into acquiescence, he figured his longevity was best served by disappearing under the table to tie his shoes. "... raise your hands."

"Anyone who wants to change the rule?" Gravenstein's hand was not the only one, but

Rumsford was already huddling with her two assistant principals.

Jeanette Candelaria later told Greg that she counted twenty votes for no hats, thirty-three who wanted the policy changed, and about half a dozen who appeared either too ambivalent or too terrified to vote.

"The vote is close, so we will retain the policy as written." And with that, the First Rebellion was crushed with ruthless efficiency.

"I feel like I just had a close encounter with Josef Stalin," whispered Jimmy Clayton as they adjourned.

Master teacher Elden Ray Fong says: *The first day is the most important day of the year.*

The rest of the afternoon, and no doubt long hours into the weekend, would be spent decorating classrooms, preparing syllabi, and trying to decide on the image one wanted to present on Day One. This was no small matter. The advice Greg received covered the entire spectrum of options. Some recommended the formal approach of slacks, dress shirt, and tie, suggesting that class would be all business. Others advocated the casual approach typified by flowered Hawaiian shirts and cute sayings on the board, such as 'Welcome to my classroom, where your brain will be happy ☺.'

When asked, Dr. Rumsford remained ambiguous. "I expect you to dress professionally" was all she said. However, the literature she distributed ("Making Children Secure," *Teacher's World*, vol. 1, June 2002) argued that the casual approach would make students feel more at ease, thus feeding their self-esteem because the classroom was so non-threatening, and hence allowing them to reach their full potential, flourishing in such a way that they could go on to Hopkins Med School, Yale Law School, or Harvard Divinity School. The article even cited the case of a Nobel Prize winner who had blossomed under just such an approach. On the other hand, a more formal classroom might intimidate students, causing them to be afraid to express themselves and then, consequently, to doubt their abilities. One case study told of a student, utterly lacking in self-worth, who barely graduated high school, dropped out of Wally Thor's Truckmaster School of Trucking after six weeks, and ended up sponging off Mom and Dad in order to avoid living in a box under the bridge.

Jeanette Candelaria had pointed out that while one can always get easier, one can never implement order if it is not in place on the first day. So Sunday evening, Greg finally decided upon a pair of khaki trousers, a powder blue dress shirt and a nice blue tie, and drifted off to sleep.

Greg found himself in front of his first period class, prepared and confident. His objectives were on the board and his syllabi were in a neat stack on a table in front of the room. After welcoming his students, he picked up his class roster and a pencil. "Roger Anderson?" he asked. "Susan Arnstadt?" Suddenly, inexplicably, students began to point, then to snicker, then to laugh robustly. Greg was confused. This was not the way master teacher Elden Ray Fong said it would work.

Finally, looking down, he realized the problem. He was standing before the class naked. He had, however, been careful to cover his ass. With a hat.

4

The beep-beep-beep of Greg's Timex one-hundred split Ultra Chronograph rescued him from his embarrassment. It was six a.m., two hours before he would begin his first day as a high school teacher, with the careers of two friends and perhaps his own physical well-being at stake.

Greg had recently rented an apartment just over a mile from Shadowcliff High School, and he could see the stadium lights from his "cozy" patio, as the leasing hostess described it. He knew "cozy" was apartment-speak for "tiny," but he had not rented this particular apartment in order to park a helicopter in his living room. It was all about location, and his proximity to school ensured that neither a power outage nor car trouble nor disorientation could possibly make him late.

The apartment was 752 square feet of bachelorness. Furniture was mismatched: a brown and white dining room table his father had kept in the garage for the past twelve years, a red fake leather chair purchased for twenty dollars at a yard sale, and a blue-and-white plaid sofa borrowed from his best friend. Eight hundred CD's were housed in the same crates in which he had moved them cross-country and back again. The living room's focal point was the TV and stereo. In the bedroom, a queen-sized mattress sat on the floor, covered in black sheets recently purchased at a Going-Out-of-Business sale at Emily's Fine Linens at the local outlet mall.

As Greg lay in bed, his mind raced at dizzying speeds. He reviewed the first day's attendance procedure: write the names of anyone on your roster but not in class on the green sheet, write the names of anyone in class but not on your roster on the yellow sheet, write the names of anyone who is tardy on the pink sheet, write the names of anyone whose name is misspelled on the blue sheet, and write the names of anyone who is on your roster, on time, with correctly spelled name on the salmon-colored sheet. He reviewed the photocopy procedure: sign in, input your teacher number, use only recycled paper due to the District's acute paper shortage. He reviewed the evacuation procedure: walk calmly and quietly out of the classroom, turn right, go down the stairs, turn left, then right, then right again, then exit the building into the parking lot where students would re-assemble in an orderly fashion. At least that was the official procedure.

The unofficial procedure, he suspected, was to run like hell.

His review completed, Greg dragged himself out of bed and waded an ocean of running shoes toward the bathroom. While showering, he cut himself twice with the brand-new razor purchased at Target the day before. After staunching the blood flow and drying off, he fished some clean underwear from a U-Haul box in the corner, then pulled his first-day outfit from his closet, the one organized place in his apartment. He read the newspaper during his breakfast of cereal, a raisin bagel, and orange juice—essentially the same breakfast he'd eaten every day since first grade—then brushed his teeth and headed out the door. It was 7:17.

Shadowcliff High School's wide, carpeted hallways, comfortable air conditioning, padded overstuffed chairs, ambiance music, and ample spaces for relaxation all resembled, perhaps purposefully, the high-dollar Sweetwater Fashion Center just a few miles south. True, there were science labs where the Sunglass Hut would otherwise be, and a library in place of Nordstrom's. Yet it seemed as if the mannequins had escaped through the front window of Abercrombie & Fitch, and now roamed the Shadowcliff halls wearing the apparently mandatory representation of teenage privilege. Greg's entire outfit, purchased piece-by-piece from various discount outlets, probably cost less than the average student's T-shirt. Greg could not comprehend how a T-shirt could sell for seventy bucks—was it spun from golden thread, or woven by unionized elves?—but he knew it represented both an object lesson in supply-and-demand, laissez-faire economics and a window into the socio-economic status of the community.

Oddly, though, the stark gray brick on the outside made Shadowcliff High School look like a prison.

This look was, however, set off just slightly by the delicate, finely machined copper fascia that was virtually invisible to the passerby but whose three-hundred-thousand-dollar cost resulted in inadequate cafeteria seating and the deletion of every single handicapped ramp and railing. So while it was possible that a skilled photographer from *Arizona Highways* magazine could frame a shot with cholla cactus in the foreground and the afternoon sun glinting off the copper facade, it was equally likely that the school would face litigation under the Americans With Disabilities Act or shutdown under the local fire code.

Greg walked through Shadowcliff's front doors at 7:30, a full half-hour before first period. A faint chemical scent stung his eyes, but this discomfort was counterbalanced by the relaxing music playing softly over the intercom. Entering the office, he pulled from his mailbox a three-page handout on which was scrawled: "Read this before class today. –CR"

Seven other multi-page articles and three shorter pieces cluttered his mailbox, each featuring the same impossible demand and inimitable scrawl of Dr. Connie Rumsford.

Bob Cockrell and Jimmy Clayton pulled similar handouts from their mailboxes. "What's with the elevator music?" Cockrell asked as he absently glanced through the papers.

"Mozart," Greg replied. "I think it's from *The Magic Flute.*"

"They should play some Bananarama," offered Clayton. "Or Total Coelho."

"I'm not sure they want to turn the first day into *Rock and Roll High School*," Greg replied. "I don't think the idea of student empowerment extends to full-blown rebellion."

"What I want to know is, why are they playing music at all?" asked Cockrell.

"Mozart is supposed to improve right-brain function and enhance creative thought."

"Another Rumsford theory?" Cockrell asked.

"No, actually, this one's pretty well-known," said Greg. "I thought everyone with a kid knew that theory. What kind of music do you play for your daughter?"

Clayton tossed the articles in the recycle bin and replied, "The soundtrack from *Deliverance.*"

Greg chuckled. "I don't know if the theory is true or not, but I do like the music."

As Clayton and Cockrell exited, Greg noticed that the recycle bin was nearly overflowing. And everything in it had the exact same scrawl on top: "Read this before class today. –CR"

Maurice walked past and patted Greg on the back. "Ready to go?" he asked.

"Ready as I'll ever be," Greg replied. And then, remembering the hideous dream of last night, he checked his zipper before heading off to class.

He had finally figured out how to arrange the desks, which sat in precise pairs. The walls were decorated with a few posters, among them his Mickey Mouse Sorcerer's Apprentice poster, which he had placed over his desk to remind himself that he had much to learn. The room was sparse and spotless; some might have judged it spartan. More than anything else, it was functional.

The first day was really nothing more than an orientation, fifteen-minute classes providing just enough time for students to find their classrooms, meet their teachers, and, if Rumsford's onslaught of research was to be believed, formulate first impressions that were immutable.

Following the advice of Elden Ray Fong, Greg stood at his doorway, welcoming and helpful as he watched the halls transform from a trickle of students to a flood. Many of them wrinkled their noses at the biting chemical odor that wafted into the air.

"What is that stink?" Greg heard one boy ask his friend.

"I don't know," said the friend, "but I think it's rotting my eyeballs."

I love the smell of carpet glue in the morning, Greg said to himself, smiling. It smells like ... pedagogy.

Students began to arrive. "Good morning," he said to the bleary-eyed kid with the baggy pants. "How are you?" he said to the perky blonde with the low-cut pink tank top and a photo of her boyfriend on her notebook. "Welcome," he said to the hulking man-child with the baseball cap over his crewcut. None said a word as they passed him. Greg thought: Lesson one, social graces.

And even though class began at 8:00, he continued greeting latecomers until 8:04, never noticing that class had started since no bell had rung. This, he learned later that day when he finally had a chance to read Rumsford's articles, was because studies show that bells are disruptive to the learning environment and produce a chemical reaction in the brain similar to a seizure.

"Attention teachers...." The announcement stopped Greg mid-greeting, although it had absolutely no success in quieting the students. "... Please turn your televisions to channel twenty for a short welcome from Dr. Rumsford." An additional five minutes had been allotted first period to allow Rumsford to briefly address the student body over the school's closed-circuit television network.

On his way to the TV, Greg stepped over a student who had chosen to lay on the floor, squeezed between two who were kissing, and twisted his ankle when he tripped over a backpack. Only upon turning on the TV did he have a chance to survey his classroom. The quick count, which he realized might have neglected one or two sitting on the floor in the back, was forty-three students. The classroom contained thirty-three desks.

"Good morning." Dr. Rumsford's shrill voice broke through the tumult "I know all of you are excited to be here, just as we are excited to have you. I just wanted to take a few minutes to welcome you and to review some of the expectations we have for you this school year."

Rumsford described the dress code: no baggy pants, no low-cut tank tops, and, of course, no hats. She described the layout of the campus and the significance of each digit in a room number. She described the proper procedure for obtaining a counselor's appointment. She described the lunch schedule. She described her philosophies on respect, self-esteem, achievement, group work, bells, bathrooms, calculus, and liverwurst. She mentioned that she loved rubrics. She did not mention the smell of carpet glue.

Amazingly, Greg noticed that while students struggled to find his classroom and were uncertain when first period began, they seemed to know exactly when it ended. Rumsford was still talking as they hurried out at 8:20 sharp.

A few minutes later, as students began to file in for second period, she was still talking. Greg was now back at his door, greeting his next group of students. In the background, he heard Rumsford say, "What do you mean first period is over? How can that be? I didn't hear any bell."

Greg's planning period was third hour, and his ankle was beginning to swell. He needed to ice it desperately, but with the day's shortened schedule, there was just enough time to limp to the nurse's office, get an ice bag, and limp back to his room for a short treatment. He hobbled down the stairs, confirming that the thirty-million-dollar campus was completely inaccessible for students with disabilities, and hopped to the nurse's office where he found a sign taped to the door: "No students allowed today." So Greg hopped back to his classroom.

Rounding the corner, fatigued from his one-legged assault on the stairs, Greg ran into Dr. Rumsford. "Oops, sorry," he said. She ignored his apology and his condition, and scrutinized him from head to painful foot.

"So this is what you decided to wear on the first day of school?" she snapped. Greg was confused by the apparent simplicity of the query. Was it a trick question, with a morsel of wisdom enveloped somewhere within an abstract riddle? Yet while Connie Rumsford was many things, a transcendental Zen philosopher she most certainly was not. So Greg considered a different angle. Could there be a giant ink stain on his shirt? A blotch of salsa on his tie? He examined his clothing, then Rumsford's accusatory face, then his clothing once again. Nothing.

"Apparently," he finally replied.

"I thought I told you that the way you dress on the first day is critical. I thought I told you that you need to set the tone for your class. I thought I told you to be non-threatening."

"With all due respect, Dr. Rumsford, I don't see a shirt and tie as 'threatening.' But maybe I don't get it. Could you provide some guidance as to exactly what you would prefer?"

"You're a teacher, not an accountant. You need to be more casual, more open, more approachable. I expect better of you tomorrow. Nothing too formal. We want to be business-like, but not intimidating."

"Of course," said Greg. And as she turned away, he added, "Your suit is very nice, by the way."

Over her shoulder she said, "Thank you. Ann Taylor." It was at this precise moment, watching her toddle down the hallway, that Greg decided Dr. Rumsford needed a nickname.

The day raced into fourth period, and it was not long after Greg had taken roll that John Woodacre stuck his head in Greg's door. Greg thought that Woody, dressed as he was in black slacks, a white shirt, and a red-and-yellow flowery tie, might just have achieved perfect sartorial balance. At least close enough to appease the boss.

"Hey, Samson, can I see you?"

"Excuse me a minute," Greg said to the class as he tried to push Woodacre out the door. "No, not out there," Woody protested. "*She's* out there."

"Who's out there?" Greg led Woody back inside.

"Rumsford. I seen her give me the stink-eye from across the building before school, but I managed to escape. She'll probably look for me in my room during prep period. That's why I thought I'd hide out here."

"Good thinking," Greg said dubiously. "Listen, Woody, you can stay here until the period is over, but you can't do this every day."

"Why not?"

"Because I have to teach class, that's why not."

"So teach it. I won't be in your way."

"Yeah, but the kids'll wonder what you're doing here. They'll—" Realizing the class was now quiet,

Greg turned around to find most of the students eavesdropping. "You could hide in the library."

Woody stayed until the period ended, and most of passing period too, before sneaking out. While Greg stood at his door greeting his next class, he watched his anguished colleague dissolve into the mob of students and quickly become invisible until emerging, unscathed, fifty feet away at the door of his own classroom.

The first day whizzed past. Greg felt as if he had spent all of it greeting people, like the social chairman at a fraternity rush party or a bellman at some mid-level hotel in Manhattan. And it was only ten-twenty. Freshmen were scheduled to arrive at eleven-thirty, but Greg taught no freshman classes, which gave him the afternoon to plan ahead, read all of Rumsford's handouts, and take a nap before cross country practice. Unlike his colleagues, who had mindlessly thrown away the readings, Greg intended to study every last word. Maybe it would make him a better teacher, and maybe not. At the very least it would allow him to better understand the enemy, and as Sun-Tzu said in *The Art of War*, there may be no better tactic for survival. Sun-Tzu, it seemed to Greg, could have taught Elden Ray Fong a few things, then kicked his ass for good measure.

Greg carried his materials into the hallway just in time to see Dr. Rumsford opening Woody's door. Damn, Greg thought, this is going to be bloody. Rumsford did not even bother to step inside, as if thinking she could gain additional valuable seconds by beginning her diatribe from afar. "Mr. Woodpecker, is that what you decided to wear on the first day of school? I thought I told you that the way you dress on the first day is critical...."

A female math teacher walked past, wearing black leggings and an oversized pink T-shirt. Greg hoped against hope that she would serve as a distraction. "Hi, Dr. Rumsford," she said. "Hi, Stacy," answered Rumsford simply, and she returned to Woody and the mutilation at hand. "You should be wearing something more dignified. That tie is hideous."

Greg hurried to the staircase and, fortunately, slipped away unnoticed. He could not bear the carnage any longer. At that moment, had someone asked him what he did for a living, he would have said carpenter or longshoreman or busboy.

Tuesday was the first real day of class. Utterly bewildered, Greg settled on a white dress shirt, blue slacks, and casual black shoes, but debated the tie for several minutes before finally deciding to go without.

Once at school, Greg skimmed his mail, stopping to read a message from Dr. Rumsford, which was printed on pink paper in order to ensure teachers' prompt attention:

> Attendance is a professional responsibility for every teacher. Since the District receives money based upon enrollment, your failure to take attendance costs the school money. It has come to my attention that during first period Monday, only a few teachers took attendance. This is a problem!

He paused to recall Dr. Rumsford's long, meandering remarks from the day before, then continued reading:

> Since we are now out of pink paper, please note that your daily tardy list will be goldenrod until further notice. –CR

Greg rolled up the pink page and lobbed it toward the wastebasket in the corner as the first students began to arrive.

He stood in his doorway once again, and as he greeted the graceless and often lifeless students who entered, he noticed a small girl trying to squeeze between the mass of humanity on her left side and the wall on her right. Her flip-flops slapped the soles of her feet as she teetered atop functionless footwear and beneath the burden of a massive backpack. When she caught the toe of her flip-flop and stumbled forward, her backpack flew over her head and spilled onto the floor. Textbooks, notebooks, electronics, pencils, lunch, and makeup splattered before her. She scurried, red-faced, to gather her belongings, and as the swirl of other students laughed at her or ignored her plight completely, she begin to cry.

Greg hurried over.

"What happened?" he asked.

"I don't know," she said between sniffles. "I tripped on something."

Greg looked behind her and there was the culprit—an almost imperceptible bubble in the carpet, a monster which had spawned overnight and now devoured its first victim. As Greg helped her collect her things and her composure, he asked, "Are you OK? Do you need to go to the nurse?"

"I thought we weren't allowed to go to the nurse during first period," she replied, and Greg recalled that she was right.

After roll call and a brief overview of his syllabus, it was time for Greg to put his multitudes to work. English students were asked to read and respond to an article on persuasive writing, his first chance to see both their analytical and writing skills. The next period, Video Production students were asked not to light anything on fire, since the studio was at least a week from being finished. He could have begun teaching terminology or assigned their first project, but with more than sixty students enrolled in the class, imparting any useful knowledge to his students was about as likely as them simultaneously winning an Emmy for best costume design. Later in the day, he would assign his Yearbook students to interview one other, a great icebreaker and an opportunity to observe the very skills they would need to produce a successful student publication. And then more writing assignments in his block English class after lunch.

During his prep period, Greg walked to the library to check out some Edgar Allen Poe anthologies. He noticed more carpet bubbles along the way, counting eleven in just his corner of school. On the way back to his classroom he absently thumbed through "Tamerlane," and just when he reached Poe's line "The rain came down upon my head, unshelter'd," he heard a crash, and shards of glass flew from a second-story window toward him. Catching a glimpse of a kid running down the hallway, Greg took off in pursuit, all the while wondering if he had made a really bad first impression. He sprinted up a stairway and ran into Maurice, who had also seen the incident and had given chase himself. "Lost him," Maurice said, smoothing out his suit.

"Hard to believe, two fast guys like us couldn't catch him," Greg replied. He wasn't even winded, just frustrated.

"Doesn't matter," Maurice replied. "I know who it is. Steven Torgemeyer. We had trouble with him before, in middle school."

Greg stayed in his room for the remainder of the day, purposefully unaware of who was being praised or picked on, who was teaching and who was playing I Spy. He only knew that after collecting written assignments in his English classes, he was already behind. And there were 181 more school days until summer vacation.

Greg found himself in Dr. Rumsford's office. The walls were lined with photographs from her younger days: a visit to the Hershey's chocolate factory as a child (she looked very happy), her college graduation (she didn't), a trip to the torture chamber inside the Tower of London (positively ecstatic). Dr. Rumsford motioned for Greg to sit, so he tentatively dropped himself into the overstuffed chair in front of her desk. It slowly enveloped him. He tried to adjust his position, but two neckties emerged like snakes from the arms of the chair and bound his wrists together. "Comfortable?" she asked.

"Well, I...."

"Good. Mr. Samson, I've called you here to tell you that you're sleeping incorrectly." Greg had now drooped so deeply into the chair that he was looking almost straight up at Rumsford, and his entire body began to mimic the softness and flexibility of the chair itself. He opened his mouth to speak, but his jaw sunk lifelessly.

"Elden Ray Fong says you should sleep for exactly eight hours a night," she continued. "No more and no less. I understand that you slept for seven hours and six minutes on Monday, and then six hours and eighteen minutes on Tuesday."

Greg's head was a big blob of mush. "Buh buh buh" was all he was able to say.

"Two hours should be spent on your back. Two hours on your stomach. Then you should sleep for two hours standing up, and finally two hours hanging upside down. This will freely circulate the blood and prevent your internal organs from settling."

Greg could only nod.

"Tonight, I expect you to sleep as Elden Ray Fong requires. Remember, eight hours, no more and no less. Shifting every two hours, exactly." And with that, the chair finally consumed Greg, pushing him through the floor and into a freefall through a dark chamber inhabited by hotel doormen and fraternity guys in Ann Taylor suits. He greeted each one as he flew past, but none responded. However, each threw a stack of papers at him, so that by the time he hit bottom, he was covered in paper cuts.

5

THE DO-OVER

Friday morning, haggard teachers dragged themselves into room 4122 for a special seven a.m. faculty meeting. The fatigue of the first week was obvious. Many teachers clasped Styrofoam coffee cups with the same urgency of senior citizens clutching bingo cards. John Woodacre sat down beside Greg, shaking badly. As he tried to slice a muffin with a plastic knife and trembling hand, the blade broke and flew across the room.

"Jeez, John, you need some help?" Greg asked. Woody could only grunt as he unsteadily brought his coffee cup to his lips.

"Good morning," Rumsford announced, although it was clear from looking around that most disagreed. Had it been possible to combine the sound of a foghorn with the screeching of fingernails on a chalkboard, Greg imagined it would sound much like Rumsford this morning.

"I see most of you got coffee, and there's muffins in the back," she said, devouring a Reese's Peanut Butter Cup in one bite. "Research shows that proper nutrition is vital to brain function. And remember, students watch everything you do. You're all role models."

Greg smiled as he sipped a bottle of Gatorade.

"Now, to make sure you're on time, there is a special prize on the bottom of one of your chairs."

Teachers moved indecisively, a few of them turning over their chairs, then a few more. Greg managed to insert his thumb into a wad of peppermint chewing gum on the bottom of his chair. Although he was a long way from fully understanding Dr. Rumsford, he was fairly certain this was not the prize. Suddenly, a shriek from the back stopped everyone cold. "I won!" someone said. "Five dollars!" A murmur went up, then some scattered applause, as if the winning teacher had just performed some remarkable act of skill or courage. Rumsford appeared delighted with herself, basking in the afterglow of a public relations stunt well-received.

Yet, in doing so, she had lost the staff's attention, so her triumph quickly metamorphosed into impatience which then dissolved into chagrin and then finally eroded into exasperation. With nowhere left to devolve and her control usurped by a five-spot, she let out a whistle that would make a dog bleed from its ears.

"Touchdown!" head football coach Frank Nixon said, standing with his arms upraised. Several people chuckled, including Rumsford. Greg heard the joke—it was difficult not to hear Nixon—but he was more concerned about Woody, whose shaky hold on his coffee was causing the hot liquid to dribble down his chin. Meanwhile, more time passed as the multitude of conversations finally trickled down to attention and silence.

"You all know that there are three major learning styles," Rumsford began. Greg looked around the room and noticed several teachers nodding vigorously. He theorized that those very teachers were completely unaware that there were three major learning styles.

The movie screen was down, and Rumsford pulled the handle in an effort to release it. The screen moved upward about six inches and then locked. She tried again, and this time only succeeded in pulling it back down. Trusty lieutenant Maurice McCullough stepped in and deftly raised the screen, which finally settled into its case above the board. Frank Nixon stood and began to applaud, and several other teachers joined in.

"As I was saying," Rumsford began again, moving aside to reveal the words written on the board, "there are three major learning styles. And a good teacher addresses all three. You will notice that I have written our journaling prompt on the board for the visual learners, and I will now read it to you as well, for the auditory learners: Which of Elden Ray Fong's ideas do you find most interesting, and why?"

Greg turned to Woody and whispered, "I wonder, will the kinesthetic learners be allowed to touch the prompt, or will there be an interpretive dance?" Woody laughed, just a bit too loud, attracting a withering glare from Rumsford.

In a futuristic, dystopian world built upon survival, like in an Arnold Schwarzenegger movie, Woody was the perfect foil for Greg, an unwitting and certainly unwilling blanket of protection. He was like the slow man in the first rule of forest survival, which is: I don't have to run faster than the bear, I just have to run faster than you. And Woody, for whatever reason, would never outrun the bear that was Connie Rumsford. But in Greg's world, the real world, he could not help but feel for the pitiful Social Studies teacher from Indiana.

Greg regretted his question and the vilification it had drawn to Woody, but at least Rumsford had moved on and the staff was now at work on their journal prompts. Greg was able to shake the gloom of her reaction—he had trained himself to retreat inside himself during the darkest of times, like on lap nineteen when the leaders surge away and you cannot do anything other than suffer through six more laps of solitude and defeat—but sadly, Woody could not. His empty stare, reminiscent of Tippi Hedren after the birds pecked her near to death, was unsalvageable. So as Rumsford began a conversation with Samantha O'Bradovich, either oblivious to or unconcerned for Woody's current condition, Greg shivered noticeably.

Rumsford's question was an easy one, really. The master teacher had spent an entire chapter on methods for gaining control of the class, and flickering lights was strictly prohibited. But, unlike his other thousands of tips, he offered no insight, no empirical evidence, no anecdotes of children scarred or saved, to support his belief. Greg was bothered by unsubstantiated arguments in general and by Fong's naked assertion in particular. So he began to write.

He began to write before many others in the room even picked up their pens, and he was still writing long after each of them had finished. He was still writing when the lights flickered, and he looked up to see Dr. Rumsford standing at the light switch. With a glance, Greg was happy to see that Woody had at least managed to scribble down a few ideas in his notebook. But still stressed from Rumsford's withering stare, Woody's handwriting was nearly indecipherable, looking more like his EKG than any known written language.

"Who would like to share their thoughts?" Rumsford asked. Her perusal of the room seemed but a charade, as if she had already chosen her victim.

"Mr. Woodpecker?" The room burst into laughter, and Greg noticed that Woody flushed with resentment. "I uh ... think his, uh ... idea...." Good God, thought Greg, what a mess. "Never mind," Rumsford said, and she moved on.

After a short break for a getting-to-know-you activity involving only grunts and elbows, Rumsford once again flickered the lights. "As you know, we have had some serious scheduling problems. We worked all summer to learn the new scheduling program, and it's obvious the program wasn't any good. The counselors have been trying to resolve the problem all week, but they're not getting the job done. How many of you have more than thirty-three students in any of your classes?"

Hands shot up across the room, and one teacher asked "How about *all* my classes?"

Rumsford continued, "The District let me down on this one, and your failure on Monday's attendance didn't give us accurate numbers." Greg wondered if she was going to blame Lee Harvey Oswald at some point in the discussion.

"We have decided to scrap the current schedules and start over," she explained. "On Monday morning, we will have arena scheduling in the gymnasium." Maurice began moving through the room, issuing a stack of handouts to everyone. "Distribute this information to your Mentor Time classes today, and before you leave this afternoon, pick up a copy of your instructions for Monday morning. Have a good day."

A buzz permeated the room. At a school which was not opening particularly smoothly, Greg recognized that a day in which students were just passing time, and knew it, was not in anyone's best interest. But what could he say? And with anywhere from five to thirty extra students in his classes, why would he want to protest anyway?

Elden Ray Fong claimed he would call every parent at the end of the first week, no matter how hectic, and tell them how wonderful Danny or Suzie or Bucky had been. But of course, Elden Ray Fong spent his entire career teaching second grade. And, Greg surmised, he had never endured a career's worth of problems in just one week, as the faculty of Shadowcliff High School had been faced with. Besides, thanks to the scheduling debacle, they would be getting all new rosters next week anyway. So, master teacher Elden Ray Fong be damned, Greg went to cross country practice, then joined Bob Cockrell, Jimmy Clayton, Keri Tanner, and some other teachers for Happy Hour.

Sunday morning, Greg returned from a ninety-minute run in the desert preserve. It was a great run. The heat kept most of the mountain bikers away, so for the most part the trails were his and his alone. He felt pretty good, too; his ankle was no longer bothering him and his legs felt fresh. His plans for the rest of the day included a shower, a huge breakfast, a nap, some schoolwork in the afternoon, and reading the first few chapters of *The Long Parade* after dinner.

The phone rang while he was in the shower. It was Woody.

"What's up?"

"I'm sorry to bother you, Samson, but I was wondering if you could give me a lift to the airport," Woody said.

"I guess so. Everything all right?" Greg dried the soap in his ear.

"It will be as soon as I get on that plane. I leave in three hours."

"Where are you going?"

"Indiana. If I leave today, I can still get my old job back."

"You sure you wanna do this?" Greg asked. But he knew it was the right thing. "Never mind. I'll be there ASAP."

No more than half an hour later, Greg piled Woody's bags into the back of his pickup. The ride to the airport was deathly silent.

As they pulled to the curb in front of Terminal 3, Woody finally said, "Get out while you can."

"Unlike you," Greg answered, "I don't have a Plan B."

"What are you talkin' about? You got something better than a Plan B. Don't you got an MBA?"

"And a JD," Greg added. "But I also have more than fifty thousand dollars in student loans."

Woody did not seem to grasp the full extent of it, so Greg continued.

"Plus, all I've ever wanted to do was work in either sports or publishing. I totally oriented my program toward exactly that objective. But now the joke's on me. As it turns out, there are some jobs I can't afford to take, others I'm apparently over-qualified for, and still others where I don't have enough experience."

"Then suck it up and get a job with IBM or something, at least till you get your loans paid off? It's gotta be better than Shadowcliff High School. Anything's gotta be better than that place."

A rental-car shuttle bus glided to a stop and belched a family of three out its back doors. Dad led the way, struggling with a garment bag. A little girl followed, proudly sporting her Elmo backpack. She smiled at Greg as she passed. Bringing up the rear, Mom pulled a wheeled valise, which tipped over as she hopped the curb.

"First of all," said Greg, returning his attention to Woody, "it'll take twenty years to pay off my loans. It's like a mortgage without the house. Second, my grades weren't good enough to get a job with IBM."

"C'mon, your grades weren't good enough? Compared to some of them dipsticks they got?"

"I learned everything my classmates did," Greg explained. "Probably more. Problem was, I was completely immersed in my athletic 'career,' if you can call it that. It's tough to get a 4.0 when you're running a hundred and forty miles a week and traveling to races every other weekend. I ate five times a day, and most nights I passed out before ten o'clock."

"That kinda sucks," Woody said.

"I wouldn't trade it for anything," Greg countered wistfully. "I competed all over the world and finished ninth in the Olympic Trials."

"Nobody was impressed by that?"

"A 28:36 10-k and a drawer-full of race T-shirts mean absolutely nothing to corporate America. So I was left with my measly 3.26 GPA, which didn't exactly light a fire under Human Resources. As far as they were concerned, I may as well have spent twenty years trying to extract sunlight from cucumbers."

Woody didn't get the literary reference. "OK, then get a job stocking shelves at the supermarket. Whatever."

There was a rap on the passenger-side window, and airport security was standing over them. "Let's move it," said the cop.

"Again, it's a matter of economics. Besides, even the best grocery stocker can't make a difference to a can of peaches."

"So you're a goddamn idealist," Woody said, almost an accusation.

"I guess. Is that so bad?"

Woody shrugged. "You'll get over it." He extended his hand for an impersonal shake, then ducked out the door. After quickly hoisting his bags from the back of Greg's truck, he disappeared into the solace of the airport, never to be seen again. He was Shadowcliff's first casualty, but there was nothing casual about his demise.

On Monday morning, Greg arrived early as directed and took his place in the gymnasium. It occurred to him that arena scheduling was a process that would ensure the biggest, strongest, and most aggressive students were rewarded with their perfect schedule while the small and meek ended up with scraps. He thought particularly of the girl with the flip-flops and the massive backpack; if she could not defeat the carpet monsters in the hallway, what chance would she have in the arena?

As twelve hundred students gathered outside the gymnasium door, the noise level grew and grew until, like the Oklahoma land rush, the doors were pushed open a few minutes early and the stampede was on.

Tables were arranged in a semi-circle by department, and students scurried from one table to the next to gather cards as symbols of their enrollment.

Greg was barely able to keep up, but in one moment, he managed to sneak a glance at the Social Studies table, where Woody's empty chair stood as a stark contrast against the madness all around.

"Mr. Samson?" came a familiar shrillness, jerking Greg from his momentary reverie. It was Rumsford. "What do you know about Mr. Woodpecker?

"Not that much."

"What do you mean, not much?"

"Well, I know he's thirty-three years old and he graduated from Purdue. I know he enjoys teaching Economics but isn't so fond of Government. And one more thing. I know his last name is 'Woodacre.' Not 'Woodpecker.'"

"Do you know where he is today?"

"Assuming no problems with his flight, I'm guessing he's in Muncie."

"I'll be watching you, Samson," she said, then spun on her heels so sharply she left a mark on the newly lacquered gym floor.

An hour later, the gym floor was covered in paper, like Fifth Avenue after a World Series victory parade. Arena scheduling was winding down but the custodians' work was just beginning. The last few students trickled out of the gym with the teachers right behind them. Until Greg was stopped by a small voice.

"Excuse me?" asked a shy boy. Greg stopped and looked down at him. "I got English first hour, and math sixth hour, but all the social studies and Spanish classes are full. What do I do now?"

Tuesday morning, Greg once again stood at his door greeting students. Once again they displayed a remarkable lack of social graces. Once again Dr. Rumsford rambled for far too long on the TV. It was, without a doubt, the most colossal do-over Greg had ever been part of. Seventeen hundred miles away, John "Woody" Woodacre was getting his own opportunity for a do-over. Greg wished him the best.

6

THE FIRST RACE

I f all went to plan, no longer would there be kids sitting on the floor or two-to-a-seat, both of which were officially *verböten* according to the Sweetwater Unified School District No. 43 Safe Schools Initiative and a directive handed down by Rumsford herself. The fact that Edie Walker ordered one thousand desks for a school with an enrollment of more than twelve hundred apparently did not matter to Rumsford. The choir teacher dealt with the shortage by playing a daily game of musical chairs, a rather cutthroat version in which the first five losers were required to stand for the rest of the period. Battles in this game were often fierce, and more than one choir student had been sent to the nurse with a contusion, jammed finger, or bloody nose. Fortunately, choir class was second period, when the nurse's office was open for business. So, for Rumsford, if the choir teacher could figure out a way to solve the problem, then everyone else could be just as creative.

Or they could ignore the directive out of sheer necessity. Teachers were forced into using banquet tables and folding chairs, sofas purchased at garage sales, or patio furniture from their own back yards. Some were meeting in the cafeteria or the rear steps. Greg was one of the lucky ones, having begun the year with a full complement of thirty-three desks in his classroom. Yet that was counterbalanced by the fact that his average class size during the first week—"The week that never happened," as it came to be known—had been forty-three students.

Thirty-three was the magic number negotiated by the Sweetwater Teachers' Association, a point trumpeted on www.sweetwaterteachers.com. The Association was empowered to make recommendations regarding salaries and policies and work conditions, and because Arizona is a right-to-work state, the School Board was empowered to ignore them, a power routinely exercised. The Association would then express its indignation that the School Board would dare do exactly what it was allowed by law, and the website's message board would overflow with comments expressing bitterness and outrage.

"And then," Jeanette Candelaria pointed out, "the President of the Association will be promoted to some newly created District-level job, and everything will be forgotten until the next time."

But this morning, as Greg picked up his new rosters from his mailbox, he noticed that every one of his classes had thirty-three or fewer students, a first in his brief high school teaching career and, as far as he knew, a first in the brief lifetime of Shadowcliff High School. So, District risk-management levels and bargained-for class limits now resolved, it was time for Greg to find out if he could actually have some sort of impact on young people at a curricular level, rather than that of riot patrol and glorified babysitter.

"What is the purpose of language?" he began, a questioned designed to lead into a discussion of effective essay writing and, soon, their first essay.

Silence.

"I guess that illustrates my point, sort of," he continued, haltingly. "Let's try again. If nobody could communicate with you, and you couldn't communicate with anyone else, what would your world be like?"

"Kinda like this class," a kid said from the back row. He was dressed in ripped black baggy pants, a black T-shirt badly in need of washing, and a pair of black work boots. The official uniform of the disaffected.

"How so?"

"Boring." Several kids laughed.

"I have to apologize to the class. It's going to take a while for me to learn everyone's name. You are...."

"Kyle Friese."

"Thank you. Mr. Friese, you're certainly welcome to drop this class and try to get into another one," Greg said, "although I doubt there's space available elsewhere. You can always take night school."

"Night school sucks," he said.

"Good," responded Greg. "Then as long as you have developed such keen evaluative power, why don't you use it for good rather than for evil?"

"Huh? What does that mean?"

"Stop being the class clown and see if you can actually contribute something useful."

Greg began to describe Plato's Allegory of the Cave, the story of a man whose entire existence is defined by two-dimensional shadow pictures cast onto a cave wall but who finally ventures outside and encounters, for the first time, a full-color, three-dimensional world. Frightened by this abrupt change to his perception, he retreats back into his cave.

One girl raised her hand, and Greg called on her. "Is this Plato thing really about writing?"

Greg smiled slightly and replied, "What do you think?" It was a technique he recalled from his high school chemistry teacher, who bounced virtually every question back to the person who asked it. Many students suspected the teacher was just as confused as they were about covalent bonding, but Greg later figured out that he was simply forcing students to reflect and consider and reason, which was, after all, what a good teacher does ever since Plato himself was a student and Socrates his teacher.

The girl scrunched up her face at Greg's unexpected reply, but then offered, "I think it's about your comfort zone. When the guy went outside his cave, he didn't like it. So he went back inside the cave where he was comfortable."

"I agree," Greg continued. "And does that have anything to do with the writing process?"

"Maybe you think that we need to get uncomfortable if we're going to learn to write better."

"Perfect," said Greg, and she beamed at her success. "You see, real learning happens in a place of discomfort. For example, when you almost get in a car accident, you learn more about driving in that moment than you did in all the time spent reading the manual. Now I don't want us to be that close to danger. I want you to feel safe. However, I will push you out of your cave this year."

They did not get much farther, but that was fine. Two students waited after class to tell him that Plato sounded pretty cool, and Greg later discovered the words "Come out of your cave" written on the whiteboard in girl's curly handwriting. Meanwhile, though, Greg's rocky relationship with Kyle Friese was probably cemented.

However, the school day of any teacher must march ever-forward. So regardless of the glacier-like progress toward the writing process during first period, Greg was obligated to produce the morning announcements at the end of second period. He had been informed by Rumsford that this was among his most critical duties, and Greg certainly wanted to avoid the pandemonium of a high school devoid of vital information like the color of the day (tomorrow's was green) or the location of the Video Game Club meeting three weeks hence. But he also knew the studio had finally been wired just the previous night, allotting him a mere forty minutes to instruct his classes on equipment he was only vaguely familiar with himself.

Greg placed a mannequin on a chair in the center of the studio, behind the austere set of two milk crates. "This is Walter," he explained. "Walter is here to help us understand video production." Then he began. He taught his students the basics of the three-camera studio, how to use the switcher and the light board, and where the microphones were plugged in. He taught them about close-ups, medium shots, and long shots. He played with the Chroma key, making it appear as if Walter was broadcasting from the beach, the North Pole, and outer space. And then it was time to produce the news.

"I hope you guys got it," he said. And then, to himself: Because that's all I can tell you.

Somehow, the announcements came off with no major problems. Greg himself anchored the first show, and he kept it as simple as possible. But they survived it, and they felt good.

He still needed to learn how to use the editing deck and plan a semester's worth of assignments, but at least every student on campus was now aware that Key Club would be selling green-and-white foam index fingers saying "Go Bobcats" for five dollars. The republic could safely endure.

Planning period offered a break that seemed to vanish before he even sat down, as he knew Yearbook class was already facing an existential crisis that arena scheduling had not resolved. Self-importance was far more abundant than talent. In anticipation of that issue, and because he had no idea of each student's skill level, Greg had already opted to appoint co-editors for each section of the yearbook, reserving the title of Editor-in-Chief for himself in this, the critical first year. Yet a handful of students had already hijacked his name for the yearbook—*Umbra*—and insisted upon the more generic *Chronicle*. When Greg balked, citing the unique nature of his offering and its connection with the name of the school, three of his editors complained to Rumsford, and his decision was quickly and unilaterally reversed.

"We must always be student-centered," she explained tersely.

Rumsford had already demanded a complete list of topics to be covered, and while he managed to convince her that it was far too early to know, it was apparent she would be breathing down his neck about every little detail. Indeed, she had made it abundantly clear that he would be held completely responsible if the yearbook failed to (1) turn a profit, (2) maintain absolute editorial integrity, (3) be completely free of error, (4) have a flawless system of distribution, (5) contend for state and national awards, and (6) make everyone happy.

All of this was expected to occur with a staff of just eighteen students, few of whom held any journalistic aspirations and some of whom did not yet understand the intricate, confusing concept of nouns and verbs. In addition, his classroom contained only two working computers. Nevertheless, Rumsford demanded that every single student contribute, whether they were motivated, competent, or completely worthless. And despite his daily reminders that there was no "my part" or "your part," just "our part," the egocentrism remained tangible, as if the nineteenth member of the class. Some days it was so acrimonious, Greg was surprised one of his editors hadn't tried to name the book *The Katie*.

"I thought you were going to have that information by today," the Student Life co-editor snapped at the other co-editor.

"I had to work last night," said the other. "I told you that. Besides, you didn't do your part either."

"My part's harder than yours."

"No it isn't."

"Ladies?" Greg interrupted. "Oh ladies?" They stopped.

"As a class, we have one objective. Can either of you tell me what that objective might be?"

"To make a yearbook," one said.

"Good. Then let's do that, shall we?"

"Yeah," they both agreed. But their stares clearly conveyed their umbrage. How dare he challenge their pettiness? Perhaps he should have put forth *Umbrage* as a compromise title.

By the time Greg returned from his inauspicious lunch of chicken fried steak, which was far more fried than steak, each of their parents had left a nasty voicemail. Rumsford had also called. And their first deadline was just weeks away.

As Greg walked through the counselor's area, a frequent shortcut to the copy room, he saw a boy sitting with his mother outside Edie Walker's office. Skinny and shy, he slumped into his chair. Greg walked past with a simple "hello," then stopped suddenly. Why the hell not?, he thought.

After retracing his last five steps, he said, "You should run cross country." The kid jumped, startled, but Greg noticed a glimmer in the kid's eye. Later, he was forced to acknowledge that he might have frightened the timid fourteen-year-old who had only been in town a few hours, and the glimmer might have been a tear or just plain terror. But for now the thought never occurred to him, so Greg continued his pitch.

"It's a great group of kids," he said, now addressing the mother. "Motivated, balanced, smart." He could tell she was intrigued.

He directed his pitch back toward the kid. "What's your name?"

"Corey Hinton," he replied, although his voice cracked as he said it so it sounded more like "Co-ho-ree."

"Where are you from?"

"Macomb, Illinois."

"Freshman?"

"Yeah."

"You ever run before? I mean, not counting when the police were chasing you?" This last part was corny, Greg knew, but he thought it might break the ice.

"No," he said, now smiling. It had worked.

"Corey," his mother interrupted, "that's not true. You won the mile in fifth-grade PE class."

Corey turned slightly red. Greg did not know if he was embarrassed about the victory or because he was trapped now. Edie Walker came out of her office and invited them in, but the mother raised her hand to delay the counselor. It was at that moment that Greg, who had never before recruited someone based upon their ability to sit in a chair, knew he had found another runner.

"So, do you want to try it?" asked Mom. "Yeah," Corey said, and the next afternoon, Greg finally boasted a full complement of seven runners. True, one was asthmatic, another thought anything over half a mile was "a marathon," and one was out only until club lacrosse started in October, but there was also a promising sophomore, a new kid from California, and now the fifth-grade mile champion of Macomb Elementary School. It was certainly a long way from Greg's publicly announced goal of a state title, but progress was being made. As for the girls, he still short-handed, but he had not yet recruited out of either Home Economics class or the timeout room.

Nonetheless, there was a season to contest. Three weeks after school began, the Shadowcliff Bobcats opened their first cross country against Granite High School, one of the top teams in the state. Greg's young team was nervous.

"Listen, you guys," Greg lectured. "Success cannot be measured by wins and losses, because you can't control how the other team performs. They're older, bigger, and stronger. Our best chance to beat them would've been if their bus got lost, but the meet's on their home course so that's probably not gonna happen.

"But let me tell you how I define success," he continued. "It's doing your best under the current conditions. *Your* best. You don't have to live up to anyone else's standards. That's certainly something you *can* control."

The girls' team was finally at full strength with the addition of two more runners, but they were so desperately out-of-shape that they contributed little on this day. Only Darlene Griffin, the freshman stud who had been both coached and coddled by Maurice in club track, managed to break up Granite's top seven.

The Shadowcliff boys looked like a group of fuzz-faced, underdeveloped, acne-infested kids lining up for execution at the hands of, or rather the legs of, the men from Granite, many of whom could have posed for Gillette commercials during their summer break. Greg began his own running career as an eighty-pound freshman, so he knew that time, effort, and patience were transforming. He had tried to pass along this wisdom to his team. But today, none of those qualities would help them to avoid the imminent slaughter. When Corey struggled in after three miles, clearly spent, his twelfth-place finish was the team's best.

After the race, Greg gathered his team together. Granite's coach came over and congratulated them, offering assurances of a bright future.

"Welcome to high school cross country," Greg said. "I'm extremely proud of your efforts today. I believe you truly did your best." Smiles permeated the group. "Corey, you were awesome." At that very moment, Greg could have gotten the group to carry the bus home on their backs.

"Now, everybody put your gear on the bus, and we're gonna go for a run." Even the Granite coach turned around in surprise. Greg silenced the murmurs of protest by adding, "Remember, if you don't have anything positive to say, then don't say anything."

The run was absolutely silent, at least until they saw their bus in the parking lot of the Circle-K. Fifteen minutes later, ice cream and drinks in hand, they rode home happy. Amazing what you can get away with if there's a Slurpee waiting at the end, Greg thought.

Friday was the school's first football game in its history, a home contest against Falcon Ranch High School, a day in which the anticipation of building a new school could finally be celebrated in ritualistic high school fashion. The day at Shadowcliff featured its first assembly schedule, shortened periods that disrupted the educational flow but which were seen as vital to school spirit. Some teachers took the day as a mini-vacation during which they could show videos or allow "catch-up day." Others tried to cram fifty minutes' worth of instruction into a thirty-five minute period, unsuccessfully, so a lesson on the Battle of Hastings ended just before finding out which side was victorious. For his part, head football coach Frank Nixon did not even pretend to teach. He just schmoozed with his students and relished being the center of attention for the day.

It would not have mattered if the game were against the Dallas Cowboys or the Phoenix School for the Blind. Both Rumsford and Student Government thought the event worthy of festivity, so the entire day was centered around the game. The pep band roamed the halls during first period, interrupting classes when it broke into the school fight song. At lunch, groups of cheerleaders circulated around the tables, attempting to teach their new cheer—"We are the Bobcats, mighty mighty Bobcats, Shadowcliff Bobcats, ROAR!"—to the student body. And at one-thirty, students were herded down to the gym for Shadowcliff's first pep rally. As classes merged in the wide Shadowcliff hallways into an indistinct mass of students, many peeled off and disappeared through various doors like rats fleeing the Titanic.

When Greg entered the gym with his class, Randy Smith grabbed him by the arm. "I need you to guard the locker room," he said. "Don't let anyone in, OK?"

"Sure. What's up?" asked Greg.

Randy smiled mischievously. "You'll see."

"C'mon Randy. If I don't know the mission I might screw it up."

"Arizona Cardinals cheerleaders are performing during the pep rally," Randy explained. "Last thing we need is somebody walking in by accident. Or on purpose."

"How do you know I won't walk in?" asked Greg.

"Because I trust you more than anyone on this campus," Randy replied.

"You got me there. I'm on it."

Greg stood guard for a long time. He missed the speech by the football captain promising victory, the speech by the cheer captain promising spirit, and the speech by the president of the parents' booster club promising pizza and snow cones at the concession stand. He missed the pom squad's dance routine to remixed hip-hop and the cheer squad's disastrous attempt at a human pyramid. He missed performances by the pep band and the drum line. He missed the dance troupe. He missed the inter-class competition, in which two boys and two girls raced through an obstacle course consisting of dizzy bat, pie eating, hula hoops, sitting on balloons, and other challenges completely unrelated to football, school, or any useful talent. He missed the obligatory yell-off, a compelling contest in which each class tries to scream louder than the others. "We are the Bobcats, mighty mighty Bobcats, Shadowcliff Bobcats, ROAR!" they yelled, back and forth until finally the freshmen were declared winners.

What he did not miss was the introduction of the volleyball, swimming, and cross country teams, because no such introductions occurred.

And then it was time for the magical moment. Randy signaled to Greg, who knocked on the locker room door. "You're on, ladies," he said. Five professional cheerleaders bounded from the locker room wearing Shadowcliff football jerseys, and Greg followed them into the gym.

The women marched to the center of the gym, paused dramatically to allow themselves to be drenched in the hoots of teenage boys, then simultaneously pulled off their jerseys to reveal outfits that defied both the laws of physics and the Sweetwater Unified School District No. 43 dress code. Halter tops appeared to be constructed from index cards. If shorts could have a negative inseam, these did. Greg was pretty sure these outfits were not dress-code approved, but when he spotted Dr. Rumsford across the gym, her smile suggested only that she was thrilled her students were enjoying the spectacle.

While the outfits were scant, the routine was perhaps even more so. It had clearly been prepared, or perhaps only debated, in just a few minutes in the locker room. The pep band began to play and the women basically shook their hips and waved their pom-poms and smiled and waved like they were Miss

America when in fact they wouldn't have lasted ten seconds on *The Gong Show.* But they certainly knew their audience; six hundred teenage boys watched, spellbound. Greg assumed six hundred cold showers would be necessary as soon as the boys arrived home. When the music ended, the women all bent over, asses thrust immodestly toward the rafters, and then ran from the gym to thunderous applause. Meanwhile, five football players were momentarily elevated to Big Man On Campus because their jerseys had touched the bodies of the five cheerleaders.

The final bell rang and Greg shook his head at the inanity of it all, then dressed for cross country practice. Greg had decided to practice immediately after school so that those who wanted to could attend the game. His team was unaware how little heed they were paid by Dr. Rumsford, they just wanted to be high school kids. Plus Greg could make it to Happy Hour for some wings before kickoff.

Greg left Wingding's around six p.m., needing to stop off at his apartment for a shower and a change of clothes before the short trip to the stadium. Keri was with him, preferring to leave her car at school and bum a ride to Happy Hour and back. Greg certainly did not mind, as she was perhaps more interesting and definitely better looking than Cockrell, Clayton, or other potential passengers. He entertained devious plans to accidentally leave the bathroom door open while he showered, but finally thought better of it. How fourth grade, he reflected, except that fourth graders don't drive, go to Happy Hour, or work at jobs so all-consuming that their entire social life is narrowed down to a handful of people one sees at staff meetings and neighborhood taverns.

It took less than ten minutes to shower and dress, so he had time to relax before their required arrival time of seven. Rumsford has requested that everyone show up to support the team on this historic occasion. More accurately, her words were, "I expect everyone at the game. No excuses. Do I make myself clear?"

"You know what's odd to me?" asked Greg. Keri sat up, a sign of genuine interest. "No such request was lodged on behalf of swimming, volleyball, or cross country, even though each of those teams began play this week."

"Did you expect it?"

"No," he replied. "Of course not. Cross country rates just below leprosy in terms of mass appeal. But we teach in a school run by a woman who says nobody should be made to feel superior or inferior to anyone else. Yet the football team was played up like they were about to take the first manned spaceship to the Sun."

"Which might not be a bad thing," Keri added. Greg knew she had withstood a major conflict with the starting middle linebacker just last week, resolved only when head coach Frank Nixon accused her of being anti-sports and anti-school.

"I wonder what would happen if we didn't go?" Keri mused. Greg looked into her eyes and saw what he thought was either an invitation or a reaction to the glare off his framed London Marathon certificate of achievement (commemorating his 2:21:46 personal best as third American finisher in 2001). He decided to take the risk, and the next thing he knew they were kissing.

Rumsford was not at all pleased when they showed up at the beginning of the second quarter.

7

THE MISSION

One day, Greg was amazed to find he had no pressing work during his planning period. No papers that needed to be graded that day, no photocopying that needed to be done for the next class, no phone calls to return or administrators to mollify or errands to complete. So he went for a short run. It was a pleasant respite from the chaos, a chance to clear his head and to avoid a lost training day in case he was unable to run with the team for one reason or another. He began to run on his planning period as often as he could.

A few weeks after his first such outing, Greg ran his favorite planning-period loop, a five-miler that gave him just enough time to quickly shower and get back to class before kids began to gather outside his door. The route encompassed a couple of residential streets, the perimeter of a nearby park, an alleyway, a sandy wash, a drainage tunnel, and finally a trail that ran behind Lariat Middle School, next-door to Shadowcliff. He was finishing this run when he caught the unmistakable aroma of marijuana.

Cresting a small hill on the trail, he came upon the source: a high school student, partially obscured behind a palo verde tree, oblivious to the world.

"Hey, what are you doing?" Greg yelled. It was a truly stupid question in retrospect, but Greg was tired from another unremitting week and rationalized this as a legitimate explanation for his inability to summon anything beyond the obvious.

The student looked at Greg, eyes big as saucers. It was Kyle Friese.

"Hi, Kyle," Greg said coldly. Idealism be damned, this was a chance to get this underachieving, lethargic, apathetic pain-in-the-ass out of his classroom for good. At least the boy's lethargy and apathy could now be explained.

Kyle took off running toward the middle school. Greg slipped and fell, costing him forty yards. By the time the pothead slipped into a side door of the middle-school gym, though, Greg was close enough to know he had him cornered. Yet as he reached for the door, he stopped. Catching this kid was the right thing to do, he was sure, but when he left for his run he had not signed out. And now, as he stood outside the middle-school gym touching the door handle, he could not avoid the suspicion that he was just as likely to get reprimanded by Rumsford for his defiance of school policy as he was to get lauded for his efforts in maintaining a drug-free school zone.

Still, driven by perhaps nothing more than the love of the hunt, Greg opened the gym door. The building was empty and dark. "Damn," he whispered. But when he spotted a door on the other side of the gym, he smiled. He tiptoed across to the door, a supply closet, and listened. Sure enough, from inside the closet: labored breathing.

Greg opened the door. "Mr. Friese, what a surprise."

"Shit, man, please don't write me up," Kyle pleaded. "My parents'll kill me if I get another detention. Please, Mr. Samson." It was almost painful for Greg to witness such groveling. For an instant he wondered if he would have to grovel that much should Rumsford confront him about being off campus. Which gave him an idea.

"I tell you what," Greg offered. "It's about four hundred meters back to school. A quarter mile. If you can beat me to the west door, I won't tell anyone. If I beat you, you'll get written up. What do you think?"

"Mr. Samson, that's not fair."

"That's the deal. Take it or leave it." And with that, Greg broke into a slow, exaggerated, goading run.

Soon, Greg could hear Kyle's clumsy foot-slapping and heavy breathing getting closer. Please hurry, Greg thought. I don't know if I can fake running fast any more slowly.

When Kyle pulled even, Greg picked up the pace just a bit. Although he sounded like he was being beaten with a sledgehammer, Kyle still managed to respond, drawing even once again. Heck, thought Greg, this guy has some grit, especially in those clunky boots. With a clean set of lungs he could be a decent distance runner.

As they continued on, Greg matched his deceleration with that of Kyle, who by now was struggling badly. Greg realized freshman PE class was on the tennis courts, watching the whole spectacle and even beginning to cheer for whichever runner was their favorite. The west door was no more than fifty meters away now, and Greg began to exaggerate his own fatigue. His arms splayed and his stride deteriorated into a shuffle. At the same time, he was actually close to oxygen debt himself, the result of having to stifle his laughter at something that must have appeared quite the exhibition.

Greg allowed himself to be passed as they crossed the school parking lot, and Kyle made it to the door mere steps ahead. He reached for the door handle and turned toward Greg with a grin. "You lost, Mr.—"

Greg had to jump in order to avoid being showered with Kyle's vomit.

Despite his best intentions, though, sometimes Greg's prep-period runs were disrupted. One day he was almost out his door when the phone rang. He paused, briefly weighed his options, and then made the mistake of answering. "Hello...? Yes, this is the cross country coach."

"Your runners were running without shirts on Friday," accused the caller, who sounded like an older woman.

"Yes, ma'am, I know."

"Even the girls," she continued. "Their boobies were hanging out."

Greg stifled a laugh. "They were in sports bras, ma'am."

"I don't like it."

"I'm sorry to hear that," he said.

"Well what are you going to do about it?"

"Nothing."

"Nothing?" she cried, astounded by Greg's callous indifference to her aesthetics. "I said I don't like it."

"I understand that," Greg explained, "but the purpose of sweat is to cool the body, and it works best on bare skin. So to prevent my runners from getting heat stroke, yes, I allow them to run without shirts. Encourage it, actually."

Naturally, he was in Rumsford's office by the end of the day. "Dr. Rumsford," he began. "I know you were a nurse before you got into education, so I know you understand human physiology. I also know you care about the well-being of your students. So I would argue that we are better off running shirtless in the heat than we are transporting kids to the ER."

She did not immediately reply, the closest to a victory he had yet achieved.

"Here is a list of articles which are on point," he continued, handing her an annotated bibliography he had prepared following the phone call. "I promise you that we will wear shirts when we're on campus so we conform to dress code." Seeing what he thought might almost be the hint of a smile, he added, "Even though other Shadowcliff teams don't." As her expression quickly transformed to a scowl, he said "Thank you" and hurried out the door. For he had work to do and then, later, a vital and perilous clandestine operation.

Three days had passed since Rumsford's christening as The Wolverine. Greg completed Monday's cross country practice, then spent approximately two hours in his classroom grading papers while he waited for Rumsford to go home. While he certainly admired her energy and commitment, he was fully willing to delay his own departure as long as necessary because this just had to be done. Once she finally cleared out, he called Clayton's cell phone, and ten minutes later Clayton and Cockrell arrived in his classroom for a quick briefing. Both smelled of beer, which was all the better. Alcohol-induced courage was probably the best courage of all for this ludicrous operation, certainly better for ensuring their commitment to a conspiracy that sober people would be too wise to attempt. Cockrell, especially, should have stopped drinking a couple of beers ago.

Greg trundled down the hallway, stiff-backed and bowlegged. The bulge beneath his baggy T-shirt was obvious, and his stiff, squatty carriage looked like a robot in desperate need of a Porta-Potty. No less odd were the gloves he wore on this eighty-five degree night. Fortunately, the only other people in the building were his confederates, Cockrell and Clayton, who now occupied strategic lookout positions should the custodial help actually decide to do some custoding rather than smoking cigarettes and playing Texas Hold 'Em.

From his late nights at school, Greg knew Rumsford never closed her door when she left—he suspected that her keys were lost beneath the pile of educational journals on the front seat of her Buick—so access was easy.

"Thish is fun stuff," Cockrell slurred, much too loudly in Greg's opinion, since he was the one truly putting his neck on the line. Clayton answered,

"Holy God, did you know Samantha O'Bradovich gets the *Victoria's Secret* catalog delivered to school?"

"Would you guys shut up?" Greg said. "You're supposed to be lookouts. So more looking and less talking, please."

"Sorry," Cockrell said. And with that he started to hum.

Greg rolled his eyes. "I don't need a soundtrack," he snapped. "This is not a movie." Clayton began to snicker.

The downside of drunken accomplices growing evermore apparent, Greg quickened his pace. Spreading wide, he slowly withdrew the rectangle from underneath his shirt, entangling it for a moment before finally completing the task. He leaned it against Rumsford's desk and was about to advance to the next step when voices made him freeze.

"What are you guys doin' here?" Greg recognized the voice as Louie, one of the school's stellar custodians. He was no more than twenty feet away, but Greg hoped his drunken colleagues would provide at least a momentary delay.

"I'm ... uh...," Cockrell slurred. And then louder, "I jusht cleaning out my mailbosh and waiting for Grug Ssssamson." The signal was not much for subtlety, Greg thought, but it was certainly loud and clear.

"And I'm looking for my contact lens," Clayton added.

"Inside a titty magazine?" Louie asked.

Greg assumed he was busted, but unwilling to admit defeat just yet, he crawled underneath Rumsford's desk and pulled his cargo over the opening. Considering the tiny space, he was very glad he had stretched with the team after practice that night.

"OK, gotta go," Greg heard Clayton say, and then the outside door slammed closed.

"Teachers are weird," Louie said.

"You ain't kiddin'," replied a second voice, which Greg recognized as Gus, the custodian on his floor. The two men were far from their posts.

Greg heard the two custodians enter Rumsford's office. Years of aerobic conditioning were about to be put to the test as he calmed himself and breathed slowly, rhythmically, quietly. In order to stay calm, he picked up an educational journal from the stack underneath Rumsford's desk and, in the dim light, silently began reading about science lab ergonomics. Then he heard a strange rattling sound, as if large New York rats were dragging dog skeletons inside the walls. Rattle, grunt, scrape, and then Louie said, "Bring 'er down easy." A moment later, he added, "Let's get the broken one," followed by more scraping, grunting, and rattling.

"I love Monday Night Football," Gus said.

"Me, too," agreed Louie. "Especially since now we got the biggest TV in the whole school."

"You think she'll figure it out?" asked Gus.

"Nah," replied Louie. "She don't even know where the custodian office is at."

Greg wondered what would happen if he were discovered now, how he would explain himself to the custodians, and to Rumsford. Did he face legal liability as an accessory? He noticed the scratch in the wood—or is that particle board?—on the underside of Rumsford's desk. He became aware of a breath mint that had been dropped and, neglected, was now covered in carpet fuzz. Considering a freckle on his knee which was pressing against his cheekbone, he recalled the time he crawled inside a dryer in his dorm, just to see if he could do it. At that moment, Greg realized a vital truth worthy of inclusion in one of those *How to Survive in the Real World* books that seemed to be on every table at Barnes & Noble: Anyone who says college fails to prepare you for real life has never pretzeled himself underneath his boss's desk while two unskilled laborers steal her TV.

Greg watched their feet from underneath the desk.

"Let's get some candy, too," Louie suggested.

"I didn't bring no money."

"Don't need none. This is where she keeps her stash," Louie said, and then with the scraping of a desk drawer, he announced, "Jackpot." Greg could have reached out and tied the custodian's shoelaces together if he wanted, and truth be told, the idea definitely crossed his mind.

"Hey, Kit Kats. My favorite," Gus said. "Get one for everybody, my treat."

Greg heard the drawer scrape closed again, but then stop.

"What's with this?" Louie asked. He picked up Greg's cargo. Greg's contorted body was now in plain view, had they just bothered to look. Greg held his breath.

"Nice picture," Gus said. "Wouldja look at them teeth?"

"Must be a mean fucker," Louie said. "What is it?"

"Hell if I know."

Louie replaced the item in front of the desk, never noticing the teacher a foot away.

"Should we empty her trash can?" Gus asked.

"Later," replied Louie. "We're gonna miss the second-half kickoff."

And with that, they hurried from the office, allowing Greg a chance to finally relax. His exhale must have contained several quarts of air.

It was time to finish the mission, and quickly. His lookouts, whatever they were worth, were now a thing of the past, and were probably enjoying their next draft beer already. His nerves were frazzled and, with the exception of his gloved hands, he was getting cold.

He slid the cargo to the side and clambered out from underneath the desk. Next, he removed the large picture from above her desk and replaced it with the contraband he had brought with him. Maneuvering the original artwork underneath his T-shirt, he stood back to examine the fruits of his labor. Rumsford's bobcat picture was no more. In its place: a large picture of a wolverine. Mission accomplished. Christening official.

But Greg had no time to gloat, nor the desire. He still needed to copyedit six yearbook pages for tomorrow's deadline and then maybe get to the Taco Bell drive-through before it closed.

8

THE APOLOGY

Rumsford was relentless in her quest to lead the perfect school, placing blind reliance in the hope that every Shadowcliff student wanted the same. This was counterintuitive, of course, since teenagers are not well-known for thinking in abstract, social utopian terms. Charles Fourier they are not. Besides, there was a small but not insignificant portion of the Shadowcliff population which had been asked to leave their previous high schools, which meant that Shadowcliff High School was the educational equivalent of Australia. Sure, it might eventually grow to be paradise, but not yet. Unfortunately, because of Rumsford's inexplicable faith and her need to micromanage a zillion other things, school security was an afterthought.

Security guards were paid nine dollars an hour, not much more than a worker at the local

Jack-in-the-Box, making the job of protecting students about as important as producing bad fast-food tacos for the two a.m. drunk crowd. At that rate of pay, the selection criteria were, out of necessity, rather lax. Shadowcliff's first security hire was Jack, a short, sixty-year-old man with a limp and a bad heart. He had retired from his job as a truck driver when he could no longer read the highway signs, but Shadowcliff students loved him, mostly because he was utterly powerless to stop their shenanigans, a fact he did not dispute. So he spent most of his time sitting in the center of campus, telling road stories to kids who were supposed to be in the bathroom. Shadowcliff's second security hire was Jesse, a mountain of a man but a gentle soul. Jesse worked the family ranch each summer, and could lift a bale of hay onto the back of his truck with only one hand but could not walk back to the house when the truck was loaded, unless dinner was at stake. At Shadowcliff, Jesse dipped Skoal openly while Jack popped his heart pills and, occasionally, snuck a nip of Wild Turkey. They were such physical opposites that they made Mutt and Jeff look like twins, and together, they teamed up to keep the center of campus more secure than Fort Knox. Unfortunately, anything beyond that fifty-foot radius was like the Wild West.

So Maurice McCullough and Zoey Crandall walked the school as much as they could, while Rumsford informed teachers they were expected to spend passing periods in the hallways and serve as additional eyes and ears during their preps. With too much already on their plates, though, few could accommodate this additional request.

For all she expected of her staff, Rumsford always looked stressed, her lips pursed so tightly that it appeared she was trying to suck a brick through a drinking straw. Phrases such as "thank you" and "good job" did not seem to be part of her vocabulary. Seldom was heard an encouraging word.

What was heard, frequently, was the fire alarm. In Greg's class, the first of these rang, or more accurately shrieked, during a student presentation on the Good and Evil Manitos. It was the most ear-splitting yelp Greg had ever experienced, and he actually felt the bones in his nose begin to vibrate. He had experienced this sensation twice before, once while crossing the tarmac to board an aging 727 in Sofia, Bulgaria, and a second time when he managed to get third-row tickets to a Metallica concert in Los Angeles. In both those instances, his nose only tickled. This time was genuinely painful.

"Sorry, guys, we'll need to call timeout and get out of here." He had to yell to carry over the alarm, but it was unnecessary since his students were fleeing the howl as quickly as possible. As they began the intricate evacuation route, Greg's students merged with class after class of young people with hands clasped over their ears like characters auditioning for Edvard Munch's *The Scream*. Without a doubt, the alarm was effective in accomplishing its purpose, as the building cleared with remarkable rapidity. Even so, Greg wondered, if bells cause seizure reactions, what just happened on the inside of my head?

Twenty minutes later, amidst unbridled speculation as to the cause of the fire, the loudspeaker announced "All clear" and students and teachers were directed back to their classrooms. Twelve hundred people re-entered the building just as two were seen departing: Officer Mike escorting Steven Torgemeyer, in handcuffs, out the back door. "I knew it!" one kid shouted, and Steven Torgemeyer looked back contemptuously. Meanwhile, paramedics were placing on oxygen mask over Jesse's face while school nurse Kim Purcell, clearly annoyed that Steven Torgemeyer had such impudence to set the fire during first period, checked Jack's heart with a stethoscope.

As the days and weeks moved past, Rumsford's passion and her fury remained unrelenting, and in equal measure. The novelty of the opening had worn off, and teachers settled into a routine of hard work with only occasional respites, which were called weekends. But even these were seldom restful for Greg, between cross country practice and meets, a shred of personal time, and trying to keep up with the workload of his four different classes. By late September, as he was locking up his classroom well after dark, he realized he had spent every Sunday at school, too.

A scant nine hours later, he was back at school for the weekly Monday morning staff meeting. Even as the most vociferous of Shadowcliff's union people began to complain about the number of meetings—this made fifteen in the first seven weeks of school—Rumsford continued them unabated, as if the school were doomed without its weekly prescription of inane activities and recitation of professional responsibilities. At each and every staff meeting, Rumsford would explain why it was incumbent upon the teachers to patrol the bathrooms or chaperone the winter formal. She also reminded them that one of their most important professional responsibilities was to attend staff meetings.

"Alright, everybody," Rumsford began. "The first thing I need to tell you is this: remember that it's important to listen. Listening makes your students feel valued and respected. It gives them confidence to express their viewpoints, and we want to make every student feel they have something worthwhile to say."

Ike Gravenstein, the faculty's built-in bullshit meter, raised his hand. He had been quiet for the past several weeks, but he just could not let this one pass. "Connie?" he asked, and once again Rumsford winced at the informality. "You and I have been on the earth a long time," he said, turning the dagger. "We all know that some people don't have anything worthwhile to say." Murmurs of agreement sprung up throughout the room. "What do you suggest we do about them?"

Rumsford did not respond, but neither did she miss a beat. She continued, "And it encourages them to ask questions, because they know you'll be responsive to them."

Some teachers nodded their heads knowingly, while others were too wrapped up in their own private conversations to realize what had just been said.

"Secondly, I need to tell you to be open to possibilities. Every student can learn. It's your job to make sure that they do.

"Now, in your journals, write down the name of a student who has stood out for you the first six weeks of school. First names only."

"Do you want first and last names, or just first names?" one teacher asked.

"First names only," Rumsford replied.

Another teacher raised her hand. "What if we can't spell their last name?"

"I just want first names," Rumsford replied.

"Do you mean 'stood out' in a good way or a bad way?" a third teacher asked. But by this time, Rumsford was into conversation with Maurice, and this teacher never received a response.

Greg spent a moment pondering the prompt. What *did* Rumsford mean, exactly, by "stood out"? Was she looking for personality, helpfulness, politeness, mode of dress, or just run-of-the-mill academic excellence? Would he need a rubric to decide?

Looking around, Greg noticed the two math teachers across from him had already written down names. One had written "Bob." The other, "Dan." Greg decided it might be more interesting if he wrote "Tariq-Muhammed," a boy in his first-period English class, and so he did.

The lights flickered. "Now, team up with the teacher next to you."

So Greg joined forces with Donny Elmendorf. Elmendorf had been on the interview committee the past summer, impressing Greg as a competent and caring professional and maybe the smartest person in the department. The student he chose was "Elizabeth."

"You and your partner now have five minutes to make as many words as you can out of the letters. Go."

Greg and Donny worked furiously, coming up with AIM, AIR, AM, AT, MU, TI, TRIM, ATRIUM, QUIT, QUART, QUIRT, QUARTZ, MAIZE, MERIT, IRATE, MEAT, MAZE, MATE, MART, MARE, TEAM, TEAR, TERM, TIER, TIMER, MITER, RE, BE, HAZEL, HALE, HAUL, LIEU, ZEAL, HULA, BATHE, HEATH, ABET, ABED, MATH, BRAIZE, BREATHE, and ZEBRA.

"Time's up," Rumsford announced.

"Damn!" said Greg. "We forgot BEAT."

"Count up the number of words you made," said Rumsford.

Greg looked across at the list compiled by the two math teachers who had been forced to work with "Bob" and "Dan." Their list contained only five words: AND, BAD, BAN, BAND and NOB. Greg did not have the heart to tell them they missed BOND, ADO, and NABOB, among others.

"I have a special prize for the group with the most words," Rumsford continued. "Did any group get more than ten?"

Greg and Danny were still counting, finally raising their hands when they came up with a total of forty-two. But the negotiations had already begun. "Is REBO a word?" "Do we get triple word scores?" "Can I trade in my letters for some new ones?" The meeting soon became so chaotic that Greg and Danny's remarkable total was never acknowledged.

Rumsford's whistle finally silenced everyone. "Does anyone know the purpose of this activity?" she asked, but then answered herself, "The purpose of this activity was to demonstrate that we must never underestimate any student. Every child can learn, so we must be mindful of their potential by seeing things in a different way. Any other reason?" Again, she did not hesitate. "The other reason is to show the value of group work. Two heads are better than one."

"Yeah, I wouldn't have come up with NOB in a million years," joked the younger of the two math teachers. "Thanks for your help."

"No problem," said his partner, raising his hand. "Dr. Rumsford, doesn't it also demonstrate the inherent limitations of group work?" She regarded him dubiously, but he continued.

"I mean, wouldn't math teachers be disadvantaged *vis-à-vis* English teachers on a word-building activity? And wouldn't a group that happened to choose shorter names be handicapped as well? These guys had..."

He reached across for Greg's journal, and Greg handed it to him happily. This could get interesting, he thought.

"... Tariq-Muhammed and Elizabeth. We chose Bob and Dan. We had as much chance to win as—"

He noticed that Rumsford was once again in conversation with Maurice, oblivious to his point. Everyone began to talk and soon it was a free-for-all. She finally turned around and shouted, above the noise, "Remember to listen! Every child can learn!"

But Greg had already realized the gap, or more accurately the chasm, between the ability to learn and the desire. He could give a student a blank piece of paper and a pen, he could instruct, inspire, and nurture, and he could provide explicit directions for auditory, visual, and kinesthetic learners. Yet it was entirely possible the student would produce nothing more than a few random inkblots, sketches of lightning bolts or creatures from *The Lord of the Rings*, or in some cases, a pageful of wrinkles.

Too many times, Greg took their neglect personally, and more than once his frustration from one class oozed into the next. This was, as Jeanette Candelaria explained, a classic sign of a rookie teacher. "I'm pretty sure they don't sit at the dinner table saying, 'I wonder how I can piss off Mr. Samson tomorrow,'" she reasoned.

Other days, he took their disconnect as a challenge to his competitive spirit, the fierce determination that served him well as an athlete and that willingly embraced even the most quixotic of quests. Once, in college, he made it a point to say "hello" to a certain black teammate every day without ever receiving a reply. There was no telling if the man was inattentive, spoke only a foreign language, hated white people, or was stone deaf, but Greg persevered. Finally, late in the season, he earned a simple "Hey Samson," and that was enough. Greg knew he would never be best man at the guy's wedding—nor was that the objective— but in remaining undaunted he had made a breakthrough and, eventually, a friend. Like the idealist Woody accused him of being, Greg strove to apply that same spirit in the classroom, to break through the walls of indifference. But it was seldom easy and often frustrating.

Then there were times when a student's neglect enlarged itself into dishonesty, a transaction Greg refused to tolerate.

"Mr. Zeiss, may I see you for a moment?" Greg asked as his students, drained from a challenging exam, filed out of class. Zeiss hid his lack of self-confidence behind a blustery, mischievous exterior and a perpetual wardrobe two sizes too large. He bullied other kids into submission, distracting those who wanted to learn and insulting those who wanted to behave. According to a memo from the counseling department, it seemed this child only needed to be patted on the head and told to click his heels together three times in order for him to reach Self-Actualization and then, as day follows night, Principal's List. Greg knew better, since Zeiss could not spell, construct a coherent sentence, or read much beyond *Diary of a Wimpy Kid*, which was not on Greg's class reading list. At least he was "high-spirited," in the words of the counseling memo. Greg knew this was nothing more than educational double-talk, guessing that schools seldom received grant money when they describe a student as "a first-class prick."

With this particular student, Greg was in no mood to be diplomatic. Sarcasm suited him much better, the mandates of Connie Rumsford and Elden Ray Fong be damned.

"Mr. Zeiss, how's your neck?"

"Huh?"

"I'm just worried about your health. I thought you might have injured your neck during the test."

"Huh? No."

"I mean, you were looking around so much, twisting to look at your neighbor's test paper, that it must be sore. I think a good chiropractic adjustment is just what you need," Greg continued, thumbing through the test.

"I don't—"

"—Mr. Zeiss, can you tell me the name of the antagonist in the play?"

"Uh, it says so right there, Mr. Samson." He looked nervous.

"I know that, but I'm having trouble reading your handwriting. Why don't you tell me?"

"I ... uh ... I don't know."

"You don't know," Samson repeated. "Even though you wrote down an answer on the test?"

"I knew it then," he said defiantly.

"Has the answer changed?"

"I don't need that information no more, so I dumped it."

"*Any* more. See, what I find interesting is that you wrote the exact same answer as your neighbor. In fact, most of your answers are identical to your neighbor's. The only ones that are different are wrong."

"The dude cheated off me!"

"Now that's a distinct possibility, Mr. Zeiss. It's fairly typical that 'A' students cheat off students with an F. Why else would they have A's?" Zeiss smiled, comforted by Greg's logic. But his smile disappeared when Greg snapped, "Let's cut the charade, Mr. Zeiss. You cheated off him. We both know it, and I can prove it."

Zeiss gathered his backpack and stormed out of the room, turning around only to say, "I'm telling my dad."

"Good," replied Greg. "Have him call me. We'll do lunch."

It took no more than a few hours for the issue to be resolved.

"Sit down," Rumsford said. Her look was stern, all business. But Greg could not help but steal a glance at the wolverine print above her desk. For a man who had trained in the heat, in snow, in driving rain, who had raced with the flu and with tendinitis and with a nasty gash in his shin, and remained focused through each and every potential distraction, it took all his considerable willpower to avoid staring at the picture and cracking up.

"I just got a call from Howard Zeiss," Rumsford explained impatiently. "His son is in your English class."

"Yes, I know," Greg replied.

She continued, "He said you accused his son of cheating."

"That's correct."

"I take cheating very seriously," Rumsford assured him. "Very seriously. Shadowcliff High School will not tolerate cheaters. And we cannot aspire to academic greatness if we allow cheating. So why would you have the impertinence to accuse him of cheating?"

"Because he cheated," Greg explained. He saw no reason to elaborate.

"That's an interesting answer," she pondered. "Certainly not what I expected. Because if he did cheat, of course, there would be severe consequences. But the father says his son has never cheated on anything, and we have no record of him ever having cheated before."

"So? Statistically, one hundred percent of all first-time killers have never killed before."

"Let's stick to the point," Rumsford continued, somewhat irritated. "We're not talking about anyone killing anyone. What's wrong with you?"

"Too metaphorical, I guess."

"The father has hired an attorney."

"For what?"

"You slandered his son—"

"—First of all, it's not slander because it was said privately. That's fundamental. Hopefully, his attorney at least knows that much law." He leaned forward in his chair, emphatically. "Second, for crying out loud, truth is always a defense in a defamation case."

"Point being?" she probed.

"Point being, he did it!"

"Can you prove it? Because cheating is very difficult to prove."

"On the contrary. In this case, at least, cheating is very easy to prove. First of all, I saw him looking at another student's test, three different times. And not just looking, but staring. Amazingly, that was the only time he did any writing. I think that's pretty strong evidence. And their answers matched exactly. Exactly. Also pretty conclusive, wouldn't you say? Then he couldn't answer the very same questions ten minutes later."

"And how does that prove cheating?"

"I'm no psychologist, but I'm fairly certain that neither short-term nor long-term memory completely evaporates in just a few minutes."

"Mr. Samson, that's the first intelligent thing you've said today." Greg smiled and sat back in his chair, and Rumsford continued. "You are definitely not a psychologist. Because if you were, you'd know how damaging such an accusation can be to a teenager." She paused to unwrap a Twinkie. "And they're demanding an A."

"That's ridiculous! Both the kid and the parent signed the District Code of Conduct, which includes a section on academic integrity. They also signed my class expectations, which define cheating. Besides, everyone knows—"

"—They claim the test didn't specifically prohibit collaboration."

"Collaboration, huh? Nice euphemism. The teacher handbook doesn't specifically prohibit me from teaching class naked, either. What the hell?"

"Mr. Samson, please stick to the subject at hand! And watch your goddamn language! I don't know what point you're trying to make, Mr. Samson, but you're going to have to give him the A."

"You've got to be kidding."

"I never kid about cheating. I take cheating very seriously. In fact, I abhor cheating. That's why I'll be putting this incident in your personnel file. And you're also going to write him a letter of apology."

She reached into her desk drawer and withdrew a rainbow of form letters, which she studied intently for a few seconds. "Here, use this one," she said, passing one of the papers across the desk. It was goldenrod.

Greg took the page and stood wearily. "Well, I certainly thank you for your time, Dr. Rumsford."

"Remember," she called after him, "our parents are our customers."

A few hours later, Greg took a chair at Wingding's. The usual crowd was there—Clayton, Cockrell, Keri Tanner—along with other teachers in what was becoming a rapidly expanding circle of fatigue and commiseration. Things between himself and Keri Tanner had been awkward the past couple of weeks, but with ten others there, they could maintain a cordial distance while they worked out their feelings in private. Greg was most pleased that Jeanette Candelaria had chosen to join them; he found her cynicism rooted in years of experience and disappointment to be a refreshing change from the others, whose own cynicism was the product of only a few weeks on the job.

Greg began to tell the story of the afternoon's meeting with Rumsford. As he described the cheating incident, Jeanette said, "Good for you. Too many teachers won't take a stand."

"I'm not so sure," Greg replied. "I know I'm right, both philosophically and in this specific instance, but I wonder if it was worth it."

The others looked at him quizzically, so he continued.

"Rumsford basically tore me apart for it. Seems I stole the kid's self-esteem, and now he's probably doomed to a career behind the counter at Circle-K when he could be Secretary General of the United Nations. Not to mention how I exposed the entire District to litigation."

"Damn lawyers," Cockrell said. Then, looking at Greg, he caught himself. "Sorry."

"Don't be. Slime is still slime, even driving a Mercedes-Benz. *Especially* driving a Mercedes-Benz."

"So what happened?" asked Jeanette.

"To make a long story short, I have to give the kid an A.... Hell, I graded it just for kicks, and he only got a sixty-eight. He couldn't even cheat well."

"I wouldn't do it," Clayton announced defiantly. "Here's what I'd do. I'd give him another test, and it'd be the hardest fucking test I've ever written."

"I'm not sure I have that option," Greg explained amidst murmurs of discontent. "Oh, yeah, one more thing. I have to send him a letter of apology. Like *I* was in the wrong."

Jeanette suddenly began to laugh hysterically, nodding her head vigorously with each cackle. Everyone was puzzled, and patrons at the bar looked at her, then searched desperately for the manager. Was the woman having an epileptic fit? Was she choking to death on a cocktail weenie? While Greg knew she was not in danger, he was no less confused by her reaction.

"Jeanette," he said, "what's so funny?"

She finally calmed her breathing enough that she could speak. "You have to send him a letter of apology?"

"That's right."

She reached beneath the table. "Is yours...," she asked, pulling something from her purse and then thrusting it triumphantly into the air, "goldenrod?"

9

THE BATTLE OF GETTYSBURG

"W e're your new anchors," said the red-haired freshman as he walked into the TV studio the next morning, his insincere smile showcasing a mouthful of braces. The day's broadcast of the morning announcements was five minutes away, and Greg would not have acknowledged him if not for the rather smug, matter-of-fact manner of his introduction.

"I don't recall asking for new anchors," Greg said brusquely as he rushed past with a videotape in hand.

"Where's the copy?" asked a second boy, thinner and darker than the first, pushing his way into the control room.

Stopping him, Greg asked, "Who are you?"

"I'm Paul Coates," said the dark-haired boy. "This is Andy Varner," he added, indicating the redhead who flashed his braces once again. "We did the announcements in middle school."

"Dr. Rumsford said we were supposed to help you," added Andy.

While the announcements were a chaotic daily event, and some additional technical expertise and dedication would have been appreciated, Greg was certain he had not asked God, or Rumsford, to drop a couple of nerdy kids on him for babysitting.

"Thanks, but we don't need your help," he told them.

"That's not what Dr. Rumsford says," the redhead offered. "She says you need someone with experience. She said the announcements suck—"

"—She didn't say 'suck,' you moron," interrupted Paul. "She said 'stink.' There's a difference."

"What's the difference, genius?" Andy responded.

"Suck is worse than stink."

"Is not."

"Is too. There's stink," he said, his right hand down by his knees, "then bite, then suck, then blow chunks." With each of these, he moved his hand higher up the ladder to indicate the various levels in this critical hierarchy of teen vocabulary. "See? Suck is two levels worse."

"You guys," said Greg, trying to close the control-room door. "You'll pardon me if I don't find this conversation fascinating. In fact, it stinks, bites, sucks, *and* blows chunks. Please go away."

"Mr. Samson, Frank doesn't want to read the announcements," he heard a student say from behind him. "And if he won't, then I don't want to either."

"Crap," said Greg, under his breath. But when he looked up, there was Andy Varner, his braces gleaming in the fluorescent lights, and Paul Coates, arms crossed in one of those superior "what are you waiting for?" poses.

Greg jerked his thumb over his shoulder. "Get miked up."

Moments later, the countdown began. "In five, four, three, two, one. Cue talent." And with that, Andy Varner and Doug Coates were on the air.

The next five minutes were filled with misreadings, mispronunciations, inside jokes that couldn't even be considered sophomoric, and finally Andy's "shout out to my homeboys," which sounded particularly ridiculous coming from a red-haired adolescent wearing a Tommy Hilfiger shirt and sporting five thousand dollars' worth of metal in his mouth, and whose mother dropped him off at school every day in a Volvo.

When the broadcast ended, Paul gave Andy a high five. Greg entered from the control room, flabbergasted at their blithe attitude at having just reduced the announcements to an exercise is self-glorification that contained absolutely nothing of value for anyone else. "You're fired," Greg said simply, then turned quickly and left the studio.

That afternoon, Greg received the following e-mail:

> From: Connie Rumsford, EdD
> To: Greg Samson
> Subject: Andy Varner and Paul Coates
> Sent: October 11, 1:44:21
>
> Andy and Paul tell me you "fired" them. This is not acceptable!! We are a student centered school! –CR

To which Greg replied:

> From: Greg Samson
> To: Connie Rumsford, EdD
> Subject: RE: Andy Varner and Paul Coates
> Sent: October 11, 1:51:18
>
> Andy and Paul were "fired" because they turned the announcements into a personal forum for their immaturity. Isn't "student-centered" about what's best for all 1200 students, not just two? And since I will be evaluated based upon these announcements, shouldn't I be permitted to made decisions which will impact their quality?

Greg thought he raised some interesting philosophical questions, and Rumsford dealt with them in an equally philosophical manner:

> From: Connie Rumsford, EdD
> To: Greg Samson
> Subject: RE: RE: Andy Varner and Paul Coates
> Sent: October 11, 1:56:38
>
> NO! Put them back on the air immediately. –CR

The entire process took just over twelve minutes, but at least Greg had not been subjected to another stint in that stupid office chair of hers.

Greg's Bobcats went to the starting line for their second competition against Granite, six weeks after the first. While they still looked younger, scrawnier, and less mature than their opponents, they were also beginning to demonstrate the earmarks of success— even winning a meet a couple of weeks earlier. The junior from California, who had emerged as unofficial captain because he was the oldest of the varsity runners, called the other Bobcats together for a pre-race huddle. Greg knew he was also a team leader because he had a car and often gave teammates a ride home after practice. The promising sophomore broke from his stretching routine and jogged over to the huddle. And Corey, whose voice still broke on occasion, now cracked jokes on the way to join his teammates. Greg was smiling at what he saw.

The head coach for Granite walked past Greg. "You guys don't even look like the same team as six weeks ago."

Greg never took his eyes off his runners as they met behind the starting line. "Thanks, but we both know that efficient warm-ups and team huddles don't make a successful program." But we're headed in the right direction, he added to himself.

The race began with ten Granite runners going immediately to the front, but Greg had told his guys to work together and remain patient. He had run during his planning period earlier today, so he was warmed up. As soon as his last guy raced past, Greg sprinted out a gate and cut through the desert, emerging at the mile mark just in time to see the ten Granite guys run past. Shadowcliff's top three were still running together, and more important, they appeared to be gaining. "You guys look great," he said, quietly and calmly. "Keep moving up." Greg stayed until his last man ran past again, then it was another dead sprint to the picnic ramada on the far side of the lake. Two miles into the three-mile race, and now the Granite squad was split into two groups.

Between them were Shadowcliff's top three. This time, Greg's excitement could not be contained. "You guys are awesome. Stay aggressive!" He waited impatiently as long as he could, cheering each of his runners as they passed. While well-intentioned parents shouted "Keep it up" or "Way to go, Tommy" or the ever-useless "Go!" Greg tried to offer something of value to each runner: "Stay tall" or "Relax your hands" or "Focus on the red shirt in front of you." The uninitiated probably wouldn't see those as any more meaningful, but Greg knew from several hundred of his own races that they provided a specific point of focus, and perhaps kept a suffering runner from the destructive morass of self-pity that always loomed around the next corner.

He cheered for as many runners as he could, then sprinted back across the park toward the finish line. He missed the first two Granite runners come across, but managed to get there in time to see Corey narrowly beaten on the sprint by Granite's number three guy. Shadowcliff's next two runners came in soon thereafter, in seventh and eighth. While Greg's two remaining scorers still struggled, and this day's score of 17-42 appeared little better than the previous 15-50 whitewashing, Greg was overjoyed.

Thirty minutes later, Darlene won her race handily. "Nicely done," Greg said simply.

"I felt so bad on the hill," she replied. "And I think they mismarked the course."

"Really?" asked Greg.

"And that one girl from Granite is a total bitch. She was running, like, right next to me at the start. I couldn't believe it."

Always a charming and gracious winner, Greg thought to himself.

Like the boys' race, the girls fared much better, the product of fitness and confidence borne from the shared toil of young people with a common purpose. Shadowcliff had three other girls in the top ten, and lost to one of the state's better teams by just a few points.

"You guys have come so far," Greg began their post-race meeting. "I wish the season were another three months long. Unfortunately it's not. Next week is our District championships, which will be the final competition of the season for some of you. I just hope you realize the magnitude of what you've done. You've trusted me and believed in yourselves, and I'm incredibly proud of you."

"Are we running to the bus today?" Corey asked.

"What's the team rule?"

"We run to the bus after any race on a day that ends in Y," said the team, most of them anyway. Darlene, sitting behind everyone else, was listening to her headphones, oblivious to his remarks until she saw her teammates begin their post-race run. Greg looked at her inquisitively, which she answered by digging into her bag and pulling out a crumpled sheet of yellow legal paper. She gave the paper to Greg before nonchalantly picking up her bag and climbing the stairs onto the bus. Greg's jaw dropped as he read:

> Darlene does not need to do any long
> run's after races. It will hurt her speed.
> Maurice.

Greg knew Darlene often visited Maurice to complain about Greg's coaching decisions, and Maurice always sided with her. Always. As he explained to Greg, "She's like my daughter. I have her back." To which Greg often thought, if she's like your daughter, perhaps you should stop indulging her and teach her some responsibility. And maybe some teamwork and sportsmanship while you're at it. However, valuing his job, he kept his mouth shut and watched with self-satisfaction as she continued to progress even despite her best efforts at resistance. He wondered how good she would be if she actually submitted to Greg's training plan, but he recognized that to be pointless speculation.

After reading the note, it took Greg several minutes to recover from this usurpation of his coaching authority and from Maurice's blatant misunderstanding of exercise physiology, the bioenergetic demands of racing, and the rules of grammar. Twenty-five minutes later, their run completed and drinks in hand, all the other kids were now chatting happily as the bus pulled out of Circle-K and onto the free-way. Meanwhile, Darlene slouched inside her head-phones, insulated in her passive-aggressive world.

One day at lunch, Jimmy Clayton offered a remark-able proposal.

"I'm studying the Battle of Gettysburg right now," he began. "You're reading Walt Whitman's Civil War poetry. Dr. Rumsford wants us to be innovative and student-centered. She loves integration. You up for it?"

"Up for what?" Greg asked. He understood vaguely where Clayton was going, but wanted to see how much forethought had gone into the details. He forgot that Clayton was probably the most anal per-son he had ever met.

"Fifth hour block," Clayton began. You've got English, I've got American History. My class ver-sus your class, Union versus Confederacy. We'll re-enact the Battle of Gettysburg in the main mall." As Clayton continued, Greg decided it was a grand idea. If it succeeded, it would be a really cool event. And if it failed, Rumsford would certainly be there to ob-serve, and the debriefing was sure to be a riot.

A few days later, Greg's thirty-one confeder-ate soldiers lined up on one side while Clayton's thirty union soldiers lined up on the other. Greg's numerical advantage was mitigated by the fact that two of his girls were wearing shorts skirts—thus minimizing their ability to attack with any degree of gallantry, confidence, or dignity. He also faced the obstacle of historical fact. Yet he considered this far less of an impediment, and was tempered by grave doubts that anything in the next thirty minutes would remotely resemble any recorded history.

Clayton directed the confederates toward Missionary Ridge, symbolized by three desks, and Little Round Top, a garbage can. Students raised imaginary Colt revolvers or Springfield rifles and began shooting. Some even added their own soundtracks: "Pchew! Kabloom! Aaah!" Soldiers from both sides died heroically while others advanced with a sense of great pride and purpose. Greg sat back, enjoying the show, and noticed that many of the "dead" soldiers were now listening to their iPods or sharing photos with members of the opposing army. So much for patriotism.

After Samson's final Confederate assault was repelled, Clayton stood atop a desk, donned a stovepipe hat, and delivered "The Gettysburg Address" to three score and one young people. Greg had gone to the second floor, where he called out "Revenge for the South!" and then, brandishing a water pistol he had picked up at Mick's Corner Store that morning, "shot" the erstwhile Mr. Lincoln. As the president crumpled before the astonished witnesses, Greg ran

out the back door, playing his role as the crazed as-
sassin John Wilkes Booth for all it was worth. He did,
however, decide to deviate from the facts in at least
one area. Since jumping down from the balcony
and breaking his leg was not particularly vital to the
simulation, nor in his own best interest, he took the
stairs instead.

One hundred feet away, Dr. Rumsford shook her
head in disgust and trudged back to her office.

Later that day, Greg walked through the office lobby,
somewhat lost in the swirl of contradictions he had,
once more, been forced to suffer. A vaguely familiar
voice broke his trance.

"Greg Samson!"

Greg turned and saw a large, bespectacled man,
cheeks rounded and chins drooping from too many
expense-account dinners. He wore a slick gray
Armani suit that, without a doubt, cost more than
Greg's next two paychecks. It was Darnell Lyon, former law-school classmate of Greg's and the name-
sake of "the law firm with teeth." This last part, Greg
realized too late, he should have thought of more
dramatically.

"What are you doing here?" Lyon continued.

"I work here. I'm a teacher." And then, after a
pause, he added, "I guess that makes you the enemy."

Lyon forced a smile. "Why aren't you practicing law?"

"Never took the bar exam," replied Greg. Anticipating the next question, he continued, "I figured out halfway through the program that I didn't want to practice."

"Really? Then why didn't you drop out?"

"I tend to finish things I start," explained Greg. "I suppose it's some sort of character defect."

"Well, you should consider becoming an education lawyer," Lyon said. "There's lots of work, and you'd be a natural."

There was an awkward silence, finally broken when Greg said, "I need to get to class. It was nice to see you, Darnell."

The lawyer was now searching through his thousand-dollar alligator briefcase. "See you around," he answered simply.

As Greg walked to class, he entertained contradicting emotions as he tried to ascertain whether Lyon's final words were prophetic, or merely friendly. The idea of practicing Ed Law was certainly intriguing, for many reasons. On the other hand, he would not have minded squaring off against this guy in a debate over student rights versus academic responsibility, assuming he had the backing of Dr. Rumsford. With that final caveat, though, he dismissed the middle ground as logistically impossible. For the ostensible case of *Samson v. Zeiss* made it abundantly clear that Rumsford had allowed the school's prevailing climate to become one of compliance and submission, especially to whichever parents could afford a high-priced lawyer like Darnell Lyon. And in a community where many parents were attorneys, lived next door to attorneys, or provided orthodontia or acne prescriptions to the children of attorneys, most of them could.

Greg found himself inside room 4122, which was no more than half the size he remembered it to be. Faculty were packed in shoulder-to-shoulder. A bird flew in the door and lit on top of a bookshelf in the corner. While he was no ornithologist, the bird appeared to Greg to be a woodpecker.

Standing in front of the group, Rumsford said, "*Umpjay onay ouryay eftlay ootfay.*" Greg found it an odd request and Pig Latin an even odder way of making it. But always happy to exercise and always a team player, he joined his colleagues in jumping on his left foot.

"*Κτυπήστε ελαφρά το κεφάλι σας και τρίψτε στόμαχος σας,*" Rumsford said next. Greg recognized it as Greek, which he experienced when he traveled to Thessaloniki to run a race in 1997. Since all the Greek he picked up was "please," "thank you," and "third place," he was actually quite pleased to even recognize the language. As he looked around to see the reactions of the others, he noticed Lydia Scanlon, the librarian who knew everything, rapidly taking notes with one hand while she used the other to flip through a Greek-to-English dictionary at exactly five-eighths the speed of light. Meanwhile, every other member of the faculty somehow understood the command, and all began patting their heads and rubbing their tummies while Maurice McCullough tossed rewards of pita bread, Kalamata olives, and baklava to the teachers like fish guts to a trained seal act.

Rumsford frowned at Greg before she continued. "*Timro bia koota betra rock, timro bia koota bira rock, Timro bia koota betra rock, ra sabi tira halouna,*" she said. Greg was not certain, but he believed Rumsford was speaking Nepali. He had caught a snippet of the language last Saturday night while watching a Discovery Channel documentary on climbing Mt. Everest. Lydia Scanlon was again taking furious notes while rifling through a well-worn Nepali-to-Greek dictionary. And once more, Greg's vague recognition of the language was no match for the veracity of the others, who put their left foot in, took their left foot out, put their left foot in, and then shook it all about, while Maurice McCullough made small talk with a Sherpa who had just trekked in from outside.

Her nostrils flaring as she stared straight at Greg, Rumsford now said, "*Ickpling gloffthrobb squutserumm blhiop mlashnalt zwin tonobalkguffh slhiophad gurdlubh asht.*" Greg recognized this as Luggnaggian, and he was absolutely certain that nobody in the room understood a language that existed only inside a three-hundred-year-old satirical novel. Again, Lydia Scanlon was writing and thumbing through an antique Luggnaggian-to-Nepali dictionary. Maurice McCullough, dressed as Gulliver, was leading the staff in Luggnaggian cheers. The other teachers were shouting things like "*Frestum!*" and "*Yariputh edlak!*" until, finally, someone cried "*Maldodrost er pliffnesh!*" and Rumsford pointed and nodded that nod of infinite superiority while everyone else licked the floor in front of her.

Rumsford bared her teeth at Greg. Drops of saliva fell from her lower lip as she began her final remarks. "*Wah wah wah wah. Wah wah wah. Wah wah wah wah wah.*" Charlie Brown's teacher. He expected most to recognize this language. He was, however, absolutely befuddled—yet not the least bit surprised—how everyone else knew to get out of their chairs and march out of the room without swinging their arms. Moments later, even Lydia Scanlon took her leave, juggling what appeared to be an entire library with just one hand, so Greg was left all alone.

And from atop the bookcase, the woodpecker said, "Nevermore."

10

THE CONDUCT REFERRAL

Greg Samson had been subpoenaed to Dr. Rumsford's office so many times in his short professional life that he finally stopped counting in early February, settling on a number somewhere between "a shit ton" and "infinity." He yearned for the day when every possible inquisition was exhausted, even as he conceded her ability to manufacture crisis from virtually any choice he made. As usual, she did not disappoint.

Before he could even take a seat, Dr. Rumsford thrust a paper at him aggressively. "Mr. Samson, can you explain ... this?" The last word she spit out, like poison. Greg took what she offered and recognized it as an assignment from a few weeks ago.

"Cade Ralston's essay," he identified, mystified that it was now in her possession.

"What was the assignment?"

"It was a persuasive essay. They were allowed to pick their topic."

"Why?"

"Why did I let them pick their topic?" Greg asked.

Rumsford nodded as she pulled a yellow pad from her desk drawer. She never went anywhere without a yellow pad. Greg followed her hand as she picked up a pen and began taking notes.

"Students should write about something that concerns them. For Cade, that's the fact that Shadowcliff doesn't have honors classes. He feels," indicating the essay, "as if he isn't being challenged."

"So challenge him."

"I have challenged him all year within the parameters of our model. I give him higher-level assignments than the other kids. I made him rewrite this essay twice. But he feels heterogeneous grouping isn't working."

"Who is Cade Ralston to decide such a thing?"

"Well, I would say Cade Ralston is a kid who is experiencing it first-hand. Heterogeneous grouping may be good for the self-esteem of some kids, but he's just coasting."

"Have him help the dumb kids, then."

"I don't have any dumb kids in my classes," replied Greg, "as per school philosophy." Rumsford's eyes enflamed at that. "So having him eviscerate 'The Love Song of J. Alfred Prufrock' into 'a guy is trying to decide if he should eat a peach' really isn't in Cade's best interest.... In his opinion, that is." Greg was unsure if he said this last part in time.

"If I say it is, then it is. Your job is to do what I say," Rumsford shot back.

"And I do. I support every one of our programs. My Mentor Time class is one of the few on campus that actually does anything. I continue to develop ways to challenge my strong students. But like Voltaire, I also support Cade's right to express his beliefs."

"Who's this Voltaire? What class is he in?"

Dr. Rumsford's phone rang, and Greg sat back to catch his breath. Through all his visits to Rumsford's office during the school year, his greatest challenge had been to avoid looking at the wolverine poster. Now, he made the mistake of a quick glance, and stifled a laugh just in the nick of time.

"Where were we?" Rumsford asked as she hung up the phone. "Oh, yeah, the essay. How could you give it an A? Did you even read it?"

"I read it several times. Like I said, I made him rewrite it twice. It's a good essay."

"It's a terrible essay," she countered. "Not a shred of proof. There's not a journal article or an expert opinion in there anywhere."

"The assignment was to support it with your best argument, not someone else's. It wasn't a research paper. Cade is a sophomore, not a senior. He did exactly what he was supposed to do."

"I'd like to see the rubric you used to evaluate this."

"I don't have it," Greg replied. "I gave it back to Cade when I returned the essay."

"I bet you didn't even have a rubric. So I made one myself." She pulled out another of her ubiquitous yellow legal pads. "Ideas, D. Organization, F. Mechanics, D."

"Whoa," Greg jumped in. "A 'D' in Mechanics? The only grammatical error in the entire essay is a misplaced comma. And an 'F' in Organization? He wrote five paragraphs—intro, three body, and conclusion. He had a strong thesis statement. The entire essay was clear and coherent. If you don't agree with the point, well, I wouldn't expect you to. But he offers some valid ideas."

"I don't care about anyone else's ideas," Rumsford replied. "I only care about my own."

The battle was lost—that much Greg had known since the beginning—but it no longer mattered. He sat back and crossed his arms.

"Mr. Samson, let me make myself clear. You are to stop this nonsense. The student will receive an F for this essay. And I suggest you re-evaluate your teaching practices. There will be no more of this essay-writing nonsense. An English class is not an appropriate venue for a student to express his opinion. From now on, I expect you to spend your time doing valuable activities ... and nothing else."

Still mystified as to how Rumsford ended up with the essay, Greg ran into Cade Ralston on his way back to class. Cade was eating a hamburger. "I gave it to her because I wanted her to know how I felt," he explained. "Did you get in trouble?"

"Don't worry about it, Cade. I have a long list of transgressions."

"Could you get fired?" Cade asked, genuinely concerned. "I'd feel terrible if that happened."

"I guess I could," replied Greg. He had not even considered that possibility. "But if that's the straw that breaks the camel's back, then the fault is with the camel as much as the straw. See you in class tomorrow." And with that, Greg proceeded to his classroom and recorded Cade's A in the gradebook.

But every time Greg thought the system was going to squeeze the last drop of life from him, every time he grew fatigued of juggling too many balls for too many hours with too much criticism on too little sleep for too few dollars, something magical would happen. One morning, Kyle Friese walked into first period five minutes early. The last time Kyle had been early for class was probably the day they issued scissors in kindergarten, Greg thought. And not only was Kyle early, he was dressed in a shirt with actual buttons. And then the kicker: "Hi, Mr. Samson."

Greg was stunned. "H – hi, Kyle," he finally got out.

"Mr. Samson, you ever read *Cat's Cradle* by Kurt Something-or-Other?"

Greg began to correct him on the author's name, but stopped. At this moment, it really did not matter if Kyle thought the guy's name was Zeke Wifflesnoffer, did it?

"Why? Are you thinking about reading it?"

"I read it over the weekend."

"Really?" Greg said. He hoped his surprise wouldn't come off as doubt. "What did you think of it?"

"Pretty freaky. Newt cracked me up. And that whole ice-nine thing. Whoa."

"Yeah, I liked Newt, too," Greg replied. While it would never land him a gig on *Book-TV*, Kyle's comments seemed to Greg no less profound than the words of Vonnegut himself.

"What should I read next?" Kyle asked.

Greg suppressed a full-on heart attack. "If you want more Vonnegut, I'd go with *Slaughterhouse-Five*. Or do you want a different author?" Greg asked.

"I'm up for someone different," answered Kyle.

"OK, I'm thinking something by Tom Robbins. Maybe *Half Asleep in Frog Pajamas*."

"What's it about?"

"What's it about?" asked Greg rhetorically. "Let's see. It's about a monkey and a stock broker and a three-hundred pound psychic and amphibians and outer space and—"

"—Whoa," said Kyle. "Sounds totally wacked. You think I'll like it?"

"I think you'll love it."

Even the most engaging teachers struggle with classroom management, because even the most motivated class and the most dynamic lesson can be subverted by a single outlier. Throughout the year, Greg tried to decipher the vague bromides offered by Dr. Rumsford while simultaneously plumbing his own academic memory. His most outstanding recollection was of his American History teacher who, upon catching a student asleep in class, would erase the entire chalkboard and then send the loaded eraser airborne. Students would watch, transfixed, as it sailed end-over-end and then, invariably, land on the head of the offending student. Unfortunately, in this day and age, the eraser technique was no longer utilitarian, for two main reasons. First, schools now utilized white boards, so a direct hit no longer produced the white chalk mushroom cloud of victory. Second, in this community, litigation was a near certainty. When he asked colleagues what to do in certain situations, most of them simply said, "Write him up." But the recurrence of the same names and the same issues—the "frequent fliers," as they were called—proved that Conduct Referrals were an ineffective deterrent. They also added more paper to an already overwhelming stack on his desk. So Greg returned a dozen blank forms to the office and kept a single one for show. This he kept on permanent exhibit, tacked to the bulletin board behind his desk.

By springtime, Greg had discovered that he cut a commanding and often intimidating presence, even at one hundred forty-eight pounds, and he used that knowledge to his advantage. This was not always for the best, as Rumsford often reminded him to "be more nurturing," but he did find that he was usually able to keep his classes focused and on-task. Greg heard enough comments from students to realize this was true, most of which began, "We get so much more done than we do in Mrs. ___'s class."

Greg was willing to use any tool at his disposal, and he became more resourceful with each passing week. When one of his students responded to F. Scott Fitzgerald by calling him "a fuckin' fag," Greg asked, or more accurately demanded, that the student stay after class.

"Brent, you have a choice," he explained after everyone else had left. "I can write you a Conduct Referral, or we can call your parents. You realize, of course, that if I write a Referral, Mr. McCullough will be calling your parents anyway." Then he added, "But I'm sure you know that already." The student's barely perceptible wince told Greg he had guessed correctly.

"Fine," the boy said, maintaining his bravado amidst his self-betrayal. "Call my mom." It seemed almost a dare, and Greg had no intention of losing a game of chicken with a fifteen-year-old with a cesspool where his vocabulary ought to be.

"As you wish." Greg dialed the number while the boy shifted uneasily. Greg guessed he had never experienced this method of discipline before.

"Hello, this is Greg Samson, Brent's English teacher at Shadowcliff.... We had an incident in class today and, well, I'd like Brent to explain it to you himself." Thrusting the phone at the boy, Greg said, "Tell her what you said."

Brent took the phone, his bravado melting. "Hi Mom.... I cursed in class today. I—"

"—No," Greg interrupted. "Tell her *exactly* what you said."

The boy covered the phone and looked at Greg, almost pleading. To clinch the deal, Greg pulled the Conduct Referral down from the bulletin board. "Use the exact words," he said, firmly.

"This writer we were studying, I called him a bad name." He looked at Greg as if to say, "Is that good enough?"

"Word for word," said Greg.

"I said that F. Scott Fitzgerald was a fuckin' fag," Brent finally told his mother, barely above a whisper. And with that, Greg motioned for the phone.

"This is Mr. Samson again. For what it's worth, I don't like the first word and I definitely don't like the second word. But I'm willing to let you and Brent discuss whether you think this was appropriate language for the classroom.... No Conduct Referral.... Yes, ma'am. Thank you for your time. I'm sorry to bother you." He hung up the phone and turned to face Brent.

"She says she'll speak with you at home." The boy sat, motionless, his mouth agape and his final protest frozen deep within his throat. "You're free to go now," said Greg, and he returned the Conduct Referral to its place of display on his bulletin board. At the end of the year, it was still there.

Armed with this and other simple techniques, Greg became the champion of the downtrodden and dispirited. Over the course of the year, the chubby kid who had spent years being rebuked by other students now willingly shared his views on poetry. The mousy girl with the out-of-date eyeglasses became unafraid to demonstrate that she was, as everyone had long suspected, the smartest girl in class. And even the black-clad, head-banging fringe kids were occasionally drawn in, and it turned out they often had a quirky, creative bent that sometimes concerned Greg in its nihilism but other times captivated him as a revelation of lost innocence.

Meanwhile, the cute, the trendy, and the popular—the "in crowd" who had been allowed to skate since junior high school on the basis of their charm or their affiliations—now were forced to earn their keep like everyone else. And while it turned out that many were insightful and articulate, others could offer nothing more substantial than "I agree with Jimmy," and they knew the jig was up, their cover blown, and their free ride terminated.

Not that this guaranteed Greg a strong teaching evaluation. Like everything else, these were handled almost exclusively by Rumsford. Despite her position as assistant principal, Zoey Crandall was not involved in the process whatsoever, apparently having been dispatched to critique the merits of each of the three new Chinese restaurants that had opened nearby. Maurice McCullough, the other assistant principal, handled a few of the evaluations for veteran teachers, especially those within Rumsford's inner circle. Rumsford was indifferent whether anyone would accuse her of cronyism. She just knew what those teachers did in class and knew they were too old to change, and thus felt it unnecessary to evaluate them herself.

But the rookies, that was another story entirely.

Greg discussed the process with Bob Cockrell, Jimmy Clayton, and Kerri Tanner one spring night at Wingding's.

"If she gives us a bad evaluation, we can dispute it, right?" asked Clayton.

"I don't think so," Cockrell replied. "I think we're stuck with it."

"She'll probably give some kid a candy bar to be purposely disruptive in my class," Clayton theorized, "then rake me over the coals for poor classroom management."

"Then we'd all better be at our best," Keri suggested.

So even though Greg knew his classes were meaningful and his students generally engaged and well-behaved, he still wanted to include some additional flair to increase his likelihood of a strong evaluation. On the day scheduled, on which his students would analyze twentieth-century American poetry, Greg set the mood with dim lighting and soft jazz, then utilized both individual response and a rotating pair strategy he invented on a run last weekend. It went so well that, as she left, Rumsford said, "That was a pretty good class, Samson." She even noted in her evaluation that Greg was "dedicated" and "spends a lot of time at the school," something he did not think she had ever noticed.

With the exception of the night custodians, in fact, Greg and Dr. Rumsford were almost always the last two people in the building. It was not quite as bad during track season in the spring, since weather allowed them to practice earlier, but with yearbook's final deadline bearing down on him, Greg often stayed well into the night. One especially late evening, which he spent preparing a group activity for English and then proofreading yearbook captions, Greg finally shut off the lights and was headed home when he witnessed Rumsford on her hands and knees, scrubbing the carpet in Shadowcliff's main mall. A bottle of bluish-green liquid was at her left elbow, a mayonnaise jar full of thick purple sludge to her right. It appeared to be some sort of cleaning solution challenge, and always the fan of honest competition, he watched intently. Indeed, at this moment he was obliged to admire her thoroughness and acknowledge her as a kindred spirit, just as inadequate at delegating as he was. He watched her for a moment as she scrubbed vigorously, one solution and then the other, until the purple sludge seemed to emerge victorious. With that, he decided it was best to leave through a different door, quickly and silently, for fear he would be spotted, given a rag and a mayonnaise jar full of purple goop, and assigned to scrub the carpeting alongside her while they discussed educational theory like long-lost pals.

11

THE ACID TEST

Spring rains in Arizona are rare, but when they happen they swoop in with suddenness and violence. Just such a rainstorm struck one early morning in April, its ferocity alarming to students and teachers and death to their umbrellas. Greg hurried into the sanctuary of the building, where blue plastic garbage cans were scattered about the hallway, ten or fifteen of them dispersed like a small blue forest, each rapidly filling with a golden liquid which looked like beer but smelled of sulphur and waste. Certainly ceiling leakage was not part of Rumsford's grand design. Certainly the Environmental Protection Agency would have reason to be concerned about the toxicity of these drips.

The rain stopped by mid-morning, fortuitously since the barrels were nearly full. Maintenance Supervisor Teddy "T.R." Raszko stroked his chin thoughtfully, struggling to calculate the weight of fifty-five gallons of water and, worse, how to relocate the drums without spillage. After consultation with Dr. Rumsford, he disappeared.

Shadowcliff's mechanical room was housed in a large brick building abutting the stadium. Greg occasionally needed to borrow a golf cart and bags of chalk to mark the home cross country course, so he had an almost exclusive ticket to the mechanical room. He knew it contained a poker table, a side-by-side refrigerator, and the largest television on campus. Of course, he knew that last one anyway.

But Teddy "T.R." Raszko, the overlord of the mechanical room, remained an enigma. Lurking unseen in the shadows, he emerged only to magically fix problems, then disappeared, often to the lake. Rumors followed T.R. over the years as he moved up the ladder from grounds crew at Palomino Elementary School to Maintenance Assistant at Reata Middle School and now to Shadowcliff. It seems items were frequently missing from his inventory: fertilizer, table saws, air conditioning units, rolls of carpeting, sheets of glass, pallets of bricks. But, given time, he always managed to cobble something together so the schools kept running. Equally mysterious was his cohort Rob, whose entire job consisted of mowing the athletic fields. Every week, five acres of grass were mowed, so Frank Nixon's and Jeff Dunleavy's fields looked great, so Shadowcliff looked great, so Rumsford loved him even though she did not even know his last name.

Greg had considered an investigative piece for the yearbook, but he knew that asking his editors to engage in some actual reportage would be a pointless and frustrating request.

An hour later—enough time to watch *Family Feud* and still resolve the problem before lunch—T.R. reappeared to implement his solution. As students walked toward the cafeteria, each of the blue plastic drums was now surrounded by four orange highway cones, an unequivocal statement that T.R. had absolutely no idea what to do. But at least students were aware of the grave danger, and could avoid any great peril on their trek to lunch.

After lunch, students wore the cones on their heads or utilized them as megaphones, calling words of encouragement like "Hey dickweed, have fun in math!" to their friends. Soon, the cones were scattered everywhere, their already questionable utility now rendered moot.

As the last of the stragglers made their way to class, the air was pierced by Jesse's sharp whistle from the center of campus. Fifty yards away, Steven Torgemeyer looked up but did not stop rocking one of the blue garbage cans, sloshing water onto the carpet until he finally managed to capsize the whole thing and send four hundred and forty pounds of putrid water cascading across the floor.

Jack responded to the whistle and was already giving chase, as much chase as a sixty-year-old man with a limp can give. Steven Torgemeyer, who had age, speed, mobility, and motivation all to his advantage, simply walked down a side hallway, so Jack stopped, giving up the ghost as he breathlessly clutched at his heart. But in the spirit of teamwork, Jesse had procured his new bicycle from the storage room, a fresh steed for the pursuit, a gift from the Parent-Teacher Association at Rumsford's behest since there was no way Jesse could cover the campus without it. Unfortunately, the first pedal stroke by the three-hundred-pound man was also his last. Snap! went the pedal, the victim of too much force, too much weight, and too much cheap alloy. As Jesse reached down to pick up the broken piece, the chase was over before it ever really began.

In every culture, one guy holds a scepter to rule the tribe while another holds a shovel so he can clean up after the livestock. Some people are simply more accomplished than others—whether the task is running long distances or playing the guitar or painting a landscape or remembering the names of every man who died at the Alamo. Greg was good at running and he knew Bowie, Travis and Crockett, but his paintings looked like a mix between bad tie-dye and livestock shovelings and, to his great regret, he could not play an instrument. So Greg could qualify for elite status at most races but would never make the Louvre or the Country Music Hall of Fame. Everyone has his own talents, and his own deficiencies.

In some cases, these are subjective in nature. People thought Van Gogh was a hack until well after his death, and now his paintings fetch tens of millions. Others are completely objective; Greg ran faster for 10,000 meters than his Italian friend Marcello Perroni, and no amount of beer or argument could alter the numbers. Then there were academic grades. An F signified that a student was less successful than one who earned a D, and both were significantly less successful than one who earned straight A's. National Honor Society was established to acknowledge those students, whose niche of success was measured by their grade point averages.

Until Dr. Connie Rumsford got ahold of it.

One day a student asked Greg if he would sign her National Honor Society application.

"But you're getting a D in this class," Greg said, genuinely confused. He was a member of NHS at Bonanza High School and he never earned below a B, and that only rarely.

"So?"

"So that's not really an NHS-level grade. I'm sorry."

The girl turned away, but not before Greg noticed her eyes welling with tears.

The next morning, as expected, Greg and every other Shadowcliff teacher received Rumsford's e-mail on the subject:

> From: Connie Rumsford, EdD
> To: Shadowcliff staff
> Subject: National Honor Society
> Sent: March 26, 7:19:32
>
> It has been brought to my attention that many of you are not signing NHS applications for our students. NHS will be open to all students who wish to join. Being a member of an academic honor society will help their self-esteem and make them want to earn better grades, which is our goal. If a student presents you with an NHS application, sign it! –CR

"I'm curious," Greg said to Jimmy Clayton at lunch. "If you don't need to earn good grades in order to join National Honor Society, why would you be motivated to earn good grades once you're in?"

"Fuck if I know," Clayton said simply. "When I was in National Honor Society, it meant something."

"Well, it's still national, and it's still a society," observed Cockrell. "Two out of three ain't bad."

"Yeah," said Greg. It's sixty-seven percent, a D, which at Shadowcliff High School is apparently good enough for membership in National Honor Society."

Greg skooched his chair back. "I'm still hungry."

"More lasagna?" asked Clayton. "Isn't that your third plate?"

"Small portions," he explained. "I definitely cannot afford to do this every day."

He returned to the table moments later with another rectangle of lasagna and a glass of water. "I wish they had tea," he said. "Or juice."

"Probably too expensive," Cockrell said. "Rumor has it they lose hundreds of thousands of dollars on school lunches."

Greg pointed at his plate, which now contained only half as much food as a moment before. "When they sell microscopic pieces of lasagna for two-fifty? I seriously doubt it."

But the question haunted him, so the next day Greg submitted a Freedom of Information request for Sweetwater Unified School District No. 43's financial records and cafeteria serving guidelines. A thick manila envelope welcomed him home a week later, and Greg spent dinner learning more about District food service than any man ought to know. The next day, he shared his results.

"According to District financial records, Shadowcliff averages four thousand dollars a week in profits. The District as a whole makes about twenty-five thousand a week. We're exploiting students' hunger as a profit center."

"That doesn't seem fair," Cockrell observed. Greg bit into a peanut butter and jelly sandwich, one of three he brought as a personal protest against the faculty lunchroom. He had vowed not to buy lunch for the rest of the year.

"I agree," said Greg, muffled by the peanut butter in his mouth. After he swallowed, he added, "Not only that, we still seem to run out of food most days. Which means, according to the law of supply and demand—"

"—They can raise prices!" Clayton exclaimed.

"Exactly. Then there's the lack of vegetables. District guidelines require two vegetable selections per day. Unless this is a vegetable," he added, holding up a ketchup packet.

"And of course, the issue that started this whole inquiry, the lasagna question. According to District guidelines, there are supposed to be nine servings of lasagna in a pan. They cut it so there's twelve."

When Greg got fired up about something, he was notorious for seeing it through to its natural conclusion. Even when that conclusion might not be in his best interest. The lasagna question was one of those instances. That night, he wrote a letter to the

District Director of Food Service, describing the issues with food shortage, lack of beverage and vegetable options, and serving size.

So it came to pass that the next time they served lasagna, there were nine servings in a pan. However, Greg noticed they also had new pans, eight inches square instead of the previous ten. Keri Tanner's quick calculations revealed that, by conforming to requirements, the District had actually managed to reduce the serving size by fifteen percent.

"Genius!" said Greg, who at least was smart enough to know when he was beaten. "Our District Director of Food Service is an unadulterated genius."

"Must have been a member of National Honor Society," Keri asserted.

Yet the faculty lunchroom was more than a place for failed attempts at culinary militancy. It was also the nerve center of faculty gossip, and occasionally actual news.

"Did you hear what happened to Shelley?" The faculty lunchroom was abuzz. Some said she was fine, while others proclaimed her near death. Some categorized her as an innocent victim, others as heroic Superteacher who risked her own well-being to protect the welfare of her precious students. Indeed, the story-lines were endless. But eventually, Greg pieced together the following facts: Science teacher Shelley Banyan had been sitting at her desk while her students were doing a lab on acids and bases. She was called to the back of the classroom in order to answer a student's question. When she returned to her desk, she took a sip of coffee and immediately felt some sort of violent acid reflux reaction. She guessed, correctly, that a student had put concentrated lemon juice in her cup, so she quickly ran (Greg suspected it was more of a fast wobble) to the teacher's lounge, pulled a box of baking soda from the refrigerator, and shoveled the whole thing into her mouth one spoonful after another. Apparently, the base of the soda crudely counteracted the acid in the lemon juice, averting disaster. But now she was on the way to the hospital for observation, with a really bad stomach ache and a massive case of flatulence.

Greg knew the implications of this unfortunate event. As expected, an announcement came through just before the end of the day. "Attention teachers, please report to room 4122 for a mandatory meeting after school." And so, once more, teachers dutifully filed into the room, where they were given that exact recitation of the facts, an assessment of Ms. Banyan's condition, and an assurance that the perpetrators would be dealt with swiftly and firmly.

At the next faculty meeting, Dr. Rumsford gave an update on the whole situation. "Shelley Banyan is fine. She was discharged from the hospital. She had diarrhea for three days. She has asked for and received administrative leave. My offer of a reward was successful. Steven Torgemeyer came to me personally and identified the young man who put the substance in her mug. I'm not at liberty to tell you his name, but he's been suspended, the District has ordered him to attend mandatory counseling, and he may be facing criminal charges."

Teachers began to speak amongst themselves and the buzz grew.

"At the request of the District," Rumsford silenced them with her tone, "we will have a guest speaker at today's meeting. This is Detective Jerry Travers from the Sweetwater Police Department." While Rumsford lauded the detective for his extraordinary work, his years of service, and his fine rapport with the community, Officer Mike distributed a multi-page handout befitting Dr. Rumsford's standards for volume and imaginative waste of colored paper. The title: "Drug Abuse and You." Greg believed this sounded too much like a public relations brochure, which, he was guessing, was not the point of the presentation.

"Good afternoon," the detective began. "Recent events involving one of your teachers have, uh, prompted the school district to ask me to, uh, speak about drug abuse issues. Specifically, how can you, the teachers, spot drug usage, uh, among your students?"

"What recent events?" Clayton whispered to Greg, who just shrugged in reply. He looked around the room and saw puzzled looks everywhere.

But the detective continued anyway, leading the teachers on a long, meandering, and absolutely uh-ful expedition through marijuana, cocaine, pain-killers, muscle relaxers, and heroin. He offered considerable detail, including a discussion of the history of each substance and the chemical structure and bonding patterns of each molecule. Greg's butt was becoming, uh, numb.

"Our last category of drugs that I want to discuss is the hallucinogens. These are also known as, uh, psychedelics. I didn't realize it, but apparently Lysergic acid diethyl—, uh, diethylamide, or LSD, is making a comeback here in eastern Sweetwater," he said. "That's not unusual, since this is a more up-scale or, uh, wealthy community. So this is the drug I would like to spend the most time on."

Ike Gravenstein raised his hand. "We've been sitting here for half an hour. I don't deny that drugs are nasty things. But can you tell me what this has to do with the Shelley Banyan situation?"

"What does it have...," the detective replied. "Why, everything!" He continued for several minutes, discussing the cost, form, synthesis, methods of use, tell-tale signs, and dangers of taking LSD. He continued, "As you probably know, LSD is known on the street as—"

"—Acid!" said Greg, louder than he anticipated.

"That's, uh, that's right," said the detective. But Greg was not trying to play fill-in-the-blank. It was, in fact, a moment of clarity. He leaned over so Clayton could hear him, and whispered, "Acid. The boneheads at the District office think he put LSD in Shelley's mug. The kid's gonna get two to four years in the state penitentiary for unlawful possession of a citrus juice."

Greg rushed into the copy room one morning, needing only thirty copies of a vital handout to complete his end-of-year choice novel assignment. Class was scheduled to begin in ten minutes. When he found all three copy machines broken, he hurried over to the office, hoping for clemency to use the administrative machine. Ramona Thurlow was on the machine at the time. Surely she'll understand, Greg thought. "This machine is only for important administrative things," Ramona told him as she finished her job.

"But I need this for my next class," Greg replied, checking his watch, "and all three copiers are down."

"Sorry. Important administrative things only," she barked, and punched a button to clear her access code. In her haste, she left her original document on the glass. Greg waited until she rounded the corner, then withdrew her original. "US Airways flight itinerary," it was entitled. She was flying to Florida on Wednesday.

Copiers were not fixed for several days, forcing teachers to improvise. This was not a practical problem for Greg, who could easily tweak an assignment or shuffle things around, but it bothered him because the textbook was really low-level. If Rumsford wanted to create a system that guaranteed no child would be excluded from the learning process, a system that manifested itself in a complete void of educational rigor, then she certainly chose the ideal text to accomplish those goals. One of Greg's favorite Questions for Understanding from the junior-level Language Arts text, which followed an excerpt from *Moby Dick*, was as follows: "What kind of animal was Moby Dick, and what was his unique characteristic?" The answer, a white whale, was found word-for-word seven times in the three-page excerpt. There were no higher-level questions posed, nothing that asked students to interpret or evaluate. Nothing about how the men felt toward Captain Ahab or Ishmael's growing concerns regarding the morality of Ahab's quest or male bonding experiences that bring men like Ishmael and Queequeg together. Not only were the questions extremely superficial, but the reading selections were often questionable and the thematic organization confusing. On top of all that, the supply of texts was vastly insufficient. This forced students to share books and guaranteed that the more skillful readers would need to pause, often for several minutes, while they waited for their reading partner to catch up and turn the page. Strong readers often spent more time waiting than reading.

Thus, stronger students faced one more handicap, one more disincentive to reach their potential, while the weaker ones often skipped half the text because they did not want to keep their partner on hold. The end result of the textbook shortage was that instead of being lifted up by heterogeneous grouping, the weaker students actually fell further behind.

The copiers' malaise seemed to inspire the same attitude in many of Shadowcliff's teachers. It was not unusual to see half a dozen combing the shelves at Blockbuster in search of a video they could show in class. Greg could not fathom how *Monsters, Inc.* related to Earth Science or what *The Chronicles of Narnia* had to do with Geometry, but that was not his issue. Unlike many of his colleagues, Greg could not afford to rest. His first yearbook was delivered two weeks before final exams, requiring his physical labor in moving more than sixty boxes to different locations around the school and absolving the faculty of any pressure to teach the last few days of school.

Greg's Yearbook class was busy enjoying their creation. Although they were finding typographical errors, missing captions, and other mistakes, they were generally proud of the finished product. "And you should be," Greg told them. "For a first-year book, this is very good. Definitely something we can build on for next—"

"—Attention, students." It was Dr. Rumsford over the loudspeaker. "I have two important announcements for you today," she continued. "First of all, it is my pleasure to announce that we have selected our very first Student of the Year. He is a fine young person who demonstrated considerable moral courage, self-discipline, and school spirit. He will be awarded a five-hundred dollar gift certificate from Sweetwater Mall. That young man's name is Steven Torgemeyer."

The groans could be heard even from the classroom next door.

"My second announcement is this. Anyone who wants their money back because they are unhappy with the yearbook should see Mr. Samson in room 3290. That is all."

The day after final exams, the teachers gathered for teacher checkout. The day began with a brief meeting, of course. Greg ended up sitting at the same table as Donny Elmendorf. Greg had not seen much of Elmendorf that year other than at department meetings, and they had not spoken since the SCRABBLE activity in October.

Greg waited for Elmendorf to finish his conversation with another teacher. "Hey Donny, you had something do with me getting hired last summer, right?"

"Only a little," he replied. "Why?"

"I don't know whether to thank you or shoot you." Elmendorf laughed, and they spent the next few minutes chatting about their respective school years, small talk between two guys who both just wanted to finish cleaning their classrooms so they could get on the road to Colorado or San Diego or, hell, even Goodyear. Finally, though, Greg asked the sixty-four-thousand-dollar question. "You comin' back next year?"

Elmendorf chuckled. "I'd rather cut off my penis with a plastic butter knife."

12

THE GIRLFRIEND

The moment they finished checkout, Bob Cockrell, Jimmy Clayton, and Keri Tanner piled into Clayton's Honda Accord, opened the sunroof, popped in a U2 CD, and headed northwest to Las Vegas. It was a trip with two purposes. First, there was the belated fête in honor of Keri's divorce, and second, a well-deserved celebration of the fact that each had made it through the school year without significant physical ailments, mental breakdowns, or existential crises. Greg's bag was in Clayton's trunk and he would fly in later that evening, after the all-star track meet in which Shadowcliff's freshman sensation Darlene Griffin was invited to compete.

A few minutes after eight o'clock on a warm Arizona night, Darlene crushed the Colorado girl she dubbed "the slut in the purple socks" as well as the top milers from New Mexico, Utah, and Nevada, missing the state record by less than one second. She had improved her mile time by thirty-eight seconds in just one year of training with Greg. "I did it!" she exclaimed, rushing to the rail to embrace her parents and Maurice McCullough, the club coach for whom she had enjoyed only moderate success but who treated her like the Queen of France. Greg waited patiently a few yards away. When she finally turned toward him, Greg smiled and mouthed the words "great race." With barely an acknowledgement, she immediately returned her attention to Maurice, and Greg recognized that his work was done.

Greg pulled into Sky Harbor Airport fifteen minutes later. He recalled his last trip there, nearly nine months ago, when he helped John Woodacre flee the state like a felon. Even though he never heard from Woody again, Greg had still taken some of his suggestions to heart. He had sent out, by his count, one hundred sixty-three résumés since Labor Day, and received exactly seven responses. Six said, in essence, "thanks but no thanks." The seventh offered him the opportunity to "triple your income while building a firm client base and a consistent cash flow." Greg distrusted vagaries in general and pyramid schemes in particular, so he dismissed that one out of hand. And this was not the time to worry about it, either. Two hours later, after the flight to McCarran and a twenty-minute run to the Tropicana, Greg was ready to play, to celebrate, and to momentarily forget.

He quickly showered, dressed, and met up with the others at the blackjack tables. Clayton, fueled by some unfathomable blue-and-red double rum drink in a twisty plastic souvenir glass, spent the next twenty minutes offering his assessment of the trip so far. "Un-fucking-believable," he explained, and Greg nodded knowingly. Clayton was down nearly two hundred dollars.

Later, Cockrell offered, "I hear there's a really good midnight buffet at Bally's." So even though it was well past midnight, they began the northward trek on Las Vegas Boulevard. Clayton called their attention to something remarkable, pointing emphatically at a stoplight. His speech had deteriorated to a strange language consisting mostly of consonant sounds, profanity, and spittle. "Look at the K—" he implored.

"The what?" asked Cockrell. He had probably drank just as much, but his extra fifty pounds bought him some leeway.

"The K-f-thh. It's—"

"—Unbelievable?" asked Keri. Her last name was now Zabriskie.

"Un-*fucking*-believable," corrected Clayton as he grabbed onto Cockrell for support.

As they crossed Tropicana Avenue, a hooker held an eye shadow brush as she squinted into a compact mirror. The mirror seemed much too small, and even the bright neon of the Strip failed to provide enough illumination.

"Can I help you with that?" asked Keri, startling the hooker.

After a moment of uncertainty, the hooker offered her makeup to Keri, who skillfully applied a subtle touch-up of reds, purples, and blacks.

"Thank you, honey," said the hooker. "Any o' y'all want some company?" She cocked her hip to one side, seductive-like, and with the gold chain of her miniature sequined purse wrapped around her index finger, swung the bag in circles.

Clayton started to stumble forward, but Keri put her hand on his chest. "No thanks," she said.

As they resumed walking, Cockrell looked over his shoulder. "Kind of reminds me of my first sexual experience," he offered.

"Oh, do tell," Keri said.

So Cockrell began, "I was in this bar, the Wagon Spoke, in Coeur d'Alene, Idaho. I was seventeen. There was this lumberjack who kept buying me shots of Jack Daniels. I guess he thought it would be funny to get the underage kid drunk. I think I had nine. Then, I don't know how it happened, I end up dancing with the house transvestite."

"They have house transvestites in Idaho?" asked Keri, incredulous.

"Very progressive state," offered Greg. "I think it's some kind of social service program."

"Anyway, I was dancing with her ... him ... and suddenly he ... she ... tells me to get a piece of rope. Six-foot long, no more and no less."

"I think I'm gonna be sick," Clayton said, dashing to the bushes in front of the Imperial Palace.

"She tied you up?" asked Greg.

"Or did you tie her up?" posed Keri.

Clayton looked up from his puking, intrigued, then wiped his mouth and rejoined the others on their northbound trek. He seemed less unstable now.

"Neither one," answered Cockrell. "I kicked her ... him ... in the balls, then passed out near the juke-box. The lady bartender took me home and made me a man."

Hours later, sobriety achieved via a meal of luke-warm waffles and insipid bacon, they returned to their hotel with the task of figuring out how to apportion two queen-sized beds among four people when three were single men and the other an attractive recent divorcee who had a sexual history with at least one of them. The sky was already growing lighter. Jimmy Clayton and Greg finally volunteered to sleep on the floor. While they all brushed their teeth, Greg's summary of the evening made Keri laugh so hard that toothpaste flew out her nostrils and onto Clayton's chest. He looked at his chest, then at the others, who were now in hysterics. "Unbelievable," he declared, shaking his head.

For the rest of the weekend, Greg instigated when necessary but otherwise flew just under the radar, winning a few bucks, out-eating several behemoths at the buffets, and having a generally glorious time that ended far too quickly. On Memorial Day they headed back to Arizona, and Greg headed back to work.

The last place Greg wanted to spend the first week of his precious and well-deserved summer vacation was in a meeting room with a hundred other teachers. Yet here he was, rubbing the sleep from his eyes as he entered the gymnasium of the West Phoenix YMCA for day one of a five-day seminar on "Integrating the Curriculum" taught by L. Fred Mandeville. Greg questioned whether Mandeville possessed the imposing credentials of, say, Elden Ray Fong, but he did know Mandeville's article on integrated instruction was the most interesting of the two-hundred-plus Rumsford articles he had read over the course of the year. This was the penance he was required to pay Dr. Rumsford in exchange for a full-blown, year-long integrated class. For the next year, he and Clayton would be teaching "The American Story," giving them license to re-enact Gettysburg, tame the wild west, or construct their very own Hooverville as appropriate. They had convinced Rumsford that it would be an effective method of teaching, that it would appeal to a variety of learning styles, that it would implicate all levels of Bloom's Taxonomy, and that it would fulfill all the District's curricular objectives, and she agreed. They really believed it, too. But they also knew, regardless of whether it turned out to be a rousing success or a Hindenburg-like crash-and-burn, that it would be a helluva lot of fun. So while he was not sure this was the profession he wanted to be in, Greg was willing to make himself the most competent professional he could during his stay, however lengthy or brief it might turn out to be.

Besides, he rationalized, there might be a decent-looking and reasonably interesting single female teacher taking the seminar, too. His luck certainly could get no worse.

The room was filled with round tables, most of which were already surrounded by a gaggle of teachers: old and young, male and female, thin and fat, peppy and weary. Greg found an empty chair and began to chat with the others at his table. One was a third-grade teacher fascinated with tropical insects. Another was a middle-school art teacher whose students had won awards for their watercolors. Yet another was a high school math teacher whose great uncle had been among the pioneers in researching Cantor's Continuum Hypothesis. Greg expounded on his love for John Steinbeck, finding a sense of inclusion due only to their shared circumstance of having virtually nothing in common.

Mandeville stepped to the microphone and introduced himself. He was balding and somewhat pudgy, and wore a wide tie that looked like a TV test pattern. "Not the most inspiring character," Greg whispered. As it turned out, though, he was also a successful honors teacher at an upper-middle class school in Illinois, one that featured similar demographics to Shadowcliff's. He maintained ambitious expectations for his students, and for those taking his seminars as well. "This will be a working session, people," he explained, "and by Friday, you will be expected to have produced a usable curriculum unit on a topic of your choice." Greg was relieved, knowing that forty hours of lecture would have driven him to contemplate suicide, even if that meant jumping from the nearby first-floor window, coming back inside, and repeating the process until dead. But he noticed many of those in attendance murmuring their discontent amongst themselves, displeased at the prospect of actually having to produce work in exchange for their Certificate of Completion. It was apparent they would rather fulfill their professional development requirements with the least development possible, and instead spend the next five days reading the latest John Grisham drivel or filling out the *New York Times* crossword.

"While you're welcome to seek out those with similar interests," Mandeville continued, "sometimes you gain the most from the diversity of other teachers. So I would encourage you to consider working with the people at your table, regardless of what you teach. The process of finding common ground can be interesting indeed."

As Greg reached into his bag to get a notebook and pencil, wondering if any other human actually used the word "indeed" in spoken English, the woman behind him backed her chair into his. "Sorry," she said.

"No problem." He smiled at her.

"We heard you talking about Steinbeck. We're going to work on an American history and literature unit, if you want to join us."

Greg weighed Mandeville's words against the woman's invitation and realized this new group was exactly what he needed to prepare for The American Story. Besides, the woman herself was kind of flirty, and not half-bad to look at. She had dark hair, welcoming brown eyes, full lips that produced a quirky smile, and firm, tanned legs.

"Sure," he said finally, then excused himself from his table and wished the others a successful week. As it turned out, they eventually spent the entire day trying to find that common ground of which Mandeville had spoken, eventually arriving at a project entitled "Light-and-Shadow Perspectives on the Non-Euclidian Geometry of Insect Mud Nests: An Interdisciplinary Unit." In retrospect, Greg was very glad he had bailed out.

"Hi, everyone," he said as he slid into a chair at the new table. "My name is Greg Samson."

"Tracey Dobberman," replied one. "Rex Foster." "Adrienne Walsh." And finally, "Amanda Moretti." That was the pretty woman who had invited him to join.

As it turned out, there was a significant amount of brainpower at this table. Tracey seemed to know more about American politics than George Will, and radiated a strong sense of liberal purpose. Rex had spent two years teaching on the reservation before he moved to the small mining town he now called home. He spoke fluent Navajo and collected bottle caps. Adrienne was older, having already retired from a teaching job on the east coast before moving to Arizona to be closer to her grandchildren. Her knowledge was remarkably diverse, from history to microbiology. Greg still thought he could beat her at Trivial Pursuit, but only because he would get more of the Sports and Leisure questions. Amanda was the most social of the group, with an encyclopedic knowledge of Virginia Woolf. And she touched him softly on the arm in that strange way, innately pro-grammed into women, that confuses the absolute be-jeezus out of men in general and Greg in particular.

By the end of the week, Greg had his Certificate of Completion in one hand and Amanda's phone num-ber in the other. A three-hour phone conversation preceded their first date, during which they spent the evening discussing everything from Shakespeare to sports. Although their professional lives seemed to have little in common—she taught honors English at an inner-city high school while Greg taught everything under the sun in wealthy white-flight suburbia—they shared much in common personally. When school started again in August, they were officially a couple.

When they walked into room 4122 for their first orientation session preceding the new school year, every Shadowcliff teacher was given a thick yellow book. Greg's reaction was instantaneous; no good could possibly come of this. Dr. Rumsford soon explained that it was a phone log, in which teachers were to record each and every phone call they made throughout the year. "We're not doing this to keep you from using the phone," she explained. "On the contrary, it's a system to monitor that you're making the expected number of parent contacts. It can only help you."

One year of such practices and pronouncements, of Rumsford offering ways for teachers to help themselves that ended up being more work, more hassle, and more exposure, had trained Greg to be perpetually skeptical. Yet he was still a non-tenured teacher, so he had also trained himself to keep his mouth shut even though it was often difficult. Greg turned to look for Ike Gravenstein, who held the same skepticism but not the same reservations, but as Greg surveyed the room, Ike was nowhere to be found. As it turned out, Ike had joined Donny Elmendorf and a handful of others in bolting for greener pastures. Rumsford had effectively squelched the dissent.

With nobody willing to ask the obvious question, Greg wondered exactly what she meant by "the expected number of parent contacts." Greg knew Elden Ray Fong's theory. He also knew various theories on time, all of which concluded that time is a finite commodity. Especially his.

Greg then looked at the food line. He spotted a bucket of plastic butter knives and thought of Donny Elmendorf wistfully.

"Next item. We will have a new assistant principal this year," stated Rumsford. "Zoey Crandall has accepted a position at the District office." Amidst the murmurs, Jeanette Candelaria whispered to Greg, "In education, incompetence always gets promoted." Greg now sat next to Jeanette at meetings as often as possible, always picking up some nugget of truth about the world of education that was the by-product of her twenty-plus years of experience. He aspired to her wisdom, although not necessarily to her longevity. Now, processing her latest offering, he shook his head, then asked, "But who'll be in charge of ordering lunch for Dr. Rumsford?"

As they adjourned, Rumsford shouted above the noise, "Oh, yeah, we also added the Global Scholars

Program this year," as if it were no more important than a new pencil sharpener.

Greg found himself in front of his first period class, prepared and confident. His objectives were on the board and his syllabi were in a neat stack on a table in front of the room. After welcoming his students, he picked up his class roster and a pencil. "Roger Anderson?" he asked. "Susan Arnstadt?" He realized these same students had been on his roster last year, too.

Suddenly, inexplicably, students began to point, then to snicker, then to laugh robustly. Greg was confused. This was not the way master teacher Elden Ray Fong said it would work.

Finally, looking down, he realized the problem. He was standing before the class naked. Again. And this time he had even forgotten to bring his hat.

2006 - 2007

13

THE LITTLE BLACK DRESS

We are told that you never get a second chance to make a first impression. Greg remembered that bit of wisdom from a Head & Shoulders shampoo commercial, and later confirmed it from encounters with any number of women who had rejected him in cities ranging from Albuquerque to Zurich.

Over the summer, Shadowcliff had clearly taken a big step with regard to first impressions, hiring an attractive new receptionist as the office's first point-of-contact with the public. Rumsford was always keen on enlisting the aid of her constituency when certain of their support, so Greg could only imagine the number of fathers who had selflessly volunteered to screen applicants.

"Who's the new lady?" Greg asked Bob Cockrell as they walked through the office half an hour before the first class of year two of Shadowcliff High School.

"Kelli Westin," Cockrell replied. "I was on the interview committee."

"You did good," replied Greg, pulling the usual stack of *Sports Illustrated* teacher subscription cards, video catalogs, and Rumsford handouts from his slot.

Cockrell held up an article entitled, "Turning Digital Natives Into Digital Superfreaks," then another entitled "Behavior Interventions That Work" and a third entitled "Cutting Paperwork and Other Proven Stress-Reducers." Missing the irony, Cockrell said, "I guess it's time to break in my new filing cabinet."

"You save her articles?" asked Greg.

"Every one," he answered. "Even the ones I don't read ... which is most of them."

"I read them all," replied Greg. "But I only save a few."

"It helps that you read about eight thousand words a minute," said Cockrell. "I've seen you."

"Absolutely vital tool to survive law school," Greg answered. How else, he thought, can you get through five one-thousand-page textbooks every semester when they are filled with the opinions of judges who, *ipso facto*, write in a manner whereupon their sentences notwithstanding nouns and verbs shall hereinafter cease and desist *in re* clarity, thereunto appertaining, subordinate to a legion of footnotes, *infra*? Sometimes he frightened himself with the things he thought.

But instead, he submitted, "You never know when a paper airplane war is going to break out. And your room will be our last line of defense. I'm glad we're friends."

With that, they waved their goodbyes, first period beckoning.

Three hours later, now on his prep, Greg walked through the office and stopped at the front desk. As he waited until Kelli Westin finished a phone call, his eyes were drawn to her left hand, on which he noticed a diamond only slightly smaller than one of the moons of Jupiter. Not that he cared—he and Amanda were getting along great, so the look was simply bachelor instinct—but it did provide an important piece of the puzzle. Her kids probably attended Shadowcliff, and she probably drove to school in a BMW. In other words, about par for the neighborhood.

"Yes, ma'am," she said patiently. "The bus maps are online.... There's a tab at the top of the homepage.... That's the one.... My pleasure. Have a nice day."

As she hung up the phone, Greg stepped forward. "I just wanted to introduce myself. I'm—"

"—You're Greg Samson." The surprise must have shown on Greg's face, so she explained. "I've already heard about you."

"Uh oh. Good or bad?"

"Depends who you ask." Her smile hinted of mischievousness.

"And who did you ask?"

"My name's Kelli Westin," she said instead.

"Welcome," said Greg. He then glanced down the hallway, where he caught a glimpse of Rumsford's scowl. Even that much was sufficient. "I'd best get to the copy room."

Skyscrapers in New York City house financial concerns that convert dollars to yen to euros to baht to francs to rubles to pounds and back to dollars, somehow generating millions in profits without ever producing anything tangible. Down the street are advertising agencies purposed with convincing Americans that WhackO's are a better breakfast cereal than ZowieFlakes when both are, in fact, primarily wheat, corn syrup, and red dye No. 5. Fortunes are made and men become powerful in these offices, while the real work takes place fifty floors below.

On a smaller scale, schools work the same way. Not in terms of the vacuousness of the process—certainly it is more vital to convert curiosity into knowledge and to convince young people of their infinite potential—but in terms of the behind-the-scenes work that powers the process.

During Shadowcliff's first year, the school's myriad maintenance issues were overshadowed by its problems with schedules, unruly students, stressed out teachers, pointless assistant principals, and overbearing parents. From the outside, the physical aspect of the school seemed its best asset. So naturally, Teddy "T.R." Raszko was bumped up once again, this time to the Sweetwater Unified School District No. 43 District office. Rob went with him. Jeanette Candelaria's theory about incompetence being promoted was again proven.

T.R.'s replacement at Shadowcliff was a sour, stooped older man named Skip McGregor. McGregor was in the early stages of liver failure and was consistent in that he was mean to everyone. But at the same time, the mechanical situation at Shadowcliff improved significantly. Materials seemed more readily available, so projects that used to take a week were now done in one day. The roof stopped leaking. Carpet bubbles became a thing of the past. Problems were solved with ingenuity and attentiveness, not orange cones. And from his visits to the mechanical room to borrow the golf cart and chalk liner, Greg came to recognize that Shadowcliff High School provided Skip with both health insurance and a sense of purpose, no matter how lonely it might be.

Also behind the scenes, yet every bit as essential, was the copy room. Tens of thousands of sheets of paper passed through the three faculty Xerox machines each week, and with machines operating far above capacity, failure was inevitable. The failure of one copier was enough to disrupt the school profoundly; the failure of two was catastrophic. Often, teachers could be found with their arms buried deep inside a Xerox machine, searching for an elusive scrap of paper which was gumming up the works. After a while, teachers stopped saying "hello" to one another, their greetings replaced with things like "Copier two's out of toner" or "Jam in number three." Despite the fact that teachers were required to be trained in the use of the copy machines, and were retrained by District mandate after each major repair, it was not unusual for at least one of the copy machines to be on the fritz at any given time.

"I've been through so many trainings, I think I could work at Kinko's," said Bob Cockrell one day.

Greg added, "Well at least we have a fallback plan if the teaching gig doesn't work out."

In an effort to alleviate the copy room frustration, Shadowcliff instituted one more change. "Copy Moms," trained on the copiers, would be responsible for handling all the teachers' duplicating needs. On Tuesdays, Susie Cooter worked the copy room. She was pretty, kind, extremely efficient, and had a terrific body. Many of her friends called her "Hooter," but she was so nice that it was never said with animosity.

One day at lunch, the topic of conversation turned to the Copy Mom program.

"I think the Copy Moms are great," said Keri. She was now officially Keri Zabriskie, her maiden name.

"Yeah," agreed Clayton. "That Tuesday mom has a great rack."

Keri rolled her eyes.

"Suzi Cooter," said Greg, and everyone looked at him curiously. "The mom on Tuesday. Her name is Suzi Cooter."

After a bite of his pulled pork sandwich, he continued. "Do you think dads are welcome to work in the copy room, too?"

"I don't know," said Keri. "Why do you ask?"

"Suzi Cooter is divorced," replied Greg. "She's seldom in dress code. This week she was wearing short cutoffs and a tight tank top, with heels."

"Is that why you always do your copies on Tuesday?" asked Cockrell.

Greg smiled and continued. "I actually do my copies on Tuesday because they always get done correctly. Kelli Westin and Suzi Cooter have made for a nice campus beautification project, but they're also both damn good at what they do. Skip McGregor, too, although he's not quite as pretty."

One Tuesday morning, on his way to the copy room, Greg passed through the front office. Kelli looked up from her work and said, "Hey Greg, I just found out you have a law degree. Are you ever going to use it?" And while he recognized early in the third year of his four-year MBA/JD program that he was unlikely to practice, it was a question he still sporadically returned to when times were especially challenging or money especially tight. Despite his denials, he occasionally wondered if he should take the bar exam and join guys like Darnell Lyon in the world of expensive suits, expensed lunches, and 2200 billable hours a year.

The purpose of the Global Scholars Program was "To cultivate an elite community of lifelong, impassioned, and principled learners with an international perspective on knowledge." This came from the organization's own website. Greg assumed they actually meant "passionate," and that something had been lost in the translation from the French spoken at Global Scholars headquarters in Paris. But then again, knowing the reputation of the French, it was possible they actually expected high school students to maintain an intimate relationship with their homework.

The Global Scholars Program was certainly alluring, as sexy as an educational program can be. It was like Shadowcliff High School's little black cocktail dress—a seductive invention designed to emphasize a beautiful woman's best assets while simultaneously inciting jealousy in her slightly less gifted friends. While Rumsford did not boast the legs for the real thing, she certainly held the resources and the backing for the metaphorical version.

And thus, Shadowcliff became the fourth high school in Arizona to implement the Global Scholars Program, beginning in the school's second fall.

Never mind that Shadowcliff still had not mastered the intricacies of registration, lunch, or carpet cleaning. Rumsford had decided the previous January that Shadowcliff would become a Global Scholars school, so a Global Scholars school it became.

At that point in time, still on their honeymoon, the District probably would have allowed Rumsford to make Shadowcliff into whatever she could conceive—be it a music conservatory, a training camp for left-handed astronauts, or the world's first oceanographic institute in the middle of the desert. Indeed, Superintendent Lew Vincennes was quoted numerous times endorsing the Global Scholars Program, describing how it would bring "world-class curriculum to an already cutting-edge school." He had pushed the School Board to approve its adoption and boasted that it would be the crowning achievement of his career.

But that was back in January. It was now August, and the shine was coming off Rumsford's apple.

While many teachers discussed the paradox, none was actually courageous enough to ask how an academically exclusive program was in keeping with Rumsford's theories about homogeneity. What about the potential self-esteem hazards of identifying some students as "elite" and others as lesser mortals? Perhaps Ike Gravenstein would have questioned such a profound and fundamental paradigm shift, but Ike had chosen to relocate to the Sweetwater Classical Academy, a brand-new red brick private school located less than ten minutes north of Shadowcliff on a small plot of desert land surrounded by coyotes and creosote.

Free public education has been a staple of American democracy since the 1820s, but never without its critics. Whether those who did not want to pay the taxes or those who believed teachers were simply failures at any other decent profession, the detractors have always been legion. The recent manifestation of this criticism was the rise of small private schools, often christened "academies," which sacrificed economies of scale in favor of exorbitantly high tuition. But the owners of these private schools knew from their expensive consultants what wealthy parents desired. Marketing studies and focus groups revealed that the word "academy" was key, invoking wistful thoughts of ancient Greece and olive groves and the glorification of Athena. Students at these academies wore uniforms (although not Greek togas, which Greg thought would be more appropriate), sat in classes of no more than twenty-four students, and were offered an education rich with "rigor," the educational buzzword of the hour even as it remained undefined. Did it mean more homework, or less? Did it mean greater depth of inquiry, or more breadth? Did it mean more group project-based learning, or more individualized instruction?

So academies sprung forth like Athena from Zeus's head, dotting the landscape of Phoenix's most affluent suburbs. The mix of competition and their inability to define rigor led to the death of many of these schools, and new buildings already sat abandoned, rigor having been replaced by *rigor mortis.*

However, a few of these private schools had become successful, a fact which alarmed school boards who saw a handful of their best-and-brightest students being siphoned off by the interloping academies. In response, school districts began to diversify, offering programs or angles designed to set themselves apart.

Toward this end, Sweetwater Unified School District No. 43 hired an administrator whose only job was marketing. One week, the Director of Marketing enthusiastically trumpeted the achievement of Elise Fenwick, who was victorious in Sweetwater's spelling bee and would represent the District in state competition. The next, it was Samuel Downs, a seventh-grade teacher who successfully completed a summer internship. Unfortunately, one notice identified the internship with NASA while another said it was with NSA. That extra A proved a critical distinction, as some colleagues envied Downs for his experience working with rocket scientists while others mistrusted him, wondering if his complicity with the government included spying on teachers in search of copyright violations or the misappropriation of school supplies. As it turned out, Downs actually interned with the NSAA—the National Ski Area Association—and was befuddled by his colleagues' strange reactions to a summer spent preparing for his retirement job as a snowboarding instructor in Vail.

Over time, the Director of Marketing ended up devoting most of her time to securing half-price baseball tickets or discounts on wedding cakes. Thus, in its efforts to keep up with competition in the educational marketplace, Sweetwater Unified School District No. 43 essentially became Groupon.

Greg and Bob Cockrell were discussing this fact at lunch one day when the topic turned to the Global Scholars Program.

"It seems like we're trying to become the educational equivalent of Wal-Mart," said Cockrell. Greg, having just put a forkful of salad into his mouth, simply waved his fork as invitation to continue. "I just hope that by trying to be everything, we don't end up as nothing."

To be fair, the Global Scholars Program was a lot more than nothing. One could tell it was admirable just from looking at its website: pictures of exotic locales and happy adolescents, testimonials by former Global Scholars students who were now neurosurgeons or CEOs, lists of great books that everyone talked about but few people actually read, and quotations about the value of a liberal arts education from Socrates, Jean-Paul Sartre, and George W. Bush. All spoke volumes about the prestige of the program. So, by God, Shadowcliff just had to have it.

But it did not take long for Greg to recognize that the real purpose of the Global Scholars Program, at least at Shadowcliff, was appeasement. It would appease those students like Cade Ralston who demanded more challenging classes. Ironically, though, Cade did not enroll in the Global Scholars Program, choosing instead to spend his time on varsity basketball, a job, community service at a local food bank, and an internship in which he was researching possible cures for childhood leukemia. Privately, Rumsford condemned him for being "average."

More important, Global Scholars was meant to appease the parents. Their success—measured by the price tags on their cars, the square footage of their homes, and the type of precious metal associated with their health club memberships—often led them to impose unrealistic expectations upon their children and unreasonable demands on teachers who knew that no amount of wealth could buy true intellect.

This is not to say that Shadowcliff was devoid of highly motivated, intellectually gifted students. It had its share, and then some. Many of these children had grown up with every advantage, and now manifested those benefits as true scholars. But not all. Some parents refused to accept that their aspirations were not always shared by, or even appropriate for, their kids. Nor would they accept that frequent parental nudging would not guarantee their children admission into Stanford (the ultimate symbol of successful parenting), no matter how much cash the parents threw at tutors.

Indeed, Shadowcliff's parents often acted as if tutoring was the magic elixir. No matter whether their child couldn't grasp trinomials, struggled with sentence fluency, or was unable to keep straight the battles of the American Revolution, a tutor was called. These young men and women, like valiant knights atop their trusty steeds, would ride in, slay the dragon of uncertainty and rescue the beautiful damsel of opportunity, and then ride away several months later with hundreds or more likely thousands of dollars in their pockets. In fact, while many of them did render a valuable service to Shadowcliff students, most acknowledged that their major contribution was to help students find stuff in their backpacks, an apparently esoteric skill for which they were being paid upwards of a hundred bucks an hour.

Undeterred, parents kept tutors on speed dial and ramrodded their children (many of whom would have preferred to practice with their garage band or join the lacrosse team) into the maelstrom of geniuses, semi-geniuses, pseudo-geniuses, and not-really-geniuses-at-all that populated the Global Scholars Program.

The Program began with fully one-ninth of the student population at Shadowcliff. The fact that, by definition, only two percent of students meet the empirical standard of "gifted" did not deter parents from their ambitions. Neither did the fact that little Johnny earned all C's during his freshman year at Shadowcliff. No, in the third grade he once managed to draw five concentric circles, each in a different Crayola color, and if that did not prove the boy was a genius then what did?

Finally, it appeared Global Scholars was meant to appease Ramona Thurlow. Greg understood the belief system of the parents: We spent too damn much money for a house in this fancy neighborhood in this well-respected school district because we want the best for our kids, and if we are this successful then we want to make sure our kids are doubly so. As for Thurlow, though, her sense of entitlement was a complete mystery. Greg's best guess was that it evolved from three facts: (1) that she was a twenty-three year veteran of Sweetwater Unified School District No. 43, (2) that she helped to open the school, and (3) that she once earned an A in a college class entitled Contemporary World Issues. Of course, when she was enrolled in this class, a contemporary world issue was Watergate, or maybe the Cuban Missile Crisis. Nevertheless, armed with the necessary perspective, Ramona Thurlow was now the Global Scholars Coordinator, charged with the grave responsibility of ordering books and arranging training for the Global Scholars teachers.

Sadly, she neglected to arrange this training until all the sessions were full, meaning the program began without a single teacher who understood the curricular expectations of the program, the Socratic method it utilized, or the lofty requirements for the Global Scholars diploma. But she promised they would get trained next summer, so they only needed to fake it for one year. Who would know?

Well, who besides one-ninth of the Shadowcliff student population, who may not have been smart enough to truly belong in the program but were certainly smart enough to recognize if their teacher really knew her stuff or was making things up on the fly?

And who besides any Global Scholars auditor who happened to stop by the school? Instructions for a secret code were circulated throughout the front office; an announcement of "Please turn in your green stapler" actually meant, "Holy shit, the people from Global Scholars are here." Global Scholars teachers worked in a constant state of fear, which of course made Rumsford deliriously happy.

But if Thurlow herself was on edge due to her tiny oversight, she managed to hide it well, with her own office, no teaching responsibilities, and the opportunity to leave during the day anytime she felt so compelled. Although required to view a weekly webcast for all Global Scholars Coordinators, she usually just let it run while she ate a sandwich, Skyped her best friend in Massachusetts, or took hour-long midday hikes through the nearby mountains in a thorough and painstaking search for the shadows and the cliffs that gave the high school its name.

Besides, she reasoned as she kicked a rock off the trail, Global Scholars teachers were all reasonably intelligent, had been hand-picked by Rumsford, and were being paid a stipend of one thousand dollars. So they would just need to figure out a way to handle the stress. Most did so by spending their stipend (and more) on tequila.

Nevertheless, as the semester trudged on, both teachers and students settled into the Global Scholars routine, much of which focused upon the ability to get very little sleep.

Ramona Thurlow provided occasional curricular advice, from which the students created fictitious newspaper accounts of Napoleon's conquest of Europe, revised the text of *The Cherry Orchard* using rap beats or SAT prep words, and made mobiles out of coat hangers and magazine clippings to demonstrate the seven circles of hell. Few noticed when one student represented the seventh circle with photos of Rumsford and Thurlow.

And occasionally, students read the story in the textbook and answered questions.

But the Global Scholars Program was having a profound difference in one regard. Since they were writing newspaper articles and revising text and making mobiles under the umbrella of such a prestigious educational opportunity, these students were being molded into "an elite community of lifelong, impassioned, and principled learners with a global perspective on knowledge." They were also finding it necessary to quit the football team or marching band because of the inordinate demands on their time. In exchange, though, their grades were being augmented one full point for honors classes as reward for nothing more than endurance, as the rigor of Shadowcliff's version of Global Scholars was found only in the amount of work, not the critical thinking it generated. Thanks to the grade augmentation, Greg realized that Global Scholars had managed to appease the parents in a most superficial and inaccurate way: by convincing them of their child's success through a class ranking system which completely distorted the true abilities of Shadowcliff's students.

In early September, at Greg's urging, Amanda Moretti applied for a position with Shadowcliff's

Global Scholars Program. She was bright, motivated, a world traveler who spoke fluent Italian and passable French, certified in Gifted Education, and she brought letters of reference attesting to her ability to challenge students with true rigor and critical thinking skills. Rumsford gave only a cursory look at her CV, told Thurlow, "This girl clearly doesn't have what it takes," and turned her down without an interview.

14

THE NERDS

One-ninth of Shadowcliff's student body in the Global Scholars Program meant that eight-ninths of the student body was not. Rumsford said this majority was just as capable, just as talented, just as valuable as Global Scholars students, but everyone knew it was only lip service. The *Sweetwater Sentinel* never published stories about kids getting B's in regular-level English. Within a matter of days, students began to view the Global Scholars Program as a separate entity altogether, so the academic freaks could spend their lunches memorizing Fibonacci's Sequence or interpreting Renaissance poetry while the normal kids could talk about far more important stuff.

Like Autumn Kessler's tits.

Autumn's summer trip to Paris, an annual mother-daughter bonding experience intended to relieve several clothiers of their inventory, yielded more this year than shoes and dresses and extra baggage fees for the flight home. This time around, she and Mom also returned sporting certain anatomical modifications, the exceptional work of the Merci Beaucoup Breast Enhancement Center in the Montparnasse District. Autumn's boobs were now, in the words of one boy, "freakin' epic"—just in time for the start of school.

The school year in Arizona begins in early August, for reasons that remain difficult to fathom. Perhaps it is because Arizonans are proud of their air conditioning, and thus feel some primal need to chill gigantic buildings. Or maybe parents just need a legal way to dispose of their kids, given that summer temperatures probably kept everyone inside for the past two months and Mom is probably spent from washing dishes and doing laundry and listening to teenagers scream about their favorite band and their latest zit, or exhausted from having to pay the maid and the landscaper. In any event, when school starts at a time of year when temperatures are still over one hundred and ten, girls' outfits tend to be provocatively minimalist.

Autumn Kessler showed up the first day wearing tiny shorts and a tank top. Only some sort of dark magic, conjured to torment any student with a Y chromosome, kept things contained. On the second day, she wore a short skirt and a sleeveless blouse whose top button held only by willpower.

"God, I want to be that button," said one boy.

"She didn't have those last year," said his friend.

"I heard her parents bought her new jugs for her birthday."

"Shit, all I got was a skateboard."

Rumors abounded, but the facts did not matter anyway. Girls just wanted to hate her for the attention she now received, while boys just wanted to appreciate her new melons. They attacked this glorious objective with a heroic sense of purpose, but their ideas were mostly uninspired: Twister games, chicken fights at pool parties, Jägermeister, and the like. Ultimately, none came to fruition. But as Greg Samson once observed, one of the greatest qualities of young people is their combination of optimism and resilience. And in this particular quest, hope certainly was eternal.

Attendance at football games nearly doubled, and the front-row seats closest to the cheerleaders became prime real estate, more precious than parking spaces on Black Friday. Frank Nixon thought it was because of the team's improved play, and Rumsford was of course delighted at this significant uptick in school spirit even though she was oblivious as to the reason.

During the first quarter of the game against West Ridge High School, the Shadowcliff offense was on the move and the cheer squad offered its support. During a stunt at the end of their cheer, Autumn slipped and was caught by another cheerleader, exposing for milliseconds what might have been her left nipple. Some boys still consider it the highlight of their high school careers.

Meanwhile, the envy of the school was Autumn's boyfriend, the football captain, whom everyone incorrectly assumed was granted *carte blanche.* In reality, he was as frustrated as everyone else, and Autumn Kessler's assets remained the Holy Grail.

They were also the impetus for renewed discussion of dress code. Although nobody mentioned Autumn by name, the general topic took up most of the allotted time at the first staff meeting of the year.

"You know, it's really uncomfortable for us male teachers to enforce dress code," said one. "I don't want to be considered a perv if I tell some girl her ... you know ... are hanging out."

"You won't be considered a ... a what?" asked Rumsford.

"A perv," he replied. "Pervert."

"Nobody is saying you're a pervert just because you enforce dress code," said Rumsford.

"I'm not even sure some of the girls are wearing bras," Cockrell added.

Jimmy Clayton offered a solution. "For some reason, my classroom is really cold this year," he said. "Send 'em to me. I'll let you know if they're wearing bras or not."

As Cockrell tried not to laugh, a female teacher spoke up. "It's no easier for us. I'm tired of seeing boys' underwear all the time. The wedgie should not be a fashion statement."

The discussion continued unchecked for a moment, until Rumsford raised her hand to quiet the throng. "Are any of the Global Scholars students out of dress code?"

There was no response, so the meeting was adjourned.

Although spared from the prestige of the Global Scholars Program, its demanding parents, and the threat of the green stapler, Greg had his own issues to worry about. But he also had his own victories.

For one, he was no longer teaching Video Production. Jimmy Clayton, who as it turned out had an Associate's degree in TV and Video, had taken over that class (how he managed to avoid it during the first year was still a mystery). Paul Coates and Andy Varner were now regular anchors, and Rumsford claimed to be thrilled with the improved quality of the production. Greg harbored doubts that she truly knew whether the quality had improved or not, as he speculated that her office still contained the same broken television installed by Louie and Gus during Greg's clandestine Operation Wolverine the previous fall. This was a doubt he harbored singularly, for he never told anyone else about the exercise, and Clayton and Cockrell scarcely recalled its details.

One of Clayton's Video Production innovations was "Faculty Feature Friday," for which one lucky teacher was interviewed each week. Early on, Clayton chose Greg Samson and assigned Paul and Andy to the piece.

Questions ranged from Samson's teaching methods to whether he preferred dogs or cats. Some of the questions were thought-provoking while others were inane, but he answered them all earnestly. Finally, the topic now on Greg's coaching, Andy asked, "Distance running seems like such a crazy sport, especially in Arizona where it's so hot. So why would people choose to be distance runners?"

Greg had answered this question before and thought about it often. He had innumerable answers to the question—from personal challenge to aptitude to individual opportunities within a team context. He could answer the question physiologically, psychologically, philosophically, sociologically, or theologically. He could answer it in one minute or one hour. But he knew they wanted something different for Faculty Feature Friday. So instead, he went for the laugh, explaining, "It's like hitting yourself in the head multiple times with a hammer." And off Andy's curious look, he continued, "It feels great when you finally stop."

A couple of days later, Greg was summoned to Rumsford's office. He had not been for more than a week, so he figured he was due.

"I just previewed the footage for Fun Friday Faculty Video Thingee, or whatever the hell it's called, and I must say, I'm very disappointed," she said. "For the life of me, I can't figure out why you were selected ahead of some of the other teachers."

This Greg expected, so he chose not to respond.

Then she continued, "But that's not the biggest disappointment. The biggest disappointment is the incredibly poor judgment you used."

"Excuse me?" replied Greg, now truly perplexed.

"You said running was like hitting yourself on the head with a hammer?"

"Yes," he said uncertainly.

"I directed Jimmy Clayton to remove that part of the interview."

"As you wish. But I'm not sure why."

"Don't be so dense, Mr. Samson. If you tell kids that running is like hitting yourself in the head with a hammer, kids are going to go home and hit them-selves in the head with a hammer."

What Greg thought was: If kids are dumb enough to watch my interview and then go home and hit themselves in the head with a hammer, maybe they deserve to be hit in the head with a hammer.

What he said was: "Umm, OK."

But unless Paul Coates and Andy Varner chose to hit themselves in the head with hammers—a hobby they might already enjoy—this was not his problem. In fact, since it did not result in a goldenrod apology sent to either the American Cranium Guild for dam-age inflicted or Ace Hardware for misuse of hand tools, he counted it a win.

In another victory, Greg was also rid of Yearbook. The class was now being taught by Lawrence de Vries, a 27-year-old graphic artist hired on a part-time ba-sis with one specific charge. According to the job posting on Sweetwater Unified School District No. 43's website, de Vries was to be responsible for "The production of an annual yearbook within District guidelines and appropriate financial constraints." According to Rumsford, de Vries's job was to make sure "the damn thing isn't a piece of crap like last year." When de Vries assured her that he could do better, the job was his.

De Vries's letter of application cited his design experience, his Silver T-square Award from the Phoenix Society of Young Graphic Artists, and his ability to do any number of things that Greg knew were far too expensive for the current yearbook treasury. Sure, full color, gold foil typography, pre-paid downloads of the year's most popular songs, and an embossed textured jigsaw cover all sounded sensational, but the modest $1478.53 net profit Greg had produced would never cover such luxuries. Mr. de Vries pledged a dazzling visual product, but he could make no such promises as to its editorial integrity. In fact, he had applied for the position with the following statement: "I can guarranty the year book will reflect the latest and gratest in typography, lay out, and photography." Rumsford was thrilled. Greg, however, figured if this was de Vries's typical level of editorial skill, there would be lots of refunds to kids whose names were mangled into incomprehensibility.

So despite Rumsford's aspersions on what was really a pretty good yearbook under the circumstances, Greg was not the least bit disappointed when de Vries was hired.

With both Video Production and Yearbook no longer among his teaching load, Greg was now teaching two classes of The American Story with

Clayton, two senior English classes, and one section of Business Law.

As a requirement for being given The American Story, one of Rumsford's demands was that lesson plans be submitted on a daily basis. Since Clayton was even more obsessive and methodical than Greg, this was a painless obligation. The pair produced a handout for the benefit of students, distributed at the beginning of each thematic unit, which described each day's topic, all graded assignments for the unit, various project options, and questions for reflection. This, too, was submitted to Rumsford.

In September, they finished writing their "Quest for Liberty" unit, encompassing the American Revolution and the Declaration of Independence. It reflected a truly integrated approach to learning, the product of two curious and diverse teachers and the previous summer's week-long curriculum workshop which provided Samson with valuable perspective on how to structure an integrated curricular unit. And a girlfriend. He dropped a unit handout in Rumsford's mailbox on his way to cross country practice that evening.

The next morning, it was already back in his mailbox. One of the reflection questions posed the following: "Which man was most important to the creation of the new nation during the Second Continental Congress?" Rumsford had circled this question with a red Sharpie and added: "What about women? SEE ME." Greg walked to the front desk and borrowed a pen, then added his answer: "There were no women at the Second Continental Congress ... unless you want to count visits from Benjamin Franklin's various female professional acquaintances." He thought this last phrase would be clear enough, but the handout was back in his mailbox by lunch, with this notation: "Yes, you definitely need to include those women!"

And that is why Greg Samson and Jimmy Clayton spent an entire afternoon debating whether or not to teach the role of prostitutes during the Second Continental Congress. Final score: Common Sense 1, Rumsford 0.

At this point, Greg decided to utilize Rumsford's own tactic of overwhelming the opponent with paperwork, so he began to submit every handout, article, assignment, page of lecture notes, review, test, and rubric, often more than once. For several months, he was unsure know how much Rumsford read; occasionally, a piece might end up back in his mailbox, but as the year progressed, they were more or less given free reign. Ever suspicious, and now going two to three weeks between visits to Rumsford's office, Greg refused to get comfortable, until one day when he found several units' worth of paper-work unmarked, unwrinkled, and clearly unread, all in the recycle bin outside Rumsford's office. Just like the first year with Rumsford's handouts, Shadowcliff High School could be proud of the fact that its principal was keeping Arizona's recycling centers in business.

Chang Yi and Matt Ramirez were freshmen in the Global Scholars program, friends since astronomy camp when they were eight years old. Both loved math even more than dinner. They created complex mathematical models just for fun, the way other kids played basketball in the driveway or Madden on their X-Box. If they could not sleep, they would text equations to each other until one of them made an error, which generally meant they were at it until their morning alarms. They were short and pimpled and their voices still cracked when they were excited, which typically involved trigonometric functions. They could calculate in their heads the point at which the train leaving New York and the train leaving Chicago crossed paths. They were usually ignored unless some kid wanted to copy their homework. They were nerds with a capital N. The Global Scholars Program was perfect for them.

One weekend, Chang and Matt began working on a project for their Pre-Calculus class, in which they were the youngest students by at least a year. Sequestered behind closed doors, their discussion and the tickety-tickety of their computer keyboard lasted well into the night, and they resumed the project the following morning. It was a simple problem, actually, nothing more than creating the equation for a paraboloid, a three-dimensional parabolic function. But the math needed to be exact.

They presented their findings on Monday. Their presentation was simple, yet technologically dazzling: rotating, three-dimensional mapping to demonstrate paraboloids in non-linear space. "Excellent work," said the teacher. Chang and Matt smiled shyly at the accolades. "Your calculations are elegant and your presentation is most impressive." Ever practical, the teacher thought the project might be applicable to modeling of grain storage facilities or military fortifications. The rest of the class, however, recognized that the paraboloids represented exactly what they were intended to represent, and challenged the freshmen to take the next step.

That afternoon, the nerds waited outside cheer practice until Autumn Kessler emerged.

"Hi," Chang said, nervously. His voice cracked and Autumn laughed, and Chang's face flushed.

"I'm sorry," she said. "Do I know you guys?"

"No," answered Matt. "That's Chang. I'm Matt. You're Autumn, right?"

"Uh-huh."

"Hi. See, we love math," Matt continued. "Can we show you something?"

"Ummm ... OK. I'm not that good at math."

"You don't have to be," said Chang. "We just need you to look at this model we created."

Minutes later, sitting in Autumn's car, the boys opened Matt's iMac to show her their 3-D projection. "So they're paraboloids?" asked Autumn, suitably impressed, pulling up her shirt to reveal her new breasts. And while Chang Yi and Matt Ramirez all but experienced spontaneous combustion, Jack the security guard remained ever-vigilant from across the parking lot, earning his nine dollars an hour by courageously nipping Wild Turkey and valiantly watching Autumn's car through his binoculars.

15

P retty receptionists, efficient maintenance, and buxom Copy Moms were just some of the reasons that school started with greater success than it had a year ago. Scheduling was far smoother, even despite the school's tremendous growth. Teachers were in possession of valid rosters from the beginning and Rumsford did not destroy student morale with a twenty-minute speech the first day. At the end of the first week, Greg left with high hopes for a smoother, less traumatic, more enjoyable school year.

Then he got the call.

"Greg, this is Lily." It was his stepmother, his father's wife for six years since the death of Greg's mother. "Your father is in the hospital."

Half an hour later, Greg was bedside in the VA Hospital in Phoenix, his father a gaunt, spotted commingling of limbs and tubes beneath a stark white bedsheet and thin blanket. He looked years older than their last visit a week ago. Greg knew his father was beginning to get sickly. Two years before, when he came back from his college teaching engagement, Greg spent the summer playing golf with his father just to help him build up his strength after he had suffered a stroke. Greg did not even like golf, but it worked, at least in the short-term. More recently, however, his father was falling more often, bruising himself regularly, and occasionally slurring his words and complaining of a light-headed feeling which, despite his father's denials, sounded suspiciously like another stroke.

Amanda showed up a few minutes later. "I came as soon as I got your message," she said. Greg knew she had lots of work to do; she always did. Yet she dropped it for him. What a girl.

Later, his father in no danger, they paused for a drink in the hospital cafeteria. Amanda drank coffee, Greg orange juice. They discussed their week and the weeks and months ahead, the students they knew would challenge them, the assignments they knew would inspire them, the administrative expectations they knew would aggravate them. They questioned and they speculated and they laughed, a lot. One thing they did not discuss was their future. But it was clearly there, bubbling not far beneath the surface.

They saw each other as often as they could, as often as their teaching loads and their perfectionism would allow. Sometimes it was once a week, usually more. To Greg's great surprise, and the great pleasure of his father, she began to go with Greg to the hospital more and more frequently, until she became such a fixture that other patients began to call her by name. Once, she brought her otherworldly "chocolate cake to die for" to Thursday night Bingo, not recognizing the horrid implications of that title until after she served everyone. The nurses were mortified, but the patients thought it was the funniest thing ever, and Old Man Skinner even withdrew his dentures so he could flash not one, but two separate smiles. Meanwhile, Greg's father took to her in his own special way.

"How are you feeling?" Greg would ask him. "Oh, I feel pretty good," he would respond, the tubes in his nose shaking with his every word. Then he would slide over in bed, pat the open space, and offer, "Amanda, why don't you lay down right here?" Greg was uncertain whether he should be offended or proud as hell, but Amanda said the old man's spunk was the coolest thing ever.

Amidst these frequent visits were real dates, and during those times Greg began to learn more about her school. She told stories of greed, hypocrisy, self-interest, and abject incompetence. In other words, an average day at Shadowcliff. "You mean it's like that everywhere?" Greg asked, and Amanda, with exactly one more year of experience, nodded wisely.

In the history of Shadowcliff High School, fourteen teachers had been selected by Dr. Connie Rumsford as Teacher of the Month. Ramona Thurlow had won for, as the plaque stated, her "imaginative and cutting-edge teaching practices" because, apparently, nobody had ever thought to read the stories and answer the questions in the textbook. Frank Nixon had won for his "exceptionally high standards that have pushed all students to excel," since completing worksheets with a partner was a clear manifestation of the best practices of cooperative learning, especially on game days. Ike Gravenstein never won, despite the fact that his class featured weekly Socratic seminars that tied current affairs to historical events in a compelling manner. His classroom featured comfortable beanbag chairs, too. And even though Greg Samson had worked harder than he ever thought possible, and created the framework for a unique interdisciplinary class, and coached Shadowcliff's most successful team ... well, apparently he had not done enough ass-kissing, and never would, so he knew the award was far out-of-reach.

Greg had long been about the process, not the product, a lesson he learned the hard way many times. One example was the Bix Road Race in Davenport, Iowa, which he entered only because of its prize money but then wilted in the heat. As he sat in the medical tent, Greg swore he would never again choose a race simply for its extrinsic rewards. Now, like the idealist Woody correctly pegged him to be, he was comfortable in the intrinsic knowledge that the rewards at Shadowcliff were a student's opened mind and improved skills, and his own self-satisfaction of a job well-done. He had enough plaques at home.

With the retirement of several members of Rumsford's inner circle at the end of the previous school year—"It was just too fucking hard," said the demure sixty-three-year-old Olivia Schrader—Bob Cockrell was chosen for Shadowcliff's Leadership Team. This elite group was directed to formulate school policy and shape the methods by which Shadowcliff was to become an even greater school. Explained Cockrell, "It's mostly ceremonial. She tells us what she wants, and we say OK."

Greg recognized that Rumsford's unilateral decisions would appear even more democratically authoritative with the imprimatur of the entire Leadership Team, so in essence the members of the team were nothing more than a giant human rubber stamp. Except in this case, the prestige of their position also carried with it the obligation of a two-hour meeting and as many as half a dozen readings each week. Cockrell kept his readings in pristine condition, hoping that someday he would be able to sell an entire lot of mint educational theory articles on eBay. However, while Cockrell lost two hours a week, he kept his sense of humor.

"I'd like to nominate Greg Samson for Teacher of the Month," he said at the October Leadership Team meeting.

"Pfft," replied Rumsford. "You nominated him last month. And the month before that."

"And I'll keep nominating him," said Cockrell, who had become one of Greg's closest friends on campus. Cockrell's love of fly fishing had taught him perseverance. "I think he's a great teacher."

"Stacy Johnston will be our Teacher of the Month," stated Rumsford authoritatively, completely unconcerned as to whether any other member of the team agreed. After all, Stacy wore leggings. Maybe she taught a decent math class. What the hell; that was good enough for Rumsford. Meanwhile, thanks to Cockrell's persistence, Greg was becoming the Adlai Stevenson of the teaching profession.

"Now, let's discuss the new standardized test we'll be using...."

Some teachers at Shadowcliff saw teaching as a call-ing. Most of those teachers were very good, and some had even been recognized as Teacher of the Month. Others saw teaching as a job that allowed them summers off, and they complained every time they were required to take an in-service in July when they should have been lounging on a Mexican beach while a young man named Pedro de Alcaríz Hispaniola y Cruz, or something exotic like that, served them margaritas as they worked on their tans while stretching their legs toward the tranquil aqua sea. Most of those teachers were decent but uninspiring, just good enough that it was nearly impossible to replace them under the personnel system in place. A third group saw teaching as a hellish chore replete with demonic creatures whose sole purpose on earth was to suck the very life-blood out of adults. Most of this group of teachers, thankfully, left the profession after only a couple of years. Greg occasionally saw one of them working as Second Assistant Night Manager at Toys R Us, where they now manifested that same perception of customers.

Greg recognized that teaching was not a calling to him—he could have been very happy as a busi-nessman, an advertising copywriter, an engineer, an Army cartographer, or especially a novelist—but perhaps more like a craft, something for which he had some aptitude and which he could learn to do with greater skill. Plus it fed his sense of idealism more than map reading for the Eighth Regimental Command ever could. He was growing in the profession, and like everything else in his life, would ultimately become pretty good at it through sheer repetition, work ethic, and force of will. He also recognized that, like most distance runners, he worked best in his own little world, so each day he shut his door, taught his students, and hoped the administrivia would not intrude. On days it did not, he was satisfied that he had not chosen Darnell Lyon's path. But like gray hair and cockroaches, administrivia has a way of showing up without either invitation or forewarning.

In addition to The American Story and his senior English classes, Greg was now teaching an elective which allowed him to use his legal training and perhaps to satisfy Kelli Westin's enquiry, if not his own occasional questioning. He pitched the class as a Social Studies course entitled "American Law and You," citing national and state standards in history, government, and economics as well as recommendations from the National Council for Social Studies and the American Bar Association. Both the Social Studies department chair and the new Assistant Principal for Academic Services endorsed the new class, and Greg's course synopsis and proposed syllabus were submitted to Sweetwater Unified School District No. 43.

Conrad Luper decided it needed to be called Business Law, and so it was.

Thirty years before, Luper had earned a degree in Geology from Bemidji State University. He soon found that the demand for geologists was not particularly robust, although he was offered a position as an unpaid intern. So instead he began his adult working life in the fast food industry, where two years of diligence and a flair for the deep-fryer enabled him to work his way up to a part-time assistant manager position while simultaneously destroying his already pasty complexion. He then succeeded in networking his way into a lesser position at a different fast food chain. Realizing his path to prosperity had already stalled twice while he was still only in his mid-twenties, he went back to school to earn a teaching certification, eventually selecting Business Education due to his managerial experience.

Now Luper taught typing (officially called Beginning Computer Applications) at Rancho High School, but as the most senior business teacher within Sweetwater Unified School District No. 43, was also given the additional duties of overseeing the District's Vocational Education program. This enabled him to spend the month of July lounging on a Mexican beach while a young man named Pedro de Alcaríz Hispaniola y Cruz served him margaritas as he stretched his pale, hairy legs toward the sea.

William Shakespeare wrote, "Some men are born great, some achieve greatness, and some have greatness thrust upon them." Conrad Luper was none of those men.

But he did enjoy his margaritas. And he was now Dr. Conrad Luper, EdD, having finally completed his dissertation entitled "Advantages of Hunt-and-Peck in a Digital World." The awarding of the doctorate was proclaimed by Sweetwater Unified School District No. 43's website. Later in the year, Greg did a quick Google search and found the abstract of Luper's dissertation. As expected, it was about teaching typing.

The administrivia began the first week of school when Luper dropped by. His position as Director of Vocational Education afforded him afternoons off. He taught three morning classes and then oversaw a dozen or so teachers throughout the District. In Luper's case, "oversaw" was apparently a synonym for "forwarded e-mails to." But occasionally he made rounds, accounting for every mile (to the exact tenth) lest he be shorted forty-four cents in expenses by the District. Greg was in the middle of The American Story when Luper slipped in the door. Luper's expression suggested profound discontent with the fact that nobody was typing at the time.

As Greg continued class, Luper passed the time by looking at last year's *Chronicle* yearbook. Greg occasionally noticed Luper jotting down notes, a confusing development since the man had not even introduced himself. Perhaps he was from the World Yearbook Federation, here to award one of the prizes Rumsford so desperately craved and so clearly did not deserve. Maybe he was there to ask for refunds on behalf of everyone who failed to ask last year. Maybe he just had a strong fascination with typography.

At the end of the day, as the final student packed up and shuffled out of class, Luper finally introduced himself.

"I'm Dr. Conrad Luper, District Director of Vocational Education." This cannot be good, Greg thought to himself. Luper continued, "My son Kyle was in your English class last year."

"I don't recall a Kyle Luper," said Greg.

"Kyle Friese," said Luper. "His mother is remarried."

"Oh, how can I forget Kyle Friese?" Greg said. "Who does he have for English this year?"

"I have no idea. They sent him to Barksdale Military School."

Greg never did ascertain the reason for Luper's visit, and in retrospect, was not sure if Luper even knew the reason for Luper's visit. It did not seem to be about typography, nor about Barksdale Military School. It did not seem to be about anything, really. And those visits, Greg knew, were ones fraught with the most danger. Suddenly, this pale specter which had spent more than an hour in his classroom took on an ominous visage in his mind, and the haunting had begun.

Yet even when troubled by administrivia, ghosts, or the ghosts of administrivia, cross country practice always offered new life, a chance for Greg to share the joy of the sport which had meant so much to his own life. Greg was proud of his cross country team's accomplishments during the first year, but he knew there was still a long journey in order to achieve his goal of a state title. The boys team was developing rapidly, although still a year or two away from great things. But the girls' team was bolstered by a move-in from North Carolina, an outstanding freshman, and a soccer player whose only real soccer skill was her ability to run forever, and emboldened by a strong summer of training and by leadership which had developed a culture of team success rather than individual glory.

Meanwhile, Greg recruited like never before. He recruited based upon recommendations from the middle school coaches. He recruited kids who were cut from volleyball and football and cheerleading. He recruited kids out of P.E. classes based upon their endomorphic bodies, their efficiency of stride, and their ability to complete more than two laps of the gym before detouring to the water fountain. He recruited kids out of registration lines and his English classes. He encouraged each returning member of the team to bring a friend. And by the end of the first week of practice, he had thirty-seven boys and girls out for cross country.

One notable exception: Darlene Griffin, who only months before had proven herself to be the best girl in Arizona, was a no-show.

The shrieking violins of the *Psycho* theme woke Greg from a Saturday afternoon nap. This was Greg's current ringtone, a sound he felt certain no other shoppers at the Big Town Supermarket would confuse with their own. Over the summer he had used "War" by Edwin Starr, which was truly distinctive but which he abandoned when his phone rang in the milk aisle and an elderly shopper nearly suffered cardiac arrest.

With the second violin screech, Greg reached for his phone. "Hello?"

"Hello, Coach, this is Mary Jo Griffin-Goldberg.... Darlene's mother."

"Yes, ma'am. How are you?"

"I'm fine. The reason I'm calling is to let you know why Darlene hasn't been at practice."

"Great," said Greg. "I was ... we were all wondering what was going on."

"My husband and myself were talking with Darlene, and we have decided that she's not going to run for Shadowcliff this year."

"Just cross country, or both cross country and track?" asked Greg.

"Both."

"And when you say 'we have decided,' does that mean Darlene decided?"

"Yes, my husband and myself. And Darlene." And Maurice, too, guessed Greg.

"Um, may I inquire as to why not?" he asked instead.

"We just think she needs to keep it real," replied Mrs. Griffin-Goldberg.

"Keep it real. Ohhh-kay." Greg shook his head and continued. "Can you tell me exactly what you mean by that?"

"She needs to chill out. You know, chillax."

"I see," said Greg, wondering why a forty-year-old mother whose third husband was a real estate attorney chose to express herself like a cast member on some trashy MTV reality show.

"But she's still going to run club track, so she can work on her speed," she explained. "With Maurice," as if that needed mention.

"You realize that she beat the best milers in the southwest last year, right?" Greg posed. "You realize that even in our endurance-based program, Darlene improved her 400 and 800 times considerably, and she barely missed the state record in the 1600?"

"Darlene wants to focus on the 800," Mrs. Griffin-Goldberg replied.

"She was ranked number forty-six in the U.S. in the 800 and number eleven in the 1600. I already have college coaches wanting to offer her full rides. As a miler, not a half-miler. Not to mention that current research says the 800 is sixty percent aerobic. The 1600, more than seventy-five percent. She'll benefit a lot more, both short-term and long-term, from continued aerobic development."

"Maurice says she needs to work on her speed."

It occurred to Greg that if Maurice suggested Darlene join the circus, Mrs. Griffin-Goldberg would at that very moment be speeding toward Zampini's Circus Outlet to pick out a pair of sequined tights in whichever color Maurice advised.

"Just out of curiosity, who is she going to race against?"

"Other kids in club track," answered Darlene's mom, like Greg had just asked the dumbest question in history.

"Kids who are either younger than her or else too slow to run on their high school teams?"

"Maurice says she needs to work on her speed."

"Of course. If I may ask one more thing, Mrs. Griffin-Goldberg. Why didn't Darlene call me herself?"

There was a long pause, which Greg finally broke. "Never mind. No matter. Please tell her I wish her the best. And thank you for the call."

He hung up the phone and began dancing around the room as if a thousand candirus were invading his pants. He screamed "Yes! Yes! Yes!" until his downstairs neighbors began beating on their ceiling with a broom handle and hollering, "Will you two please keep it down?" Although it was only himself, this moment was no less orgasmic.

16

THE OLIGARCHY

The whispers began a few weeks into the semester. Not whispers about Thurlow's tan or Rumsford's philosophical one-eighty, but rather, about the Global Scholars Program's first-ever academic scandal.

While Greg had no actual involvement in the situation, he nevertheless had interest. He championed academic integrity, of course, but he also knew that whatever happened to one teacher or one program was destined to affect others. From the lasagna question to the Shelley Banyan incident, nothing at Shadowcliff happened in a vacuum. Even the mere hint of transgression made Greg shudder at the potential school-wide implications.

Assigned a research project on the Crusades, Global Scholars freshmen had allegedly hacked the code to make an academic website appear to be their own. Apparently the Global Scholars Program frowned on such shenanigans, no matter how ingenious they might be, no matter the level of technological wizardry they might demonstrate. Now seventeen students were on the verge of banishment from the program. So was their teacher, who in the District's eyes had made the unconscionable errors of (1) assigning that particular topic, and (2) catching the perpetrators.

There were accusations, meetings, conference calls, and of course lawyers. Darnell Lyon became such a fixture in the Shadowcliff lobby that Kelli Westin brought him daily morning coffee. Greg waved at Darnell on his way to his mailbox each morning and again on his way to cross country practice each evening. In one week, Darnell put in more hours at Shadowcliff than virtually any of the teachers—but did so at three hundred bucks an hour. Greg, who could multiply, began to wonder if his aversion toward Ed Law was hasty. Yet every afternoon, as he spent time with his rapidly improving cross country team, those misgivings quickly passed.

Then, suddenly, Darnell Lyon was gone, as if extinct. The whispers quieted, the students returned to the program, and the "elite community of lifelong, impassioned, and principled learners" was back at full force. Conspicuously absent, the teacher had been reassigned to a school in the opposite corner of Sweetwater Unified School District No. 43, teaching

C-track Earth Science (or "Rocks for Dummies," as the class was often called) and serving as assistant pom coach—two positions for which she had absolutely no qualifications.

It was only then that Greg noticed: Shadowcliff's supply of goldenrod paper had been exhausted.

Throughout the wealthiest neighborhoods of northeast Sweetwater, seventeen parents held thick goldenrod packets in their hands—packets which exonerated their children from obvious culpability, which offered apologies for the annoyance that had been created, and which (in keeping with their golden color) made this coterie of seventeen parents the *de facto* oligarchy of Shadowcliff High School.

In mid-October, during fall break when most Global Scholars students were vacationing with their parents at their San Diego beach houses, eating too much pizza on their Caribbean cruises, or engaging in all-night World of Warcraft competitions, Superintendent Lew Vincennes was fired. While the official reason was the ever-evasive "wanting to go in a different direction," everyone knew it was because of Global Scholars.

"Whoever they get won't be as bad as Vincennes," Jimmy Clayton said to Greg as they were planning their unit on utopian societies and Romanticism. "That guy was an idiot."

"Don't forget the old expression," replied Greg. "The enemy you know is better than the enemy you don't know."

A week later, Assistant Superintendent Lucille Scholz, a tiny, gray-haired grandmother fond of knitting during School Board meetings, a lifelong employee of the Sweetwater Unified School District No. 43, and a champion of Connie Rumsford and her vision for Shadowcliff High School, was elevated to the corner office. The *Sweetwater Sentinel* ("Editorial excellence in the east Valley for 32 years") opined that Lucille Scholz was the best choice for Superintendent because she was the only person who could handle Rumsford.

Although the most successful, the seventeen families of the Oligarchy were not alone in their efforts to exercise dominion from the outside. One day, Greg's American Story class was in Jimmy Clayton's classroom, working on group projects. When Greg's English section combined with Clayton's history section, there were more than sixty kids in one room, yet it was easily monitored by one teacher. Today was Clayton's turn to supervise, enabling Greg to remain in his classroom and grade essays. As he was writing a comment about a student's exceptional use of textual support, Greg's phone rang.

"Hello...? Yes, this is Coach Samson."

"Your runners blocked the driveway at the grocery store yesterday." The voice and delivery sounded familiar.

"I don't understand," answered Greg. "You mean they stood in the driveway so you couldn't leave?"

"Well, no," said the caller. "But when they ran past I had to wait for them."

"Were they on the sidewalk?"

"Yes."

"So they were running where they were legally allowed to be, and they didn't purposely stop to block you in...? I apologize for the inconvenience, but that doesn't sound any different than any other legal pedestrian."

"But I had to wait for them."

"Is this the same woman who called last year to complain about us running without shirts?" There was no answer. "Ma'am, I'll be sure to speak with my team about our running etiquette. And I certainly appreciate your ongoing concern for our safety. Have a great day."

He hung up the phone, put away his grading, and began to prepare an annotated bibliography about pedestrian right-of-way laws.

Greg still struggled to engage the students for whom school was an ordeal, the students with no interest in learning or contributing, who were unmotivated by fear of failure or lectures by their counselors or parents about their futures, the students who consumed oxygen and resources and attention but produced little besides exasperation in return. It seemed as though ten percent of his students consumed ninety percent of his energy, but he knew the rules: You don't get to choose your students. So he pressed on in vague hopes of even a single victory, one Kyle Friese among the bunch.

Jeanette Candelaria called them "bottom feeders by choice," even though the accepted term was "at risk." Lucille Scholz prided herself on reaching these at-risk students, so she sent weekly e-mails about inclusion strategies and planned faculty in-service sessions to help teachers address the unique needs of these students.

Nevertheless, some tasks are so ingrained in the high school curriculum that they become immutable, unique needs be damned. One such task is the senior research paper, which Greg assigned during the first quarter. The four senior English teachers had decided to stagger the process in order to maximize library time and resources, so Greg's students submitted their papers at the end of October while those for other teachers were due at various times later in the year. Some papers were exceptional, such as one student's analysis of how the poetry of John Keats was a reflection of his painful childhood or another student's historical survey of Japanese imperialism leading up to Pearl Harbor. Some barely met the minimum standard but were just adequate enough to merit a D. Others failed to achieve even that low threshold. One student, for example, wrote a research paper entitled "Three Uses of Hemp," which contained exactly one citation, averaged nine misspellings per paragraph, and fell more than eleven hundred words short of the fifteen-hundred word requirement. Greg had prepared a detailed rubric for the assignment, a Rumsford-quality document even more exhaustive than those of his colleagues, and every student received a copy at the beginning of the process so they could ensure their paper was satisfactory. According to Greg's rubric, this paper earned a score of twenty-seven percent.

"Mr. Samson," the student complained after grades were returned, "you failed me? That's completely bogus."

"Let's talk at lunch, Blaine," Greg told the boy. "Right now I need to share some thoughts with the entire class." But as Greg began to describe his reactions to the research process and offer some takeaways, it was obvious that Blaine had completely tuned him out in resentment.

Unexpectedly, Blaine actually returned at lunch, although the pizza he ate had not improved his mood. Greg indicated that the boy needed to clean some sauce from the corner of his mouth, then said, "Can you please take out the assignment?"

In his effort to be as thorough as possible, Greg used both words and pictures to explain every step in the process in detail, creating an imposing fifteen-page document on which Suzi Cooter took great care to ensure its timely duplication. While the best students would have been able to pull a pristine copy from their notebooks, Blaine's was buried in the depths of his backpack, stained and tattered, the first page nearly torn off, subsequent pages crinkled, thick dark drawings of geometric patterns filling the margins of most pages.

"We went through this entire packet in class, right?"

"I guess so," said Blaine.

"Let's look at the list of graded assignments first, OK?" Greg watched as the boy turned through the pages.

"This here?" he asked.

"That's the one," answered Greg. "Now let's go through each step. The first requirement was to get your topic approved."

"I done that!" he said.

"Well, yes and no," replied Greg, checking his notes. "You did submit a topic, but the topic I approved was on the evolution of the bow and arrow as a combat weapon."

"Because I always use a crossbow as my primary weapon in video games. You said that was a cool topic."

"It is. But that's not what you wrote about."

"I couldn't find no information on it," Blaine said, "so I changed topics."

"OK, but I explained that if you changed topics, you needed to get your new topic approved. You never did, and I never would have approved it anyway. You also never asked me for any research help on the original topic. I bet I could find a million hits on Google in less than five seconds. Then, for your new topic, you didn't submit the required outline, or any bibliography cards, or any note cards, or a rough draft. I could have helped you at any of those intermediate steps."

"I didn't think I needed no help," Blaine replied.

"So all along, you thought you were good?"

"Look here, Mr. Samson," said Blaine, turning to the copy of the grading rubric included in the packet. "I even graded it myself to make sure I done it right. I gave myself a ninety-one."

Greg was astounded. He would expect a student to grade himself a little higher, of course, but the gap here was colossal.

It took him a moment to recover, which only seemed to vitalize Blaine. "This school is supposed to be student-centered, right? So my grade should count for something."

"We obviously have very different perspectives on the quality of this essay," Greg finally said. "So let's go through your rubric and see where we diverge."

Blaine offered the document to Greg and sat back, awaiting redemption.

"OK, let's start with length. Fifteen hundred words were required. You were nowhere close, but you gave yourself ten out of ten."

"Don't you always say 'It needs to be however long it needs to be?' Well this was as long as it needs to be."

"It wasn't, actually," said Greg. "You clearly wrote it off the top of your head. If you had done any research, you could have added several hundred words plus made your points a lot stronger. Let's look at the number of sources. Ten different sources were required. You used one. And—"

"—I only used one because that source gave me all the information I needed," argued Blaine.

"You have one quotation from it, that quotation adds nothing to the essay, and you cite it incorrectly. Then you didn't even include a Works Cited page."

"Did we need one?"

"What do you think?"

"I don't know," Blaine replied, the standard teenage equivocation. Greg stared at him but said nothing. The boy grew uncomfortable as the silence stretched out, and finally he acknowledged, "I guess you wouldn't have made it part of the grade if we didn't need one."

"Very good. Nor would I have spent two days teaching you how to write one. Yet you still gave yourself ten out of ten."

"OK, so maybe I didn't deserve that."

"Blaine, I gotta be honest with you. As I look through this paper a second time, I'm not sure it deserves a grade of twenty-seven." As Blaine sat up, victorious, Greg continued, "I think that grade is actually much too high." And Blaine slumped right back down in his chair.

"Now here's the problem," said Greg. "This is required by the District for seniors, so you can't pass senior English with a failing research paper."

"Can't pass? That's not fair."

"It is, actually," Greg said, "but it's not my goal to fail you. It's my goal to teach you how to write a decent research paper. So I will give you the opportunity to redo this. We'll go back to your original topic of the bow and arrow. You'll need to complete each of the steps before you submit your final paper. I will help you, but you'll need to do the work on your own time. You'll have until Christmas break, so about six weeks."

"What if I don't do it?" Blaine asked.

"Then the current grade of twenty-seven will stand, and next year you'll be a fifth-year senior. So I hope you'll take advantage of my offer."

The very next day, Greg was summoned to Rumsford's office as he expected.

"I got a phone call from a parent this morning," she said. "You failed her son on his senior research paper?"

"I did," said Greg. "Quite frankly, it was embarrassingly horrible."

"And you said he wouldn't graduate?"

"I gave him the opportunity to re-do his paper, but yes, if he doesn't get a passing score on the paper then he doesn't pass the class, and the class is required for graduation."

"Says who?" Rumsford demanded.

"The District, for one," Greg answered. "I'm not sure if it's a state requirement. But it's in the District curriculum guide that students are required to master the research paper. He didn't."

Rumsford tramped over to her bookshelf and began scouring the selections, finally choosing a thick black binder. When she found the appropriate document, she read with such wrath that the words themselves were probably terrified.

"It doesn't say that at all," she said finally, almost spitting the words.

"Of course it does," he replied, offering the photocopied page of the curriculum guide. She ignored it and thrust the black notebook at him.

"Show me in here," she demanded.

Reading, Greg realized that Rumsford's document did not, in fact, say anything about mastery. But something was amiss. After a moment, he turned to the front of the folder he was reading, and there was his answer.

"Dr. Rumsford," Greg said. "This is not the District curriculum guide. This is just the catalog that gets passed out at registration."

"Well, that's good enough for me," she snarled.

Three days later, on the second Saturday in November, Shadowcliff's seven varsity girls won the state cross country championship, and Greg's bold prediction had been affirmed.

Yet at Shadowcliff's weekly staff meeting—Rumsford still held a wellspring of superfluity with which to bore them—it was announced that the football team was playing its first-ever playoff game on Friday, and that everyone was expected to support "the most successful team on campus." Frank Nixon, who barely taught during the season, bullied other teachers into giving his players passing grades, and skipped out on bar tabs at every opportunity, graciously stood to accept the applause of colleagues while Rumsford fawned over him. Greg noticed Athletic Director Randy Smith begin to raise his hand. Greg caught Randy's eye and shook his head. Randy knew. Greg knew. And seven amazing girls knew. That was enough.

When the football team lost its first-ever playoff game 49-6, Greg was in the stands as directed. He was not necessarily disappointed at the outcome.

On the drive home, he called Amanda, who was at her own school's playoff game.

"Hey baby," he said. "How's it going?"

"We lost," she replied. Her favorite student was the starting left tackle.

"So did we," said Greg. "You want to meet somewhere for a late dinner?"

"I'm tired," she answered. "I'd rather just get home. We're going see your dad in the morning, right?"

"Yeah. I'll pick you up about nine."

"Perfect," she said. "Gives me time to go to the gym. And you can get a run."

"I'll see you in the morning then."

"I love you," she said.

"I love you too."

As he pulled into the parking lot at his apartment complex, Greg's *Psycho* ringtone punctured the air. It was Lily, his stepmother.

"Hi Lily," Greg said, maneuvering into his parking stall. She was crying. "Lily, what's going on? Lily?"

A few minutes later, still in the driver's seat, Greg called Amanda.

"My dad is dead," he said.

17

THE PAYBACK

Greg slept fitfully that night. Over and over he reviewed his relationship with his father. The ballgames when he was younger. His father's thirst for cheap Scotch. The friends his father approved of, and those he did not. His sharp tone, which could reduce the adolescent Greg to a cowering mess when delivered appropriately. The backhand that sometimes followed. His father's remarriage to Lily. There was so much to run through the filter, and no telling what would come out the other side.

Greg's father had taught him how to ride a bike and drive a car. His mother had taught him the Lord's Prayer and how to cook and swim and read and fold a fitted sheet. His father had taught him anger, his mother, compassion. Greg wondered how much he was like his dad, and how much like his mom.

And then there was the time Greg announced that he would no longer play baseball because he wanted to focus on becoming a distance runner. His father never missed one of Greg's baseball games, even toward the end when the boy spent most of his time on the bench, cheering for Randy Smith and the rest of his Bonanza High School teammates. Following the switch, Greg's father never watched him race and had no idea what was even his best event. He did not understand why Greg needed a new pair of running shoes every few months, so Greg ran in them until the soles were so worn that he may as well have been running barefoot.

But the man had a sense of humor sharper than his chin. After leaving the Army, he worked as a banker for more than twenty-five years, never complaining despite his obvious dissatisfaction. He paid the grocery bill and the mortgage and Greg's college tuition. He came home every night and kissed his wife every morning and took her to dinner every Saturday. He cared for her on her deathbed with a gentleness that Greg had never before witnessed, and when the cancer finally conquered the last of her resolve, the strong man cried for days.

During Greg's frequent visits to the VA Hospital, he had begun to see his father in all his facets, like a piece of cut crystal: robust yet vulnerable, brave yet fearful, glib yet thoughtful, angry yet accepting. And as his father shone through the glass, he exploded into a rainbow of colors, the full spectrum of a man far more complex than Greg had ever considered. Now, that spectrum was left only to memory, reflection, and photographs dulled by time.

"We never had closure," Greg said to Amanda. "We never said our peace. We never brought all the conflicting emotions together and put 'em in a neat box and tied it with a ribbon like you're supposed to do."

"Who says that's what you're supposed to do?" she asked. "You spent quality time with him. And you did it for him and he loved it."

"Is that enough?" asked Greg.

"It'll have to be."

"But I never got through his shell. He was a hard man, impenetrable almost. I should have tried harder."

Amanda stared tenderly at him, her warm brown eyes like soft pillows he could fall into and sleep for a thousand years. But not yet.

"I don't even know how he felt about me, really."

"He loved you," she replied. "He was happy for you. He was happy for your running and your teaching and coaching. And he was happy that you found me."

"How do you know?"

"I know because women are about five-hundred-billion times better at emotional intelligence than men," she chuckled, an obvious answer to an absurd question.

Greg cocked his head as he looked at her, and she continued, "And I know because he told me. He told me he's proud of you. He told me that a lot."

"He never told me."

"Greg, your father was born during the Great Depression, then he fought in the Korean War. Men like that don't talk. They work, they serve, they struggle, they persevere. They don't explain."

"I wish he had."

"I know." She held him close as he began to cry.

"I'm all alone now," Greg said.

"No," Amanda responded. "You are absolutely not alone. You've got your friends and your students and your team. And you've got me."

"I'm no picnic," he said.

"I know," she affirmed. "Just like your dad."

Bottom-feeders were not limited to Greg's senior English class, or even to Shadowcliff's senior class as a whole. In fact, they come in all species: talkative freshman boys and sullen junior girls, kids from stable two-parent homes and others who shuttled between divorced parents, pretty girls and overweight boys and popular kids and outcasts. Even the integrated, project-based American Story class had a few.

"What they need is a kick in the ass," Jimmy Clayton suggested as he read a notice for an upcoming Lucille Scholz in-service entitled "Empathy for the At-Risk Student." He and Greg were grading westward expansion projects. "I hate how they screw up group projects for everyone else."

"I wonder what would happen if we put all the bottom feeders in one group," Greg offered. "I'm just thinking out loud here, but maybe they would see what a drag it is to work with other people like themselves. Or," he paused, his index finger in the air for emphasis, "maybe they would come up with something really creative."

"Maybe they would burn down the school," said Clayton.

"I'd like to take that chance," said Greg. "Besides, it'll make classroom management easier since they'll all be at the same table. I say we do it."

As an athlete, Greg loved when more-talented athletes diminished themselves with poor choices or inferior work habits, because that was one more guy he could beat. As a coach he felt the same way, confident that his teams would out-prepare their opponents. But as a teacher, he exercised far less control over the process.

Greg was convinced that some of his students had not read an actual book since, perhaps, *Go, Dog, Go!* He was sure they scrolled through items on the internet, so they were at least exposed to words, but their reading experience was probably limited to skimming the dialog box to see if their wizard had been upgraded to level six before the Enchanted Bandits could ransack the Forbidden Forest and steal the treasure of the Cave People. So Greg decided that every Friday would be free reading day in the English component of The American Story, allowing Jimmy Clayton a day to rally on the History component, which always seemed to have more content. The only catch for free reading was that it must be a novel. There were plenty of grumbles the first couple of weeks, but most of the class began to adapt and even enjoy the opportunity. Greg began to cherish Fridays as well, a chance to indulge his own love of reading during the school year without guilt or loss of sleep.

Two boys, however, were unmoved. The first time they arrived without a novel, Greg allowed them to read a magazine. When it happened again the next week, he sent them to the library, but they were gone for most of the period and still returned empty-handed. The third week, same thing, so he made them sit in their chairs for an hour. "You can count the holes in the ceiling tile," he said, and at the end of the period one of them actually had a number.

On Friday of the fourth week, Greg was stapling his new "Read A Book, Grow A Mind" poster to his bulletin board when class began. While their classmates quietly opened their novels, the two boys arrived late and noisily took their seats on opposites sides of the classroom. One plopped his backpack defiantly on his desk, crossed his arms, and began counting holes in the ceiling tile. The other began to spin his pencil on his desktop, each spin somehow louder than the one before.

"I have had it with you guys!" Greg finally bellowed. Every head jerked toward his voice. "Get out a piece of notebook paper and follow me," Greg commanded them. Then he addressed the rest of the class. "You guys carry on. Sorry for the disturbance."

As Greg led the two boys into the hallway, they snickered like nine-year-olds who farted at the dinner table. "I'm so glad you think this is funny," he said, barely containing himself. "Illiteracy and ignorance and apathy are all hilarious, especially when you're serving fries at McDonald's. A sense of humor and a full day's work will earn you, what, twenty bucks?"

One shrugged while the other mumbled, "Idunno," crammed together into one inarticulate sound.

"This is not an optional exercise," Greg continued. "You are expected to have a book, and you are expected to read it. That is, assuming you actually know how to read." He paused, waiting for some sort of verification.

"I know how to read," the mumbler said finally.

"Excellent," said Greg. "Yet you choose not to. Voluntary is the worst kind of ignorance."

"I am not ignorant," the boy replied.

"Actually, you are. Which you would understand if you looked up the definition in the dictionary. Of course, that would require you to *open a freaking book!*"

A freshman walked past on his way to the bathroom, his eyes never leaving the conversation as if recording a mental note that he must avoid Mr. Samson's class in the future, at all costs.

Greg continued, "Now, write the following note to yourselves: Bring a novel every Friday." He watched as they did as directed, the tiled wall serving as their desks. Only then did he realize he was still holding his stapler. When they finished writing, Greg stapled the notes to each boy's shirt and assigned them a remedial grammar worksheet, which they chose not to complete.

By the end of class, Greg knew he had messed up. Badly. He had acted without thinking, and in so doing, violated a cardinal rule of teaching by failing to respect his students' dignity. He wondered what kind of job a disgraced teacher would be able to find, especially when he would never get a recommendation from his principal.

That night, so worried was he by his egregious lapse in judgment, Greg did not dream. In fact, he barely slept. At two a.m., after lying in bed for hours while his mind raced with possibilities, he finally moved to the living room, where he watched an old movie until he passed out on the sofa for a couple of fitful hours before waking for Saturday morning cross country practice. The next night it was three a.m. when he staggered in his fatigue to the living room, then finally drifted off to an Ab Roller infomercial half an hour later. Over the two nights he considered every justification for his actions, and every repercussion. Suffice it to say that the justification column contained virtually no entries, whereas the repercussion column required a second page.

"I let two students get my goat," he explained to Amanda. "Two guys with the combined intellect of a badger and the combined ambition of a pebble made me lose my temper."

"Greg, teachers lose their tempers all the time," she reassured. "And you've been under a lot of stress."

"With more to come," he said. "First I'm gonna get nasty phone calls, then Darnell Lyon'll get a crack at me, and then Rumsford's gonna cut out my heart. Slowly."

He began the next week in a state of profound disquietude, fully cognizant that, when finally called before Rumsford's inquisition, his conduct would be indefensible. He hoped the school had replenished its goldenrod paper, although between his exhaustion and culpability he was incapable of crafting a lucid statement anyway. He hoped he could afford to replace the boys' shirts, that they were not spun from golden thread or woven by unionized elves. He worried that if he joined the Peace Corps, he would be assigned to someplace very cold, like Lapland or Yakutsk. He wondered if Amanda would wait for him until he returned. He doubted that his dad would be proud of him now.

Remarkably, though, he received not one single phone call, nor was he bidden to Rumsford's office. With each passing day he slept a little more and worried a little less until, finally, more pressing matters pushed the event from his consciousness. It was, he eventually decided, some sort of karmic payback for all the times he had gotten into trouble when he was right.

But as much as his terrible judgment, what gnawed at him was the fact that he still could not motivate the two boys to read.

Greg found himself sitting in a cramped, suffocating little booth, no larger than a Porta-Potty but without a door. How he managed to get inside did not matter. Dr. Rumsford sat beside him, two people sharing a space barely large enough for one. Rumsford wore tan slacks with a red smock and yellow hat, and her nametag identified her as "The Wolverine." Greg looked through the window, small enough that it could have been covered by a piece of notebook paper. Before him stretched a nearly endless line of vehicles—American luxury cars and sporty European models worth more than he would earn this year and next—snaking around the parking lot, down the street, and around the corner.

As each fancy car and its faceless driver pulled up to Greg's booth, Rumsford wordlessly handed them a souvenir from the school. The driver of the black Escalade was given a row of desks and a case of Scantron answer sheets. The Porsche 911 received a Xerox machine and three rolls of purple bulletin board trim. The SL550 collected a soda machine and a pallet of algebra textbooks. Size was irrelevant; everything fit somehow. A Harley-Davidson motorcycle was given an entire computer lab, and all thirty-two machines, tables, and chairs managed to fit into its saddlebags. And every one of the drivers had no face but perfect hair.

The school supplies were soon extinguished but, like the house at Halloween that gives out the best candy, the vehicles just kept coming, as if word of Rumsford's largesse was the hottest thing on the evening news.

A Lexus pulled up and Rumsford presented it with a plastic grocery bag, overflowing with an

indistinct but odoriferous red blob. A Hummer received what appeared to be the same nauseating gift.
Greg fought to suppress the churning in his belly. As
the next vehicle approached the window, Rumsford
reached into her chest and withdrew a handful of
vital organs, plopped them into a grocery bag, and
passed them out the window. Greg was not the least
bit surprised.

The line of cars now reached beyond the horizon
as Greg's colleagues appeared in the booth. One-
by-one, Rumsford harvested their innards and sent
them back to work with a dismissive wave. The black
Escalade returned, followed by the 911. Each left
with a bag of teacher guts and then magically re-ap-
peared in line a few cars back. The line never progressed. It only grew longer, cutting deeper into the
horizon, while the same seventeen vehicles passed
the booth in an endless loop.

Finally—he knew it would be only a matter of
time—Rumsford turned toward Greg and reached
out for him. His last thought was that he hoped he
ended up in the 911, since he had always wanted one
of those. And then he felt her hand plunge inside
his chest.

18

THE REVOLVING DOOR

"**A**nything else we need to talk about?" asked Ramona Thurlow. She was anxious to end the department meeting because she had not yet hiked today and the sun was dipping in the western sky.

"I have something," said Greg, raising his hand. "How many copies of *The Adventures of Huckleberry Finn* do we have?"

"About a hundred, I think," responded Thurlow. "But why? You're not planning to teach it, are you?"

"I am."

"I thought we decided we were going to get past the dead white men and teach literature that's relevant," she countered.

"Well, I would argue that just because it's written by a dead white guy, doesn't mean it's not relevant," Greg said. "*Huck Finn* is about friendship, peer pressure, abusive parents, individual integrity against groupthink, conscience, betrayal, racism, ignorance, intolerance, greed.... I'd say those are all just as relevant today as they were in 1885. Besides, Ernest Hemingway once said it's the greatest American novel every written."

"He did?" said Thurlow.

"He sure did." Greg pulled out a sheet of paper on which he had written his notes. "All modern American literature comes from one book by Mark Twain called *Huckleberry Finn*. American writing comes from that. There was nothing before. There has been nothing as good since." As the other English teachers stared at him, he added, "I wanted to make sure I didn't misquote."

Thurlow checked her watch. "If I say OK, how do you propose to teach it?" she asked impatiently.

"First I'll spend a couple of days describing and giving examples of various humorous devices, so students can look for them in the novel. I had to do that in a college class with *Catch-22* and it was a great exercise."

"What's a humorous device?" asked Katherine Bogard.

"Specific techniques used to create humor. Things like comic repetition or incongruity or comic deflation. I could share my materials if you'd like."

"No, that's alright."

"Anyway, we'll discuss the different kinds of irony, which leads into a discussion of satire. And tone. From there, I figure I'll talk about the traditions of local color in American fiction and how *Huck* fits into that. You know, what is realism and so forth? And that's a great lead-in to the discussion of the N-word and racism and why Twain isn't a racist."

"But he is," argued Katherine. "That word is racist, by definition."

"We have to consider the context of its use," Greg replied. "At the time the novel was set, it was the word of choice to describe African-Americans. We also have to consider whether Twain is using the characters to express his own beliefs, or to make fun of Southern ignorance. For crying out loud, Jim's the kindest, most gentle, most honest character in the book."

"OK, maybe," said Katherine.

"Anyway, then we'll talk about the various themes of the novel, and finish up with some sort of Socratic seminar."

"Sounds awfully high-level," Thurlow said, uncertain.

"Why yes," replied Greg, in a tone much different than Thurlow had used. "Yes it does."

And so Greg introduced *The Adventures of Huckleberry Finn* the Monday after Thanksgiving, beginning with Hemingway's verification of its worth. "This novel is guaranteed to offend many of you, entertain most of you, and if I do my job right, educate all of you," he said. "The thing is, classic literature is timeless. In other words, the themes are just as important today as they were when the book was written. I think every one of you will identify with something that Huck Finn goes through."

"Isn't this about the kid and the slave going down the river on a raft?" asked one student. "I saw the movie once. I'm never going down the river on a raft."

"Let me clarify," said Greg. "I didn't mean you'll do the same things Huck does in the book. What I mean is that you'll have to deal with the same issues as Huck. Like feelings that you don't fit in. Or how do you know if someone is a real friend? We'll identify the themes after we read the book, then we'll see if they apply to your life. Does that work?" The student shrugged in vague affirmation.

"Good," Greg said. "Along the way, we'll learn about humor, and history, and most of all about perspective."

"Wait a minute," said another student. "This book uses the N-word, doesn't it?"

"Two hundred and nineteen times," Greg acknowledged.

The student frowned. "Check it out, Mr. Samson. I'm the only black dude in the class, and Twain's a white guy, right?"

"He is," said Greg.

"So when a white guy uses the N-word, that's offensive," the student continued. "Not like I haven't heard it around here before," he added, looking around the room. Greg noticed a couple of students avert their eyes.

"Richie, I understand your concern. The best I can tell you is that, despite the word, I think it's not a racist book and I think I can prove it. But if you're uncomfortable reading it, talk to your parents and I'll let you choose another novel. But understand that you'll be flying solo if you do."

"You can prove it's not racist?" Richie challenged.

"If you give me a chance," Greg replied.

Richie crossed his arms and sat up assertively. "You haven't lied to me yet, Mr. Samson. Don't mess up now."

Greg smiled at the challenge, then picked up a handout from his desk. "We'll begin with a question-naire about racial beliefs. This is not for a grade, but it's an important part of our learning. There are no right or wrong answers, so please answer the ques-tions honestly. I repeat, please answer the questions honestly. I will collect it, but I promise you that no-body will see your answers. Not even me. It will be locked up in my filing cabinet until we're finished with *Huck Finn*. Any questions?"

The questionnaire, created by an educational publisher as a companion to teaching *Huck Finn*, proposed to assess changes in attitudes as students processed the novel. Greg purposely left the words "© Thinking Resources Workshop, San Diego, CA. May be duplicated for educational use" at the bottom of the page in case the copyright police stopped by. Some questions were easy, such as, "Would you consider yourself racially tolerant?" Others were more challenging, such as, "How do you feel about Affirmative Action?" But the most troublesome were those which were meant to arouse passions on either side, questions like, "Should black men be allowed to date white women?" The questionnaire was lengthy, and many students needed to take it home because they did not finish during the class period.

The next day, he received a phone call. During his lifetime, he had been called by agitated bill collectors with a quota to fill, pesky salesmen with a goal to achieve, and pissed off ex-girlfriends with an axe to grind. He had been jeered by Romanians when he beat their national champion in a 5-k and heckled by Chinese when he ran bare-chested through the streets of Beijing at sunrise. He had been called every name imaginable for every offense fathomable, few of which he was actually guilty of. By now, a couple years shy of forty, he had heard it all.

Or so he thought.

"What the fuck are you teaching?" it began.

"Excuse me?" Greg asked, more confused than offended.

"I cannot fucking believe that questionnaire you're making your students fill out. You have a lot of nerve getting that information from teenagers and then selling it to that racist organization."

"I'm sorry, ma'am, but I have absolutely no idea what you are talking about."

"Like fucking fuck you don't," she continued. Greg used his yellow telephone log to keep tally of her f-bombs, already up to four and the conversation less than one minute old.

"Should black men be allowed to date white women? What kind of fucking fuck is that?"

"Excuse me, ma'am, may I first ask who I'm talking to?"

"This is Gloria Fucking Jones. David's mother. And I want you to know that I'm going to call the fucking newspaper and the fucking School Board and tell them what you're doing."

"You're going to tell the newspaper that I'm teaching *Huck Finn?*"

"I'm going to tell them that you're a fucking racist and that you're selling information to the Thinking Resources Group, whoever the fuck they are, so they can send more racist garbage to my son."

Eleven so far.

"Mrs. Jones, that company provides educational resources. Nothing more than that. This particular item is—"

"—Don't you fucking cut me off, mister. You may think you're safe in your fucktopia, but as God is my witness I'm going to do every fucking thing I can to get you fired."

Fucktopia? Greg wondered. Fourteen. "Listen, Mrs. Jones, you don't know me but I can assure you I'm no racist, and either is the novel. The purpose of the—"

"—I told you not to cut me off. I've read *Fuckleberry Finn*, I mean, *Huckleberry Hinn*, *Finn*, fuck, whatever, and they say 'nigger' a lot."

"Mrs. Jones, I offered my one African-American student the opportunity to read a different novel. I'll make the same offer to you if you want your son to read—"

"—Fuck that! And fuck you and your racist KKK organization and your fucking survey and I'm not going to rest until you are fucking unemployed."

A late flurry to get to twenty. And Greg, who knew a thing or two about defamation, really wanted to tell her to go ahead and contact the press and the School Board, since he would love to win that lawsuit and be able to afford a house rather than his dinky apartment. More than once he opened his mouth to encourage her. But instead, he just said, "Thank you for your input, ma'am," and hung up. Then he wondered if he should wash his ears out with soap.

Over the next few days, Mrs. Jones called her son's Mentor Time teacher and let fly another barrage of f-bombs. When that failed to accomplish anything—and why would it?—Mrs. Jones then called Maurice McCullough, who simply said, "Greg Samson is not racist." When she started to protest, he added, "And I'm a black man."

"Fuck," she muttered, and hung up the phone.

The next day, Maurice found Greg during his prep period.

"What the fuck are you doing, man?" he whispered.

"Huh?" said Greg, shocked. "What?"

"I had to put my ass on the line for you with some foul-mouthed mother who thinks you're in the KKK. And I'm not even sure she's wrong."

"Oh, please, Maurice. Is this about *Huck Finn*? It's just a book. As we're reading it, I'll prove that the book is not racist. I guess that'll have to do for proving that *I'm* not racist. Although I think you know better."

"You won't prove anything because you're not gonna teach it. I will not go down with you."

"What if I duly note your warning but I teach it anyway?" Greg posed. "You're safe, and I'm just an impertinent employee."

"You'll be an imper—. What does that word mean?"

"Impertinent. It means disrespectful."

"If you teach the book, you'll be an impertinent former employee. I'll see to it that Dr. Rumsford cans your ass."

As Greg returned to class to retool, he was genuinely regretful that his students were being deprived of the opportunity for a change in perspective or, for some, a profound paradigm shift. What a fucktacular waste, he thought.

Another waste, minus the profanity, was the Vocational Education matrix Greg was required to complete for his Business Law class. This document was mandated by Sweetwater Unified School District No. 43 for all Vocational Ed classes, whether Child Development or Woodshop or Computer Applications. A dizzying array of squares colored either green or yellow, with asterisks and footnotes and subheadings, the document was so busy it was difficult to complete without getting a headache. And it was made even more difficult by the fact that it was originally developed in the early nineties to ascertain whether business classes were actually teaching business, and had never been updated to reflect the expansion of Vocational Education. Now, the Family Studies teacher needed to assess whether or not she was "Incorporating appropriate business case studies" into her curriculum, and the Woodshop teacher was forced to evaluate whether or not his students were "Engaged in strategic planning to anticipate future business needs." At least it gave Conrad Luper something to do, for he had spent the semester turning a paper document into the current multi-colored chart, a fact of which he was extremely proud.

When Greg checked his e-mail that afternoon, Luper's matrix was there. And it was due in three days.

But another e-mail was more pressing, this one from Dr. Rumsford: "See me before you leave today. —CR"

Another day in the life.

As Greg walked to her office that afternoon, he doubted that she would even listen to his explanation of the *Huck Finn* questionnaire extravaganza. Weary of the angst, he deliberated whether he should just resign.

"Is this about Mrs. Jones?" he asked, cutting to the chase.

"Who?" said Rumsford. Turns out Maurice had settled that one after all, albeit unsatisfactorily. So Greg considered alternate possibilities. Maybe he was double-parked. Maybe Rumsford wanted to shave his head.

"I just wanted to tell you that the Leadership Team has named you Teacher of the Month," she said.

"I'm sorry," said Greg, astounded. "What was that?"

"You are December Teacher of the Month," she repeated. "Congratulations."

"Thank you," he said, still thinking this was some sort of cruel joke.

"And this is for you," she said, offering him a potted houseplant. "I'm sorry about your father."

How ironic, Greg thought, that after busting his tail for a year and a half and teaching whatever Rumsford demanded and coaching a state championship team, it took his father dying for any of his work to get recognized. And how ironic too, he thought, that the remembrance of his father's death would be a houseplant he could probably keep alive for only a few weeks.

"By the way," Rumsford added, "no more stapling notes to students, OK?"

When Amanda came to Greg's apartment for dinner on Saturday, the plant was sitting on an end table and Greg told her the story. "I'm going to call it Harold," he said.

"After your dad?"

Greg smiled and hugged her so she would not see his tears.

Only days later, interim Superintendent Lucille Scholz fired Dr. Connie Rumsford. "As the last Teacher of the Month," Cockrell said to Greg, "I guess you're now Teacher of the Decade."

Two weeks later, after complaints about her lack of leadership from exactly seventeen Shadowcliff parents, Lucille Scholz was fired. And a lifetime of service to Sweetwater was instantly expunged before she had even unpacked her new office.

One would think the backlash would be cataclysmic, but in fact much of the daily business of schools goes on without the meddling of, indeed without the need for, administrators. Plus Maurice was still there, now as acting Principal. Otherwise, except for Greg's weekly visits with Rumsford, it was business as usual, which by the end of the semester meant fatigue was a constant, like a thirty-fourth student who never left.

Greg sat wearily at his desk at the end of the day. His month-long study of *The Adventures of Huckleberry Finn* had been replaced by an overview of Twain's other works, but a jumping frog and a time-traveling colonist were an unfulfilling replacement for the greatest novel in American history. Still, Christmas break was just days away, his students were bringing him cookies and gift cards, and he had outlasted Rumsford at Shadowcliff High School. When he realized that Gloria Fucking Jones had never called to apologize, he did not even care.

Dr. Robert Halter was a lifelong educator who had progressed from Science teacher to assistant principal to principal to the Sweetwater Unified School District No. 43 District office, where he now served as Administrator in charge of Secondary Schools. Following the most recent purge, he was also one of the last remaining EdD's at the District office, which made him next in line to ascend to the Superintendent position.

Vinnie Pantuzzi was a well-respected and even much-loved principal at Mustang High School, eighteen months from retirement and hoping to live out his administrative career with as little drama as possible. Which made him the logical choice to take over at Shadowcliff High School. He was also Dr. Halter's best friend, so he could hardly say no.

Pantuzzi was visiting his mother in Pittsburgh when the call came, and while he debated his fate he knew his argument was ultimately in vain. So when school resumed in January, Vinnie Pantuzzi was now in charge at Shadowcliff.

He was a good listener, but a man with his own convictions. He was firm but eminently fair. He maintained a sense of humor to go along with his sense of purpose. So while he may not have wanted to be at Shadowcliff High School, he was the man they needed.

One day Greg received an e-mail from Pantuzzi: "Please see me before you leave today."

It was, except for the word "please," no different than dozens if not hundreds of e-mails he had received from Rumsford. He wondered if this was the beginning of a similar relationship. But when he arrived at Pantuzzi's office, the man was actually civil. No, he was actually friendly.

"What's the matter?" Pantuzzi asked.

"You just smiled," Greg said.

"Is that a bad thing?"

"Well, this is my first high school teaching job, so my experience is limited," Greg explained. "But based upon that experience, I didn't think administrators were allowed to be human. I thought the job description required daggers and venom and laser beams."

"So I've heard," Pantuzzi replied. "We'll see how it works out."

He picked up a piece of paper from his desk. "I understand you know a young lady named Amanda Moretti."

"She's my girlfriend."

"Nice going. You think you could work at the same school as her?"

"Of course. We're both too busy and too directed to spend our time making googly eyes. Why do you ask?"

"I was going through some papers today, still trying to get moved in," Pantuzzi said, a sweep of his hand indicating the mess left behind by Dr. Rumsford. "And I found this." He held out the paper.

"Amanda's résumé," said Greg.

"When I read it, I thought, 'If this girl wants to work here, we sure as hell need to make it happen.' I'm going to call her and offer her a job for next year."

"Awesome," said Greg.

"By the way," said Pantuzzi. "Great work with the cross country team."

When he left Pantuzzi's office, Greg's smile was so bright that Kelli Weston spotted him from across the office.

"What are you so happy about?" she asked.

"Good day," he said. "Very good day."

"When are you going to use your law degree?" she continued.

"That's what I want to know," chirped Darnell Lyons, who was sitting in the lobby in his powder blue Italian suit. "Have you given any more thought to Ed Law?"

"Not interested," replied Greg coldly. "That would require my becoming a lawyer."

Already yapping on his cell phone, Lyon did not even hear Greg's answer. His flagrant violation of unenforced school policy exuded a smug confidence that whichever administrator was in power would capitulate as soon as Lyon unlatched his briefcase.

Yet the expensive lawyer soon found that Vinnie Pantuzzi was a more difficult nut to crack than Rumsford ever was. Lyon remained an integral part of the school's ethos, of course, but a less visible one, as Pantuzzi quickly revoked the privilege of free coffee and free office space in the Shadowcliff High School lobby. So Darnell Lyon relocated to the local

Chili's, where he poured over cases while billing his clients for his deep fried calamari.

Greg found himself at a rally of white supremists, only this one did not involve hoods and burning crosses and thirty packs of Bud Light and guys named Bubba and Jim Ed. Instead, there were couples with names such as Rance and Kimberly, imported silk shirts and two-hundred-dollar yoga pants, glasses of Pappy Van Winkle bourbon and crystal stemware filled with 1998 Dom Pérignon.

In the center of the room sat Socrates, attempting to engage the others in conversation. They were unimpressed. One by one they placed their glasses on fancy marble coasters, then stapled a football to Elden Ray Fong's shirt. None of them was chastised, and within minutes the Master Teacher was covered in pigskin.

Greg watched from the corner, occasionally hitting himself in the head with a geology hammer he had borrowed from Conrad Luper's toolbox. Meanwhile, Greg's dad, whose hospital gown flew open in the back with every step, flirted shamelessly with the maid.

Amanda arrived and suggested to Greg that they leave. Vinnie Pantuzzi held open the door, allowing them to quietly slip away. The Shadowcliff girls' cross country team ran past, and Darnell Lyon, waving a writ of mandamus, gave futile chase.

19

THE FOUR WORDS

Pantuzzi provided a sense of calm previously unknown at Shadowcliff. Teachers breathed and students smiled. Micromanaging was replaced by big picture thinking, negativity and fear by hope and goodwill. But this was still Sweetwater Unified School District No. 43 and still the government, so the new principal's superpowers extended only so far.

Greg's inauspicious morning was followed by a quick lunch of two PBJs and some applesauce, then a visit to his mailbox. Amidst the items accumulated since morning, he immediately recognized Randy Smith's handwriting, neat block letters he had known since childhood. The note said simply: "We need to talk."

The four most dreadful words in the English language are "We need to talk." These four catastrophic words induce physiological reactions ranging from whimpering to panic attacks. They have made brave men quiver and brought hearty men to their knees. Gloom and despair are their constant companions, dejection and ruination their unvarying conclusions. They represent the verbal apocalypse of the modern world.

These four words always precede the most dire of proclamations. When your dentist tells you, "We need to talk," he usually follows with, "You need a root canal." When your plumber tells you, "We need to talk," you can be sure that your sewer is about to explode. Your oncologist will assert that you have a tumor the size of a golf ball, and the IRS will inform you that you need to show up on Monday morning with your last five years of tax records. And of course, when spoken by your girlfriend, those four words are lead-in to, "I think we should see other people," which is dating code for "I think you are a complete loser." Then it's only drinking, misery, and Jerry Springer reruns, thus proving she was right.

Randy's and Greg's lengthy history had engendered between them a level of mutual honesty, confidence, and protection. Yet Greg had now been employed by Sweetwater Unified School District No. 43 for long enough that his trust in Randy was overridden by mistrust in the myriad administrative levels above him. With twenty minutes left in lunch period, Greg figured he may as well face his Judgment Day.

Passing the copy room, he noticed Marcia Hibbing, squatting ingloriously, her hand deep inside one of the copy machines. Marcia was a pretty young student teacher whom boys swooned over and fantasized about taking to prom, whom girls admired for her kindness and empathy, and whom her supervising teacher believed was going to make a fabulous educator. "Goddamn fucking piece of shit," she snarled, and Greg chuckled, knowing that Marcia Hibbing was gaining valuable experience in one of the many daily frustrations of her chosen field.

When Greg arrived at Randy's office, his friend was on the phone but waved him inside, passing him an ominous-looking envelope from the United States Office of Civil Rights.

Tens of thousands of solitary miles had cultivated in Greg a remarkable imagination. Many considered his imagination to be rather peculiar; some even called it bizarre. Yet he had traveled more than any of them and had plumbed the depths of oxygen debt and his own soul and fiber and sanity more than any of them, so he rationalized that his imagination was excusable. His first thought was this: Mrs. Jones has not given up her warped but glorious objective.

In mere seconds he envisioned the whole scenario. Mrs. Jones called the Office of Civil Rights and unleashed a twenty-minute expletive-filled diatribe.

The profane complaint made its way through the labyrinth of the federal bureaucracy, eventually landing on the desk of a sympathetic law clerk who prepared a memorandum which cited statutes, case law, and examples of Greg's bigotry and intolerance. Perhaps the complaint was buffeted by evidence of him stapling notes to his students' shirts or his horrible and misguided insistence on academic integrity. Soon there was an entire dossier of Greg's egregious lack of racial and social empathy. Greg knew that a civil rights violation was both a civil and criminal case, so he was facing hundreds of thousands of dollars in fines along with a hefty jail sentence in which he would share a cell with a large, hairy man who had not been hugged enough as a child. Greg wondered if Bob Cockrell would serve as a character reference.

But Greg finally realized that such a letter would probably come through the principal or even the Superintendent, whomever it was that day, so he put aside his exhausting speculation and opened the envelope. He found not a summons, not a criminal complaint, not a petition signed by thousands of aggrieved. Instead, he found a questionnaire. But since this was a questionnaire from the United States Office of Civil Rights, not merely a survey on carpooling or favorite bakery goods, it was still troubling. Not troubling in the nature of forced sodomy in the prison shower, but probably not a questionnaire he should blithely toss into the recycle bin either.

And, with more than one hundred questions, definitely not a survey he could complete in a few minutes. So he figured he would visit with Randy Smith now and worry about the OCR business after school.

Randy hung up the phone and turned to Greg. "Thanks for coming to see me," he said.

"What's going on?" asked Greg. "Am I fired?"

"Not likely," laughed Randy. "I just need to make you aware of the civil rights complaint we received. I've been given a directive by the District office to make sure I speak with each coach individually, and to ensure that they complete the required paperwork."

"This?" asked Greg, waving the questionnaire. "What's the deal?"

Randy shook his head at the absurdity. "Baseball," he said.

"What did Jeff do now?" asked Greg. Except for not knowing that baseball caps cause hair loss and strokes, baseball coach Jeff Dunleavy was one of the most fair and honest men Greg knew.

"Raised money," explained Randy. "The baseball booster club raised sixty-seven thousand dollars to install nice bleachers at the varsity baseball field. They had camps, solicited donations, you name it. Then the softball booster club filed a complaint.

They think the baseball boosters should split their proceeds fifty-fifty with softball."

"Why not?" said Greg. "They were considerate enough to stay out of the way so that baseball could maximize its revenue. It's only fair."

"Problem is, baseball already installed the bleachers. They wanted to get them done in time for the playoffs. But the Office of Civil Rights says they can't actually use them until they help softball raise enough money for an equivalent set of bleachers."

"Can't use them? Is there going to be some sort of bleacher police at home games?"

"Actually, yes."

"And what if someone decides to defy the bleacher police and sit in them?" asked Greg. "Will they get pepper sprayed? Beaten with a nightstick?"

"I don't know," Randy replied. "I don't want to find out. The District doesn't want to find out."

"So it doesn't matter that a good crowd for softball is ten parents and a dog?"

"Nope," said Randy.

"And it doesn't matter that when the school opened, there were no bleachers whatsoever at the baseball field, so everyone had to bring folding chairs?"

"Negative. It does make us look bush league, though."

Greg nodded, then continued, "I suppose now the boys and girls basketball teams will have to pool concessions revenue even though the boys probably generate twice as much."

"Correct, except it's more like four times as much."

Randy smiled weakly, and Greg knew his friend well enough to know it was forced, that the softball boosters and the District and the federal government had made this a priority issue and Randy now had to clean up the mess.

"Amazing," said Greg. "The school isn't even ADA compliant, so the two kids in wheelchairs have to wait outside until someone opens the door for them. But *this* is our biggest issue?"

"Apparently," Randy replied.

"Maybe the fans should start holding rallies and singing 'We Shall Overcome,'" Greg suggested. "Maybe girls' volleyball should sue and try to get half of the football revenue."

"Please don't encourage that," Randy said, grimacing.

"I promise," Greg assured him. "But what does this have to do with me?"

"Probably nothing," said Randy. "But every coach has to fill out the OCR questionnaire. You'll need to prove that all the money you raise for cross country and track is used equally for the boys and girls programs."

"So if I buy a three-hundred-dollar pole vault pole for an experienced, elite boy pole vaulter, I need to buy a three-hundred-dollar pole for a beginning girl who won't bend the pole anyway so she could probably use a two-by-four?"

"That's how I understand it," Randy said, shaking his head.

Throughout the rest of the day, Greg skimmed the OCR questionnaire. There were questions about equipment, transportation, and other routine administrative items. While his class was busy writing about the effect of rioting in Chicago on public perception of the Vietnam War, Greg discovered a question about uniform colors that concerned him slightly.

Was green (Shadowcliff's main color) a civil rights violation in-and-of itself under some case with which he was unfamiliar? Did it favor one gender over the other? Did it marginalize a protected class of people? Ultimately, though, he was unable to arrive at any reasonable conclusion, so he decided the question must be more about sufficiency of uniforms, and numbers, and age, although he was left to wonder if his choice of black shorts would lead to greater civil rights scrutiny in the future.

That afternoon, curious, Greg wandered over to the baseball game after track practice ended. This was a big game, against the very same Granite High School that Greg's cross country team defeated for the state championship last fall. Granite was a sports powerhouse, and its baseball team featured one of the state's top pitchers. Lawn chairs ringed the field, making it look more like a demolition derby or a pee-wee soccer match than a high school baseball game featuring two of Arizona's premier players.

There was only one place where people were not sitting. The brand-new bleachers were empty, cordoned off by yellow police tape and guarded by two school security officers and an armed United States marshal. The OCR was serious.

Greg stayed long enough to watch Shadowcliff's best hitter, Reid Harkness, a tall left-handed senior who, like Granite's pitcher, was being mentioned as a candidate for the Major League Baseball draft in June. The Shadowcliff community felt this would be a great thing because of the attention it would bring to the second-year school. The Shadowcliff faculty felt this would be a great thing because, while Harkness could hit a hanging curve ball four hundred feet, he could not write an essay or solve a simple algebraic equation or keep his hands to himself in the lunch line.

The first pitch was a slider, low and outside, and Harkness sliced it down the left-field foul line. Parents scattered as the ball rattled amongst the lawn chairs, and more than one parent's beverage flew from their hands. For a drug-and-alcohol-free campus, some of those beverages looked suspiciously frothy and golden. Harkness stepped out of the batter's box and surveyed the damage he had caused.

An impish smile came to his face and he turned to speak briefly to the catcher. As the parents returned to their lawn chairs and refilled their cups, Granite's catcher set his target for the next pitch. Again it was low and outside, in the exact spot as the last, and again Harkness sliced it foul down the left-field line. Parents again scattered, drinks again spewed, and the ball again clattered amongst the chairs.

As Harkness and the Granite pitcher exchanged surreptitious nods to confirm a brief conspiracy well-engineered, Greg saw several parents moving toward the cordoned-off bleachers. They were immediately stopped by the federal marshal, who offered only deaf ears to their arguments even as more parents arrived and the most adamant pushed forward. Randy hurried toward the bleachers to keep things from escalating, but a loud crack!—the unmistakable sound of Reid Harkness's bat crushing a baseball—stopped the debate mid-sentence. Heads swiveled simultaneously to watch the ball clear the right-field fence and land in lane three on the adjacent track, the exact spot where Greg's relay team had been practicing baton passes a short while before.

Shadowcliff parents began high-fiving. A few men, probably scouts, took notes. The Granite pitcher kicked the mound dejectedly while his catcher trotted out to talk. Parents retreated to their places along the left-field foul line, allowing the federal marshal to draw a relieved breath. And Greg wondered which federal agency would be involved if a member of his relay team had been killed by Harkness's blast.

Happy that question could remain unanswered, Greg retreated to his classroom, called Amanda, and began the questionnaire. An hour later, satisfied he was in compliance, he inserted the document into its envelope and began grading essays.

20

THE POCKET VETO

The next morning Greg dropped the OCR envelope into Outgoing Mail and then went in search of Samantha O'Bradovich. Typically, it worked the other way around. Once, she spent an entire day camped outside Greg's door in order to advocate for one of her Special Ed students. And that was not a story unique to Greg's class. O'Bradovich was relentless, and most teachers muted their annoyance at her interruptions with genuine respect for her tenacious advocacy.

They also appreciated her husband Stan, a hardy Irish-German-Australian who played his didgeridoo at the annual staff Christmas party. Because most of the teachers got pretty sloshed at the Christmas party, they likely would have been impressed by any sounds coming from an intricately painted hollow log. But, in fact, Stan was actually pretty good.

After Stan's dramatic finish to "Rudolph the Red-Nosed Reindeer," a few of the less-intoxicated teachers applauded and an overweight dachshund barked. "Isn't he wonderful?" Samantha asked rhetorically. She had six egg nogs in her by this point, all liberally embellished with Captain Morgan. Most murmured their agreement, although Frank Nixon announced that Stan's didgeridoo playing "sounds like a camel with bad farts."

Stan smiled wanly but Samantha was not so forgiving. She was on Nixon in a flash, and spent the next ten minutes lecturing him about Christmas music, Australian culture, aboriginal people, kindness, traditions, and the nutritional value of egg nog.

"She's quite persistent, isn't she?" Stan chuckled, a mix of pride and amusement.

"Yeah," Greg agreed, "whether advocating for her students or, apparently, the didgeridoo."

"Actually, she hates the didgeridoo," said Stan. "But she loves her students."

"You can tell. She's like a bulldog. And I mean that in a good way."

"I'll tell you something, though," confided Stan. "It's different now. Parents threaten her with lawsuits, and the District won't back her. So sometimes she feels like she has to advocate for students that don't even deserve it. It's wearing her down."

Greg remembered this conversation distinctly as he waited outside her door more than a year later.

"Hi, Greg," said Samantha. "Come on in. What do you need?"

"I'm here to discuss Troy Vandevort," he replied. Troy was a blonde boy in Greg's integrated American Story class who combined an infectious happy-go-lucky attitude with a burning desire to succeed in class. His friends called him Voldemort.

"I don't think I know him. Is he Special Ed?"

"I don't believe so," answered Greg. "But he should be." Off her questioning look, he added, "I'm pretty sure he's dyslexic."

With that, Samantha began typing on her computer. "What's the boy's name again?"

"Troy Volde ... Vandevort," said Greg, laughing at his own mistake. "V-A-N-D-E-V-O-R-T."

"Got it," Samantha replied after a moment, now reading the screen while Greg examined the posters on her wall. One talked about persistence, another about character. Then there was a photo of her and her husband and her husband's didgeridoo.

Greg was not a patient man by nature, but his distance running career had taught him the value of perseverance, since a ten-mile run today might not pay dividends for months or even years. So as he grew as a distance runner, he also became better at enduring horrible restaurant service or slow supermarket checkout lines. Awaiting a drink refill or paying for milk became meditative opportunities to hone his skill at staying focused upon distant objectives. But he never completely surrendered himself to the tranquility of the process; he was still a goal-oriented person. He wanted the refill, the milk, or the good race.

And now he would wait as long as it took, because he liked Troy Vandevort and respected the boy's work ethic and wanted him to receive the services he so desperately deserved.

So Greg reread the quotations about persistence and character and tried to figure out where the photos were taken and tried to recall other quotes about persistence and character and thought about the workouts his track kids would do leading up to the state championships and wondered why he never tried to play the didgeridoo. He thought about Amanda. Most of all, though, he thought about Troy Vandevort.

"Troy Vandevort can't be dyslexic," Sharon finally announced.

"Why do you say that?" asked Greg. "I mean, I recognize this is your area of expertise, but since you don't know him and I have him in class, I would respectfully disagree with you."

"His grades are almost all A's and B's," she replied, "even in text-intensive classes. He got a B in your class last semester, and I know you don't skimp on the reading."

"True, but—"

"—And his scores on the state reading tests all exceed the standard," she continued. "He was in the eighty-fifth percentile last year."

Greg was unconvinced. "But the state reading test does not have a time limit. I'll bet he needed extra time to finish. Maybe hours."

"All that proves is that he's a slow reader," she replied. "Lots of kids are slow readers. There's no way you can convince the District office or the Department of Education that a kid with these reading scores is dyslexic."

"Let's put this in terms I understand," said Greg, and Samantha nodded for him to continue. "Let's say I have a kid on the track team who has only one leg. And let's say this kid runs ... hops ... the mile in four minutes and twenty seconds, which would be fast enough to score at the state meet. And everyone would be pointing, going 'hey, that kid has only one leg.' But despite the obvious evidence that he has only one leg, the District office and the Department of Education would decide that because he ran really fast, he must actually have two legs. Is this an accurate analogy?"

"Yes and no," said Samantha, thoughtful. "See, there is no evidence that Troy has one leg, I mean, has dyslexia. Plus, as I said, he's always been a strong student."

"So the fact that Troy works his butt off to overcome his disability and get B's proves—"

"—He's a junior in high school and nobody has ever asked for him to be tested," Samantha said.

"And nobody has ever threatened litigation on his behalf," added Greg.

"That's true, too. But officially, he cannot be dyslexic."

Greg reached into his pocket, pulled out a piece of paper, and offered it to Samantha. "Troy's class notes." Samantha read the first line:

> The Chcigao roits invloved Yippies prosteting the Veitnam War during the covnentoin to choose the Democatric nominee for Predisent.

"Troy Vandevort has dyslexia," she concluded, the four words he most wanted to hear.

At any high school, some students are simply more visible than others, and some more invisible. When Joe Schmoe is absent, nobody really gives a damn. Troy Vandevort, as much as people like him, is still only missed by a few. But when Autumn Kessler is absent, people notice. Especially when they find out she is on another trip to Paris.

Just like in August, speculation intensified quickly. She was eloping with a rich European, or with George Clooney. She was filming a movie. She was going to be on the cover of *Maxim*. Most were disappointed to find out her only purpose was to buy a dress.

But what a dress.

With its pricey limos and fancy dinners and rented suits and uncomfortable backyard photos and liquor purloined from Dad's bar, prom season always brings hope to high school juniors and seniors. It had better, when tickets cost a hundred dollars a couple and guys routinely drop a grand just for a date with a girl they thought was cute in March but now, in April, are not that into, and vice versa.

Autumn's sheer electric blue prom dress was custom designed in Paris to accentuate her remarkable paraboloids, a perfect example of the distinction between the letter of the law and the spirit, a dress intended to be as revealing as possible while still conforming to the guidelines of the school dress code. The tension between her anatomy, the forces of gravity, and whatever support was being somehow provided by the strapless gown was really an object lesson in the interplay between engineering and Newtonian physics. Autumn Kessler had no idea about Newton's laws, and probably would have guessed they had something to do with figs. Chang Yi and Matt Ramirez could have explained it to her and even done the calculations, but they were not at prom.

People gawked when she arrived, people tried to brush against her on the dance floor, and people she had never met wanted to take pictures with her. It was almost criminal to be her date—her longtime boyfriend, the football captain, ever-stymied by Autumn's strict No Trespassing policy. And prom night, despite its potential and the assistance of Dad's vodka, proved no different. A single millimeter of French silk stood in his way, an electric blue size six fortification as impenetrable as the Soviets outside Leningrad. If the rest of the student body had been aware of this cruelty, they would have collectively wept on his behalf.

Three weeks later, the week before final exams, Autumn Kessler received official invitation to become a member of the University of Arizona cheerleading squad, on two conditions. The first, of course, was that she graduate high school, so she enlisted Chang Yi and Matt Ramirez to provide some last-minute math tutoring. The boys worked for free, and happily, probably because the tutoring sessions took place at Autumn's swimming pool and her damp bikini reminded them of the glory of that fateful October afternoon. Thanks to their enthusiastic assistance, she earned a C in Algebra two, and her diploma.

The second condition, also involving breasts, was much more expensive to fulfill. The day after graduation, Autumn Kessler took her third flight to Paris within the past year, where she visited the Merci Beaucoup Breast Enhancement Center in order to have her celebrated tits reduced by two cup sizes. Her father had now spent the combined annual salaries of Jimmy Clayton, Bob Cockrell, and Keri Zabriskie with the net gain of one expensive custom dress Autumn could no longer wear. But at least she now fit into a U of A cheer uniform. Plus she graduated as Shadowcliff High School's first *bona fide* legend. Maybe they would put her bra in the trophy case. As an added bonus, having accumulated more than thirty thousand frequent flier miles, Autumn earned a free trip to visit her boyfriend at his college in Indiana in the fall, a trip she never used.

Meanwhile, among the mortals, Sweetwater Unified School District No. 43 exercised its pocket veto and Troy Vandevort remained officially non-dyslexic.

Greg found himself at an IRS audit, where an amorphous ex-girlfriend called him a fucker for being a loser who spent too much time in supermarket checkout lines. The IRS agent attempted to perform a root canal on Greg, with Voldemort assisting. Unfortunately, Voldemort only provided written directions, which were indecipherable, so he called Greg a fukcer.

The phone rang, Greg answered, and Mrs. Jones called him a fucker. Autumn Kessler, her breasts inflating and deflating, recited Newton's Law of Universal Gravitation: "F equals G times the quantity m sub one times m sub two divided by d squared!" An armed federal marshal kept the crowds away. Everyone cheered, then called Greg a fucker.

As it began to rain, an old lady rode in on a farting camel and, on the phone, called Greg a fucker. Then Frank Nixon threw a didgeridoo onto the track, killing Greg's relay team just before the sewer exploded.

2007 - 2008

21

THE MESS FROM TEXAS

Yet another school year brought yet more change to Sweetwater Unified School District No. 43, this time in the person of yet another Superintendent. But this Superintendent was different. She wore heels and spoke with a drawl. She was an outsider. She was recommended by Elite Educational Talent Search LLC, an administrative headhunter which matched her résumé with the needs of Sweetwater Unified School District No. 43 and received a fifty-thousand dollar fee for doing so. Recruited from a suburb of Dallas, Dr. Patty Sue Morning was chosen on the basis of her leadership, innovation, communication, integration of technology, and perhaps most of all, her ability to inspire the public. A crucial bond election was looming, only three months hence.

As one of the shining stars of Arizona education, Sweetwater Unified School District No. 43 had never worried about funding before now. A young, vibrant community, most of its residents had kids in the District. The success of these schools—whether measured by empirical data such as graduation rates, SAT scores, acceptance to top-tier universities, or property values, or by less concrete but no-less-important metrics like prestige value—virtually guaranteed the passage of any measure that would ensure continued excellence for just a few extra dollars per year. For more than a generation, newcomers had selected Sweetwater as their landing-point-of-choice due to its stellar reputation, and families in other parts of town aspired to purchase a home within the Sweetwater attendance boundaries. But the landscape was changing.

First of all, school districts in other Phoenix suburbs were creeping up on Sweetwater Unified School District No. 43 in the various objective measurements. Second, the situation at the state legislature was alarming. A conservative wing of the state Senate had managed to control the education debate by bullying the opposition into submission. Suddenly, funding for public schools found itself slashed and the money diverted to private school vouchers and subsidies for charter school construction. Angry letters and picketing followed, but accomplished little.

Finally, the carousel of leadership at the top of Sweetwater's hierarchy was disconcerting to many, and dysfunctions which were unimportant when Sweetwater represented the gold standard suddenly found voice as the competition ratcheted upward.

So while Dr. Morning was officially charged with recapturing the stability that had marked Sweetwater Unified School District No. 43 for decades, her biggest challenge was making sure the bond was approved by voters in the November election.

Dr. Morning was also expected to restore the flagging spirit of Sweetwater teachers, whose enthusiasm had been tangibly dissipating while the District careened aimlessly from one leader to the next. Toward that objective, she organized a "teacher retreat" for the Friday prior to the first day of school. So Greg dutifully filed into the gymnasium of Bonanza High School with Amanda Moretti, new teacher in Shadowcliff's Global Scholars Program and, as of June, his live-in girlfriend.

When Amanda decided to move in, the couple relocated to a two-bedroom apartment in the same complex as Greg's previous place, just minutes from Shadowcliff. But even with an extra bedroom, they still needed to purchase new bookshelves to accommodate Amanda's massive library. After the curriculum seminar at which they met last year, Amanda had spent more than two hundred dollars on half a dozen reference books personally recommended by L. Fred Mandeville. Just a month ago, while attending a Global Scholars training (paid for out of her own pocket, since Ramona Thurlow was so busy planning her summer trip to Italy that she neglected to submit a funding request to the District office), she purchased another five books. Like a Las Vegas high roller who received valet parking, free meals, and a complimentary suite with each visit, her Amazon account permitted Amanda to order educational books with just a few clicks, something she did almost weekly. Greg wondered if they should ask for valet parking, meals, and a free room at the International Academic Publishers' trade show.

Then there was Amanda's collection of novels, including the entire Virginia Woolf collection and the books that literary people were supposed to read but never did, the ones Amanda said she would get to "someday": *Don Quixote* (unabridged version, just under one thousand pages), *An American Tragedy* by Theodore Dreiser (which became a rather dull movie, Greg thought, despite Montgomery Clift and a stunning Elizabeth Taylor), and of course Marcel Proust's *Remembrance of Things Past*, a dastardly six-volume boxed set that Greg occasionally used as a doorstop when he unloaded groceries from the car.

Greg loved to read and possessed an insatiable appetite for knowledge, but he also possessed a library card. However, Amanda argued that, over the course of the school year, they would recoup the costs of books and bookshelves by carpooling to and from school each day. Although Greg pointed out that her math was fuzzy and the two variables mutually exclusive, Amanda prevailed nonetheless.

As the couple entered the gym together, the noise was already thunderous. Teachers, whether recharged from their brief summer hiatus or complaining because they were tired from teaching summer school, carried on animated conversations describing trips to Europe or to visit grandchildren, about kids' soccer camps or travelling baseball teams, of camping in the woods or buying a new sofa. Some stories were truly exhilarating, like the teacher who hiked three hundred miles atop the Great Wall of China or the counselor who worked in an orphanage in the Caucasus region of Asia. Others were so mundane that it would almost make a person cry until she realized her life was just as boring. Henry David Thoreau famously said, "The mass of men lead lives of quiet desperation." Among them were some who actually taught Thoreau during the school year, then reorganized their storage room over the summer.

Greg led Amanda to the east bleachers, beneath a Shadowcliff banner, where forty or so teachers were already seated and the number growing rapidly. She had previously met Bob Cockrell, Keri Tanner, Jimmy Clayton, and a few other Shadowcliff teachers from having joined an occasional Happy Hour, and they began chatting like long-lost pals. Greg abhorred these environments, which made the solitude of distance running the ideal pursuit for him, but they were Amanda's forte. Within five minutes, she met the entire staff, found a new workout buddy, joined a book club, and gained invitation to a bridal shower. A bald guy Greg did not know whispered in his ear, "Your girlfriend is awesome." Greg turned to agree, but at that moment a tall, confident, well-coifed woman in a burnt-orange skirt and flowered blouse took to the podium.

"Good morning everyone," the woman said, voice oozing central Texas. The raucousness dropped to a low hum, and many of the teachers in attendance answered "Good morning." "Now y'all know something about me," she continued. "I like when people say 'good morning' to me because, you know, that's my name. So let's try it again, shall we?" And then, authoritatively: "Everyone."

"Good morning!" the audience responded as one. Greg turned to Amanda and said, "I sincerely hope this isn't the first step in the indoctrination of the Hitler Youth." He was answered with "Shh!"

"Welcome to a new school year," she said. "As y'all have probably figured out, I'm Dr. Patty Sue Morning, y'all's new Superintendent. And I'm guessin' y'all have figured out I'm from Texas. But I am honored to be here as y'all's leader." Greg cringed at the overly autocratic sound of that. "I would now like to introduce some people y'all'll be learnin' more about as the year goes on," she continued.

"First, this is Dr. Beatrice Rayburn." Dr. Rayburn stood up and waved. She was a smartly dressed woman with short, dark hair and perhaps a bit too much makeup. "I brought her with me from Texas because she's the best staff development professional I know. As Assistant Superintendent, she'll be in charge of curriculum development and teacher training programs." The applause was underwhelming, teacher training programs being about as popular as rectal exams.

"Next, this here is Dr. Dave Jesperson. Dr. J will be my right-hand man, working on technology and student services." The welcome was, again, less than enthusiastic, because many people knew that two of Sweetwater's best administrators, including previous interim Superintendent Dr. Robert Halter, had been jettisoned to make room (and salary) for Dr. J.

"One o' the things I'm committed to doing is improving the experience for all of our stakeholders. That's parents, students, and the community...."

"She missed teachers," noted Greg.

"... Words are empowering, and we want to empower people. Toward that goal, y'all'll find that some people have new job titles. For example, bus drivers will now be known as Transporters of Learners." A buzz started among the crowd. "And front office staff are now Directors of First Impressions. But let's remember that all o' y'all is responsible for making a good first impression. And every one of us," she continued, indicating the sharply dressed, highly salaried imports around her, "is responsible for helpin' y'all have a great year. One o' my goals is to improve communication. So if any of y'all need anything from me personally, I would invite y'all to call me or send me an e-mail, and I'll get right back to you.

"And now, I'd like to allow Dr. Rayburn and Dr. Jesperson to speak to y'all for a few moments. Thank you kindly for y'all's time, and I wish you a great school year."

Dr. Rayburn and Dr. Jesperson each addressed the crowd for a few moments, rather superficial remarks in Greg's view. Then, for the next hour, an endless succession of District administrators took to the podium. The District Director of Pedestrian Safety (formerly a part-time position in charge of training crossing guards) promised increased supervision of drop-off and pick-up areas around school. The District Director of Horticultural Enhancement and Community-Space Aesthetics (formerly head groundskeeper) promised the grass would be mowed. The District Director of Lubrication (formerly oil-change guy) promised school buses would run better. Vapidness filled the gym, and as the teachers grew evermore restless, the low buzz of muffled conversations became louder and louder until finally the District Director of First Impressions could not be heard. She smiled feebly, stepped away from the microphone without another word, and several minutes passed before the teachers realized the "retreat" was adjourned and it was time to report to school.

Vinnie Pantuzzi opened that afternoon's faculty in-service with words of promise. "I want to make sure we get finished quickly so you'll have time in your classrooms this afternoon." Next to free food, time was probably the most precious commodity an administrator could bestow upon his staff. As always, there were desks to arrange, syllabi to copy, and first-day activities to plan, all under the constraints of the fact that students would report in two-and-one-half days and, already, one of the three copy machines was out of service.

"Also, I just want to say that I hope we have a smooth and trouble-free year. As most of you are aware, this is my last year before retirement, and I'd like to make it an easy one." Then, after a pause, he added, "As if that's possible."

Pantuzzi allowed that one to linger awhile, then said, "Now I need to introduce some new staff members." In fact, there were nearly thirty new teachers among a staff of about eighty, so Pantuzzi added, "We've had some turnover, and we also added about five hundred new students, so this is gonna take a while." As returning teachers swiveled in their chairs to survey the new meat, Pantuzzi began. Amanda, who was scheduled to teach five classes in the Global Scholars Program, was warmly received by all the new friends she made at Dr. Morning's good morning group hug. Ben Koch, the bald guy who had spoken to Greg in the bleachers, was the new Theater teacher, the son of northern California hippies. It took nearly a quarter of an hour for Pantuzzi to get through the entire list, which was not a good sign when he had just promised to keep things short.

Most schools in the District needed to replace only about ten teachers each year: a few due to retirement, some to transfers, others due to marriage or babies, and occasionally because a teacher found a more attractive job selling real estate or working at Costco. Shadowcliff's disproportionately high number should have alarmed anyone at the Sweetwater Unified School District No. 43 offices who bothered to pay attention to such statistics. While the new Superintendent and her Texas cronies were probably unaware of Shadowcliff's turnover rate, those who worked in Human Resources and Payroll were acutely conscious that teachers were bailing out of Shadowcliff at unprecedented frequency. At least now their alarm was tempered by the esteem of their new titles, such as Director of Risk Protection Programs (formerly insurance tech) and Director of Computational Analytics (formerly bookkeeper).

Greg's own endeavor at changing his job title was a half-hearted one this time around. With a conviction that a champion should do its best to defend its title, he wanted to be part of the cross country team's efforts to repeat. Plus Pantuzzi had given him the opportunity to teach Advanced Placement Literature in addition to his American Story and Business Law classes. Clearly the original concept of Shadowcliff, that of eschewing honors classes in fear of hurting someone's feelings, had been abrogated in just two short years in favor of a more traditional approach.

Thurlow pushed Greg for the AP class with the logic that it was a college-level course and that, in addition to his recent college experience, Greg had years before also taught a couple of composition classes as an adjunct at a local community college. As the school year progressed and Greg learned more about the expectations of AP and the abilities of his students, he recognized Thurlow's folly. Sure, he loved teaching the class and thought he was doing a good job, but the AP students were so far above the community college students that it was like he had been chosen as President of the United States because he was once a tour guide at the White House.

By the time Pantuzzi finished introducing the new teachers, the applause for the newcomers had grown faint and everyone had grown restless. "Sorry, that was long," Pantuzzi said, "but we need to keep going. This is the big one." And with that, he began describing the various technology upgrades and innovations available for teachers. "They've promised lots of resources, along with trainings to introduce them to you. I know change doesn't come overnight. It'll be a process, but by the end of the semester, Dr. Morning expects you to be utilizing many of these tools in your classrooms."

Reactions varied. Younger teachers, far more technologically savvy, seemed to have no issues with the new edict, but Greg noticed Thelma Bourdain, a veteran World History teacher, shaking her head vigorously. Counting on the fact that the history of ancient Mesopotamia was unlikely to change thousands of years after the fact, Thelma assigned worksheets in class nearly every day, most of them Xerox copies of smeared and faded dittos first created in the 1980s. This might have been a good thing, actually, since when she wrote on the board the jiggling flab underneath her arm was revoltingly hypnotic. Because they were close friends, Dr. Rumsford deflected the criticism and allowed Thelma to continue her onslaught of worksheets. New leadership might not be so accommodating.

Pantuzzi continued, "There are also some technological changes that will be more immediate. This year, you'll each have an individual website and you'll have the ability to post assignments." This garnered mostly positive responses. Some teachers immediately recognized the time savings in not having to make extra copies of everything. Others simply ascertained that the distinction between "ability" and "requirement" gave them a semantic loophole if necessary.

"Starting from the very first week, you'll be required to update grades at least once a week and post them to the internet. As I said, this is a requirement."

"This is bullshit is what it is," said Jimmy Clayton, louder than he wanted.

"I'm sorry, Mr. Clayton? You care to comment?"

Clayton probably did not wish to elaborate, but now he was stuck. "I just think all this is going to take a lot of extra time, which we don't really have as it is. I mean, I teach The American Story and Video Production and run the campus TV station."

"For Christ sakes, Jimmy," Frank Nixon blurted out, checking his watch. "We don't need your résumé. We all do extra stuff around here." He had told anyone who would listen that he had a three o'clock appointment with a new quarterback transferring in from Iowa Falls Central High School.

"Yeah, but you get paid, what, six thousand bucks for your extra stuff?" Clayton responded.

"I did the math on it," Nixon said. Keri Tanner had once told Greg she was uncertain if Nixon could multiply, so now she sat up alertly while Greg turned to Amanda and said, "We know he can't do the math on bar tabs."

"I figure I make fifty-eight cents an hour as a coach," Nixon averred. "Fifty-eight cents an hour. So it's not like I'm getting rich."

Greg looked at Keri and shook his head, knowing Nixon just fabricated that number for dramatic effect. The calculations were easy. The coach's alleged rate of pay would have required him to coach ten thousand hours per year, hardly possible in the 8,544-hour year of the Gregorian calendar used in the United States and throughout most of the world, including every country that played football. Plus Nixon had teaching obligations to ignore, worksheets to photocopy, and golf to play on Sundays. And it was a fair bet that he slept. If you require every possible hour plus another fifteen hundred that don't even exist in order to win five or six games a year, Greg mused, perhaps you aren't a very good coach.

Pantuzzi waited for the mini-drama to play out before continuing. "The thing is," Pantuzzi explained, "many teachers become comfortable with their routines, and that's understandable. But the world is a different place than when we were in school or when we started our teaching careers. Our students are different, our resources are different, our technology is different, and like it or not we need to keep up. There is no other industry on earth where people do things the same way they did a generation ago. The door-to-door salesman is dead." Some teachers nodded, acknowledging his logic.

"Not only that, how many phone calls or notes do you get from parents asking about grades? Five a week? Ten? You post grades on the internet, you don't have to deal with that anymore."

Over the summer, Pantuzzi revealed, a committee consisting of parents and District-level administrators had met several times to discuss grades. "Now I'm supposed to show you a video," he said.

"Good morning!" the video began cheerfully, even though it was mid-afternoon. In the video, Dr. Morning explained that the goal of the grading committee was to create a consistent and transparent system for evaluating students, so that an A in one teacher's class demonstrated the same level of mastery as an A in another teacher's class, and an F at one school demonstrated the same lack of mastery as an F at another school. She further explained that she had listened to their concerns and offered some ideas based upon her own experiences in Texas. By the end of the summer, the committee made its recommendations, the School Board approved, and now assessments counted as two-thirds of a student's grade while homework and classwork counted one-third. The computer grading program would be locked to these proportions, she said, concluding that the work of the grading committee would make everyone's job easier. Although she never said how.

When the video concluded, Pantuzzi offered his take. "Now, if a student complains about his grade, all you have to say is, 'I'm just doing what the grading committee tells me.'" He smiled wryly as he did when he knew things didn't quite add up.

Pantuzzi went on to emphasize that the new technology directive was more than just posting grades. Dr. Dave Jesperson, new Associate Superintendent, would lead efforts to incorporate technology as a teaching tool through the use of projectors, laptops, tablets, websites, virtual classrooms, and subject-appropriate technology-based curriculum. It sounded dazzling, challenging, captivating, and a bit overwhelming.

"Mr. Koch?"

The bald man stood up like the trained actor he was. "I think incorporating technology into our classes is great, although it's easier in some subjects than others of course. My question is: Will I be penalized if I don't use technology as often as an English teacher?"

"For now, there is a handout available at the back of the room explaining how to get started," Pantuzzi explained. "Going forward, teachers will be trained by the District on appropriate uses of technology in their classrooms. Then you'll be expected to do what you can. Which brings me to the next item.

"Evaluation. A reminder, this is the first year of the state's new pay-for-performance system. Your performance will be evaluated by several measures. These include, uh...." He pulled out his notes before continuing. "These include parent and student surveys, differentiation of your instruction, and scores on state standardized tests."

Again Mr. Koch's hand shot up. "So just to clarify," he said, standing, "we are being asked to differentiate our instruction but standardize our evaluation. Is that correct?"

"That's correct," Pantuzzi replied. "Remember—"

"—But that's absurd," interrupted Koch. "It's completely nonsensical." From this point forward, Greg referred to the new Theater teacher as Mr. Kochlöffel, a German cooking spoon. A spoon to stir things up. After a year's hiatus, the spirit of Ike Gravenstein had returned to Shadowcliff.

"Mr. Koch," said Pantuzzi calmly. "Let me explain it this way. If you want the world to make sense, you need to get out of public education."

And the veteran teachers, for all intents and purposes, shouted "Amen."

For the first time in three years, Greg did not have bizarre, vivid dreams the night before the first day of school. He was unsure if this was because he was getting comfortable or because he now had Amanda's soft breathing beside him. It certainly was not because of disinterest. Greg told his athletes that butterflies were to be expected before races; they showed that a runner cared about his performance. Over time, the butterflies would calm down but would always be there. When they completely disappeared, it was time to retire, which explained why Greg ran just a few local road races these days. But the first day of school still held a sense of excitement for him, even though he was glad to be rid of the nightmare.

As had now become a District-wide procedure, Monday was fifteen-minute getting to know you periods with little stress and absolutely no expectations. Rumsford was gone but not forgotten, this being one of her ideas. The day began with a brief welcome video from Dr. Morning, all business in her all-black outfit. She welcomed everyone to school and taught them to greet her with a hearty "Good morning!" Greg was a bit concerned about the new students moving to Arizona from the east, those who arrived in late August only to discover that school was already two weeks going because it started when the air temperature was still well into hellish triple digits. How would they learn to greet the commandant as expected?

Otherwise, Greg enjoyed an easy morning, ate lunch with Amanda, and then spent the afternoon trying to recruit distance runners from the freshman PE classes. That evening, he had six new freshmen at cross country practice and went home tired but contented.

Greg found himself in front of his first period class, prepared and confident. His objectives were on the board and his syllabi were in a neat stack on a table in front of the room. After welcoming his students, he picked up his class roster and a pencil. "Roger Anderson?" he asked. "Susan Arnstadt?" He realized these same students had been on his roster each of the last two years.

Suddenly, students began to point, then to snicker, then to laugh robustly. He was standing before the class naked. Again.

Greg was no longer confused, since this had happened before. This was not the way master teacher Elden Ray Fong said it would work, but Greg, as a third-year teacher, had learned to adapt.

But before he could remedy the situation, Dr. Patty Sue Morning rushed through the door. She was wearing a black leather corset, black fishnet stockings, black gloves, and jet-black cowboy boots. A Dallas dominatrix. In one hand she carried a grade book, in the other a black leather riding crop. "Good morning!" said the students in unison, but Greg, dumbfounded at her intrusion, said nothing. Dr. Morning looked at him mischievously.

"Mr. Samson, you naughty boy," she said. "You didn't say the magic words." And then she began to whip him.

22

THE IN-SERVICE

The second day was the first "real" day of classes, a day for teachers to distribute their course syllabi and then read them word-for-word. This procedure, formulated years ago by some long-retired District-level administrator, was considered the best methodology to ensure against any potential misunderstandings and the litigation that sometimes followed. The practice was now entrenched, without question or deviation, throughout Sweetwater Unified School District No. 43. At the end of each period, students shuffled off to another class where that teacher would once again read his syllabus word-for-word, while their previous teacher would read her syllabus word-for-word to another group of students who had just been subjected to the same experience in their previous class. It seemed like a giant hamster wheel, except that every hour more hamsters and more wheels are added so that, by the end of the day, a million hamsters have run on a million wheels and nobody has gotten anywhere. Students quickly learned to tune out the whole process, rationalizing that they could text their friends now and read the syllabus later. Of course, they seldom did. Sometimes the really smart kids who wore glasses and sat in the front row on the first day actually paid attention, but by lunchtime even they were beaten down. In fact, the only things produced by this process were hoarse, exhausted teachers and bored, uninformed students. Actual brain activity on the second day of school was but a rumor.

Greg despised this methodology and finally decided to ditch it in favor of a more hands-on activity in the computer lab. Instead of the standard routine of distribute-read-bore-repeat, Greg uploaded his documents to his class website. Students were to log in, download the syllabus and the assignment, and then utilize the syllabus to answer questions about class expectations. His content was no different than that of any other teacher on campus—bathroom passes and late work policies and other procedural banalities—but his method of delivery was both consistent with the District's commitment to technology and a more engaging way for students to learn. Of course, that was a very low bar on this day. Additionally, the activity allowed Greg to get an early glimpse at his students' basic computer skills, and it allowed every student the opportunity to begin the year with an A, since the answers were all right in front of them if they were the least bit thorough.

Best of all, it was a lot less stressful than talking for five straight hours. Greg explained the assignment and then sat back to watch.

The first problem arose within seconds. "My login isn't working," one student said. "Either is mine," said another. As Greg circulated around the room to trouble-shoot, more and more hands went up. After ten minutes of fruitless effort, Greg decided to call the District Director of Digital Facilitation (formerly tech coordinator), who informed him curtly that the logins were not yet activated.

Throughout the week, Greg found he was unable to post any more documents, update grades as required, or even add a simple message to his school website. Suddenly, the shoe was on the other foot, as veteran teachers were able to safely retreat into their anachronistic pencil-and-paper world while digital natives floundered in desperation, their lesson plans reduced to "read the textbook and answer the questions." E-mails started to fly between teachers, first in the same department, then at the same school, then District-wide. The exchanges began as pleas for help, but when help proved unattainable, the tone changed to frustration and eventually to anger. Meanwhile, Site-Based Technology Managers (formerly campus techs) were being called upon to fix problems that were above their pay grade and, often, their knowledge.

At the end of the second week, teachers throughout the District received the following e-mail:

> From: Dr. David Jesperson
> To: Sweetwater Unified School District
> No. 43 staff
> Subject: Technology concerns
> Sent: August 21, 7:29:53
>
> We understand that the current technology issues are challenging for many of you. We are aware of your concerns and are working on a solution. Please be assured we have a target date in mind. Thank you for your patience.

Greg opined that the first day of school might have been a nice target date, but too late for that now.

At its first meeting of the year, the School Board offered a stern rebuke to the District Director of Technology (a legitimate title), commanding him to do whatever Dr. Jesperson directed in order to rectify the situation.

"If Dr. Jesperson says jump, you say 'how high?'" commanded the School Board President, who worked as a criminal defense attorney. "If he says stay until midnight, you stay until one a.m. If he says you need to walk to Alaska to get a piece of equipment, you start walking. Are we clear?"

"Yes, ma'am," said the Director of Technology numbly.

Unfortunately, Dr. Jesperson had left town that morning in order to drive his daughter to college at Texas Tech, leaving his cell phone on his desk in Sweetwater.

The School Board also commanded Dr. Morning to manage the onslaught of angry teacher e-mails, so the next day she ordered the District Director of Electronic Communication (formerly e-mail tech) to limit staff messages to no more than three recipients. This did nothing to resolve the actual crisis, and made departmental collaboration far more problematic, but at least it minimized the unfettered District-wide complaining and appeased the School Board for the time being.

With his job at stake, the Director of Technology unveiled a plan to rotate the Site-Based Technology Managers between schools. This made little sense, as both principals and Site-Based Technology Managers themselves tried to clarify, and certainly failed to address the problem at hand. The Director of Technology explained that the current system was inequitable, since some of the Site-Based Technology Managers were far more skilled than others. Rotating them, he explained, would put each school on equal footing. Dr. Morning endorsed his idea enthusiastically.

"Great plan," said Greg the next day at lunch. "Now nobody's technology will work."

"Like it already doesn't?" Cockrell asked.

"Seems to me we have some teachers who are better than others," Greg continued, "yet we don't rotate them."

"That's a good point," said Keri. "We train them."

"That is, assuming Dr. Rayburn is better at her job than Dr. Jesperson seems to be at his," Greg answered.

"And then what about the students?" asked Keri. "Some of them are certainly smarter than others."

"Also true," said Greg. "Maybe we should just rotate everyone. Each week, students change schools, teachers change schools, administrators change schools...."

"I like it," said Clayton. "But only if District administrators change districts."

On Thursday of the third week of school, every teacher in Sweetwater Unified School District No. 43 mustered in Shadowcliff High School's spacious auditorium for the first professional development session of the Morning regime. Shadowcliff was selected because it had the best facility, but it was also at the farthest extreme of the District, so teachers would need to drive as much as forty-five minutes to get there. That meant the in-service could not begin until four p.m. and was scheduled to last until six. Greg hoped it would end a few minutes early so he could make it to cross country practice, but just in case, he had instructed his assistant coach on the day's training. He spent ninety minutes grading and planning, then called Amanda's cell phone to make sure she would arrive on time. With her remarkable focus, she could get lost in planning and not even realize she missed an appointment, meal, and once or twice an entire night's sleep.

"Thanks for calling," she said as she met Greg outside the auditorium. "I didn't even look at the clock. I would have worked right through it."

"I know," he said. One evening over the summer, Amanda was sprawled out on the sofa reading *The Grapes of Wrath*, part of her quest to complete the entire Steinbeck catalog during the month of June. "I'm going for a run," Greg announced. "Be back in about an hour." Sixty-two minutes later, he walked in the door and she was still reading. He showered, microwaved a burrito, and opened a beer. Only then did she look up, saying, "Were you going to run tonight?" She stayed up until three a.m. to finish the book. The next night, when she was in the same position reading *East of Eden*, Greg sat down next to her, gently held her face like the Little Nutbrown Hare so she was looking directly at him, and told her "I'm going for a run." She nodded, but her nod was so vacant that he was doubtful if it ever registered that he was gone.

As they entered the auditorium, they were handed an agenda by the District Duplication Process Coordinator (formerly photocopy person). Greg thought Suzi Cooter deserved such a title, but her daughter had graduated so she no longer worked as a Copy Mom. Greg and Amanda slid in next to Keri Tanner and waited for the show to begin.

"Our first presenter is not...," Dr. Morning began, only to be silenced by a tremendous wave of feedback. Many of the teachers plugged their ears at the sonic assault. "Don't get so close to the microphone," Dr. Jesperson suggested, so she tried again from farther away. "Our first presenter...." H-u-m-m-m-m-m-m went the sound system, ever louder to match her growing impatience. She glared at the District Audio Coordinator (formerly AV assistant) who was working the sound board at the rear of the auditorium, but he was too busy turning knobs and adjusting slides to notice her ire.

"I said, our first...." Now the sound system responded with an ear-splitting click-click-click, a horrible sound which finally convinced the District guy to throw up his hands in defeat. Koch jumped from his seat and ran up the stairs to the sound board, pushed the Coordinator out of the way, and made the necessary adjustments.

Audio issues finally resolved, Dr. Morning continued. "Our first presenter is not on y'all's agenda. We just hired her, and she's done a fabulous job of sifting through all the data for today's session. So I'd like to introduce Dr. Fiona Carvalho to y'all. Dr. Carvalho has a bachelor's degree in Psychology, a master's in Applied Mathematics, and a doctorate in Analytical Statistics. She is an expert on standard deviation, linear regression, univariate and ... what's that word?"

"Multivariate," said Dr. Carvalho.

"Oh, of course. Univariate and multivariate functions. She wrote her dissertation on, uh, Cheb— ... Cheb—"

"—Chebyshev's Theorem?" offered Neil Fortune, Shadowcliff's AP Calculus teacher. He was wicked smart.

"That's right!" said Dr. Carvalho, who had apparently just made a new math geek friend.

"Chebyshev's Theorem is my second-favorite unknown Russian postulate," Greg whispered.

"You know more than one?" asked Keri Tanner.

"Sure. Yakovlev's Model of Supercompensation. It's the foundational theory of physiological adaptation to training." Amanda, not surprised in the least, could only smile and nod.

"And what's Chebyshev's Theorem about?" Keri asked.

"No clue," said Greg. "You're the math teacher. You tell me."

Dr. Morning continued, "Dr. Carvalho has worked as an insurance actuary and in market research. She brings a wealth of insights about how we can use statistics to inform our work."

"Notice what she doesn't bring?" Amanda whispered. "Teaching experience. The woman's never been in front of a classroom in her life."

"You mean that's important?" asked Greg facetiously.

"And now," said Dr. Morning, "let me formally welcome Dr. Fiona Carvalho." A few people applauded as Dr. Carvalho approached the podium. She had a pale complexion, sturdy legs, and a bottom that spent too much time in an office chair. She moved the computer mouse and a blue screen was projected behind her.

"Hello everyone," Dr. Carvalho said. "I'm sorry I couldn't be here for the teacher retreat. I was in transit from Minnesota."

And now she was typing.

"I can't seem to log in," she said, then tried again with the same result as the audience grew restless. Dr. Morning glared at Dr. Jesperson. Finally she said, "But fortunately I have copies of my PowerPoint for you to follow along." Jesperson quickly volunteered to distribute the thick packets.

Dr. Carvalho spent more than half an hour explaining various statistical measures she had analyzed, including grading trends over the past decade, absentee rates, and Pearson product-moment correlation coefficients to illuminate relationships between family income, education, and student achievement. It was way over most teachers' heads, and most returned to grading quizzes or playing solitaire on their smartphones. Even the math teachers began to get antsy. Greg possessed the great ability to endure pain like nobody else in the building, plus he brought neither a smart phone nor papers to grade, so he hung on like grim death. Only Neil Fortune was able to follow her entire presentation, and he found her captivating.

She read almost every word on every PowerPoint slide, which were duplicated nine to a page, so small that most of the text and all of the data were unreadable. But she seemed to have the numbers memorized. "The correlation coefficient is 0.93641," she said, not even consulting her notes. As you know, any r value over 0.7 is considered a high degree of correlation."

"You knew that, right?" Greg asked Amanda, who appeared to be in a numerically induced stupor.

"Knew what?" she replied, speaking on behalf of everyone.

But eventually the blitzkrieg of numbers came to an end and Dr. Carvalho relinquished the podium to Dr. Morning. "Thank you for that most enlightening overview," Dr. Morning said. "I'm sure everyone gained a greater understanding of the mountains of statistical data we analyze every day." Greg noticed that Dr. Morning sported the same glassy-eyed look as Amanda and most of the audience.

"I need to run back to the office. I'm sure y'all understand that I'm busy," she said, managing to simultaneously insult nine hundred busy teachers in less than ten seconds, which Dr. Carvalho would have believed to be statistically impossible. "Before I leave, though, I'd like to introduce Dr. Beatrice Rayburn." As Dr. Rayburn came to the podium and began typing, Dr. Morning slipped out a side exit. "Logins aren't working, remember?" reminded Dr. Jesperson, who looked as if he wished he were utilizing the same side exit as his boss.

"Oh, right," she growled. But when she turned toward the audience, she immediately became Miss Perky. "Hello everyone," Rayburn began. "Thanks for your attention so far. My job today is to take Dr. Carvalho's statistics and apply them to our immediate issues. Unfortunately, since I thought I would be able to use my PowerPoint, I don't have a handout for you to follow along." Her quick sideways glance at Dr. Jesperson was obvious.

"I will be focusing on our District objectives and aligning them with measurable state standards," she continued, reading from her notes. "While what you teachers do is certainly an art, it has also been enhanced with the advent of modern analytics. The Texas ... I mean Arizona ... Board of Education has developed a number of statistical measures to ensure our students are getting the education they deserve. These standards quantify student performance and allow accurate measurement of every district, every school, and every student in the state.

"Now, I don't think it's any surprise that Dr. Morning expects Sweetwater to be the best district in Arizona, so let's take a look at these numbers."

Greg had received his teaching certification through a little-known quirk in the licensing process rather than a conventional teacher training program in college. Unencumbered by traditional methodologies, he had little use for the concept of teaching to the test. "To clarify," Greg whispered contemptuously, "teaching is now just a computational exercise?"

For the next hour, at least, it was. It sounded more like finance class, where every decision is guided by a strict risk analysis and numbers rule the day. But they were dealing with young people, by God, with hopes and dreams and fears and challenges and phobias and anxieties and talents often beyond our comprehension, living and breathing human beings not as easily quantified as annual rate of return.

Dr. Rayburn's talk finally concluded, it was now Dr. Jesperson's turn. Teachers shifted in their seats, their butts tingling like Novocain and their minds a Zen teacup overflowing numbers. It was quarter to six, and they had been bombarded with data for more than ninety minutes.

"We want to make sure we respect your time," said Dr. Jesperson. "And my colleagues have done such a brilliant job under difficult circumstances that I think maybe we've had enough for one day. I'll be doing site visits in the next couple of weeks, and we can talk more at that time. Thank you for—"

Nobody heard the rest amidst the mad dash for the exits. Greg ducked out another side door and managed to make it to cross country practice on time. Twenty minutes into the run, he noticed Dr. Patty Sue Morning through the window at Starbuck's, where she appeared to be reading *Vogue* magazine and enjoying some sort of Frappuccino.

23

THE PANTY BANDIT

Greg finally met Dr. Jesperson a couple of weeks later, during Dr. J's site visit. The administrator was scheduled to spend his entire day at Shadowcliff, with a few minutes in each class and more as necessary. Although he termed this a "fact-finding mission," he never failed in his attempt to impart some Solomonic wisdom or point out a teacher's particular shortcomings.

"This would be better in small groups," Jesperson fact-found a math teacher during her lesson on polynomials, oblivious to the fact that small-group work is particularly ineffective if nobody in the group knows how to do polynomials. "This would be more authentic with a guest speaker," Jesperson fact-found the Physics teacher during his lecture on Archimedes' Principle, as if the ancient Greek himself were currently working the drive-through window at the local Taco Bell, just waiting to put down the chalupa and explain the concept of displacement. "You really should differentiate this," Jesperson fact-found the Special Ed English teacher, who taught a class of twenty-six kids ranging from AD-HD to autistic, from emotionally disturbed to learning disabled, all with their own Individualized Education Programs.

Greg's turn to meet Dr. Jesperson came just before lunch. His fact-finding began with the recognition that Greg was the cross country coach, a fact he likely divined from the cross country team bulletin board in the back of Greg's classroom. Moments later the bell rang and students hurried to lunch, leaving Greg and Dr. Jesperson alone.

"You're the cross country coach, huh?" he began.

"I am."

"I didn't like to run myself," Dr. J said. "I figure I only got so many heartbeats in my lifetime, and I don't want to waste any of 'em."

Greg knew that his one hundred fifty beats per minute for two hours a day plus forty beats per minute for the rest meant he gained three full days of heartbeats every week compared to Dr. Jesperson's constant eighty beats per minute. But since he was not yet clear on either the purpose or the hierarchical dynamics of this meeting, Greg chose not to respond to Jesperson's chuckle.

"I played baseball instead. North Plano High School. Started in center field for three years. I was pretty fast, though."

Greg had run for much of his lifetime, and had been in too many social interactions where people felt compelled to explain their own views on running, always unsolicited. He labored through them in the same painful way he was able to endure workouts turned ugly. This, he thought, was looking like such a workout.

"In fact, I was the fastest guy in school," Dr. J continued. Greg, who knew exactly where this conversation was heading, hoped Dr. J would not notice his lips moving. "Coulda anchored the relay if I wanted to, but like I said, I didn't like to run." The words "didn't like to run" flashed through Greg's head nanoseconds before Jesperson delivered them.

This was familiar ground now, so no more difficult than a blister. He knew this would be uncomfortable but not unmanageable. Greg nodded involuntarily at that notion, which Jesperson took as an invitation to continue.

"I remember one day in PE class, I ran the four-forty in forty-five flat." Since that would have made the Olympic final back in 1972, or whenever Jesperson was in high school, Greg assumed they simply ran once around the field and decided that was close enough.

While Greg's running career was never an occupation, it was certainly a commitment, plus in his best years he actually won enough prize money to pay his bills. So he wondered how, for example, a doctor would respond if Greg began to explain why he distrusted medicine, or an auto mechanic if Greg began to explain why he disliked cars, or Dr. Jesperson himself if Greg began to lecture him on the questionable scientific research about education.

Worse, Jesperson was nowhere near finished. "Then I went to college at North Texas State and majored in education," he said. "I could have started on the baseball team if I went out, but I decided to focus on my academics. You know how it is." And Greg, who made Dean's List every semester as an undergraduate while also training year-round and working a part-time job, said simply, "Of course."

"Plus running is bad for your knees," Jesperson continued. "That's a medical fact." Although never supported by any respectable medical research, Greg had heard this one the most. Determined not to betray himself with an absent nod of the head or an inadvertent movement, he held his breath, something he was capable of doing for a very long time. Yet Dr. J sat patiently until Greg finally broke. "I guess that's true," he said. "Every old cheetah I've seen is in a wheelchair."

Some people never actually listen but, interested only in the sound of their own voice, simply wait for their turn to talk. Clearly, Jesperson was one of those. And, having grown uninterested, he missed Greg's sarcasm completely. He now surveyed the walls of Greg's classroom, as if they would allow him to divine the quality of Greg's teaching and per-haps even of his soul. If so, Greg's soul was in trou-ble, since he spurned the posters, colored bulletin boards, glittery borders, and cute tchotchkes favored by his colleagues. He preferred to leave the walls mostly bare, to be filled up with student work over the course of the year.

"Well, I need to go now," said Jesperson finally. "I have lots of ideas for making your classes better. Nice talking to you."

As Dr. J scurried out the door, Greg realized the administrator had never even asked what classes Greg taught.

The next day, Greg decided to eat in the faculty lunchroom, where the consensus on Dr. Jesperson's fact-finding mission seemed to be one inescapable fact: the man talked too damn much.

"Of course he talks too much," offered Greg, pausing from his homemade turkey sandwich. He had not bought lunch since the lasagna question dur-ing Shadowcliff's first year. "He has administritus."

"What the hell's administritus?" asked Clayton.

"I just made it up," Greg answered. "A disease found only in school administrators. Too much pow-er and too little empathy, too many answers and too few questions."

"Good one," said Jeanette Candelaria, taking a bite from her Cobb salad.

After they finished eating, Jeanette and Greg walked toward the office together.

"I'm glad I'm out soon," she said.

"Wait," said Greg. "You're leaving us?"

Jeanette nodded. "One more year after this."

"And then what?"

"Lots and lots of golf."

"That was my dad's retirement, too," said Greg. "One summer he decided he wanted to play Hilton Head, so he drove straight through, forty-five hours with a couple of naps in his car. He gets there and it's raining. He checks into his hotel and it rains for two days. So he gets back in his car and drives forty-five hours back to Arizona. The day after he leaves South Carolina it's seventy-five degrees and sunny. He gets home and it rains for three days here."

Jeanette laughed. "I just plan on playing Sweetwater Country Club a lot," she said.

As they passed Kelli Weston's desk, the pretty receptionist looked up from her computer and asked, "Greg, when are you going to use your law degree?"

Greg shrugged. "I promise, whenever I do, you'll be the first to know."

Greg and Jeanette continued on, and Greg explained, "She asks me that all the time."

"If you're going to do it," offered Jeanette, "you'd better do it soon. Because teaching sucks you in and you never get out."

Greg realized he had never considered her choices. "You tried?"

"I have a Marketing degree, but I thought I would teach for a couple of years," she replied. "I got certified and got a job and now here I am, twenty-seven years later."

"You're really good at it. Any regrets?" asked Greg as they arrived in the mailroom.

"Teaching is one of the most noble and rewarding professions on earth, and don't let anyone tell you any different. It's the business of education that sucks the life out of you."

Greg withdrew a catalog of educational videos, whose back cover offered: *This month's special— Diarrhea Is No Laughing Matter, only $24.99.* "Jeanette, you think I could work this into my curriculum? Maybe during my Civil War poetry unit?"

"Well," she snickered, "if anyone can do it, you can."

Greg's AP English class was watching a video clip from the Orson Welles version of *Othello* when his phone rang.

"Hello...? Yes, this is Coach Samson." The caller was the same crabby old lady.

"There were more than one hundred of your kids in my front yard yesterday," she complained. And this time, she sounded like she was ready for bear.

Greg crawled underneath his desk to muffle the call. "One hundred kids?" he asked for verification.

"That's right."

"In your yard?"

"Yes."

"I'm afraid that can't be correct. You see, we have forty-three kids on the team, plus two coaches. One kid was absent yesterday, and we had two parent volunteers. One kid was late. By my math, that's forty-five, which is a lot less than one hundred."

"It's about the same," Crabby Lady protested.

"Really it's not. Besides, the hill we were running is a public street, and there are gated communities on both sides of the road, so I'm guessing you live behind one wall or the other. Which means that unless every one of my kids called a friend and then they all hopped your fence, you must be mistaken."

"I know what I saw."

With Pantuzzi now in charge, Greg realized that an annotated bibliography was no longer necessary and a more assertive approach was warranted. "Ma'am, you've now called me three years in a row. Cross country is kind of overlooked, so I'm delighted that you're aware of our existence. But may I ask, is your entire premise that all teenagers are evil?"

"Well, um...." Crabby Lady paused for a moment, then finally affirmed, "Yes."

"Then I recommend you call our principal, Mr. Pantuzzi," said Greg. "He's a dedicated lifelong educator, so I'm sure he'll be totally receptive to that theory."

Greg told Amanda about the call, and his history with Crabby Lady, as they shared highlights of their respective days.

"At least I have become the nation's greatest expert on runner right-of-way laws," he said, referring to last year's annotated bibliography. "Maybe I'll retire from this nonsense and become a professional expert witness."

Amanda smiled. "I'm sure that sounds much more lucrative than it really is."

Amanda Moretti had run competitively as a high school student in Long Island, New York, then recreationally through college for both physical and mental health. Now, with a teaching load of five Global Scholars classes, she had lots of work to do and little time to run, but she made it a point to put aside her Type A personality and join the cross country team for a couple of runs each week. That was a great arrangement for Greg; not only did he get to see his girlfriend more frequently, she was also a great fit for some of the girls. Cross country runners tend to be introverted and cerebral, and many established an easy rapport with the bright, personable, outgoing new teacher. When they ran together, they discussed philosophy and politics and literature and boys.

Soon, the first words many of them said at practice were, "Is Ms. Moretti coming today?" Greg was often tempted to say, "Hey, I'm smart too," but he knew that on the days Amanda showed up, everything worked better. He could assign his assistant coach to run mid-pack and then sprinkle various parent volunteers throughout the group, allowing him to push the top boys toward the success the girls' team had already achieved.

Since Amanda was not an official coach, she did not have a locker in the coaches' locker room. Instead, she simply locked her door, turned out her lights, and changed into her running gear in the most remote corner of her classroom. After completing the run, she would return to her room to plan tomorrow's lessons while Greg stretched with the team, then they would preserve the book budget by carpooling home together. Occasionally Amanda needed to stay late, so on those days Greg ran an easy two miles home and then prepared dinner for when she dragged herself in the door. She was a great teacher, and along with three other new teachers was doing magic in the Global Scholars Program, transforming it into the high-level, critical-thinking, inquiry-based program it was supposed to be. But she was already dragging a lot.

Ramona Thurlow, on the other hand, who had virtually nothing to do with the transformation but who still took credit, appeared to be more energetic than ever.

One evening, Amanda finished running with the team and then retreated to her room to prepare for tomorrow's classes, while Greg finished up at practice and then made sure everyone had a ride home. After the last kid was picked up, Greg walked through the building, pausing just a moment to notice a bare spot in the carpet. He recognized it as the exact location where, two years before, he saw Dr. Rumsford on hands and knees with the thick purple cleaning solution. Her stuff had eaten through the carpet.

When he arrived at Amanda's classroom, the lights were out and the door locked. This was unusual for her to go home so early, early being a relative term. But it was no great inconvenience; Greg could easily run home in about twelve minutes. He turned to leave but then decided to take one more peek inside, contorting himself to look through the narrow window. And there she was, sitting silently at her desk in the dark.

Greg was perplexed. He had never seen her at rest unless there was a novel in front of her face, a beach below her chair, or a pillow beneath her head, so he doubted she was meditating. When he tapped lightly on the window, she gasped and popped straight up, like toast.

Fanning herself with one hand while placing the other on her chest to calm her heart, she finally made her way to the door and opened it for Greg to enter.

"Honey, what's wrong?" Greg quickly asked. "Why were you sitting in the dark like that?"

"I am really freaked out right now," she answered.

"I'm sorry. I didn't mean to—"

"—No," she said. "It's not you. It's...."

"It's what?"

There was a lengthy pause as Amanda struggled to regain her composure. Then, finally, she said, "Someone stole my panties."

"What? Are you sure?"

"I am now. This isn't the first time."

"It happened before? Why didn't you tell me?"

"I thought maybe I accidentally dropped them," Amanda explained, "or I was so tired that I spaced out somehow. But ever since then, I've been careful. So now I know they were stolen."

The next day, Amanda knocked on Pantuzzi's door to deliver the uncomfortable news.

"Someone has been stealing my underwear," she said.

"Someone has been...?," Pantuzzi replied, a little red-faced. "How is that possible?"

"When I was at cross country practice. Someone came in the room and stole them."

It did not take long to cross-reference the list of people with keys to her classroom against the list of people who were on campus after six p.m. the previous evening. The bandit was undeniably Paco, the custodian responsible for cleaning the section of Shadowcliff that included Amanda's classroom. Pantuzzi picked up the phone and placed a call to the District office. When he got Errol Strothers, District Director of Advocacy, Policy, and Regulatory Affairs (formerly general counsel) on the line, he put the call on speakerphone.

After explaining the situation, Pantuzzi concluded, "I want that guy fired, immediately."

"Can't do it," Strothers responded. "First of all, you have no proof. He has rights. And I assume he's Mexican. We'll get sued for sure. I think the case *Higgins v. Assmann Electronics, Inc.* is on point."

"Assmann?" repeated Pantuzzi, trying not to laugh. "You've gotta be kidding me."

"That's a real case," Strothers affirmed.

"OK, fine," continued Pantuzzi. "Then I want him suspended."

"Can't do that either. Since we contract out our custodial services, we have no direct legal control over his employment. *Taylor v. Graham County Chamber of Commerce.*"

"Then what do you propose we do?" asked Pantuzzi, his patience wearing thin. "Wait until he does something worse?"

"You'll need to catch him in the act," said Strothers. "Maybe plant a hidden camera. Or tell the teacher to be more careful. In fact, from what you've told me, I'm pretty sure the teacher is in violation of the Teacher Code of Conduct. I think it's on page sixty-seven."

"Wait a minute," Amanda cried. "You're saying this is *my* fault? That's ridicu—"

"—Sorry, it's page sixty-five. 'A teacher will demonstrate proper manner of dress when on duty, on school property, or at off-campus school functions.' You'll need to submit a TDR, a Teacher Discipline Report."

"I know what a TDR is," Pantuzzi responded. "Thank you for your time." He angrily punched the speakerphone to disconnect, then stood seething for a moment.

Finally, Amanda asked, "You're going to write me up?" She struggled to hold back tears.

"The hell with that," Pantuzzi said. "They can kiss my meatballs."

"But won't you get in trouble?"

Vinnie shook his head. "I'll tell them I misunderstood. You actually said 'candies,' not 'panties.' I'm old. My bad."

Amanda smiled at this island of compassion amidst a vast ocean of idiocracy.

Pantuzzi continued, "I'll keep an eye on the guy. In the meantime, can I make a suggestion?"

She nodded.

"Keep your underwear in your desk drawer, OK? And lock it."

Amanda smiled and dabbed at her eyes, then moved in for a hug.

"No hugs," Pantuzzi said. "Go teach. Go be wonderful."

Stifling a laugh, Amanda said, "That guy's name was 'Assmann.'"

"Can you imagine going through life with that name?" Pantuzzi asked. "I thought I had it rough."

As technology issues inched toward resolution, teachers were not the only ones exasperated. Parents grew evermore frustrated at both the problems themselves and the lack of communication about them, prompting the Oligarchy to organize a community coalition armed with time, vitriol, and Dr. Morning's e-mail address. The Superintendent soon grew so tired of responding to nasty e-mails that she finally ordered the District Director of Physical Assets (formerly inventory clerk) to remove the computer from her office.

At one point, the District Director of Technology was asked by a reporter from the *Sweetwater Sentinel* about complaints by the Site-Based Technology Supervisors, who pointed out work was more difficult now that they were disconnected from their schools. He answered, "They don't work for the school, they work for me." The reporter's follow-up question, why they were still referred to as "site-based," went unanswered. The next morning's edition featured an op-ed piece in which the Editor stated, "In fact, due to profound mismanagement, they don't really work at all," and noted that Dr. Morning could not be reached for comment.

It was not until the sixth week of school before Sweetwater Unified School District No. 43 finally resolved its technology problems. The next day, Dr. Jesperson fired the District Technology Director.

Now that the problems were fixed, grades were being posted to the internet on a regular basis. And now the problems inherent in the new grading proportions became apparent. While one-third homework and classwork and two-thirds assessments seemed easy enough, it was in fact fraught with gray area. Did a project count as homework or assessment? Was an essay written in class an assessment, or was it classwork? What about simulations? What about extra credit?

Shadowcliff parents seized on every discrepancy, contacting teachers in order to exploit each inconsistency for their sons' and daughters' best advantage. One night, Amanda told the story of Elida Singh, a first-generation American whose parents and grandparents emigrated from India following the Union Carbide disaster at Bhopal. Amanda had assigned her junior-level Global Scholars classes an in-class activity in which groups of students were to analyze five different translations of *The Decameron* to observe distinctions in diction, syntax, and organization, and ultimately discuss whether these distinctions impacted Boccaccio's meaning in any way. Elida received a C on this activity, which brought her class grade down to a B.

Online grades were sold to teachers as a tool to avoid unnecessary parent inquiries. Parents would no longer need to ask the teacher, "Have you graded Suzie's math test yet?" because they could just check the website. What was not conveyed, and perhaps not even considered, was that parents would now have instantaneous access to any grade fluctuations and, as a result, teachers would have real-time complaints to deal with.

Elida's father called Amanda and demanded to know why his daughter now had a B. Amanda explained that Elida's performance on the in-class activity caused her overall grade to drop. Elida's father then demanded to know why this activity was classified as Classwork/Homework rather than Assessment. Amanda explained that it was completed entirely in class and was meant as a tool to teach students about the power and delicacy and specificity of language. Elida's father then demanded that it be reclassified because Elida's test scores were nearly perfect so, if this counted as Assessment, she would keep her A in the class. Amanda refused. He asked why. She said because it was not an assessment. He said Amanda should give his daughter a better grade. Amanda refused. He asked why. She said because Elida had not done her best work on the activity and did not learn all she might have. He again demanded the assignment be reclassified. Finally, Amanda asked the million-dollar question: "The goal of Global Scholars is to teach kids to become thinkers. Are you telling me that Elida's grade is more important than that?"

"Elida is going to Cornell," the father answered. "To become a doctor. All we care about is her grade."

To her credit, Amanda held firm and the grade remained as classified. Mr. Singh, unsatisfied, called Vinnie Pantuzzi, then Dr. Jesperson, then finally Dr. Morning herself. Dr. Morning then called Pantuzzi and directed him to speak with Amanda.

"You're confident this is an accurate grade?" Vinnie asked her.

"I am."

"And it definitely belongs as classwork?"

"Absolutely."

"OK then," he said. And that was all.

A week later, Elida aced her test on *The Decameron* (Amanda feared the consequences at home if she didn't) and got her A anyway. That night, as a reward for her integrity, Greg took Amanda out for Italian food at a local place called Boccaccio's. He loved the irony, plus their garlic bread was outstanding.

Greg himself had to deal with a parent phone call on occasion, but utilized Pantuzzi's suggestion as his best defense and simply blamed the District's grading committee.

As the end of the quarter drew near, it became apparent from the chatter that parent complaints about the grading system were increasing. In the faculty lunchroom, most teachers could offer a story about a recent uncomfortable conversation. Pantuzzi related that he had fielded many such phone calls himself. So had Dr. Morning, who grew so tired of the annoying interruptions from concerned parents that she finally ordered the District Director of Physical Assets to remove the telephone from her office.

One week before the end of the quarter, the District Director of Parent Communication (formerly PR assistant) sent a letter home to each parent explaining that online grades would be taken offline for a couple of weeks to allow teachers to concentrate on their last-minute grading. With more than twenty thousand families in the District, costs for printing, envelopes, postage, and manpower exceeded ten thousand dollars. Greg wondered why they could not just post the notice on each teacher's website, since that's exactly where the parents would be going to check grades if they cared anyway.

To many parents, this rationale sounded completely bogus. Because it was. In fact, Dr. Morning had ordered each principal to examine each teacher's grades to ensure that every assignment was properly classified. Parents did not know the actual reason, but when a program that has been put forth as being entirely transparent suddenly goes dark, questions are bound to arise.

In the northeastern edges of Sweetwater Unified School District No. 43, the Oligarchy of seventeen parents simultaneously called "bullshit" and sent Darnell Lyon on a three hundred dollar an hour visit to Dr. Morning. The meeting was brief, and Errol Strothers, District Director of Advocacy, Policy, and Regulatory Affairs, advised Dr. Morning to heed Lyon's advice. That evening, online grades were live once again.

24

THE ELECTION

"Greg, did you see this?" screamed Amanda. Since Greg was in the shower, he could not ascertain if "this" was a dead cockroach or an alien encampment on the patio furniture. "What 'this' are you talking about?" he responded.

When he opened the shower door, she was standing in the bathroom with the newspaper. "This," she said, thrusting it at him. But before he could even dry off his hands, she continued. "Paco, the custodian who stole my underwear."

"Yeah?"

"They arrested him last night for sexual assault."

According to the newspaper, one of the members of the girls' volleyball team had forgotten her math book in her locker, so after practice she went to retrieve it. Next thing she knew, she was being pushed into the girls' bathroom in a remote corner of the building, where her cries for help echoed loudly off the tiled walls but were muffled to the outside world. Not that it would have mattered anyway; Amanda and Greg had left school half an hour earlier, so campus was pretty much deserted by that time.

"Remember when I told Vinnie?" Amanda asked.

"The lawyer for the District basically said it was your fault, right?"

"Vinnie asked if we needed to wait until the guy did something worse. And now...," she trailed off.

"And now the lawyer will get to negotiate a settlement with the victim," said Greg.

"What if I would have still been there? I wonder if I could have prevented it." She sounded remorseful for not doing so.

"Maybe," Greg replied. "Or maybe it would have been you instead." He meant that to assuage Amanda's guilt, but it seemed to have a much different effect. Breakfast and the ride to school were nearly silent as Amanda sifted through various "what if" scenarios in her mind. When they arrived at school, they found a notice for a mandatory after-school meeting in their mailboxes. Then, on their way to class, they walked past Vinnie Pantuzzi's office. The door was closed, the lights were dim, and Pantuzzi's head was down. When he looked up ever so briefly, his expression was one of utter powerlessness and despair. Amanda, who bore witness to his fateful phone conversation with the District Director of Advocacy, Policy, and Regulatory Affairs, wiped a single tear from her cheek. She knew the man in the office was a decent human being who deserved better.

All day long, Pantuzzi stayed in his office with the door closed. During her prep, Amanda stood outside for several minutes, more than once bringing her hand up to knock but then bringing it back down again. Ultimately, she realized there was nothing she could say or do, so she left him alone in his misery.

Miles away, a reporter from the *Sweetwater Sentinel* arrived at the Sweetwater Unified School District No. 43 headquarters as soon as it opened for business. The District Director of First Impressions told the reporter that she would need to wait, and so the reporter sat in the lobby for more than an hour, going through the questions she would ask Dr. Morning when she finally was granted audience. That time came a few minutes after nine a.m.

The reporter was buzzed through the security doors and within moments was in Dr. Morning's office—a large, oak-paneled room with a desk the size of an aircraft carrier and comfortable blue seating to match the thick blue carpeting. The drapes were open, revealing a lovely view of the distant mountains against which Shadowcliff High School was set. With neither a computer nor a telephone taking up desk space, everything seemed almost too neat.

Dr. Morning, an insincere smile plastered to her face, motioned for the reporter to sit. The reporter did not say "Good morning!" but was not chastised.

"The District Director of Advocacy, Policy, and Regulatory Affairs and the District Director of Marketing are on their way. While we wait, would y'all like a snack?" She motioned toward a corner of the office, where a tray of oatmeal cookies and a freshly made pitcher of lemonade sat on a small table, like this was a social visit to grandma's house.

"Cookies and lemonade?"

"No reason to be uncivil," Dr. Morning replied. "I think we—"

At that moment there was a knock on her door. "Come in," she said, and the door opened to reveal Errol Strothers, the District's lawyer, and Nancy Youngblood, the District Director of Marketing (a legitimate title). They entered the office but then stopped, and the reporter noticed Dr. Morning glaring at them.

"Good morning!" they both said finally, and Morning's eyes softened. She waited as they took chairs next to the reporter.

"Now, what would you like to know?" asked Dr. Morning. Her cheerfulness, while clearly artificial, was unsettling.

"May I record our conversation?" asked the reporter. Errol Strothers nodded, so Dr. Morning said, "Of course. We want to make sure everything is accurate."

The reporter pulled out her mini-recorder, switched it on, and set it atop Dr. Morning's desk. "First of all," said the reporter, "I'm curious why the Marketing Director is here. Doesn't quite seem appropriate for a situation like this."

"I asked Nancy to be here because we want to make sure we convey a positive message," said Dr. Morning. "We—"

"—A positive message? A girl was raped last night. I guess I'm curious as to what sort of positive spin you can put on this, so why don't you go ahead and make a statement."

"There's no reason to get upset," Dr. Morning said. Then she looked toward the Director of Marketing. "Nancy, do you have our statement?"

Nancy nodded and passed a sheet of paper to the reporter, who began reading. The page was still warm, fresh from the copy machine. Dr. Morning drummed her expensive fingernails on her desktop and Errol Strothers clicked his ballpoint pen. Finally, the reporter looked up and said, "This is filled with platitudes."

"Why thank you!" smiled the Director of Marketing.

The reporter shook her head and turned toward Dr. Morning. "May I ask you some questions?"

"Of course," said Dr. Morning. "I'll be happy to answer anything y'all want to know."

"Great," said the reporter. "To begin, can you tell me why there isn't security present at all times when students are on campus?"

"Well, you see," Dr. Morning began. "We made a decision—"

Out of the corner of her eye, the reporter could see Errol Strothers shaking his head.

"We have no comment on that one," Dr. Morning continued. "Next question?"

"After this event, how are you going to assure parents and students that the schools are safe?"

Dr. Morning replied, "We pride ourselves on the safety of our students, and we are part of the Safe Schools Initiative." She was still smiling, but with such effort that her mouth began to twitch slightly.

"But you were part of the Safe Schools Initiative yesterday, too," continued the reporter. "And obviously Shadowcliff High School really wasn't safe after all. So how are you going to assure parents and students that—"

"—We will always take measures in our constant quest to ensure safety," Strothers said.

"What sort of measures, exactly?" asked the reporter.

"Appropriate measures," Strothers replied.

"What would you say to the young woman and her parents if they were here right now?" asked the reporter.

"They're not," said Strothers, "so let's focus on actual issues." Dr. Morning shuffled through some paperwork while leaning back in her chair.

"Will the contract with the cleaning company come under scrutiny?" the reporter asked.

"Every contract comes under scrutiny," Strothers replied.

"But wouldn't you say this contract and this company present some unique issues today?" the reporter followed up.

"Every issue is unique in the eyes of the law," Strothers replied, clearly tiring of this.

"I'm sure it is," said the reporter, growing frustrated at his evasiveness. "OK, let's talk more about security. Can we really expect schools to be safe when security guards get paid so little?"

"Our security guards are professionals," said Strothers. "They are trained and they are prepared to respond to any situation, regardless of their rate of pay."

"And just to clarify from before, how many security guards were on duty at the time of the incident?" the reporter probed.

"The number of security guards isn't the issue," Strothers responded. "The case *Hill v. Safford Unified School District* describes the standard of care."

The reporter sighed, scratched her head, and began to examine her notes. Strothers caught Morning's eye and nodded slightly, indicating that things were going well, and she smiled in response.

"So you're saying that having a contracted custodial company working a large building at night with no security on campus is sufficient to meet the standard of care?" the reporter finally asked.

"It's all about foreseeability," Strothers replied. "It's complicated legal stuff. You probably wouldn't understand."

"If you say so. Final question. Did you have any inkling of this, any sort of evidence that the suspect might be a danger before this event occurred?"

Strothers opened his mouth to answer but did not respond for several seconds. "Dr. Morning?" the reporter redirected.

"I'm sorry," Dr. Morning said, rejoining the conversation. "What was the question?"

"Did you have any inkling that the suspect might present a danger prior to this event?"

"Of course not," Dr. Morning said. "Don't be silly." Strothers leaned back in his chair, his relief obvious.

That afternoon, before Vinnie Pantuzzi prepared to address the teachers, Amanda finally was able to speak with him.

"Vinnie, there was nothing you could have done," she said.

"Of course there was. We knew the guy was rotten. I shoulda gotten rid of him."

"They wouldn't let you."

"Yeah, but if I had any backbone, I woulda done it anyway."

"Vinnie, you stood up for me like a champion. You have plenty of backbone."

"No I don't," he concluded. "As an administrator, I had my backbone removed long ago."

Fall break could not come soon enough for Vinnie Pantuzzi, who booked a flight to Pittsburgh to visit his mother. As his departure drew near, though, it was clear the sexual assault was still weighing heavily on him. Nevertheless, the school year was obliged to march forward. Papers needed to be written, projects needed to be finished, sports events needed to be played, theater productions needed to be rehearsed, and Arizona standardized pre-tests needed to be administered. These pre-tests were meant to establish a baseline of knowledge for students, and would then be compared to post-test scores to evaluate student growth and teacher effectiveness. Dr. Rayburn had explained this at the in-service, but most of the teachers were probably comatose by then. Measuring student growth was a great yardstick in theory, but in reality there were just too many human variables, both innocent and pernicious.

First of all, there was the illusion that an entire year's worth of material could be captured in a forty-five question multiple choice test. That fallacy was compounded by the further illusion that the test was even representative. Jimmy Clayton told Greg that the American history test contained six questions about the American Revolution and nine about the Civil War, meaning that one-third of the entire test was devoted to ten years of American history. Meanwhile, the robber barons, World War I, the space race, and the Middle East were not represented by a single question, as if they were meaningless to the trajectory of the nation. The English test for Greg's class was not much better, containing far too many questions about similes and metaphors and not enough about information literacy, the pitfalls of plagiarism, or how to construct a vibrant thesis statement.

There was also that population of unmotivated students, Jeanette Candelaria's "bottom feeders by choice," who were more likely to blacken the bubbles in the shape of a penis than to take the pre-test seriously. By District decree, pre-tests could not be used for a class grade, virtually guaranteeing low scores. This meant that even minimal effort on the post-test in May would yield huge gains. On the other hand, Greg's AP students never met a test they sloughed off, and with their high pre-test scores the opportunity to demonstrate growth would be severely compromised.

Beyond that, teachers certainly understood the import of these test scores on their livelihood, and a few came up with creative ways to manipulate the data. One ambitious teacher combed through the answer sheets and changed correct answers to incorrect answers, but that process ultimately proved too time-consuming. One enterprising teacher offered extra credit points for the lowest pre-test score in each class, and more than half his students accepted the challenge with a score of zero. One patient teacher decided it would be easiest to wait until the post-test, provide his students with the correct answers under the pretense of a "review session," and demonstrate growth scores to make him look like Teacher of the Millennium.

And most, including Greg and Amanda, gave the pre-test and then set about to increase performance by teaching as well as they could, figuring if that did not satisfy the state of Arizona then the state of Arizona could go screw itself because maybe they were in the wrong profession.

The day of his pre-tests, Greg was visited by Conrad Luper. Luper had more or less left him alone for the past twelve months, apparently satisfied by the quality of Greg's Business Law matrix and the fact that nobody had complained too loudly about the class. His visit was unwelcome but, Greg knew, essential for Luper to earn his administrative stipend. So Greg prepared himself, a bit concerned by Luper's overly friendly manner.

"Mr. Samson, how are you?" he asked.

"I'm great, Conrad. And you?"

"Fine," he said. "Just dandy. Listen, I know you're busy with state testing today, so I'll get right to the point. You've been selected as site coordinator for Business Education. Congratulations."

"Ummm," Greg said, confused. "I didn't apply for the position."

"You were appointed!" Luper boomed. "You'll be perfect. Your matrices are exceptional."

"With all due respect, that doesn't seem like much of a qualification," Greg answered. "Besides, I only teach one business class, and it's only kinda-sorta businessy. Why not someone who's full-time business?"

"You'll need to go to the state convention in November," Luper said, ignoring the question.

"State convention?" Greg faltered, still trying to figure if he had grounds for appeal.

"Then it's settled," said Luper, extending his hand. "Mr. Site Coordinator." Like it was some great honor.

"Don't I at least get a better title than that?" asked Greg.

Luper again ignored the question. "I'll send you the information on the state convention. We'll pay your registration fees, naturally."

"Naturally," said Greg, as Luper shook his hand once more before leaving. Greg entertained a sneaking suspicion that he had just been appointed to do the boring parts of Luper's job, and if so he really wanted that better title. He chose Director of Absurd Matrix Numbers, or DAMN for short.

Pantuzzi seemed far more relaxed when he returned from fall break, plus a few pounds heavier. "Mama Pantuzzi is eighty years old, but she can still cook like nobody's business," he explained simply.

But Vinnie's relaxed mood was tempered by the bond election in just a couple of weeks. His job was not in jeopardy, of course, but he was concerned for the future of the school district he had so capably served for so long. He reminded Shadowcliff teachers of the Arizona statute which prohibited them from politicking in class, but he encouraged them to do all they wanted on their own time. Kochlöffel penned an impressive letter to the editor, while other Shadowcliff teachers trekked door-to-door to solicit voter support.

For his part, Greg harbored additional concerns. The first was keeping Amanda from going over the edge. While some teachers used fall break as a chance to go to the mountains or the beach and recharge, Greg and Amanda remained in Sweetwater. Greg faced a small stack of essays and was in the midst of preparing a criminal law activity which he would use on the Vocational Ed matrix as "Provides adequate opportunities for students to consider career choices." But for the most part, his fall break would be devoted to cross country practice. The state meet was just a few weeks away, and he believed it could be a special day.

Amanda spent the entire week planning, researching, and revising. Frustrated by her students' inadequate theme statements, she borrowed Greg's Theme-O-Matic®, a tool he created two years earlier and had been using with great success ever since. She devoted an entire day to revising the Theme-O-Matic® in order to make it appropriate for her Global Scholars students. In the morning, her efforts resulted in the change of exactly two words and the relocation of an arrow about one-quarter of an inch. In the afternoon, she changed the title font and returned the arrow to its original position. Then she and Greg spent two hours trekking door-to-door in their apartment complex to solicit voter support for the school bond.

"Your perfectionism is part of what makes you a fabulous teacher," Greg said, "but I worry that it's going to kill you." She had no grounds to dispute him. Although caught up as the second quarter began, Amanda desperately needed a few days off. The question was whether she would take them.

Meanwhile, the *Sweetwater Sentinel* began to run editorials about the bond election. While the newspaper was anything but complimentary about Dr. Morning, it still encouraged the bond's adoption, opining that a well-funded district with deficient leadership is still more likely to succeed than a poorly funded district with the same deficiency. At the final School Board meeting before Election Day, Dr. Morning spotted the Editor of the *Sweetwater Sentinel* across the room and mumbled something to Dr. Rayburn. One bystander thought she may have said the word "a-hole."

The vote on the bond was not even close. Sweetwater, long known as a city that supported education and took pride in the quality of its schools, a city of comparative wealth in which a small tax increase would scarcely be felt by most residents, a city which had never failed to pass a school bond, voted overwhelmingly NO.

Fortunately, the school bus still arrived the morning of the state cross country championships, alleviating another of Greg's concerns. Six hours later they were back at Sweetwater, talking of Mexican food and Pepsi, which most had sworn off for the season. The girls did not defend their title, finishing a bittersweet second place. It was good enough for a trophy and five of the seven girls won medals, but it fell nine agonizing points short of victory. Yet while second place was disappointing for the girls, the boys' third-place finish was better than winning the lottery. Corey Hinton, whom Greg had recruited from a chair in front of his counselor's office in the earliest days of Sweetwater, earned first-team All-State honors with his seventh-place finish. No Granite High School runner was within twenty seconds.

Nevertheless, the gloom of the bond defeat and the fact that Frank Nixon's football team still had a chance to make the playoffs meant the cross country team's performance went virtually unnoticed. Only Randy Smith, Shadowcliff's Athletic Director and Greg's long-time friend, was in the parking lot to congratulate the team upon its return to school.

25

THE ABSQUATULATION

Just weeks before the election, Dr. Morning promoted both Conrad Luper and Ramona Thurlow to District-level positions in Sweetwater Unified School District No. 43. Thurlow was now Director of Gifted Education. The fact that she had no background in teaching gifted students was apparently trivial, as Shadowcliff's Global Scholars Program had, under her specious direction, become almost entirely self-sufficient. In truth, this was thanks to Amanda and the other new teachers and to Vinnie Pantuzzi's calm, steadfast support, but Thurlow claimed that Rumsford's departure "left me free to run the Program the way I want." Pantuzzi knew her claim was spurious at best, but six months from retirement he felt no need to dispute it. Thurlow was even allowed to maintain her office at Shadowcliff, ostensibly better to oversee Global

Scholars and actually best for her midday hiking routine. Meanwhile, Luper's position as District Director of Vocational Education was made a full-time gig, while a long-term substitute was hired at Rancho High School to teach Luper's three typing classes, an assignment a monkey probably could handle and a trained monkey probably could handle better than Luper. As Jeanette Candelaria promised, incompetence was once again promoted.

Now, with the defeat of the bond, both feared the gravy train would be derailed after having barely left the station, and they would be unceremoniously forced to endure the walk of shame back to their previous positions. They need not have worried, though, for there were larger issues to confront.

The Sweetwater Unified School District No. 43 School Board met a week after the election. Often at odds over a budgetary decision or philosophical direction, some Board members felt genuine animosity toward one another. But on this night they spoke deliberately, in hushed tones, better for veiling their frustration and presenting a united front. Amidst tedious discussions of equipment purchases, lunch receipts, and district vehicles, they managed to keep their emotions contained.

Until the end.

"Dr. Morning," rasped the Board President, and the Superintendent stood up. She knew better than to insist on her usual greeting.

"For the first time in Sweetwater history," said the President, "the voters have voted down a school bond." Dr. Morning nodded as the President added, "Congratulations." It was clearly not meant in celebration.

"You now have a solemn task ahead of you," continued the President. "It becomes your job, and the job of your staff, to determine how to cut twenty million dollars from our budget. I assume you have given this some thought?"

"Not really," said Dr. Morning, her eyes focused on a gum stain on the carpet. "We're still compiling data and analyzing trends and whatnot, so—"

"—Well you'd better start. Are you going to increase class sizes? Fire teachers? Fire administrators? Turn off the electricity? Are you going to take a pay cut?"

Dr. Morning's head jerked with this last proposition, and she looked at the empaneled School Board for the first time all night.

"It seems to me that if I have such a grave responsibility, I'll certainly be earning my salary," Dr. Morning said. "I don't understand why y'all'd consider that."

Another Board member, a long-time Sweetwater resident whose two kids had both graduated from Eldorado High School, leaned forward and adjusted his microphone.

"Dr. Morning, your title and your salary aren't just rainbows and kitty cats. They carry accountability. The bond failed on your watch. In the public's eyes, and in the eyes of many members of this Board, that's your fault. No one else's."

"But I only came to Sweetwater four months ago," she protested. "There were issues long before I got here that I haven't had a chance to address quite yet."

"Your leadership, your problem," said the President. "In fact, and this is very interesting, we just found out that in your previous district, a bond failed there, too. That's quite a streak you've got going."

"Now that was different," Dr. Morning argued. "That was—"

"—Funny you didn't mention that on your résumé or in your interview. One might think you were being purposely, shall we say, evasive."

"I think dishonest might be a better word," said the Board's Vice President.

"I am offended by that," said Dr. Morning.

"Quite frankly, Dr. Morning, we don't really care if you're offended by that," said the President. "You were hired to make sure the bond passed. You assured us you could do exactly that. You didn't say anything about the fact that you were oh-for-one."

"I was one-for-two," she protested. "I passed a bond at my first job in Nacogdoches."

"The fact remains," said the President, "you didn't tell us."

"You didn't ask!" Dr. Morning screeched.

"This is partly our responsibility," the President admitted. "We obviously trusted the search firm too much. We should have vetted the candidates more carefully. Lesson learned. A very expensive lesson. And because it was so expensive, we're stuck with you."

Dr. Morning let out a deep breath of relief.

"For now, anyway," continued the President. "You have one week...." She looked around at the other Board members. "Is that what we decided?" Each nodded in agreement, so the President turned back toward Dr. Morning. "You have one week to submit to this Board your proposed list of cuts. Figure out how to cut twenty million dollars and not impact our kids, and maybe you save your job. Am I clear?"

Dr. Morning nodded meekly.

"Move to adjourn," said one Board member. "Seconded," said another. "In favor?" Every Board member said "Aye." "Opposed?" Silence. "We will meet in special executive session one week from to-night to review the proposed cuts," the President said. "Our next public meeting will be in four weeks. We are adjourned." With the crack of the gavel, Dr. Morning snuck out as quickly as possible, mumbling incomprehensibly. One bystander thought she may have said the word "bitch."

A few minutes later, Dr. Morning sat in the darkness of her office, contemplating the ramifications of tonight. She would have to work ridiculous hours over the next week to prepare the new budget, and no matter what she offered, people would be angry. She would have to get a computer in her office, which meant she would once again be receiving e-mails from irate parents. And she would probably ruin her manicure. Besides that, if the Board was going to insist she take a pay cut, she would have to breach the lease on her Jaguar, and she loved that car. She began to rub her temples in order to clear her chakras and to help her recall where she had hidden the good bourbon. The massage was helping with neither objective. She wished she had her computer now, so she could Google the location of the nearest liquor store.

She was startled from her contemplation by a knock at her door, and she jumped.

"What the fuck do y'all want now?" she screamed.

Only when she turned toward the door did she see the Channel 10 news crew already inside her office, the red light glowing brightly atop the camera to signal that they were live.

The following day, a Wednesday, Dr. Morning did not show up for work. She was absent Thursday as well. Friday, too. Luper submitted a purchase order for Greg's registration fees at the state Vocational Education conference, then called it a day. Thurlow went one better, skipping out altogether and missing the once-dreaded announcement that everyone needed to turn in their green staplers. In her absence, Global Scholars auditors simply rotated through various classrooms, filling pages upon pages with meticulous notes. When they finished observing Amanda teach a class on gender roles in Japanese literature, they spent half an hour with Vinnie Pantuzzi, informing him that his Global Scholars Program was one of the more impressive they had observed in recent weeks, all despite the fact that Ramona Thurlow was absent. "She is?" Pantuzzi replied. "I had no idea." He then called FTD and ordered flowers for each of his Global Scholars teachers.

By the time Dr. Morning failed to show up on Monday, news of her extended absence had spread throughout the District. Teachers were edgy, fearful of the unknown. So, too, were Dr. Rayburn and Dr. Jesperson, who assumed they would be required to complete the list of cutbacks she had neglected.

"Bea, you think we could file for an extension?" Dr. Jesperson asked. "There's no way we can do this."

"As far as we know, she's still the Superintendent," Dr. Rayburn answered. "It's not our job. Just stay busy with your stuff and I'll stay busy with mine."

"I suppose," Jesperson said. "And if we get called out, maybe we can get Carvalho assigned to it. She's the numbers person."

Dr. Morning did not show up for work on Tuesday, the day her assignment was due. The School Board was already aware of her extended absence, the timing of which troubled them greatly. To say they were displeased would be a gross understatement, and that evening's special session promised to get nasty.

"I cannot believe the deceit and ... wickedness ... of that woman," the Board President began. "I have never in my life witnessed anything so unprofessional."

"Can we all agree that she's fired?" asked the Vice President. "I mean, I assume she's skipped town, but if she shows up for some reason can we officially terminate her?"

"I'd prefer public flogging," said another Board member, and two others seemed to think that was a great idea.

"Dr. Rayburn, Dr. Jesperson, what about it?" asked the Board President, now turning her attention to Dr. Morning's Texas cronies.

"Are you asking me if she should be flogged?" replied Dr. Rayburn.

"Nobody's getting flogged," said the President, to the disappointment of the other Board members. "As tempting as it may be. Let me ask a better question. You two are closest to her. She brought you from Texas and as far as I can tell you are her closest confidantes."

"I think Dr. Carvalho should do it!" blurted Dr. Jesperson.

"Do what?" asked the Board President. "What are you talking about?"

"I'm sorry," Jesperson answered. "Go ahead and finish."

"What I want to know is whether either of you know where she is. Has she contacted you? Has she told you her plans?"

"No ma'am," said Dr. Jesperson. "Back home, we would say she absquatulated."

"Ab-what-ulated?"

"Absquatulated," repeated Jesperson. "It's a Texas word. It means ... uh ... took off. Ran away. Headed for the hills, so to speak."

"So it seems."

The next day, Sweetwater Unified School District No. 43 announced that Dr. Patty Sue Morning, Dr. Beatrice Rayburn, and Dr. David Jesperson had all been fired, a word known in more places than just Texas. Dr. Robert Halter, Vinnie Pantuzzi's best friend and one of the administrators scuttled over the summer to make room for Jesperson, was brought back to serve his second tour as interim Superintendent.

"That's number five," said Greg when he received the news at lunch. He took a bite from his sloppy joe.

"Four, actually," said Cockrell.

But Greg justified, "Since it's his second time, I counted him twice."

"He's like the Grover Cleveland of administration," Clayton added.

Then, like every other teacher in the District, Greg walked to his classroom, closed his door, and taught.

Greg was exceptionally proud of Amanda's work with the Global Scholars Program. Her creativity and passion and integrity had helped transform the Program into a major source of pride in Sweetwater Unified School District No. 43, something badly needed following the defeat of the bond. Simply by the quality of her work, she had helped to disarm seventeen too-powerful Shadowcliff parents. At the same time, her stress level had risen even beyond that of first quarter, the accumulation of perfectionism and nights with four hours sleep taking its toll. Plus, with cross country finished, she was no longer running, to the detriment of both her physical and mental health. So as the fall semester came to a merciful end, Greg knew that a vacation was essential.

His relationship with Amanda was flourishing but had failed to clear one critical hurdle: Amanda's seventy-eight-year-old Italian grandmother. "Why can't you fall in love with a nice Italian boy?" she would ask Amanda during each of their weekly phone conversations. "What about that boy Tommy Pagliaroni?"

"Grammy Luciana," Amanda protested, "I knew Tommy Pagliaroni in fourth grade." Then she would proceed to explain, again, why she had fallen for Greg. At the end of each call, Greg would shoot her an inquisitive glance, and Amanda would simply shake her head and answer, "Not yet."

So Greg decided they needed a Christmastime trip to New York. Relatives could fawn over Amanda, they could catch a Broadway play and maybe some jazz in Manhattan, and perhaps Greg could figure out how to crack Grammy Luciana.

"What do you think?" he asked Amanda.

"I haven't been home for a couple of years," she said. "I love it."

Greg paid for the airline tickets, Amanda arranged accommodations in her aunt's basement in Queens, and Greg found a ticket broker who could, on short notice, get him two seats for *RENT* at the Nederlander Theater.

Now he just needed mentoring. And he knew the perfect coach.

The next day, he tapped on Vinnie Pantuzzi's office door. "I need a small favor," Greg explained.

"What can I help you with?" asked Vinnie.

"I need to make a positive impression on an old Italian lady."

Pantuzzi rubbed his hands together, welcoming the task. "If there's anything I know, it's old Italian ladies," he affirmed.

A week later, Greg and Amanda touched down at LaGuardia Airport, and the adventure began.

They did all the touristy things like visiting the Met and the Empire State Building and Ground Zero. They caught Les Paul at the Iridium and a plethora of street performers. They drove past Amanda's old high school in East Rockaway and visited her best friend, who now lived in Hempstead. But mostly, they spent their evenings in her aunt's living room, yammering as only New Yorkers can do.

More accurately, Amanda yammered and Greg listened. He listened to Amanda yammer with her mother and aunt about politics and literature. He listened to Amanda yammer with her father and uncle about politics and the Yankees. He listened to Amanda yammer with her grandparents about politics and religion and music and education. He listened to Amanda yammer about childhood stories grown dim in the minds of some and distorted in the memory of others, but which always ended up with everyone laughing. Greg now understood how this woman could command a room in just a few minutes, and it made him happy to see how much she was enjoying herself. With one minor exception.

"He seems like a nice young man," said Grammy Luciana one night as she bundled up against the Queens winter, "but he doesn't say anything."

"He's quiet, Grammy," explained Amanda.

"I don't trust quiet," she said as she tossed her sash around her neck and led Amanda's grandfather out the door.

On their final night in New York, everyone met at Grammy Luciana's house in Massapequa for a farewell dinner. The kitchen was orchestrated chaos over which Grammy Luciana exercised absolute dominion. The men, forbidden to enter this sacred realm, sat in the living room watching the Knicks game on TV and yammering about the good old days of Patrick Ewing and John Starks, or for the older guys, Walt Frazier and Willis Reed.

And then it was time to eat. "Here, you sit at the head of the table," Grammy Luciana said to Greg, and Amanda sat to his right. He was unsure if this was a ceremonial honor or if it was designed to make it easier for the entire family to grill him all at once, but Greg knew better than to argue with Grammy Luciana.

Greg had attended pasta feeds at races around the world, but he had never seen a spread like this. Baskets of bread issued the pungent smell of garlic, which ceiling fans then hustled throughout the room. Plates of antipasto containing a garden's worth of tomatoes and a creamery's worth of provolone and taleggio cheeses rimmed the table. In the center, a tub of steaming penne sat upon a ceramic trivet that depicted an Italian vineyard. At Greg's left elbow was a pot of marinara sauce, at his right a pot of clam sauce. Two similar pots sat at the other end of the table. "This one's vodka sauce and that one's Bolognese," said Grammy Luciana. Aromatic needles of parmesan, freshly grated of course, were dispersed in glass bowls around the table. Wine glasses that would not stay empty for long nestled at the two o'clock position above each diner's plate. The smell was divine. Frank Sinatra sang "Fly Me To The Moon" in the background.

Greg was certainly in his element now. Within minutes, he polished off some antipasto, three slices of garlic bread, a plate of pasta, and a glass of wine. As an only child, he was never a fast eater, but the food tonight was so magnificent that he barely stopped to breathe while the others yammered and ate and yammered some more. Forks waved expressively and bread punctured the air as family members emphasized their opinions, which were as plentiful as the food. At one point Greg stole a glance at Grammy Luciana, who smiled back at him even as she somehow managed to watch each member of her family at once. As Greg placed his fork on his empty plate, he looked at Amanda, and she nodded at him.

"Greg would like some more, please," she said, and all conversations stopped as everyone grabbed pot or ladle or breadbasket to make sure his plate was once again full.

An hour later, the carnage was complete and the table looked like the Huns had swept through Eastern Europe. Greg had eaten three plates of pasta and was a little buzzed from the wine.

After the other women began the dishes, Grammy Luciana pulled Amanda aside. "He's a nice boy," Grammy Luciana said. "I like boys who can eat. I think you should marry him."

When Amanda told Greg later that night, he laughed. "Back when I was training, that would have been just a warmup."

Greg found himself in the Roman Colosseum, poised for battle. The gates opened, the crowd cheered, and he was suddenly surrounded by a horde of old Italian women, each of whom began a gastronomic assault. Some threw penne pasta while others threw bread or tomatoes. Their aim was true and their number so many that he was left with only one defensive option. Discarding his shield, he began to catch the food in his mouth until each of the old women ran out of things to throw.

Amanda came down from the imperial box and approached the victor, who wiped his mouth with his sleeve. As she kissed him, another cheer arose from the crowd and all heads turned to see three Texans running out the Colosseum gates, the old Italian women nipping at their boot heels.

26

THE CELEBRATION

Greg and Amanda returned to Sweetwater feeling both contented and recharged, plus Greg could put his cold-weather running gear back in storage for the year. And while the District office and interim Superintendent Dr. Halter would still be faced with the challenge of a new budget, the departure of the mess from Texas and Vinnie Pantuzzi's steady hand brought a relative calm to Sweetwater Unified School District No. 43 in general and to Shadowcliff High School in particular.

That changed as soon as semester grades were posted.

The fiasco with first-quarter grades was nothing compared to this, since these grades actually mattered. They were the ones that ended up on transcripts, that determined class rankings and academic scholarships and college acceptances and individualized rewards. They were both meat and potatoes and carrot and stick within certain families. Elida Singh earned an A in Amanda's class, thankfully, so her perfect GPA and her parents' dreams for her future medical career were both maintained. Amanda figured Elida's individualized reward was that her father would allow her dinner that night. But every teacher still had a handful of students dissatisfied with their grades, and others who did not particularly care about the grade itself but, due to their D in Biology, were now faced with the loss of their ski trip to Colorado with friends or their much-anticipated yellow Mustang convertible.

"I wish kids cared about their performance in and of itself," Greg lamented. "Not just for the perks."

"You are such an idealist," said Amanda, but without the same accusatory tone used by Woody a couple of years earlier. Hers was almost complimentary.

"I guess it's understandable, though," Greg continued. "Teenagers have never been very good at big picture. For a while, I was afraid my mom would kill me if I got a B. I didn't become interested in learning for learning's sake until college."

In fact, it was easy to ascertain who cared more about the grade—the student or the parent—based upon which one of them protested, and upon what grounds. Student protests were usually about the loss of some privilege, a protest Greg diffused quickly. "If going on the cruise really mattered to you, you would have done your work all semester and not just the last week." Kids hated him for that, even though they knew he was right. But their hatred was usually short-lived because, most often, they were able to sweet-talk their parents and explain what a jerk Mr. Samson was and could they please have just one more chance, and they ended up with a deck chair anyway.

Parents, in contrast, usually focused upon either the long-term repercussions to their child's future or the teacher's unfair practices. In the first case, they usually handled it themselves, sometimes successfully and sometimes not. In the second case, they let their attorney do the talking, and Darnell Lyon was the attorney of choice at Shadowcliff High School.

A master at scrutinizing individual teachers' grading policies as spelled out in their syllabi, this time of year was a late Christmas for Darnell Lyon. He always found an abundant supply of parents willing to pay his fee of three hundred an hour to prove that "may" and "might" and "shall" and "will" and "can" all had different meanings in the eyes of the law, and since the teachers required that both parents and students sign the syllabus to acknowledge its contents, this was a contract of adhesion in which all ambiguity would be construed against the teacher.

At least, as near as Greg could determine, that was Lyon's legal theory. He did not know if it would actually hold salt in a court of law, but no teacher ever disputed Lyon, and with their spines long-since removed, no administrator ever challenged him. And Sweetwater Unified School District No. 43 sure as hell was not interested in litigating against him. Shoddy, inexact wording and improper punctuation were manna for Darnell Lyon, and from there it was only a matter of time before he had the teacher dead to rights. The more stubborn they were, the worse he could make things, and it was said he could be merciless. His dissection of teachers' syllabi might reveal a misused semicolon; his vivisection of the teachers themselves yielded a few inches of colon, and then surrender.

Now the ambiguities of the District's new grading policy were his to exploit as well.

The week after grades were posted, Darnell Lyon put in ninety hours, the next week eight-five. He earned more money in those two weeks from tearing down teachers than virtually any of them would earn in an entire school year of building up students. In the process, he managed to retain grade point averages, ensure college admissions, and restore vacations.

Meanwhile, because their parents could not afford pricey lawyers like Darnell Lyon, students at the poorer schools in Sweetwater Unified School District No. 43 were stuck with the grades they actually earned.

But some parents felt they could handle their grading disputes without legal intervention, which is why Greg was called to in a meeting with Edie Walker, one of Shadowcliff's counselors, and Marc Weymouth, the father of one of his students.

"Thanks for coming today," Edie said to begin. "No problem," Greg replied. Mr. Weymouth simply nodded and eyed Greg scornfully.

"Mr. Weymouth, would you like to start?" she asked.

"Sure," he said. "It's very simple. I need to know why Lisa got a C in your class."

Greg replied, "Yes sir. It is very simple. She got a C in my class because her average was seventy-one percent." He offered a paper to Mr. Weymouth. "Here's a copy of her grades in case you'd like to see them."

"I've seen them already," he replied.

"Then I'm not really sure why we're here."

"You told my daughter that you thought she was capable of better, right?"

"I did," said Greg, "at the time I returned a project that, quite frankly, wasn't very good."

"Is she capable of A's?"

"I think so," Greg affirmed.

"Then why did you give her a C?" interrupted Edie Walker. Over the past two years, Greg's interactions with Edie Walker had not been particularly positive. She was nice enough, but seemed to believe that her job description began and ended with capitulation. There were always students in her office, where she allowed them to rest instead of taking the Math test that was stressing them out. If classes proved too difficult, she was always willing to help her students with schedule adjustments, even going so far as to drop a required course. She once signed off on a transaction which allowed one of Frank Nixon's football players to graduate by counting Weightlifting as a Science credit.

"Because that's what she earned," Greg said. It seemed simple enough to him.

"But what about what you said?" asked Mr. Weymouth. "You can't tell a kid she's smart and then give her a dumb kid's grade."

"Mr. Weymouth, a student's intelligence is often reflected in her performance, but often times it is not. Students don't get the grade they are capable of earning. They have to actually earn it. That's kind of like real life, wouldn't you say?"

Edie Walker reacted, apparently affirming a valid point.

"It's not your job to teach real life," argued Mr. Weymouth. "It's your job to teach English. Maybe you need to teach better."

Edie Walker reacted to this one as well. Greg realized that, for her anyway, this would probably come down to whomever got the last word.

"That would be a valid argument if nobody earned A's, but in fact, many students did. And if I may be honest, sir, they did because they had a far better work ethic than your daughter."

"Lisa has gotten A's in English every semester."

Edie Walker jumped in. "He makes a good point there, Mr. Samson. Why do you think she would suddenly drop so much?"

"And don't you dare tell me she doesn't work hard," Mr. Weymouth continued. "She earned her black belt in karate when she was fourteen. Do you know how hard that is?"

"Not exactly. I was a pretty good distance runner, though, so I do understand hard work."

"He's our cross country coach," interjected Edie Walker cheerfully.

"But in point of fact," Greg continued, "your daughter has *not* gotten A's every semester. I looked it up. As a freshman she got an A and then a B. As a sophomore she got a B and then a C. Now as a junior she barely got a C. If this trend continues, she'll get a D this spring. Which is why I told her she's capable of better."

"She will *not* get a D this spring," said Mr. Weymouth firmly. "I forbid it. How dare you say that?"

"I'm not saying I want her to get a D. I'm saying I want her to get an A. To *earn* an A," Greg clarified. "But I witness her effort level each day. She makes a lot of effort to be social, I'll give her that. But her actual classwork, not so much."

"What does that mean, social?" asked Mr. Weymouth.

"Well, first quarter she did pretty well, with an eighty-five. Then she spent most of the second quarter flirting with a boy in class and—"

"—Why didn't you move seats?"

"I did. It didn't help. And as you can see, she had a lot of low grades and missing assignments during the second quarter, which dropped her semester grade by fourteen percent. To a C."

"So you're giving her this so-called life lesson and making her keep the C?"

"Which she earned," said Greg, finally.

On his way home, Mr. Weymouth called a friend, who recommended he speak with Darnell Lyon. But the expensive lawyer refused to take the case. "I've read Mr. Samson's syllabi," Darnell explained, "and they're air-tight. Not an ambiguous phrase, misused word, or incorrect punctuation mark to be found." What he didn't mention was that Greg had received a higher score in Contracts when they were classmates in law school.

That spring, Lisa Weymouth earned a D in Greg Samson's class, needing to rally at the end to pull even that out. Plus the boy she spent the year flirting with asked another girl to prom.

Mandatory post-assessments were scheduled for late spring throughout Sweetwater Unified School District No. 43. No matter that the District was operating as only a skeleton since the absquatulation of Dr. Patty Sue Morning and the termination of her lieutenants. Sure, they had been ostensibly replaced by Ramona Thurlow and Conrad Luper, but Thurlow seldom left her office at Shadowcliff and Luper was too busy adding more colors to the Vocational Ed matrix.

Only Dr. Fiona Carvalho could explain the statistical importance of the tests, so after spring break she made a tour of the District, conducting a mandatory in-service at one school per day until she covered them all. Shadowcliff's came in mid-April. This would be her favorite stop, since she had been dating Neil Fortune, Shadowcliff's Calculus teacher, since the fall.

After she finished describing the mathematical functions that would be used to interpret the data, and the way in which this interpretation would be converted to a quantitative evaluation of each teacher, she opened up the floor to questions. Ben Koch, or Kochlöffel as Greg preferred, was the first to raise his hand, ready to stir things up.

"I asked this question back in the fall, but I never got a definitive answer," he began. "All year long we've been asked to differentiate our instruction, but now we'll be evaluated with a standardized test. How is this fair?"

"Standardized tests allow us to equitably compare one school with another and one teacher with another," she explained. "Anything else would distort the data by adding a second variable."

"But I thought you had expertise in multivariate functions," Koch continued. "Touché!" thought Greg, impressed by Kochlöffel's thrust.

"I do," she answered. "But nobody at the State does, so they would prefer we keep it as simple as possible." Nice parry.

"Other questions?" She indicated Amanda.

"I understand the need to make the statistics meaningful," Amanda began, setting the hook. "You explained that." Dr. Carvalho smiled, pleased to have gotten through. "But here's my question. What if the test itself is invalid? What if it's a bad test?"

"It's not, I can assure you," Dr. Carvalho asserted. "The test was scrutinized by the State."

"Then I respectfully disagree with the State," Amanda continued. "When I gave the pre-test, there were several questions where kids raised their hands and said, 'Ms. Moretti, none of these answers is right.'"

"Well, maybe you hadn't taught that yet."

Amanda continued, "And other questions where kids raised their hands and said, 'There are three possible answers for this question, except none of them is very good.' I looked at the test afterward, and—"

"—You looked at the test afterward?" exclaimed Dr. Carvalho. "You are not allowed to do that!"

"Under the circumstances," explained Amanda, "I thought it was a reasonable thing to do. I have a degree in Literature, with honors, so I know a little bit about my subject. One test question asked something about theme. I can't remember the exact wording. But all the answer choices were wrong. The best answer among four bad choices was really a mish-mash of plot and tone."

"Well then," said Dr. Carvalho, "you'll need to adjust your instruction."

"Theme and tone are not the same thing," protested Amanda.

"Not only are the tests used for your evaluation, they are also preparatory for state-mandated testing," Dr. Carvalho explained. "We spent a lot of money to hire EduLytics to create these tests."

Kochlöffel was the first to ask the question everyone was wondering. "What's EduLytics?"

"EduLytics is a well-respected educational assessment company. Very data-driven. Good people. I selected them myself."

"Wait a minute," asked Jeanette Candelaria. "These tests weren't even written by teachers?"

"That's correct. Less chance for bias. Each question is triple-blind tested and then cross-normed against multiple demographic factors."

"By chance is EduLytics located in Minnesota?" asked Kochlöffel pointedly. Dr. Carvalho winced.

"I assure you," she countered, "every one of the pre-test and post-test questions aligns with state curricular guidelines and summative assessments. Which, as you know, are required for students to graduate."

"So you're telling me I should teach information that I know to be incorrect?" asked Amanda incredulously.

Carvalho examined her manicure for defects, then finally took a deep breath and looked at the Shadowcliff teachers. "I'm telling you it's your job to get kids to pass the state test. Next question."

Despite protests based upon facts and logic and other such trifles, the test was of course given exactly as prepared. They all knew it would be. Forewarned, every one of Amanda's students answered the question about theme correctly, choosing B as the answer even though they knew it was erroneous. In a moral victory, none of Greg's students filled in the bubbles to make a picture of a penis. And later that summer, Darnell Lyon was able to get an injunction which invalidated the State's power to withhold graduation based upon a set of tests which were clearly flawed.

As the year drew to a close, Vinnie Pantuzzi began to clean out his office, retirement close at hand. The circumstances had been challenging, but upon reflection he decided that it had actually been one of the most enjoyable school years of his long career.

Vinnie's retirement party was held the weekend before final exams. The festivities took place in a large banquet hall filled with Shadowcliff teachers and others he knew from his years in education. Dr. Robert Halter, interim Superintendent of Sweetwater Unified School District No. 43, sat beside him. Halter was also retiring, although he had promised to stay through October, long enough to give the School Board sufficient time to hire a permanent Superintendent. But District-level administrators never have grand retirement send-offs in their honor. By that time, they don't have enough friends left. Halter's friendship with Pantuzzi remained intact, though, so he sat beside the guest of honor as the two planned a week-long fishing trip to Montana before each rode off into his respective sunset.

After dinner came boring thank-you speeches, funny stories, and entertaining skits to honor the man. In one, a thin, fit gentleman and a younger bald cooking spoon of a man who looked remarkably like Shadowcliff High School teachers spoofed Pantuzzi's life with a five-minute presentation in drag that had Vinnie red-faced and Dr. Halter crying in hysterics. Greg was glad there is no existing videotape of the performance.

Finally, Vinnie said a few words. He smiled humbly before he began.

"I want to thank you all for coming tonight, and for being part of my career. My l-o-n-g career." He chuckled. "Fact is, I loved being a principal. Even with its frustration and irritation and confusion, it was also filled with joy and satisfaction. I got to work with dedicated professionals and watch great young people become successful, and I wouldn't trade it for anything.

"You know, when Dr. Patty Sue Morning ... good morning!" Everyone laughed. "When Dr. Morning decided to take her talents elsewhere ... I think I saw her working at that bagel place next to the supermarket...." Another big laugh. "Anyway, here's a secret. When she left, the School Board asked me to be Superintendent." He turned to Dr. Halter. "You didn't know that, did you?"

"I did not know that," Halter affirmed.

"But I told 'em to—"

"—Kiss my meatballs," Amanda filled in softly, and she began to smile.

Pantuzzi introduced new principal Bryce Bishop at the end-of-year breakfast, the morning after graduation. And while this was certainly a matter of great interest to all the teachers, many of them were more fascinated by the new bauble on Amanda's left hand.

Greg found himself inside a church. Mozart was being piped in and the carpet smelled of caustic adhesive. Nevertheless, he was deliriously happy as Amanda walked down the aisle toward him. She wore a lacy off-white gown and that same quirky smile that still captured his heart. Amanda stopped for a moment in order to allow Dr. Connie Rumsford to clean a spot on the carpet, but soon she finished her triumphant procession to the altar. When she arrived, Vinnie Pantuzzi turned around, dressed in a graduation gown and a Pittsburgh Pirates baseball cap.

"Is there anyone here who sees any reason not to join this man and this woman in holy matrimony?" he asked. "And if you do, you can kiss my meatballs."

No one spoke, thankfully, so Vinnie produced the marriage license. "Here, grade this," he said to Amanda. He gave one to Greg as well, saying, "You, too." When they finished, he tried to make copies but the machine sputtered, smoked, and finally screeched to its demise.

Pantuzzi shrugged and pulled out the good book from which to read the marriage ceremony, and Greg glanced at the cover. It was Marcel Proust's *Remembrance of Things Past*.

Soon they were pronounced man and wife and transported via school bus to the reception, which was held in Shadowcliff's cafeteria. Lasagna was being served, but the portions were tiny until Grammy

Luciana arrived to take over the catering. Dr. Patty Sue Morning wandered through the crowd with a tray of cookies and lemonade. Jimmy Clayton sat in the corner, cursing at a women's bass fishing tournament on TV.

Within moments it was time to throw the bouquet and remove the garter. Dr. Elida Carvalho completed her calculations just in time to assume the statistically most likely location for the trajectory of the bouquet, and sure enough her math was dead-on. Amanda then sat down to allow Greg to remove her garter, but suddenly a man rushed from the crowd, pushed Greg aside, and disappeared underneath Amanda's dress. When she pulled back, everyone could see it was Paco, the former Shadowcliff custodian. Ramona Thurlow chased him away with a green stapler while confetti made from shredded EduLytics data reports rained down from the ceiling.

2008 - 2009

27

THE CANDIDATES

Summer, as usual, was dominated by cross country practice every morning, binge reading every evening, and naps in between. Greg attended a coaching clinic in Florida, where he lost four pounds from the humidity. Amanda spent a week at Global Scholars training, then came home and began to prepare for classes. She also spent much of her free time negotiating with an apparently infinite number of Italian women about plans for a wedding that was still eight months away. Toward the end of July they enjoyed a week in a friend's timeshare at a Mexican beach resort, where Pedro de Alcaríz Hispaniola y Cruz did not serve them margaritas.

They returned home from Mexico to a stack of mail, mostly advertising. Greg glanced through it, stopping only to pull out a letter from Shadowcliff High School, new principal Bryce Bishop welcoming him back for another year. The letter informed him of start date, staff changes, and other generalities to be fleshed out in meetings the week before school opened in early August. Fortunately, there was no teacher retreat in the Bonanza High School gym. Amanda received the identical letter. Greg tossed the rest of the mail on the table and began to sort dirty laundry while Amanda took a shower. Then they switched, ate a quick dinner, and passed out.

The next morning, amidst the mattress ads and credit card offers, Greg found a letter from the Arizona State Retirement System. His very first statement. According to their calculations, he would be eligible for retirement in twenty more years. Twenty years. He had put in three.

He had bled, both literally and figuratively. He had poured heart, soul, and energy into this job, and he had done so because it mattered, and because that was how he was wired. But the retirement letter begged the question: If I've poured everything I have into this, where will I find twenty more years' worth of everything?

He had to run.

Fifteen minutes later, he stood at his favorite trailhead. It was already one hundred and two degrees, on the way toward one-twelve. He did not care.

Over dusty boulders and through bone-dry gullies he ran. Birds circled and small reptiles searched for shade under rocks. Yet Greg saw none of it, running with a purpose on which nothing could interpose. Out here there was no standardized testing, no attendance policy, no lesson planning, no administrivia. The test was the terrain and your own willpower, and the attendance policy was that you either ran or you didn't. There was only the trail, the sun, and one hundred and forty-eight pounds of lean meat.

Yet this run was more than an exercise in physical fitness and more than a mental decontaminant. There was symbolic meaning to this run, far greater than the metronomic koosh-koosh-koosh his shoes made as they danced along the desert floor which, on this scorching day, was his alone. This was a literary run, so to speak, although Greg did not know if he was Holden Caulfield, running from something inevitable, or Yossarian, running from something he could not understand, or Nick Carraway, running from something he detested. But it did not matter, really. So he just ran.

If he stayed at Shadowcliff High School, the students would always be seventeen, and he would become an old man. Three years had felt like ten, and he was not ready to meet Santiago's fate just yet. With that, a lizard scurried just in front of his foot and he made a slight right-hand turn, accelerating up a short hill and into the distance.

Ninety minutes later, salty sweat caked his temples and dust covered his lower legs, and clarity had

returned thanks to the metaphorical value of running, of being in the moment. He need not get
through twenty more years of teaching, nor could
he. He only needed to get through one, as well as
could be done. Then he only needed to get through
one. Repeat until finished.

Besides, it couldn't get any worse, could it?

Had Bryce Bishop dressed in a T-shirt and jeans instead of a dress shirt and tie, he probably could have
asked the head cheerleader to prom. Instead, he was
now in charge of prom. And scheduling. And evaluations. And discipline. And parent communication.
And curriculum development. And staffing. And
budgeting. And a million-and-a-half other things he
had not even thought of yet.

He was twenty-seven years old.

Perhaps Bishop was so gifted a manager that, despite the budget crisis, he would lead his staff to an
esprit-de-corps never before seen in Arizona. Perhaps
he embodied the kindness of temperament mixed
with the rousing school spirit that would empower
each student to pursue his or her unique aspirations
within the greater Shadowcliff experience. Perhaps
he had the soft touch and profundity of vision to foster a sense of trust between school and community,
thus creating synergy that would propel Shadowcliff

to the apex of Arizona high schools. Perhaps Bryce Bishop was an educational savant, his age belying his skills. All this was unknown.

In fact, Bryce Bishop was the son of Sweetwater Unified School District No. 43's Assistant Director of Elementary Education. One of the School Board members had been his babysitter when he was an infant, and another was his coach in Little League. He was fondly remembered as co-captain of the Rancho High School football team when it captured the state championship ten years earlier, his gritty style of play still revered by long-time Rancho fans. "One-hundred-ninety-pound linebacker who hit like a truck," recalled one old-timer. "Toughest sonovabitch I've ever seen."

After college, he spent two years building irrigation systems in Botswana as a member of the Peace Corps, then three years as a classroom teacher while pursuing his administrative certificate. After his internship at Lariat Elementary School, he was selected for the position at Shadowcliff High School over six other candidates.

Unanimously.

Mark Twain once wrote, "Experience is overrated. The cat that sits on a hot stove will never again sit on a hot stove, but he will never again sit on a cold one, either." Maybe, thought Greg, Twain would counsel patience with Bryce Bishop. But Twain was not on the staff at Shadowcliff High School.

"I have children older than Bryce Bishop," said Jeanette Candelaria, unconvinced. By her count, seventeen other Shadowcliff teachers could say the same thing.

Some were unhappy, some even offended. Some had friends or spouses who were candidates and felt they had been disparaged. But like it or not, Bryce Bishop was the new principal of Shadowcliff High School.

"We can either give him a chance," reasoned Greg, "or we can spend our time resenting him. Which would be pointless."

Greg's perception was also buoyed by Randy Smith, who offered, "He's young, but I think he'll be good. Plus he's a sports guy."

While campus leadership had changed once again and trust needed to be rebuilt, some traditions endured. Staff meetings still took place in room 4122, so Bryce Bishop stood before his staff and whistled sharply.

"Sorry about that," he said as many members of his staff rubbed the pain from their ears. "Elden Ray Fong wouldn't approve of that method, would he?" He paused for a moment until he was sure of everyone's attention, then continued, "As usual we have lots to cover. I'm sure many of you will want to learn about me, what I believe in, and what changes you can expect this year, and that's understandable. I want to make sure you're comfortable with me as your principal, so my door will be open all afternoon. Our agenda for today's meeting is on the board," he said, indicating the neatly lettered list behind him, "and our first item of business is an announcement from Dr. Halter. So hold on."

He clicked on the computer to project the District's webcast onto the screen. Interim Superintendent Dr. Robert Halter, dressed in suit and tie, sat behind his desk, the camera frozen on him as he waited uncomfortably to begin. After a few moments, he finally began to speak.

"Good morning!" said Dr. Halter. "Wait, sorry, honest mistake." He tried to dismiss his gaffe with a guilty wave. "Let me try again. Hello, Sweetwater teachers. I hope everyone is tuned in. Welcome back to a new school year. As you know, I agreed to stay on until the District selected its new Superintendent, at which point I will be retiring from Sweetwater Unified School District.

"We have listened to your concerns and we share your goal of stable leadership that understands the Sweetwater community. Toward that goal, and because our school district is filled with so many exceptional educators, the Governing Board has decided that our next Superintendent should come from within the Sweetwater Unified School District family.

"On behalf of the Board, I am pleased to announce our three candidates for the vacant Superintendent position, in no particular order.

"Ramona Thurlow, who currently serves as head of the Global Scholars Program at Shadowcliff High School. Ms. Thurlow has now been with the District for twenty-five years and last year took on added duties as Director of Gifted Education.

"Conrad Luper, Director of Vocational Education for the District. Mr. Luper has a diverse background in both business and education and is a leader in vocational education throughout the state.

"Dr. Fiona Carvalho, District Director of Assessment. Dr. Carvalho's understanding of educational data is unparalleled, and her insights have allowed Sweetwater to become a pioneer in assessment strategies.

"There will be question and answer sessions with the candidates at each of our high schools over the next few weeks, and one final Q&A prior to the next Board meeting. We expect to have the new Superintendent in place by fall break."

The room erupted in discussion, each teacher anxious to share his or her opinions about the three finalists. Greg buried his face in his hands and considered the alternatives. The possibilities were staggering, like trying to choose between John Wilkes Booth and Lee Harvey Oswald to serve as head of the Secret Service. Thurlow was great at covering her ass, and she had a nice tan. Luper was taller and had fast-food experience. Carvalho believed in teaching to the test but could probably balance her checkbook more quickly than the others.

As far as Greg could determine, it was a three-way tie for third place.

"I think maybe we should take a short break," Bishop wisely suggested.

They reconvened half an hour later, and although Dr. Halter's announcement remained paramount in their minds, there was work to be done. Greg realized that the announcement of the candidates was perfectly timed, as it deflected trepidation about Bishop's qualifications to lead a school by provoking palpable anxiety about the ability of any of the three candidates to lead an entire school district. However, he wondered if anyone spent the half hour working on their résumé, and he checked his cell phone to see if he had received a call regarding any of the inquiries he sent out over the summer. Nothing.

Bishop began introducing new staff, the next item on his agenda. The process took less time than it had taken Pantuzzi last year, but between school growth and teacher attrition there was still a hefty number of introductions.

"Next, I want to talk about tardies," Bishop continued, again indicating the agenda. "I spent a good deal of time this summer looking at attendance reports. How many of you have a problem with students who are tardy?"

Virtually every hand in the room shot up.

"As I expected. I also walked from one end of the campus to the other several times. I found that it takes anywhere from three to six minutes, depending on walking speed. Throw in crowds and it might take four to eight. But our passing time is only seven. So we're going to add one minute to passing time this year to try to cut down on tardies."

Greg respected the fact that Bishop had actually conducted some research, not just formulated policy blindly. Last year, Greg had grown frustrated by a student who was habitually late to class. One day Greg checked the boy's schedule and found that he was coming from Economics class, not far down the hall. So while the rest of the class worked on a project, Greg brought the boy into the hallway.

"Let's do an experiment, shall we?" Greg said. "Follow me." And with that, he walked to the Economics classroom, started his stopwatch, and then began to walk as slowly as possible back toward his own. He moved glacially slow. Old people would have zoomed past. The boy grew impatient and took the lead, but Greg did not increase his pace. Finally arriving at his classroom, he stopped his watch.

"Two minutes and eleven seconds," he said. Then he turned to the boy. "Can you walk faster than that?"

"Mr. Samson, my dead grandmother can walk faster than that."

"I figured," Greg said to the boy. "So if that took us two minutes and eleven seconds, and you can walk faster than that, can you explain why you can't make it from there to here in a seven-minute passing period?"

The boy was never late to class again.

"We will also be imposing stricter discipline," Bishop added, bringing Greg back from his reverie, "including suspension if necessary, for kids with excessive tardies." A few teachers actually applauded this announcement.

"Ironic," said Greg.

"How so?" asked Amanda.

"Those are the exact kids who would rather not be here anyway."

Even with the half-hour break which began the day, Bishop covered every item on his agenda by noon, probably a record for these types of meetings. If his ability to run a meeting was any indication of his ability to run a school, he was an inspired choice.

Lunch was graciously prepared by Shadowcliff's Parent-Teacher Association. This was surely one of the bonuses of working at an upper-middle class high school. Food was often provided, and it was always good. From the "Souper Bowl" luncheon the week of the Super Bowl to the Mexican Fiesta on Cinco de Mayo, PTA meals were often the best part of the job. While they had not yet served lobster tails with drawn butter, Greg concluded that was only because National Lobster Day was June 15, long after school was released for summer vacation. Maybe I should consider teaching summer school, he thought.

Lunch also seemed to quell the teachers' concerns about the three Superintendent candidates, or at least place them on the back burner. Greg heard one teacher ask, "Did you try to roast beef? It was so good." Another responded, "I'm vegetarian, but the shiitake mushroom and white bean polenta was amazing."

They returned from lunch for department meetings. Katherine Bogard was now English department chair. After the usual mundane discussions of supplies and class sets of textbooks, Katherine began to distribute a handout.

She began, "Apparently last year there was a controversy at a school in Tucson about one of the novels they were teaching. Parents complained, lawyers got involved, then the School Board, then the Department of Education. And it finally ended up at the State Legislature."

"This can't be good," responded an older teacher whose curmudgeonly manner and wild hair caused Greg to nickname him Krusty. The old man loved to teach poetry, especially John Donne.

Greg, whose lightning reading speed had allowed him to peruse the entire handout while it was still being distributed around the room, chortled. "Jiminy Christmas," he said.

Katherine glanced at him and continued. "So the Senate Education Committee developed a model academic content policy, which is being offered as a guideline at this point. Each site is supposed to discuss whether we want to adopt it. I haven't looked at it yet, but I guess these are all things we're not supposed to teach."

"So 'model academic policy' is really a euphemism for censorship," Krusty noted, and protests soon filled the room.

"Don't shoot the messenger," Katherine said, hoping to quiet the grumbles. "First point. Stories or pictures showing a black family living in poverty."

"Why?" asked another teacher, a transfer from Reata Middle School. Katherine shrugged and looked at her colleagues for help.

"If I may," said Greg. "In law school we were taught to look at policy, so I've gotten pretty good and finding the reasons behind certain rules. Even stupid ones. I'm thinking this might be seen as portraying racial stereotypes."

"Makes sense," Katherine said. "How about this one? Dinosaurs."

"Evolution," said Greg.

"Quarreling parents or disobedient children."

"Can I play?" a new teacher, who might have been president of Beta Zeta Theta sorority as recently as last week, asked enthusiastically. "It's not happy enough?" She looked at Greg, who shrugged, nodded, and said, "Sure."

"Birthdays and holidays."

Amanda raised her hand. "Jehovah's Witnesses don't celebrate birthdays."

"Unhealthy foods or alcohol," continued Katherine. "I guess that one's easy enough." Nobody disputed her, so she continued, "Slavery."

"Also upsetting, of course," grumbled Krusty.

"Hunting and fishing."

"Animal cruelty!" said Beta Zeta Theta.

"Violence or threats of violence," continued Katherine. "Jesus Christ, this is ridiculous."

"I've read through the whole policy," Greg said. "And basically, we won't be allowed to teach anything that's, well, literature. *Les Misérables*, out. *Beloved*, out. No Hemingway or Fitzgerald. No Dante's *Inferno*. No Russians. No Shakespeare."

"No Shakespeare?" asked Krusty. "Are they serious?"

Replied Katherine, "Apparently some districts have already adopted it."

"They can have fun teaching Dr. Seuss," Krusty grumbled.

"I don't think so," Greg interjected. "No *Butter Battle Book*. No *Lorax*. No *Grinch*. I'm not even sure about *The Cat in the Hat*. Thing One and Thing Two are certainly disobedient."

"You said it's up to us if we want to adopt it, right?" asked Amanda. "So can we all agree that it's absurd and move on?"

There was no dissent. But just in case someone from the District office decided to stick their nose into what was supposed to be a site decision, Krusty began teaching *King Lear* the very first week of school.

28

THE ANNOUNCEMENT

On the semester's second Friday, Amanda was actually available for lunch, almost like a date. While the setting was the faculty lunchroom and Greg's ham-and-Swiss could never substitute for salmon and Pinot Grigio by candlelight, they were still together so it was good. On their way to lunch they did not hold hands, Amanda thinking it best to maintain a professional appearance. Yet this was the same woman who, the previous spring, had volunteered to chaperone the Shadowcliff prom with Greg. As the evening progressed, some couples had successfully identified dark and secluded corners in which to be young. Amanda discovered one such couple locked together in the throes of passion, their hands on each other's butts and their tongues in each other's throats. She quickly located Greg and pitched her idea, which he thought was fabulous.

Soon, the young lovers were startled by Greg and Amanda being similarly passionate a few feet away, and they ran away horrified, likely deterred from kissing for a good long while.

But today, decorum.

As usual, the topic of lunchtime discussion was Bryce Bishop.

"I guess he's all right," Jimmy Clayton said, "but it's weird working for a guy who still gets carded at the bar."

"Speaking of which," said Amanda as she sat down next to Clayton, "we should go to Happy Hour today. We haven't been in a long time."

Everyone agreed it was a splendid idea, so a few hours later, the original Gang of Four, plus Amanda and Zeta Beta Theta, gathered around a table at Wingding's. Zeta Beta Theta said little but smiled a lot, and she seemed to receive a text message about every twelve seconds since she checked her phone incessantly. TV's still glowed with sports, mostly baseball games but also a few soccer matches from all over the planet, for a new generation of sports fan.

Jimmy Clayton was not one of these. "I don't understand soccer," he said.

"Jeez, Jimmy, it's not very difficult," Cockrell teased. "One team tries to kick the ball in one goal and the other team tries to kick the ball in the other goal."

"I get that, you asshole," Clayton responded. "What I mean is I don't understand why it's so popular."

"It's like basketball in the inner city," Greg offered. "It doesn't take much stuff. A couple of guys with a ball and a little space is enough."

"But it's so goddamn boring. Every game ends up one-to-nothing. They oughta just play till one team scores, then declare a winner and go out for beers."

"I think the fact that goals are so rare makes it more interesting, because everything matters," Greg countered. "Every shot, every foul, every mistake could mean the game."

"But they usually don't," Clayton argued. "Usually they just kick the ball back and forth."

"Whereas in basketball, they just score back and forth so often that nothing matters," Greg countered. "In the NBA, a point is like a grain of sand. In soccer, a goal is the whole beach." He turned toward Amanda, who was deep in conversation with Keri Zabriskie and Zeta Beta Theta.

"Honey, would you rather have a grain of sand or the whole beach?"

"Is this a trick question?" replied Amanda.

Cockrell took a swig of his Rolling Rock while Clayton dipped a hot wing into ranch dressing.

"See? Right there?" Clayton jumped to his feet, waving his hot wing at the TV just beyond Cockrell's left shoulder. Ranch dressing dripped onto the table, but Clayton was too worked up to notice. "One guy had the ball and then he lost it to the other team and then they lost it back and then it went out of bounds." He sat back down and began work on the hot wing. "What a fucking pointless sport."

Cockrell turned to look until another ball went out of bounds, then turned back around and changed the subject. "So did you guys get your retirement statement in the mail?"

"Yeah. I can retire sometime in the middle of next century," Clayton said bitterly as he reached for a napkin.

Added Greg, "It was one of the most depressing things I've ever read. If we had a kid ... and this is not an announcement, by the way ... we'll both work until he's out of college, except that we probably won't be able to afford college. We're not even pregnant, and already our offspring is under pressure to get a scholarship."

"I'm sure you'll figure something out," Cockrell said. "You seem to have all the answers."

"Well sure," Greg joked, "I am reigning Teacher of the Decade. But what are you talking about, all the answers?"

"No matter what happens, you always handle it."

Amanda and Keri were now listening while Zeta Beta Theta checked her phone.

"He's right," agreed Clayton. "You always seem to have your shit together."

"First of all," Greg explained, "my shit thanks you. Even though, second of all, you are so wrong on this one." Off their looks, he continued. "I'm about six years behind on sleep. I have crazy dreams, so weird that they frighten me. I question myself constantly. Am I good enough? Is it worth it? Did I give it my best? Even if the answer is yes, what if some administrator feels otherwise? Then I have been known to staple things to children, which is not a career-enhancing move. And every time I mess up, it gnaws at me. It's the curse of the driven."

"Or the paranoid," Clayton added.

"That too," affirmed Greg. "I'm just exceptionally skilled at coping. Why do you think I still run so much? And now I start my year with a new principal and three ridiculous candidates for Superintendent." He paused for a sip of water, then continued, "No, my shit is definitely not together."

"What do you know?" Keri said. "He's just like the rest of us."

Corey Hinton had emerged as the best leader in Greg's brief coaching career. Early in the season, as he waited his turn for the ice bath, Corey sat next to Greg.

"Coach, does it ever bother you that football gets all the attention?" Cross country was currently ranked fifth in the state. Football was currently ranked sixth in its eight-team region.

"That's hard to answer, Corey," Greg replied. "On the one hand, football is king and there's nothing we can do about it. On the other hand, our team is so much more successful. You guys are great athletes, you're fantastic students, you're active in campus activities, and you're just nice people."

"You're not going to cry, are you Coach?"

Greg waved him off. "No, I'm good." After three years he knew Corey pretty well, and he observed the wistfulness that usually signaled inspiration. "What's on your mind?"

Corey smiled and said emphatically, "Cross Country Homecoming."

Greg sat forward, intrigued, so Corey continued.

"Our last home meet is in two weeks," he said. "None of the opposing teams is very strong, so we should win it easily. I know you don't like us to think that, but it's true." Greg nodded.

Six runners emerged from the ice bath and shuffled around like zombies, trying to loosen up their joints which were stiff from the cold. One of them splashed cold water on the waiting girls. Greg prohibited any major horseplay because, as he explained, "If you injure one of your teammates, a lifetime of I'm sorries won't make it better," but he allowed them a little rambunctiousness during this chilly team activity. While it was meant as a tool for recovery, Greg noticed that some of the most profound team-bonding moments happened around the ice tub.

"Since the meet's on Wednesday," Corey continued, smiling as he watched his teammates, "we can do three days of activities, just stupid stuff that won't be hard to organize."

"You have ideas?" asked Greg.

"We've come up with a few, if you're OK with them. Monday is 'Cross Country Bachelor and Bachelorette Auction,' at lunch. It can be a fundraiser, and maybe some of the guys can get dates. Then there's 'Run a Mile with the Team Tuesday.' And 'Crazy Socks Day' on Wednesday. The winners get to sit on a sofa at the finish line while our parents feed them Gatorade and cookies."

"How are we going to get a sofa to the finish line?"

"Way ahead of you, Coach. Remember that old sofa we found last week on our run, the butt-ugly one? After practice, we picked it up in my truck. It's in my back yard right now, and my parents said they'd transport it to the course."

"Ladies and gentlemen," Greg announced. "Two weeks from now will be Cross Country Homecoming!"

Overcoming the derision of some members of the football team, a few of the guys actually managed to generate bids during the auction, including one who was purchased for three dollars and ninety cents as a lunch date by a girl in his Physics class. The girls fared a little better, and when the receipts were totaled the cross country team had raised almost sixty dollars. Greg kicked in a hundred bucks and some of the parents donated as well, so the Shadowcliff High School cross country program ended up sending a nice check to Special Olympics. Ten brave souls turned out to run a mile with the team on Tuesday, an event Greg appreciated for its future recruiting possibilities. Wednesday's Crazy Socks Day turned out to be their most popular event, although they were unsure how many participants were wearing unusual socks just because that was their normal manner of dress. Nonetheless, when the Shadowcliff boys and girls cross country teams both won their Homecoming meets with perfect scores that afternoon, Corey's mom led the auxiliary that fed Gatorade and cookies to the Crazy Sock winners sitting on an absurd chartreuse sofa at the finish line. Even Bryce Bishop showed up.

As the quarter drew to a close, the staff had warmed to Bishop. He was young and impetuous and did not handle things with the diplomacy of Vinnie Pantuzzi, but he worked hard and seemed to support his teachers, and his over-the-top spirit had managed to excite students about being Shadowcliff Bobcats.

Meanwhile, Greg's AP students were reading Kafka, his Business Law students had just completed a personal injury mock trial, his American Story students knew more about the Constitution than most politicians, and his cross country team was again one of Arizona's finest. Amanda's Global Scholars students had just finished a comparison of Picaresque anti-heroes from the Spanish Golden Age, and as a bonus had learned the gentlemanly art of the tango. Amanda was now advocating for a tango at the wedding reception, which afforded Greg only five months to figure out how to not step on her toes.

While fall break was a most welcome mental break among teachers, anticipation was swelling as to the identity of the next Superintendent. Or perhaps it was apprehension. An illicit betting pool had been established by a student teacher in the PE Department, and apparently Dr. Carvalho was getting most of the action. Greg chose not to participate because he could not justify winning. Every choice, he believed, would be a loss.

As the school day ended, students dashed for the exits to begin their week of freedom while teachers throughout the District moved to their school's auditorium or meeting room or wherever they usually gathered for matters of utmost consequence. The new Superintendent was to be announced.

In room 4122, Bryce Bishop turned on the computer and projected the webcast onto the screen. On camera, Dr. Halter wore a Hawaiian shirt and a smile, quite a contrast to his last webcast in August. Clearly he was ready to begin his retirement the instant he made the unveiling. The student teacher stood in a corner of the room, holding the betting receipts in a large manila envelope. Speculation continued, and he collected a few last-minute wagers before Halter began to speak.

"We want to thank all of you for your patience with the process," Halter said, "and for your help in making our decision. As we considered each of the candidates, we continued to return to one. This candidate offers the best combination of experience, integrity, and most of all vision for Sweetwater Unified School District. So, on behalf of the Governing Board, I would like to introduce our new Superintendent."

The room was absolutely silent. As if sensing it, Dr. Halter paused dramatically and smiled, drawing out his final act as the man in charge.

"Beginning Monday morning, the new Superintendent will be ... Dr. Connie Rumsford."

Cheers stopped mid-throat, replaced by "Wait ... what?" It was positively baffling. But then, from the back of the room, Ben Koch said, "I selected 'other.' That means I win the pool, right?"

Greg found himself at his favorite trailhead. It was already one hundred and fifty-two degrees, on the way toward one-eighty-eight. He didn't care.

Buzzards circled and gigantic lizards searched for the on/off switch to their air conditioners. Yet Greg saw none of it. All he saw was the face of Dr. Connie Rumsford on every rock and cactus. Over dusty boulders and through bone-dry gullies he ran, his shoes making a metronomic koosh-koosh-koosh sound as they danced along the desert floor. Forty-five minutes into the run, he came upon Dr. Connie Rumsford standing in the middle of the trail. She stopped him and demanded that he wear a shirt.

On his return, a lizard scurried just in front of his foot and looked up at him. The lizard's face was that of Dr. Connie Rumsford. Greg made a slight right-hand turn, accelerating up a short hill and into the distance as a group of lizards, each with the face of Dr. Connie Rumsford, began to chase him.

Lydia Scanlon appeared and began running alongside him, effortlessly, informing him that a group of lizards was called a "lounge." Now the lizards were everywhere, multiple lounges, each reptile sporting Rumsford's face. They began to taunt him, one lounge calling him "unfocusedable," another calling him "distantory," and a third "digressient." The sound grew to an unrelenting cacophony of manufactured words that drowned out his footfalls and attracted a group of buzzards, hundreds of them, a "wake" according to Lydia Scanlon. Sure enough they all had Rumsford's face, too, and they munched on chocolate as they circled.

The trailhead parking lot loomed just beyond one final rise, and a wolverine chased him all the way to the parking lot. As he finished his run, salty sweat caked his temples and dust covered his lower legs. Dr. Connie Rumsford appeared with a towel. Greg unlaced his car key from his shoe and opened the driver door, and when he got in, Dr. Connie Rumsford was sitting in the passenger seat. On his way home he stopped at Circle-K to purchase a bottle of Gatorade. Dr. Connie Rumsford was working the cash register.

He arrived home to an apartment overrun by houseplants, every one an extra-large version of Harold. A picture of Dr. Connie Rumsford was on each of the pots. He decided to jump in the pool, which turned out to be populated by a million candirus. Only then did he realize he was now naked, with Roger Anderson, Susan Arnstadt, and the rest of his class pointing, snickering, and laughing.

29

THE CID

The first weekend of fall break was spent with sleepless nights and existential questioning, but fortunately his cross country team was practicing on Monday morning, which forced Greg to extricate himself from his doldrums. The team was peaking at just the right time for the upcoming District, Region, and State championships.

Greg came home from practice, showered, and poured himself a bowl of cereal. Cereal had been his breakfast of choice since he could remember, but while once Frosted Flakes, it was now granola. Amanda was the cereal warden, constantly reminding Greg that he was, after all, a few years older than her. "I would like you to stick around for a while," she insisted, but he teased, "I think you're only after my life insurance money."

Each year, Greg was becoming a more efficient teacher, so now he was caught up on grading and already planned for his first week back. Handouts were stacked on his desk ready for distribution, lecture notes were prepared, and activities were coordinated. A week of leisure stretched before him. After waking from a two-hour nap, he was already bored. There was nothing interesting on television, not even a decent old movie on Turner Classic. There were no errands to run or chores to complete. Fifty pages in, he was unimpressed with *The Red Harvest* and, quite frankly, thought Dashiell Hammett was second-rate compared to Raymond Chandler. Hammett described his characters' faces with more detail than even a dermatologist needed to know, but except for Nick Charles they were uninspired. Chandler's characters were more than facial features; they were tough and noble and they drank too much and they got beat up sometimes. Greg spent the afternoon growing evermore disenchanted with Dashiell Hammett and wondered if he should just punt and reread Chandler's *Farewell, My Lovely* so he could enjoy Philip Marlowe again. Sometimes he wished he could talk to people in the same cocksure way Marlowe did.

He decided to run again that afternoon. As he ducked out, he said to Amanda, "See you in an hour, doll face." She looked at him peculiarly. Marlowe could have pulled it off, Greg thought. After the run, he fixed chicken marsala for Amanda and himself, then sat down at his computer and opened a blank Word document.

Greg could write exceptional letters of recommendation and e-mails which were inspired in their flippancy. He once wrote a fine thesis on the antitrust implications of the European track and field circuit, which was published in a small academic journal in the Midwest. He often dashed off amusing poems to celebrate friends' birthdays or other special occasions. Tonight, though, his purpose was different. Deep down, he had known all day this was to be his destiny. If systemic iniquities could not be cured by logic, idealism, drinking, or a good run, perhaps they could be remedied, or at least soothed, by the written word.

He started three different times, each in different form, but none captured his current zeitgeist. Dissatisfied, he closed his eyes and thought back to the moment more than three years ago when he first encountered Dr. Connie Rumsford in the trailer outside Sierra Elementary School. Suddenly, words flowed like beer in an English pub: some lukewarm, some pretty good, some immensely satisfying. But they flowed.

He wrote for three hours before Amanda kissed him goodnight, then two more until he finally went to bed. The next morning, he had already written for an hour before Amanda was awake.

"What are you working on?" she asked him. She was dressed in workout clothes.

"I'm not sure yet," Greg responded, because it was true.

When she returned from the gym two hours later, he still had not eaten. She forced him to take a break and join her for breakfast, then he went back to writing.

That night, Greg took Amanda to a new restaurant in downtown Sweetwater, where he finally revealed, "It's a novel."

"About what?"

"Craziness and stupidity and passion and triumph and hard work and nutty people and absurd decisions," he said. "Just another day at work."

"Is Connie Rumsford in there?" she asked, and he replied, "More or less." "Am I?" she followed.

"Can't tell you anything else, my love. Stephen King says to write the first draft with the door closed. The door is closed."

By the time he went to bed that second night, Greg had emptied two Pepsi cans and a small box of Cheez-Its. A PowerBar wrapper lay on the floor beside his desk. He had also produced forty-five pages of manuscript and was rolling. By week's end, as they prepared to return to school for the second quarter, he had produced one hundred and nine.

He did not dream.

Maurice McCullough was not at Shadowcliff High School on the day second quarter began. He showed up for an hour on day two, then disappeared again. That afternoon, the announcement was made that Maurice was now working at the Sweetwater Unified School District No. 43 District office, as Dr. Connie Rumsford's right-hand man with a yet-to-be-determined title.

"How do you feel about Maurice joining the adminisphere?" Jeanette Candelaria asked Greg at lunch.

"Nice term," Greg laughed. "I'm not surprised. He and Rumsford were like peas and carrots."

"Nothing good ever falls from the adminisphere," she cautioned.

Within a couple of weeks, everyone at Shadowcliff recognized that the loss of Maurice turned out to be, in fact, no great loss at all.

"One more example to prove the rule," said Jeanette, and Greg knew exactly what she meant.

The timing of Maurice's departure did, however, leave Shadowcliff's Homecoming festivities entirely on Bryce Bishop's shoulders. Planning Homecoming is a massive undertaking, involving the collaborative creativity of students, teachers, administrators, and alumni. It requires a delicate balance of scheduling and a flair for the childish fun oft forgotten in the modern world. Its theme must appeal to a wide cross-section of the student body while still fitting within the school's goals and vision. It must leverage a week's worth of activities, a football game, and a dance with the ultimate goal of enhancing school pride. Student Government, for all its lofty and theoretical promises, devotes most of its attention to the success of Homecoming, and its officers often work long into the night to ensure the event is triumphant.

Most of all, Homecoming requires as its center-piece a football game that is considered a sure win-ner. Pity the school that goes 0-10 every season, as they end up being Homecoming fodder for three or four teams throughout the year. So, despite all the stakeholders involved, Frank Nixon looked at his schedule and decided Homecoming needed to be the October 31 game against Trimble High School, which had not won more than two games in a season since the turn of the millennium.

Unfortunately for Frank Nixon, this was not shaping up as one of his best seasons either. Truth is, there was yet to be a "good" football team at Shadowcliff, but this one entered Homecoming week with a moribund 3-5 record and a three-game losing streak. Trimble came in at 1-7.

At least Nixon's decision made the theme an easy one. There would be costume contests and a haunted house and scary cafeteria food. The last of these, Greg noted, was no great stretch. And there would be a pumpkin carving contest, problematic in light of the District's strict 'no weapons' policy. Greg wondered if they were going to carve pumpkins with plastic butter knives.

His bigger concern, though, was making sure the cross country team did not jeopardize its performance for the rest of the season. "No root beer chugging contests, no sumo wrestling, no doing anything that'll get you suspended." Then there was the threat of Halloween itself, which fell the night before the Region championships, the meet which qualified teams to compete at State. "Save your candy until after State, don't steal some little kid's goodies, don't soap anyone's windows." He knew he sounded like an old grandmother, but the team understood.

Homecoming week was a far greater success than Cross Country Homecoming had been, but that was unsurprising. Bryce Bishop was at school late each night to ensure things were ready for the next day's events, and his boyish enthusiasm was contagious. He also finished second in the root beer chugging contest. Unfortunately, he could do nothing to ensure the football team would be prepared for Friday. That task was left to Frank Nixon.

For Halloween night, Corey Hinton organized a team cross country party at his house. They ate like they had not seen human food in weeks. Then they went to the Homecoming game, where the gaunt, shirtless boys lent Halloween authenticity as skeletons, although these were skeletons who could run really fast. They left after halftime, Shadowcliff already down 28-7 to Trimble and on their way to a 42-20 thrashing. Their evening concluded as they all watched *Friday the Thirteenth* on the big-screen television in Corey's basement, the seven varsity boys and seven varsity girls sprawled out on the floor and the chartreuse sofa like a fourteen-piece human jigsaw puzzle. The next morning, both teams won their Region championships handily.

One week later, the Shadowcliff High School girls cross country team won its second state championship, and the boys followed with their first title. Corey Hinton closed out his high school career with a third-place finish, then cheered for each of his teammates until a seven-man blob of Shadowcliff green was congealed in the finish chute. Corey found Greg and hugged him for what seemed like hours, both as celebration of victory and recognition that their time together was nearly over.

"You're not going to cry, are you Coach?"

"I might," Greg replied. "Are you?"

When Greg was interviewed by the reporter from the *Sweetwater Sentinel*, he was still happily soaked in Corey's sweat.

As they waited for the awards ceremony an hour later, the Granite High School coach turned to Greg. "Congratulations."

"Thanks," said Greg, his grin a mile wide. "Great day for us."

"I should think so. Say, I heard the job at Long Beach State is going to open at the end of the school year," the rival coach said. "You should apply."

"Are you trying to get rid of me?" Greg joked.

"Just thought you'd be interested. You have the background as an athlete, and what you've done at Shadowcliff in four years is amazing. We used to beat you like a drum, but not anymore. Why not look at a college job?"

Greg thanked him humbly, then made sure every member of his team was dressed in their green Shadowcliff T-shirts. He loved the look of a unified team when they accepted a trophy, especially this one. Long Beach State intrigued him.

As the year progressed, so too did Greg's novel. He still saw it primarily as a therapeutic endeavor, but every week, as he added another couple of chapters, he also began to see it as a completed book. In mid-December, Greg typed the words THE END and leaned back in his chair. "It's finished," he told Amanda.

"And just in time," she said. "We've got a wedding to plan."

Amanda's mother and Grammy Luciana arrived over Christmas. The wedding was scheduled to take place in less than three months, on the second Saturday of spring break for Sweetwater Unified School District No. 43. Between now and then, there were menus to decide, centerpieces to order, and bands to hire.

"Why don't we just get a DJ?" Greg asked, and Grammy Luciana stared him into silence. "No band?" she said, shaking her head at his ignorance. "*Pazzo*," she continued. "*Mia nipote non è un barbone di strada.*"

"What did she say?" he asked Amanda.

"She called you crazy, and said I'm not a street tramp."

"A wedding with a disc jockey means you're a street tramp? I guess I'd better not suggest we serve beer."

"That would be a good idea," Amanda agreed.

"*Niente birra!*" shouted Grammy Luciana. "*Solo il vino!*"

"I think I'm going to need some help getting out of this," Greg said to Amanda.

"I'll take care of it," she assured him, then turned toward the old lady. "Grammy Luciana, *lui è solo un Arizonan stupido. Va bene,*" she said to him, and both Grammy Luciana and Amanda's mother began laughing.

"Thank you," said Greg. "Hey, wait a minute. I am not an Arizonan stupido!"

Fortunately, Greg had been running a lot since the end of cross country season, so he was always hungry. At dinner he devoured enough pasta to get back in Grammy Luciana's good graces. The next time she saw him would be the week of the wedding.

For children, each day contains infinity, packed with endless possibilities and an unending string of adventures from morning cartoons until bedtime stories. In contrast, the elderly understand the phenomenon whereby time seems like a Japanese bullet train, days so apparently short they almost overlap. Although Greg was somewhere in between, the third quarter rushed past, a blur of anticipation. There were, of course, still a few bottom feeders by choice to motivate, disgruntled parents to re-gruntle, and regrettable lapses in judgment to rehabilitate, but each day brought Greg and Amanda one day closer to being Mr. and Mrs.

They flew into Islip on Wednesday, three days before the ceremony. That would give Amanda the opportunity to attend to last-minute wedding details and Greg the opportunity to tattoo Amanda's family tree on his left arm, because trying to remember everyone was a staggering if not impossible task. This was patently unfair; since Greg's parents were both dead and he was an only child, his lineage was pretty easy to follow. On Thursday, he took the train into Manhattan to have lunch with a former high school classmate with whom he had reconnected on Facebook. The man now owned a small publishing house in Greenwich Village.

That night, Amanda and Greg dined at a seafood restaurant in Sheepshead Bay with Amanda's mother, her mother's best friend Charlotte, and Charlotte's boyfriend Ernesto. Or, as he kept reminding them, Dr. Ernesto Garcia, Assistant Professor of Spanish Literature at Long Island University in Brooklyn. Amanda's father was on a business trip until tomorrow.

Since this was Amanda's weekend, her mother continued to direct questions at her like she was a guest star on a local talk show. Greg was delighted to allow her stardom. Most of the questions Mom already knew the answer to, but she asked them for the benefit of the others. Then came the crucial mistake.

"Tell them about the Global Scholars Program," Mom suggested.

Amanda began to describe the Program, its history and theory, the rich and fascinating variety of students, and finally, some of the specific topics of study.

"Tell Ernesto about that Spanish literature thing you did," Amanda's mother suggested, her pride obvious.

Amanda explained her study of the Picaresque and glowed with gratification at the insights offered by her students. Greg smiled as she described what he thought was a really cool unit.

When she finished, Ernesto scoffed, "You don't know anything about Spanish literature."

"Excuse me?" Amanda asked. "I mean, I'm not Spanish, but the point was to get students to engage in the texts and to discover what they had in common. I don't really need to be an expert for that."

"You are definitely no expert," Ernesto continued. "Any study of Spanish literature, even one as rudimentary as yours, must begin with *The Cid*."

Greg leaned forward but said nothing, yet.

"I have a degree in Literature, with honors," Amanda protested. "Even if I don't know Spanish literature *per se*, I know enough about literature to lead my students through an inductive reasoning activity."

"No you don't. Not without *The Cid*. That's the basis of everything. Not just Spanish literature, all literature. An Italian girl attempting to teach Spanish literature without *The Cid* is offensive to us Spaniards. It's laughable."

Greg noticed a tear in Amanda's eye. "If I may interrupt," he said. "Is the problem that she's Italian, or that she neglected *El Cid*?"

"Both."

"Are you suggesting that only Spaniards can teach Spanish literature?"

"If it is to be at all authentic, yes," Ernesto said.

"So by that logic," Greg continued, "only black people can teach Black History? To make it authentic?"

"I believe that, yes."

"Then to take it one step further, only dead people can teach history?" Greg concluded as the dinner check arrived.

As Amanda and her mother said goodbye to Charlotte in the parking lot, Ernesto seethed by his car. Greg stood beside Amanda, unable to decipher Charlotte's reaction to the evening's turn of events. On the car ride home, Amanda said, "In the interest of full disclosure, if you ever insult me like that, my dad will probably punch out your lights. Good thing he was in Boston or Ernesto would have been hospitalized." Then she added, "And thank you, by the way."

"Of course," Greg said. "I loathe snobbery, and I refuse to sit back and allow an assault of it. Especially against you."

The wedding itself was an exquisite affair, even though Amanda's side of the church outnumbered Greg's side 116 to nine. He thought he could even the score at their Arizona reception in June. They were pronounced man and wife at St. William the Abbot Catholic Church, just across Sunrise Highway from the Seaford Long Island Railroad station. Then a limousine, provided by Greg's best man, whisked the bridal party to the Massapequa Elks Lodge, another mile east on Sunrise Highway and right across from the Massapequa Long Island Railroad station. It was far more romantic and wonderful than it sounds.

They ate Italian food and danced and drank and laughed and Greg tried in vain to remember everyone's name. "Is that guy your second cousin, what's his name?" asked Greg, who had never gotten around to compiling her family tree. "No, that's Robert, my friend Tammy's husband," Amanda replied. "He's Irish."

At one point, Grammy Luciana hopped up on the bandstand and took the microphone from the lead singer, announcing, "I knew he was perfect for her the moment I laid eyes on him." Then, when the applause died down, she added, "Even though he wanted a DJ instead of a band. *Pazzo.*"

The band began to play a tango, per Amanda's request, and only a few couples dared. Greg and Amanda were surprisingly good for only a few practices, she having been taught and he still maintaining the grace of a competitive athlete. Across the dance floor they heard a woman yell "Ouch!" and they looked to see Charlotte holding her toe while Ernesto apologized profusely.

The wedding cake was even better than Amanda's "chocolate cake to die for," which was saying something. Greg removed her garter without incident and then, finally, they hopped back into the limousine and were transported to their hotel for the night. Despite the fact that one of Amanda's high school friends photographed his butt and her college roommate tried to seduce one of the groomsmen—the married one—it was an otherwise glorious celebration. The only disappointment was that Greg did not get nearly enough to eat. After Sunday brunch on the waterfront, they were back in Islip for their return trip to reality. Finances, time, and the obligations of school rendered a honeymoon only a distant fantasy at this point in time.

30

THE NEGOTIATION

Adrenaline carried them through their fatigue on Monday morning, and despite their eventful weekend they both arrived at school with time to spare. Greg wore his tuxedo shirt from Saturday, a bit of wedding cake smudged on his left collar. Amanda decided that wearing her wedding dress would be extravagant and even her veil might be too excessive. But her joy was obvious. While some, especially Greg's former girlfriends, might have questioned how anyone could feel joy from marrying the man, Amanda surely glowed, a fact not unnoticed by her peers and students. Down the hall, Greg taught with a smile that made one of his students call him "Mr. Grin." His hand felt weird, his bony finger having never before been encircled by gold. But it was a good weird. Even a vague e-mail from Bryce Bishop did not diminish Greg's cheer.

Greg and Amanda decided to eat in the faculty lunchroom, where Jimmy Clayton cautioned them, "No honeymoon activities in the faculty lounge." Amanda guaranteed him it was not a temptation.

On his way back to class, Greg detoured through the office.

"So you're a married man now, huh?" asked Kelli Weston. Responding to Greg's smile, she added, "Congratulations."

"Thank you."

"Where'd you go for your honeymoon?"

"The Hilton, across the street from the airport. It had a free shuttle."

"You are such a romantic," Kelli teased.

"Yes I am," Greg agreed. "Actually, we're hoping to do something this summer. Someplace with a beach."

"By the way," she continued. "Did you know Bryce is looking for you?"

"I do," he affirmed. "Any idea why?"

"I'm not sure," she said, which was unusual. "Something about a novel and e-mails." It took the full measure of the walk back to his classroom before Greg managed to put two and two together.

A few minutes after school ended, Greg knocked on Bryce Bishop's door. He had instructed his distance runners to prepare for a hard workout, and he would arrive at some point. He just was uncertain as to what point, exactly. When it was Rumsford, he knew a visit, no matter how painful, would at least be quick, because she had nine hundred other issues to attend. A visit with Pantuzzi would involve no worse than a soft suggestion, but the friendly conversation could stretch on as long as they allowed. But Greg had little history with Bishop from which to draw conclusions.

"Come in," Bryce said, and Greg opened the door. Another man was there as well. Bryce noticed the tuxedo shirt. "And congratulations on getting married."

Greg smiled and said "Thanks."

The other man offered his hand. "I'm Errol Strothers," he said.

"The District Director of Advocacy, Policy, and Regulatory Affairs, right?" answered Greg. He shook Strothers's hand and then sat in the open chair.

"We just call me the general counsel now," he said, somewhat sheepishly, suggesting that he never really cared for Dr. Morning's enhanced job titles.

"You're the man who said my wife was at fault when her underwear was stolen," Greg said. Bishop's confused look established that he had no knowledge of the incident.

Strothers paused a moment, then replied, "We might have missed on that one. But let's get to the issue at hand." He held up a thick stack of pages, nearly an entire ream of paper. "You wrote this?"

Greg looked at the cover page and then leafed through the manuscript. It was a copy of his novel.

"I did. Although this is not the final draft."

"Doesn't matter," said Strothers.

"Why do you have it?" continued Greg.

Strothers said, "We have a serious problem here. Multiple violations of the Teacher Code of Conduct."

Greg felt as if his heart jerked. During all his visits with Rumsford, no matter how perilous, he was never accused of this. "How so?" he asked, trying to remain composed.

"Misuse of school property," Bishop explained. "They're talking about firing you." Greg's stomach knotted.

Strothers withdrew a folder from his briefcase, then said, "The Teacher Code of Conduct states ... just a minute ... 'A teacher shall not use any school property, including electronic communication, for personal use.' Page fifty-six." He showed Greg the page, pointing specifically at the clause that would implicate him.

"You wasted a lot of paper for this document," Strothers added.

"In point of fact, you copied the document, not me," Greg rebutted. "I never used school paper, never made copies on school Xerox machines, and never used contracted time to work on it. Only after school or after practice while I waited for Amanda."

"So you admit you used school equipment," affirmed Strothers. "We also checked your electronic records, and you e-mailed this document back and forth between school and home multiple times since October."

"I'm getting busted by the e-mail cops?" questioned Greg. "I thought that went out with Dr. Morning. Or the KGB."

"E-mail belongs to the company which supplies it for the use of its employees, Mr. Samson. That's explained on page fifty-eight."

"It's also really ticky-tack in this case," Greg replied. "I'm sure...." He trailed off.

"You're sure of what?" Strothers pushed.

Greg paused for a moment, the wheels turning a thousand miles an hour in his brain. The room swirled and his ears buzzed. Then, suddenly, everything locked into sharp focus, and he looked at the lawyer with a clarity he had not felt since his days as a competitive athlete.

Pointing at Bryce Bishop, Greg began, "I see Mr. Bishop here running stadium steps once in a while. He's still pretty fit. Mr. Strothers, can you tell me the difference between that and this?"

"Running stadium steps is not misuse," Strothers responded.

"Who's to judge what is and what isn't?" Greg asked. "Doesn't it still fall under the definition in the Teacher Code of Conduct?"

"That's completely different," Strothers responded. "The stadium is open to the public.

"Plus I'm still technically on duty," added Bishop.

"So which is it?" Greg probed. "Is it because Mr.
Bishop a member of the general public, or because
he's not?"

"This is not about Mr. Bishop," Strothers began
to protest.

"Agreed," said Greg.

"Then let's stick—" He was cut off when Bishop's
office telephone rang.

"Hello?" answered Bishop. He offered the receiver to Strothers. "It's for you."

As Bishop and Greg waited, Greg noticed a dozen
March Madness brackets on the corner of Bishop's
desk, with Bishop's on top of the stack.

"Yeah, I've been here all afternoon," Strothers
said into the receiver. "Why didn't you call me on my
cell?" Then, "It isn't?" He pulled out his cell phone
and glanced at it, still listening to his caller. He finally said, "Sure, I'll pick that up on the way home."

Strothers passed the phone back to Bishop and
returned his attention to the Greg Samson issue.
"Where were we?"

"Sounded like a personal call," said Greg.

"It was my wife," Strothers confirmed like it was
none of Greg's business.

"So I guessed. I'm wondering why she didn't call
you on your cell phone. Shouldn't an office phone
be for school business only?"

"It is," Strothers said. "But she needed to get in touch with me and I didn't realize my ringer was turned off."

"Page fifty-six, I believe it was?" Strothers, tight-lipped, nodded to confirm.

Greg picked up the March Madness bracket from Bishop's desk. "You really think Michigan State is going to win it all? I like Duke myself."

"I think we should stick to the point, Greg," Bishop said.

"I am, actually. Is this the same bracket that was in my mailbox? My school property mailbox? I'm wondering who made the copies. Did they do it on a school Xerox machine? And that doesn't even address issues with gambling on school property, which I'm guessing is also in the Teacher Code of Conduct." He turned to Strothers. "Is there a March Madness pool at the District office, Mr. Strothers?"

The thick silence seemed to endure for minutes.

"You've made your point," Strothers said finally. "But unfortunately for you, that's not our only concern. I've been here most of the day reading this...." He waved his hand over Greg's manuscript, like a magician trying to make it disappear. "There is absolutely no way we can allow it."

"There is absolutely no way you can stop it," Greg countered. "It doesn't fall within *Hazelwood v. Kuhlmeier*. It's not a school publication and it's not a threat to the learning environment, so it's not something you can censor. It's fully protected by the first amendment. And assuming I'm able to get it published, it's certainly not something you can fire me for."

"Are you trying to get it published?" asked Strothers.

"Some people are looking at it," Greg replied.

"I see. Fact is, it's highly inflammatory. We can fire you under the loyalty oath you signed when first hired, for starters," Strothers said. "As well as the Teacher Code of Conduct. 'A teacher shall not make any public comments which disparage the District, any school, or any employee.' I think it's on page seventy-three." He began to look through the Table of Contents.

"This is a work of fiction," Greg said.

"I'm sorry, it's on page seventy-six," Strothers said.

"Doesn't matter if it's on page one," Greg replied. "It's a work of fiction."

"Why do you keep saying that?" Bishop asked. "From what Mr. Strothers tells me, this is malicious and libelous toward the District."

"It's satire. The definition of satire is the use of humor or irony to make fun of things with the objective of making them better."

"How will this make anything better?"

"What Mr. Strothers categorizes as malicious, I call idealistic. Jeanette Candelaria once told me that teaching is the most noble profession in the world, and I agree. But it's also laden with problems." He turned to face Strothers. "If you fire me for expressing my first amendment rights, that will be interpreted as an implicit admission that the novel is accurate. Does Sweetwater Unified School District really want that public humiliation?" Greg leaned forward in his chair.

"On the other hand, if you choose to sue me for libel, the jury will either decide it's fiction and therefore can't be libelous, or else it's close enough to fact that there's an identifiable plaintiff, in which case we'll go through the manuscript page by page and see how truthful it is. Which gets us right back to square one, negative publicity." He looked at the lawyer, who dabbed a bead of sweat from his forehead and offered no refutation.

"Then there's the whistleblower statute. If this is in fact true and I'm fired for it, then by statute I am entitled to treble damages. Twenty years until retirement, times, let's say, fifty thousand a year ... I'm assuming cost-of-living increases ... that's a million dollars. Times three. Sweetwater Unified School District does not want to pay a three-million-dollar award. Although I would probably settle the case for one-point-five."

Greg scratched his chin as if in deep thought. "I wonder if the *Sweetwater Sentinel* would be interested in a story about a teacher being fired for exercising his first amendment rights. I only know the sportswriters who've interviewed me about cross country. Either of you know who their education writer is?" Neither Bishop nor Strothers offered any help. "That's OK. I can find out myself."

Greg had begun his teaching career a callow thirty-seven year old, unaware of school politics and the way things really got done. But he learned fast.

"Mr. Strothers, I want to emphasize that this is not meant as an indictment of Bryce Bishop, who has done a terrific job at Shadowcliff, but rather of the ludicrous policies and irrational decisions and senseless skull-sucking silliness passed down from the adminisphere. I submit to you that Sweetwater Unified School District does not want lawyers and it does not want media. This is my fourth year, and that much has become obvious, over and over again. In that time, I've also become a very good teacher, with strong evaluations, exceptional AP scores, and lots of parents willing to speak on my behalf. Before Dr. Rumsford was fired, I was Teacher of the Month, for crying out loud." He chuckled that he actually thought to include that among his qualifications. Pointing at Bishop's office phone, he added, "Call her and ask, if you want."

"That's not necessary," Strothers mumbled. "I've seen your evaluations."

"I'm also the most successful coach on this campus. Under those circumstances, firing me would look really fishy. Especially when other teachers have been retained despite far more egregious violations of the Teacher Code of Conduct and despite not being very good teachers, and other coaches have been rewarded for their mediocrity. So here's what I suggest instead." He reached into his back pocket and pulled out a sheet of paper. "If the book gets published, here's your press release. I took the liberty of writing it up for you." The paper was goldenrod.

"Sweetwater Unified School District No. 43 wishes to congratulate Greg Samson, teacher and coach at Shadowcliff High School, on the publication of his first novel. This satirical work of fiction is a tribute to all the hard-working educators in Sweetwater, the state of Arizona, and across the nation. The book is published by blank and is available at bookstores everywhere."

He finished reading and looked at Strothers. "You'll have to fill in the blank with the publishing company. Otherwise, no acknowledgment as to truth and no negative publicity. Hey, maybe I sell a million copies and move to Vermont and teach creative writing."

He passed the goldenrod paper to Errol Strothers.

"If the book doesn't get published, you just throw this away."

Strothers looked at the paper open-mouthed, then at Bryce Bishop.

"I need to get to track practice," Greg said. "Are we finished here?" Both men nodded.

As Greg passed through the office, Kelli Westin was packing up for the day. She looked up and smiled.

"Finally used my law degree," he chirped, and went on his way.

EPILOGUE

Dr. Connie Rumsford was Superintendent of Sweetwater Unified School District No. 43 when Sweetwater's second bond was defeated, and again when the District's third bond was defeated. After being fired, she moved to Yuma, Arizona and began teaching at Arizona Western Junior College. According to www.ratemyteacher.com, she assigns way too many readings. As a side business, she is attempting to market MiraClean, a thick purple sludge that she still cooks up on her stove and packages in used mayonnaise jars.

Jimmy Clayton became a videographer at KSBW-TV in Gilroy, California. His exposé on migrant workers and the garlic industry earned him a Golden Camera Award from the Gilroy Broadcasters Association. He serves as President of the Arizona

State University Alumni Association chapter in Gilroy, and is its only member.

Bob Cockrell completed his doctorate in education and served for two years in the Public Affairs office at Sweetwater Unified School District No. 43. Today, he is Director of Public Information at Eastern Washington University. He recently took his son Ryan on his first camping trip, during which they were attacked by bison.

Keri Zabriskie remarried and became Keri McGillicuddy, then divorced and became Keri Zabriskie. She then remarried and became Keri Kincaid. She is now separated. She still teaches math at Shadowcliff High School.

Elden Ray Fong continues to be recognized as the Master Teacher, creating an empire of educational books, software, and professional development seminars that have made him a multi-millionaire. He calls his employees' parents every day.

Lydia Scanlon retired after only two years at Shadowcliff. Despite prodding from Greg, she did not sing "Lydia the Tattooed Lady" at the end-of-year faculty breakfast. A month later, already bored with retirement, she accepted a position as Lead Research Librarian with *U.S. News and World Report* in New York City.

Maurice McCullough retired from Sweetwater Unified School District No. 43 and became Assistant Track & Field Coach at John McCain High School in another district. During his time as coach, several McCain sprinters suffered season-ending hamstring injuries. Meanwhile, John McCain lost the 2008 presidential election by one hundred ninety-two electoral votes.

Randy Smith was selected Athletic Administrator of the Year by the National Federation of High Schools, regardless of the fact that no Shadowcliff team other than cross country ever won a state championship.

Ramona Thurlow retired from Sweetwater Unified School District No. 43 when she was passed over for the Superintendent position. She spends her time doing beadwork and volunteering as a trail guide in the mountains just north of Sweetwater.

Jeanette Candelaria retired after four years at Shadowcliff. She now plays golf every day, saving her favorite goldenrod outfit for Sundays.

Samantha O'Bradovich still supervises Shadowcliff's Special Ed department, still turns thirty-second thoughts into ten-minute oratories, and still cries at least once a day.

Ike Gravenstein retired from teaching two years ago and now volunteers at his granddaughter's preschool.

John Woodacre is second assistant night manager at Toys R Us in Terre Haute, Indiana.

Stacy Johnston is now a sales rep for Lululemon yoga pants and leggings.

Steven Torgemeyer works as a security guard at Granite High School.

Frank Nixon compiled a record of 18-22 in four years as head football coach at Shadowcliff. His final teaching evaluation was equally mediocre. Nixon then became Offensive Coordinator and Head of Recruiting at Buena Vista University in Storm Lake, Iowa, but was fired after one season. He now supervises Study Hall and coaches freshman football at Iowa Falls Central High School.

Kyle Friese graduated from the United States Military Academy at West Point, New York. Commissioned as a Second Lieutenant, he is in charge of the physical training program at Fort Benning, Georgia, where he also facilitates Book Club.

Corey Hinton ran cross country at Southern Illinois University. The Saluki Cross Country T-shirt he brought home at Christmas remains one of Greg Samson's most prized possessions. He now works as a CPA in Chicago.

Darlene Griffin was arrested for underage drinking as a high school sophomore while attending a Sigma Nu party at Arizona State University. Darlene was unable to run away from police due to a hamstring injury she sustained while working on her speed with Maurice. She never ran competitively again. At trial, she received probation thanks to fair and ethical representation from **Darnell Lyon**. She later attended Phoenix Junior College for one semester but dropped out to have her first of seven children.

Andy Varner and **Paul Coates** are roommates in Los Angeles, where they produce a popular YouTube channel with more than seven million subscribers.

Cade Ralston is Director of Supply Chain Management for International Semiconductor Corporation and the youngest member of the School Board in Charlotte, North Carolina.

Teddy "T.R." Raszko worked his way up to Night Lead Maintenance Supervisor for Sweetwater Unified School District No. 43. He retired to Payson, Arizona three years ago, where he now lives in a cabin constructed piece-by-piece with items stolen from various schools in Sweetwater over a twelve-year period.

Shelley Banyan runs an Amway distributorship.

Kelli Westin became so comfortable greeting lawyers that she accepted a position as receptionist at Minkoff, Howell, Ransom & Kantor, PC. After her divorce was finalized, she married partner Michael Ransom on the beach in Maui. She occasionally slips Greg's résumé into the mailbox of senior part-ner Abe Minkoff.

Autumn Kessler's cheerleading career ended when internet photographs of her wearing only body paint went viral. During her suspension from the University of Arizona, she flew to Paris to have her breasts enlarged a second time, then started her own pornographic website, www.autumnlove.com, co-sponsored by American Airlines and the Merci Beaucoup Breast Enhancement Center.

Conrad Luper is principal at Wilson Elementary School in Florence, Arizona, an hour outside of Phoenix. His school's geology program is said to be the best in the nation.

After developing a nervous tic that made it impossible for her to knit, **Lucille Scholz** moved into Peaceful Pines Convalescent Home last year.

Vinnie Pantuzzi lives in Pittsburgh, Pennsylvania, with his wife of thirty-six years. Twice a week, he enjoys a sausage pierogi at Big Sal's, just around the corner from Duquesne University. He still goes fishing with **Robert Halter** every summer.

Reid Harkness was drafted out of Shadowcliff High School and played minor league baseball for seven years. He now works at his father's plumbing supply business.

Troy Vandevort never received help for his dyslexia and had to drop out of college as a freshman. After graduating culinary school, he is now head chef at Spencer's New American Cuisine in Seattle, Washington.

Dr. Patty Sue Morning returned to Texas as Superintendent of the San Angelo Independent School District. Although reading scores are among the lowest in the state and teacher morale continues to plummet, the District Director of Informational and Statistical Distribution informs San Angelo residents that its schools are rated "Academically Acceptable" by the Texas Department of Education.

Dr. Beatrice Rayburn and **Dr. Dave Jesperson** are partners in a company which offers corporate training, efficiency, and motivational programs. They have no repeat clients.

Dr. Fiona Carvalho returned to Minnesota to work in market research for Target. Her multivariate statistical model is generally considered the retail industry standard. She and husband **Neil Fortune** have two children, the second of whom has still not mastered his times tables.

Errol Strothers and Darnell Lyon became close friends, and Strothers eventually joined Lyon's law practice. When Lyon died from a massive heart attack while eating deep fried calamari, Strothers represented his estate and asserted that Chili's prep cooks had used too much canola oil in the batter. After winning a huge judgment, he renamed the firm "Strothers: The Law Firm Better Than All The Others."

Elida Singh left Cornell after her freshman year and later graduated from Northern Arizona University with a degree in Elementary Education. She is now a fifth-grade teacher in Prescott, Arizona.

Bryce Bishop is still principal of Shadowcliff High School, where his oldest son is the star pitcher on the varsity baseball team. Bishop can always be found sitting in a lawn chair down the left-field line with the rest of the home crowd, since the bleachers were removed several years ago. Bleachers or not, Shadowcliff is considered the best school in Sweetwater Unified School District No. 43.

Amanda Moretti won recognition from the Global Scholars Program for her excellence in the classroom and an award for outstanding teaching from the Sweetwater Vaqueros, the most prominent civic organization in the city. Amanda and Greg are the parents of a four-year-old son, Quenton, who is now almost as tall as Harold the houseplant and whose sharp wit and stubborn demeanor frequently land him in trouble at preschool.

Greg Samson is now ... well, what do you think?

As a young man, **John Prather** spent too much time in college and in running shoes. A former teacher, he is now a licensed attorney and certified curmudgeon who is decent at chess and pretty good at Trivial Pursuit. He loves movies, riding his bike, and reorganizing the storage room at his home in Scottsdale, Arizona, which he shares with his wife and son. He has broken his nose 15 times. His favorite color is orange.

Massapequa Public Library
523 Central Avenue
Massapequa, NY 11758
(516) 798-4607

Made in the USA
Columbia, SC
14 October 2018